Praise for *Soft Money*

Nar   of the Sou Burn M

"Wishnia's   train—
fast, loud, dirty, and dangerous—but it's well worth the
ride with Filomena Buscarsela in the driver's seat. . . .
A hard-edged story gracefully told." —*Booklist*

"Great fun. . . . Fil is a hyperbolic character, spewing
enough acerbic opinions to fill half a dozen average
mysteries. . . . A spirited sequel." —*Publishers Weekly*

"Sharp and sexy. . . . Hilarious and exciting. . . . [Wishnia]
has a perfect ear for female urban angst." —*Chicago Tribune*

"A distinctive voice from the barrio and an innovative
addition to the detective canon. . . . Great action
scenes, characters unlike any you've ever met before
and some of the finest writing out there. . . . One
hell of a story." —*New Orleans Times-Picayune*

"Filomena's scorched-earth tactics . . . are as effective as
her wisecracks. And what wisecracks! As his blistering
hardcover debut shows so well, Wishnia is the first
American writer to propel both his dialogue and his story
by harnessing the recent British hard-boiled school's
tidal wave of class rage." —*Kirkus* (starred review)

"Nonstop activity, wry humor, mordant characterizations,
and a solid dollop of police procedure make this a hugely
appealing follow-up to *23 Shades of Black*." —*Library Journal*

"Filomena will stick with you as you turn back and
look forward to pages of colorful prose that leave you
tingling with the joy of knowing her." —*Baltimore Sun*

SOFT MONEY

Kenneth Wishnia

Soft Money
© 2013 Kenneth Wishnia
This edition © 2013 PM Press
All rights reserved. No part of this book may be transmitted by any means without
permission in writing from the publisher.

ISBN: 978–1–60486–680–3
Library of Congress Control Number: 2012913635

Cover: John Yates / www.stealworks.com
Interior design by briandesign

10 9 8 7 6 5 4 3 2 1

PM Press
PO Box 23912
Oakland, CA 94623
www.pmpress.org

Printed in the USA on recycled paper, by the Employee Owners of Thomson-Shore
in Dexter, Michigan.
www.thomsonshore.com

For Leah, Jeremy, Steve, and Dave
And a big hug for Alison Hess
You know who you are

INTRODUCTION

There's a tradition in mystery novels of both Left and Right sociopolitical underpinnings. A hardcore example of this on the Right is Mickey Spillane's Mike Hammer, created in the Red Scare of the late forties and fifties by the World War II vet who originally conceived of his cryptofascist private eye as a comic strip—Mike Danger. Legend goes Spillane was forced to abandon the strip due to the syndicator wringing its hands about the excessive violence in the story panels. But Hammer in prose would, among other achievements, quell white male postwar disquiet of the other America on the move. This was evidenced for instance by the real life bravery of another World War II vet, Medgar Evers, murdered in his native Mississippi for daring to believe that the justice he fought for abroad should be for all at home.

"God but it was fun! It was the way I liked it. No arguing, no talking to the stupid peasants. I just walked into that room with a tommy gun and shot their guts out." So says Hammer toward the end of *One Lonely Night* after he wipes out some filthy commies torturing his Gal Friday, Velda, looking for the plans of the secret weapon. Imagine if that scene were recon-ceived and it was a black private eye saying something similar after he'd machine-gunned a viper's nest of Klansmen or White Citizen Council–types giving the works to his woman friend.

Not that Ken Wishnia's Filomena Buscarsela would ever be so brutal going after a racist polluter or a crooked teabag-ging politician, though she might have a picture in her mind of doing so. Just a passing notion, you understand. As you'll see after you read this edition of *Soft Money*, she, like Evers, is a veteran of sorts, a woman of principle. A tough, hardnosed, bighearted broad who stands up for her friends and more, she reflects on the conditions that affect her and the people she knows.

Buscarsela came along when the mystery field had, thankfully, broadened, reflecting an America in hue and gender beyond the confines of fifties and sixties crime fiction that bolstered a white chauvinist outlook on all things crime solving. It wasn't as if there hadn't been people of color characters populating mystery and crime stories before, but too often their roles were relegated to the background or presented as exotic. We didn't journey much into their heads, get to know them in a dimensional way as we did the protagonist.

To be clear, in this book—the second, after Buscarsela's debut in the Edgar-nominated *23 Shades of Black* (not exactly foreshadowing the leather and lace antics of *50 Shades of Grey*, though there are some juicy parts in the novel nonetheless)—the redoubtable Ecuadorian native is no longer an NYPD officer, but not quite a PI with her ticket just yet either. Indeed, she's the initially reluctant people's detective who's taken a grunt job with a bunch of prissy environmentalists.

But really, a woman like her, a single mother with a sardonic, protect-the-underdog sense in her bones, can't help but eventually plunge deep into the murder of a humble corner store owner when the victim's sister asks for her help. Make no mistake, Fil Buscarsela ain't no Miss Marple, amateur sleuth. Mind you, the old girl could riff off a smartass comment now and then to give her props. She didn't, though, make these kind of observations: "The train pulls in and I get on, thinking about all the lies they fed me about social mobility this society offers, about how anyone can make it if you work hard and study, if you try. In reality, the system fears innovation and only rewards those who can play along by whitewashing their alternative cultural values."

Those sentiments rang true in the novel's first incarnation. Now, after the fleecing Wall Street gave Main Street in the Great Economic Meltdown of 2008, and the more recent matters of the LIBOR dust-up and bid-rigging shakedowns by banks too big to fail, Buscarsela's words have come back to haunt us.

The burden she carries is not simply to bring to justice the one who pulled the trigger or did the deed. They're just misdirected and miseducated lumpen: if someone or some progressive group had gotten to them earlier, they'd be foot soldiers in the struggle to make the truly guilty pay. For that's the task Buscarsela's set herself, and it's a mutha. Makes Sisyphus look like a sissy, it does.

Go on, Filomena, go on.

Gary Phillips
Los Angeles

CHAPTER ONE

"He that maketh haste to be rich shall not be innocent."
— Proverbs 28:1

LÁZARO PÉREZ had a woman's heart.

I mean that. He had a heart transplant three years ago and the organ donor was a woman. He always said it made him the man every woman wants: strong back, soft heart. I needed that heart of his. His store, the only one in the *barrio* open past 1:00 A.M., was always a haven for me when I had to get out of the apartment or risk becoming a *New York Post* headline for murdering my indiscriminate fucker of a boy-friend. He also let me run up one hell of a tab when I needed it bad and no one else would give it to me. I don't think he ever knew how much he meant to me by just being there.

Lázaro was killed on April 28. Two punks held up his corner store for $211 cash and shot him dead. There was no other motive. Just two punks who lost control of the situation. Lázaro was a tough one: He got shot in the hand one time chasing two *other* punks out of his store and still managed to tackle one of them so hard the guy fingered his partner before the cops even got there.

I told the police detective these particular punks would probably party for a week until the money ran out then go and hit another place, and to watch for the same MO.

"What MO?" he said. "Two greaseballs held up a store and shot the owner. That's as common as Lincoln-head pennies."

But there's always an MO. I decided to find it.

I remember that April 28 was unseasonably cold. It rained all day and into the night. Lázaro's store was isolated on a corner facing the park. That's probably why they picked it. He had a small handwritten sign on the doorframe that read THIS IS A LEGITIMATE BUSINESS, because so many people cruised the block looking to score drugs and head back to White Plains or Jersey by way of the George Washington Bridge.

Now Lázaro has a ragged, bloody hole in that woman's heart of his. *That's* murder. Not something that happens during afternoon tea in quaint drawing rooms in the English countryside. And that's why there's a commandment against it, although sticking it alongside lying and dishonoring your parents kind of skews the priorities, if you ask me. You can always take back a lie, apologize, regain your honor. You can't bring back the dead. I've tried.

And there's always that same out-of-focus family snapshot or sickeningly sweet high school graduation photo of the smiling victim they run in the papers alongside a description of the cold, blood-stiff, fallen chest battered open with .38-caliber slugs.

He also used to give me a break on beer prices ("volume discount," he'd joke as he bagged the six-pack) while his doe-eyed younger sister Flormaría pushed a broom across the floor, sweeping her arms in wide arcs around her seven-month belly.

I have a child now, a two-year-old. A beautiful, raven-haired daughter with soft *canela* skin a shade darker than mine and a shade lighter than her father's, that bum. I used to stop up and see Antonia's father on extended "coffee breaks" back when he was unemployed and I was a cop patrolling past his building. Raúl and I went from 0 to 60 in 6.2 seconds. Then I wasn't a cop anymore thanks to a premature midlife crisis helped along by a full-blown drinking and drugging habit, and we fizzled on and off for a while before some of his sperm got loose and Antonia happened. I had learned to stop abusing myself by then, and was driving a cab for a living at the time—that had to go. For a while, Raúl did the right thing by me, moved in and started splitting the bills. It was still hot once in a while. Even after the birth we had to stop the car one time because my breasts were leaking milk. Turned him on so much we did it right there in the rest area on the New York State Thruway. But after a year he split, unable to handle the commitment. Looking back, I'm surprised he lasted that long.

I entered into a long line of unrewarding positions, which leads me to now: I quit my new job today. Working the cash register in a Komputer King chain store isn't so bad, but it's one of those discount outlets where the sales reps know *nothing* about software ("Soft where?" we call it, because so much of it disappears out the door concealed inside $250 trenchcoats), so the customers used to ask *me* questions and I had to do a lot of unpaid homework to hang on to my job. Now it's May and so hot today we went into the back room and took our five-minute coffee break standing right in front of the air conditioner. So the boss comes up to us and tells us we're talking too long and to get back to our servile positions.

"The party's over," he says, "I'm crack-i-i-i-i-n-n-g down!"

"No, you're cracking *up*," I say. Words are exchanged. I take the subway home. Short three days' pay.

Broadway. Recognized by Australian aborigines twelve thousand miles away, its meaning in midtown has been secured in thousands of films, photos, artifacts. From 42nd to 59th, The Gay White Way. North of 200th Street it has a different meaning. Like railroad tracks in the old days, west of Broadway means tree-lined streets, the old stone parish church and Catholic school, the park. East of Broadway means you're on your own. Guess which side I live on.

I trundle out of the subway looking forward to seeing my

kid a few hours early and getting to spend some time with her. Maybe I can make a real meal for her tonight. She's going to forget *mamá* can cook if I don't remind her once in a while. In front of the grocery store a guy who stinks like a damp rug that's been left in the trunk of a car for the summer offers me fifty dollars worth of food stamps for forty dollars cash so he can buy alcohol or drugs. Or maybe some rug shampoo.

I tell him, "You know, the White House is cutting food stamps to the poor because of frauds like you."

"Wha—? White House?" he asks, truly dazed.

"You know, the White House. It's that thing on the back of the twenty-dollar bill."

"Oh!" His face lights up. That. "Okay, twenty."

Oh, what the fuck. If I don't buy them, somebody else will. Little Antonia gets her favorite tonight. Shrimp.

Five flights up to *mamita* Viki's apartment. She opens the door, this mother of eight, grandmother of twenty, and great-grandmother of six (so far), working without papers on a strictly cash basis. What, did you think I can afford some fancy day care? *Mamita* Viki takes care of at least five kids all day every day because the parents have to work. She takes all ages. Gives some of these kids the only square meal they get. I squeeze past her squarish body through the narrow hallway into the living room where two boys five and six years old are trying to see how many times they have to run around the coffee table before the rug wears through to the wood.

Antonia is wobbling around the hall in her red overalls trying to master the lively art of throwing a rubber ball. She pinches the ball with remarkable strength, but isn't so good at releasing it. She's really only eighteen months, but that gets pretty tedious to repeat, so I always say she's two. For you non-parents that means she's still in diapers and speaks in priceless baby talk.

"Mommy!" she says, throwing her arms up, letting the ball bounce backwards behind her.

"Hey, beautiful!" I get the best hug I've had all day—or ever have these days.

Mamita Viki asks me point blank why I'm so early today, so we talk for a while over Spanish coffee so strong beads of sweat form on my upper lip. After a lifetime in Santo Domingo, she claims that's the best way to keep cool on a hot day. My proxy grandmother tells me a girl with my education is better off looking for another job.

Mamita Viki has the seniority to call a thirty-ish mother of one a "girl" and get away with it. She says with my law enforcement background I should try social work, she knows I'd be good at it because I do it for free all the time and why not get paid for it?

"Because I can't stand the system," I tell her in Spanish.

"Who can?" she says.

"I need a nine-to-five. How am I supposed to work an investigator's hours with a kid?"

Mamita Viki nods. "Such a waste."

"Well, we've got to be going. Tonia, where's your bottle?"

Antonia points in the direction of the moons of Mars. We look around for it. After a while *mamita* Viki crouches down in front of the refrigerator and pulls the bottle out from under it. The warm milk supplement has separated into sour water and hyperactive yogurt cultures.

"*¿Qué has hecho?*" I ask Antonia.

Mamita Viki laughs. "I telling her *que el paquete dice,* 'store under refrigerator.'"

"That's 'store under *refrigeration,*'" I tell Antonia, knowing she doesn't understand me yet. "Next time."

Five flights down to the dim haze of a city so humid you almost envy the roaches, who seem so much better prepared for it. Nothing fazes them. I'd carry her, but it's too sticky out and I'm already lugging two environment-destroying plastic bags of groceries. The paper sacks would never survive all this abuse. I cross Broadway at 207th Street and pass a group of *dominicanos* in front of a *bodega* slapping dominoes down on a card table hard enough to break them. The two old ones are content to nod at me as I pass, but the younger ones ask, "What do you want, baby? Name it!" and promise, "I'll give you half my kingdom!" At least they show some respect when I'm with the kid. When I'm by myself they say things that you won't find indexed in *Gray's Anatomy*.

Three flights up to my one-bedroom I get intercepted by Mrs. McRae, who just lost her husband of forty-three years, may he rest in peace. She is one of those white-haired little old ladies who moved in after World War II and never paid the rent late in her life. Her face is gray with agitation and fear, like she's just been robbed.

"Mrs. McRae, what's the matter?" I ask hurriedly.

"Filomena, you know the law—can they do this?"

"This" is a legal-looking letter she's holding out to me with a trembling hand that only buried her husband last Sunday. I lower the groceries onto the stairwell and take the letter, keeping hold of Antonia, who is already squirming to be set free in the apartment. (*Sesame Street* hasn't gotten around to teaching abstract concepts like "patience" yet.) It's from the landlord, writing from his office above the clouds in Trump Tower, telling Mrs. McRae that since the lease was in her dead husband's name, she has one week to clear out of the apartment that she brought two cops and a schoolteacher into the world in. They must still be at work, so I get asked the legal questions.

"They can't throw you out," I tell her first. "You're immediate family and you've been living here since 1947."

"You're sure?" she asks. The mail must have come around one o'clock. I read three hours of agony in her face.

"They can't throw you out," I reassure her.

"But can they do this?" she says, letting me give her back the letter.

"The law can't stop them from writing this garbage and hoping you believe it," I say.

So she reminds me for the forty-fifth time about how her husband helped take back Okinawa from "the Japs" and *now* look at this country, but I have to agree, Trump Tower landlords threatening little old ladies with eviction is pretty irritating. Like anyone is going to buy into this crumbling place if they ever break enough laws to go co-op.

What yuppie's going to invest in a place that's not old enough to merit preservation, just old enough to be falling apart? Elevator? 1924 was a bad year for elevators. Just six flights of stairs, honey.

This is being done to half the buildings they own, but you'd never be able to establish a pattern because they set up a different corporation for each building just to break the chain of accountability.

Finally, the apartment door is open and the baby is free. *Pyew!* I didn't have time to take the garbage with me as I dashed out with the kid this morning. Banana peels and shitty diapers—a winning combination. And the goddamn landlord must have been doing some more of his non-union "renovation" in the warehoused apartment upstairs (since when does it take twenty-nine months to renovate a one-bedroom apartment?) because the floor is covered with a fresh coating of paint chips that dislodge from the ceiling every time they have trampoline practice upstairs, or whatever the hell it is they do up there at 7:00 A.M. on Saturday mornings. What, rest after a hard day? Not for me. Now I've got to vacuum up the pre-war paint chips so the kid won't swallow them and die of pre-war lead poisoning. As an ex-cop I happen to know that no construction activities are permitted other than on weekdays between 7:00 A.M. and 6:00 P.M. as cited in section 54.14 of the NYPD's *Guide to Law*, but a knowledge of the letter of the law never bought me much consideration when I had a shield, so why should it start happening now?

Someone has shoved a leaflet under my door telling me to come to the tenants' meeting tonight to discuss the landlord's underhanded tactics. At least he hasn't hired motorcycle gangs to beat down our doors at 3:00 A.M. Yet. I put the perishables away and get out the five-dollar garage sale vacuum cleaner. It's so weak I have to bend down and stick half the paint chips down its throat by hand. It takes so long

Antonia has time to grab lots of loose chips to play with and I have to trade her for something less deadly half a dozen times. She should have come with a label: ONE BABY: ALL PARTS INCLUDED, JUST ADD LOVE.* Then in fine print: *MAY REQUIRE A LIFETIME OF MAINTENANCE.

When I'm finished vacuuming, I get to roll around on the floor with her, acting like a lunatic and talking baby talk. Hey, I have to speak in complete sentences all day long.

Cooking is a serious pain. Living with a baby has crammed so much into these two rooms that the place upholds the Puny Apartment Dwellers' Law of the Conservation of Volume: Whenever an object is placed on the shelf, another object of equal volume must fall off the shelf.

I unplug the toaster, pick the ten-inch black-and-white Korean TV off the floor, plug it in and put the toaster on top of the TV so I can catch the news while I wash and chop the vegetables. The big news is of interest to parents everywhere. Two executives are being sentenced to a year and a day for distributing chemically flavored sugar water as "100 percent apple juice." A couple of hundred thousand a year they make. You'd think six-figure salaries with five-figure bonuses would be enough money. What are these guys missing that they have to commit fraud to get more? I chop up a carrot that never stood a chance.

Local news brings a hot case from Long Island. A psychologist took the stand in a murder trial in support of the defendant's argument that he was possessed by a manipulative character from a "role-playing game"—whatever the hell that means—that forced him to kill his parents. I suddenly become aware of the chicken blood dripping from my knife to the cutting board. I was born in the highlands of Ecuador, so I know where we get our meat from, but sometimes I recall our pre-modem position somewhat further down the food chain, and I don't like being reminded.

Ecuador makes the international news! That can only mean an earthquake, a military coup, or maybe Madonna decided to buy the place. No, not Madonna, just the stuffy

8

old U.S. secretary of state taking over a meeting of Latin American leaders to express his regret at Ecuador's newly reestablished diplomatic ties with Nicaragua, as if that's any business of his. But when he gets to the chambers of the Ecuadorian congress, he is shocked and outraged by a wall-sized mural by one of our notorious commie-simp artists that apparently equates the CIA iconographically with Nazi-style fascist militarism. A spokesperson for the U.S. says this will "not send a good message to the people of the United States." Ecuador's new president says the mural stays. The camera picks out Fidel Castro for a reaction. Boy, is he getting old. Yipes! I almost slice off the tip of my forefinger with the kitchen knife.

In sports, the Mets beat out the Expos 2–0, ending Dave Cone's recent slump. Let's go Mets. They get Cone in front of the mikes to tell us if he feels his luck is changing. "It's more than a three-hundred-sixty-degree turn," says the ballplayer.

I *hope* it's more than 360 degrees, because from what I learned in geometry class, 360 degrees leaves you right back where you started. We really ought to keep a sharper eye on these sports figures. Try teaching a kid math after he hears some quarterback go on about how he gave "a hundred and ten percent." Who's the kid going to believe, some wimpy math teacher or a star quarterback?

After dinner, I go over the finances. Shit. I need a new job. Fast. Even if I got one tomorrow payday wouldn't come fast enough to cover the bills. That means I've got to shake down Antonia's dad for his court-ordered thirty-six bucks a week. A phone call won't do it, I've got to go see him. For a lousy thirty-six bucks. Wonderful.

The Worm only lives six blocks away. Not nearly far enough, but too far today with the kid and diaper bag. He's got his usual party going. Five or six of his worthless friends are there while he sits in the middle of a sagging couch I saw on the sidewalk three weeks ago, cheating on somebody with his new girlfriend. That's Antonia's dad, as volatile as ether in a bedpan. He never understood that you can't be married from 6:00 to 9:00 P.M. and be single from nine to midnight. Well, he's somebody else's problem now. Except for this weekly bullshit. He has the nerve to pull the proud father routine in front of this semi-nude 40D-breasted teenager who's still young enough to be impressed by a guy who drives a car with a stereo they can hear in North Jersey. Notice I say "drives," not "owns." It's easy to look prosperous when all it takes is ten percent down. Isn't that all a leveraged buyout is? I tell Raúl he's setting his sights too low, he should take his act down to Wall Street and score big. He laughs. She laughs. I'm glad we're all having such a great time.

"Look what Raúl bought *me*," says the talking centerfold, showing off an 18k gold chain. Raúl always had plenty of cash on hand, though I never saw him work terribly hard.

Since he's doing so well, I ask him for seventy-two dollars. I try to make it sound good, like I want this week's and next week's together so I don't have to come after him again on Monday, but I'll say this for the Worm, he knows me well enough to know we need the cash. That puts him at the advantage, so he's in no hurry to pay. Instead he starts telling the girl how we couldn't have sex right after I gave birth so we had pseudo-sex—you know, baby oil between my breasts, sixty-nine—before I shut him up. He still got out those two sentences, all in front of the kid. At least most of the terminology was vague. And this guy's on my beautiful daughter's birth certificate. I've got to mother twice as hard to make up for it.

"That was a long time ago," I say.

"Only a year," he says. Does he have to remind me?

"A year is a long time ago," I tell him. What gets me is this bronze-skinned babe-ette on his arm is a neighborhood girl, so she's got to know who he's two-timing to be with her. The proud father. He must read it in my eyes that I'm about to drag him into the bedroom and blanch him the old-fashioned way unless he comes across so he preempts me and makes a big show of getting out his wallet and tossing a few crumpled bills my way. The girl giggles. He probably spends forty to fifty dollars a night just getting her in the clubs, since she's underage. I shut the door on my way out. I just love it when I leave a roomful of people laughing at me.

Monday, Tuesday, Wednesday I spend trying to get some job interviews. I'll know it when I see the one for me, but I just haven't come across "Mattress Tester: Sleep All Day. Excellent Benefits." Wednesday turns cold and rainy. Down at Thirty-Fifth and Eighth, where handwritten cardboard signs in foreign languages taped to lampposts advertise daily piecework to illegal workers, a guy is on the corner, freezing his wet butt, proffering a clipboard full of what he claims are "Good jobs with good pay," to which all I can say is, "If the jobs are so good, why are *you* handing out leaflets on a rainy street corner?"

Wednesday night is the candlelight vigil the neighborhood arranged in front of Lázaro's shuttered *bodega*. I change Antonia, put her in a dark green dress and take her down there. This once-bright spot on an unfriendly block looks grimy and bleak under the steely gray sky reflected off the wet bricks and metal. Flowers cover some of the graffiti. The only other color is the yellow notice pasted over the metal ribs of the shutters. Next to the Police Department seal it says:

SEAL FOR DOOR OF D.O.A. PREMISES

THESE PREMISES HAVE BEEN SEALED BY THE N.Y.C. POLICE DEPT. PURSUANT TO SECTION 435, ADMINISTRATIVE CODE. ALL PERSONS ARE FORBIDDEN TO ENTER UNLESS AUTHORIZED BY THE POLICE DEPARTMENT OR PUBLIC ADMINISTRATOR.

FOR INFORMATION CONTACT:

It's a form, so they have to write in the voucher and phone number of the 34th Precinct. My old precinct. Pretty grim reminder that murder is so common they have standardized forms for it. The 34th logged seventy-five homicides last year.

Antonia wants to hold the candle, so I have to give mine

away in order to remove the temptation. It's just starting to get dark as the Dominican assistant pastor to the Irish head pastor gets up in front of everyone to say a few words about how Mr. Pérez came from Puerto Rico, how even though he was trying to reclaim this block for the community he had to keep the store open until after midnight seven days a week just to meet the $3,000-a-month rent, that he knew most of his customers by name, was shot in the back, and died while trying to dial 911, which is pretty much every human being's nightmare. I hug Antonia closer to me.

Flormaría approaches me through the crowd with her husband, Demetrio, and my stomach muscles tighten. Her face is grim and streaked with shiny wet streams as the tears roll onto her pregnant belly. There's a moment where I can't find any words for her, then she throws her arms around my shoulders and hugs Antonia and me. She loosens her grip and says, "I want you to find Lázaro's killers."

Demetrio looks at me as if he knew this was coming, had tried to prevent it, and is sorry it happened. I nod. He puts his hands on Flormaría's shoulders. She doesn't move.

"Give them time," I say. "They just started working on it."

"*Por favor, Filomena*," she says, "*tienes que ayudarnos*. You must help us."

"I will. If you need it."

"*Gracias. Gracias. Sólo confío en tí.*"

They want to take a picture with the family, so Flormaría is politely asked to stand next to the authorities. A somber photo op is still a photo op.

Mrs. Santoro gets next to me and says if only I were on the job, like in the old days, the criminals would be in jail already. I tell her the police are working on it. Old Marco must have heard the whole thing because he turns, the fire reflecting off his eyeballs, and says, "Lázaro's soul is very troubled. He has gone to the Grand Master. *Papa Legba les encontrará.*" Papa Legba will find them.

I'm cold enough without Old Marco calling up images of Lázaro's shadowy form, suffering and wandering alone through the lonely corridors of night, seeking an audience with the Voodoo god. Especially since Flormaría just asked me to get involved.

Now the Police Department's public information officer gets up to say that they are proceeding with their investigation, which at the present time shows no sign of involving Dominican mob retribution as has been rumored; it's just a robbery that went wrong. Yeah. *Real* wrong.

I scan the crowd and spot a familiar face standing along the perimeter next to the local assemblyman and city councilman, who have both turned out. It's Sergeant Betty Nichols from the Midtown South Precinct. We used to run a lot of cross-checks together because it was the lowliest dogwork our two precincts could find for us.

"Sergeant Betty," I say, going up to her, getting next to her warmth. "Your beat get extended?"

Sergeant Betty restrains herself at the scene of a homicide, but she has to tell me, "Somehow I thought you'd be around here. Is that little Antonia?" she whispers. "How big she got!" She rubs the backs of two fingers against Antonia's cheek. I put my arm around Betty's shoulders and we survey the scene.

"The feeling never changes, does it?" she says.

I nod.

"Do you know Police Officer Janette Ivins?" she asks, separating so I can shake hands.

Officer Ivins is a dark-complexioned black woman a few inches shorter than me and maybe twenty pounds heavier. She looks like she's new to the force but could probably teach the commissioner a thing or two about city living.

"She was the first officer on the scene," explains Sergeant Betty.

"Oh, so you're with the Three-four?" I say. Officer Ivins nods.

"You want to move away from here and go for a drink?" asks Sergeant Betty.

I say yes to the first part.

CHAPTER TWO

"Cuando el dinero habla, la verdad calla."
(When money talks, the truth keeps quiet.)
— Ecuadorian Proverb

"I'M HERE AS A FRIEND," says Sergeant Betty, settling into a chair behind a foamy pitcher of beer. "I've committed myself to taking one recruit out of every class and seeing she gets through her first year in one piece."

"That's very sisterly of you," I say.

"Damn fucking right it is," says Sergeant Betty, and we all laugh as she pours out three glasses of beer. The waitress brings over a bowl of peanuts for Antonia I didn't even ask for. They know me here. Some places give me a hard time about coming in with a kid, and as I walk out I overhear filthy mouthings about Hispanic mothers. Meanwhile, plenty of people in this neighborhood leave their kids unsupervised for hours just so they can hoist a few at the corner bar. It's not like I'm planning to trade her in for a pitcher of beer.

"So you two worked together?" asks Janette Ivins.

"Only off the record," says Sergeant Betty. "The only friendly face during my probation, she had five years on me when I was a spiny-haired recruit."

"And you've still got those apple cheeks," I say. Betty's a real rarity. Most sergeants turn to crap on you by the fourth or fifth paycheck.

"We'd go out for drinks after shift, right?" says Betty. "The next thing we knew it'd be 2:00 A.M. and we'd figured out how to get some slimebag to incriminate himself."

"Yeah? Tell me one," says Janette.

"Listen," says Betty, "they don't give her credit for it downtown, but Police Detective Buscarsela here invented the controversial but effective innovation of shadowing a person by walking *in front* of them."

"I almost forgot about that," I say, unable to keep from giggling.

"Oh, I'm *never* going to let you forget it," Betty says.

"So?" asks Janette.

"Well," I begin, jiggling Antonia on my knee so she won't get bored, "I was stuck sweeping the homeless out of the 175th Street Port Authority—which is a dog's detail if there ever was one—and this one transient says, 'Whaya botherin' me? Stevie Ray over there's dealin' heroin!' He points Stevie Ray out to me, so I watch this guy for a couple of days. I don't know how I missed it before. Homeboys are pulling cars right off the fuc—" Antonia is at the age where she's starting to repeat what I say. I've got to watch my language when the conversation turns to cop talk. "—right off the George Washington Bridge, steering them to the middle of the block where Stevie Ray does an awful lot of haggling with, say, forty to fifty total strangers on a good day. He's collecting a lot of loose bills in exchange for something. Having determined the high likelihood of illegal activity, I bust the guy in the act. The car leaves its rear two tires on 178th Street heading back to Jersey and never looking back. Okay, so I bust Stevie Ray with $700 in grimy bills and *mucho* heroin in his pockets."

"Twenty-nine glassine envelopes' worth, to be exact," stipulates Sergeant Betty.

"Right. So guess what? The judge throws the case out of court on the grounds that 'The officer did not furnish a basis for a reasonable belief that the defendant was in fact dealing in narcotics!' How do you like that?"

"What are you supposed to do, catch him in a Pakistani poppy field?" asks Janette.

"Well, that didn't stop Filomena," says Betty.

"It's not that he got off," I explain. "He probably would have copped down to simple possession anyway. Big deal. It was that excrement-eating grin he gave me as he walked out of court a free man. *That* got me."

"So what does she do? She calls me up and we shoot the— uh, excrement—over a couple of beers, and between the two of us, we come up with this," says Betty. "I show up on the guy's turf in full uniform to scare him off the block. Wherever he moves, I keep showing up like half a block behind him. We're both off duty, but how the hell's he gonna know that, right? We figure eventually he'll lose his nerve and take the afternoon off. Meanwhile, Filomena's in plainclothes on the other side of the street hoping that maybe when the guy *thinks* he's shaken me he'll head for his home base or leave off the stuff with whoever supplies it or something. I don't even remember what we were thinking."

"He knew my face," I say, "but only in uniform. I figured with a woman in blue on his butt, he wouldn't spot me."

"So we're playing this bit up and down ten, maybe fifteen blocks before the guy decides to give it up and head east," says Betty. "So I drop out of sight and leave the guy looking over his shoulder. The next thing I know Fil's radioing in that she's lost the guy. Then she turns around and sees that she's gotten ahead of him!"

"And the lieutenant told me I was narrow-minded," I say, while Betty starts to pour seconds. I cover my glass. One is my limit these days. One. She doesn't push it.

"You ever nail him?" asks Janette.

"Not in time. He caught fire three weeks later trying to cook up some crank or something. He'd probably be alive today if the judge had let me jail him."

"Makes you think, doesn't it?" says Betty. My beer flattens a bit.

"Listen, Fil, you should come back on the force. It's official: Headquarters has approved on-site day care."

"Yeah, and they've got computers now, too."

"Or at least get yourself a PI's license. You're too smart to be Mickey Mousing around for some chickenshit boss."

"I didn't like the men I was meeting as a cop. Somehow I don't think I'd be meeting a much better class as a private investigator."

"There's other things in the world besides men, you know."

"Yeah, Betty, I know, but I'm not going to start having sex with wallabees. But then, maybe I'm narrow-minded like the lieutenant said." Smiles form. But not for long. We remember what brought us here.

My beer flattens a bit more.

I break the silence. "So you were the first officer to respond the night Pérez was shot?"

"Yeah, but they pulled me off that and gave it to the detectives," says Janette.

"All the shit going down in this precinct and they've got you writing traffic tickets?" I say, forgetting my mouth. Antonia's asleep anyway.

"You got that right," says Janette. "When they heard the word 'mob' they kicked the case upstairs, but they soon pitched that."

"Why?" I ask.

"You want to examine the body?" asks Janette.

"That's what they have coroners for," I say.

"Well, the local hit boys always hack off a piece of the body to bring home as proof."

"And it's all there?" I ask.

"Except for—" Janette looks at Antonia. "You know, his chest. Give a shithead an Uzi and he thinks he's indestructible."

"Or a cheap .38," I say. Even the *Post* got that right.

"That's it. These punks got no family to support, no kids to think about and no future to provide for."

"And finding the right pair—" I begin.

17

"Would take a miracle," says Betty. "Refill, anyone?"

Betty takes the pitcher back to the bar. Janette turns to me. "With all the murders in this precinct, why such a mess over this one?" she asks.

"This is a quiet neighborhood. Most of those murders happened below 200th Street. The cops haven't tamed that battle zone, but they've kept it contained."

"What did he have that was so special?" Janette wants to know.

"Besides what makes any human life special," I say, cradling my sleeping child, "he was a nice guy. He made me smile. And I don't know enough people who do that."

Janette nods. The cradling motion releases a familiar fetid smell, and I carry the kid to the women's room. She's in shit up to her armpits, and she wakes up crabby and screaming. I find myself wishing the person who came up with baby-sized buttons on baby clothes should die a painful death. That's going to cost me three Hail Marys and an Act of Contrition.

Thursday I've got an interview for a managerial position with some group called the Environmental Action Foundation. I figure logging three hundred miles of police paperwork counts as managerial experience. Plus it might be socially rewarding work, although I must tell you the ad first caught my eye because to me the letters EAF stand for the Ecuadorian Air Force.

I try to explain to Antonia that I'll only be gone for a couple of hours, but she's still some months away from a serviceable concept of time. On my way to the subway a man with plastic bags wrapped around his feet asks me for some money because he's hungry. I tell him I can't stand to see that: "If you're really hungry, come on to the deli and I'll buy you whatever you want."

He says, "No, I'd rather have the money."

So would I.

With each express stop farther downtown the boom boxes get bigger and bigger and the Walkmans get smaller and smaller. You realize this is class war through stereo equipment.

The offices of the Environmental Action Foundation are in midtown, on Sixth Avenue in the thirties. I walk past the curved slab of the Grace Building glinting in the noonday sun to where the buildings get a little more crumbly. Using the pretense of construction, the police have practically shut Bryant Park down after a recent shootout.

Thanks to the subway's inexplicable punctuality, I've still got half an hour, so I go into a corner lunch counter to sip an iced tea by the window. Okay, so I gulp it down. The summer heat is coming, all right?

I notice the block has three cops on it.

I've got time to reflect on just how much I detest job interviews. Somewhere out there are lucky bastards with family connections who've never had to go through the degradation of having to cram thirty-some-odd years, 1,000 insights (998 more than *he's* ever had) and 2.8 trillion atoms of existence into a two-minute answer to "So, why do you want this job?" that expands on your gut reaction, "Because it pays, jerk." Maybe this time it'll be different.

Lunch hour subsides and the cops are gone. From out of nowhere three guys appear and set up a nearly invisible drug business. Two guys work the avenue, one keeping an eye out for customers, the other for the cops, while the third one, all 6'2" of him, waits maybe twenty feet down the side street. Times have certainly changed. They used to hawk the stuff so openly people joked about it. Now it's eye contact only. Harsh laws have pushed it deeper into the background, into the dirty corners where the broom rarely goes. There's no talking, and they've got the body of their stash hidden in a hundred different cracks in the daylight so nobody gets caught with more than a gram or two at a time—a misdemeanor in this enlightened state.

Here comes one. The guy on the northwest corner

catches his eye and nods his head away from the avenue towards the partner. A brief exchange takes place. Another customer, a white guy in a new leather jacket, gets to the corner, spots the activity, looks around and approaches the trio. He buys the stuff easily enough, is getting out the money when the cop watcher cuts around the corner and passes the group. They scatter. The big guy—the dealer—splits, so leather jacket pays the cop watcher. He starts walking away, then from where I'm sitting I can hear, "Yo! YO!!" Leather jacket figures the cops have spotted him, because he walks that stiff swift walk of panic that shows he's thinking, "Maybe if I don't break into a run 'til I get to the corner the cops won't spot me." He crosses the side street and quickens his pace, tries to disappear into the crowd. "*YO!* DUDE!" He turns. The big guy has reappeared and is calling to him. Seeing no cops, he turns around and comes back towards the avenue. The big guy wants his money. I can see leather jacket trying to say he paid the partner, but the partner isn't around, and the big guy starts slapping his upturned palm, demanding the money in *his* hand, really puffing himself up, curving his towering body so he's arching over leather jacket, practically surrounding the guy all by himself. I can hear him yelling, "Man, don't you *ever* do that!" So the buyer goes back with the seller to point out the guy he paid, which is a mistake. Now he's back on *their* turf. There's the guy! But he "disappears" into a parking garage, which is ridiculous. Nobody hides in a building with only one exit. The big guy leads leather jacket into the garage. They come out moments later arguing. The big guy says, "Hey man, I did you, now you do me!" Leather jacket answers something about having paid the partner. "Who put the stuff in your hand? Don't *never* do that! Give it back, man!" This is not one of these dealers who relies on customer satisfaction. Must be one of those crackheads who are moving in and giving drug dealing such a bad name. The drug buyer knows it's a scam, but suddenly there's two guys blocking his way and yelling at him on this open sidewalk that could have uniformed cops crawling all over it at any minute.

The ordered city has pulled back and revealed the jungle chaos beneath on a shadowy side street less than fifteen feet from the bright sunlight of Sixth Avenue. Leather jacket gives them back the stuff and they are *gone*. He stands there, slightly transfixed, staring at his empty hands, unable to believe that three guys would run a scam on him for a lousy ten-dollar bag and then hide from him. And instead of creating a center that would offer him the stuff risk-free on the condition that he enroll in treatment or at least get some counseling, we would rather have him undergo this danger.

Meanwhile, the cops have to waste their time and heart tissue chasing these guys away, dying in the street war on drugs while some people I can think of are paying for their own worldwide wars with those same drugs. I've busted crack dealers. They're hard. All sharkskin and bone and there's only one way to beat them. It's not how tough you act (because they're tougher than Pacific crocodiles), it's how *crazy* you act. Because crazy equals dangerous in a way that tough doesn't.

Maybe the human mind should just be free to do what it wants with itself. Just don't do it to anyone else.

All of this really puts me in the right frame of mind for a job interview. I smooth out my skirt, restrain those wild strands of Spanish-Inca hair that have gotten loose from their bonds in this humidity, and head to the building where the EAF is located.

Maybe I was expecting the homish sloppiness of a plywood-paneled loft full of counter-culturists, but I figured it was best to dress for an interview anyway. Sure enough, the elevator is a pre-war rattletrap that is sluggishly and uncaringly shaking itself to pieces. But the place turns out to be pretty damn spiffy. And enormous. Someone in this nonprofit organization is spending an awful lot of money on keeping up appearances. The offices must take up the entire floor, and this is one of those huge old office buildings from the forties that are short compared to today's modern gleaming ice towers, only twenty to thirty stories high, but which still take up half an avenue block. I can't even see the back wall. And I'm definitely underdressed.

I get about three feet before I'm stopped dead in my tracks: they've got three paintings on the walls by Wilson McCullough, an artist who died too soon. His hauntingly dark, environmentally themed canvases are now worth a couple of hundred thousand each. He must have donated them. Before . . .

The "managerial" position turns out to be basically typing and filing. But it's a job. I make a play for it, then go home and get Antonia from the babysitter.

When I was a kid taking high school biology in the Andes, I never understood how robins developed the instinct of neglecting eggs that had picked up the smell from some stranger's touch. You'd figure that can't be much of an aid to survival. But now I realize when I hug my daughter and she smells of some other woman's perfume that my first instinct is to wash her off so she'll smell like herself again. That smell I love.

Home. I'm in the middle of feeding her when the phone rings. It's Flormaría. She wants to see me right away. Immediately. Now.

She's due in five weeks, so I figure she's allowed a few perks. I finish feeding Antonia, and ten minutes later we're in Flormaría and Demetrio's apartment. In spite of everything, she hasn't dropped the basic rules of having someone over; she sets out some cookies that Antonia devours and brews a soothing tea of *yerba luisa*, which is good for the nerves. Turns out I need it. She wants me to drop everything and solve her brother's murder. Tonight. I tell her I'd like to, but I also need to make a living right now, and I don't think she can handle the $200 a day plus expenses that it would cost for me to start a full-time investigation. All this is in Spanish.

"Then just ask around those apartments over the store," she says. "Ask what they saw, what they heard, and in the park across the street, too, ask them what they saw and heard."

"That's the very first thing the cops will have done," I say.

"You think they care that much? Push a few doorbells, ask

a few questions—most of them don't even know *two words* of Spanish. What kinds of questions you think they can ask? What kind of answers you think they gonna get? *Lo mismo que nada.* But those people would talk to *you*, Filomena."

"Four or five buildings six stories high with five apartments on each floor? That's a hundred and fifty apartments. *And* the park? I'm telling you, Flor, that's a full-time job."

"*Bueno.* Okay. Just a few of them, then. Just the ones that are the closest to the store, facing the street."

"That's still about forty to fifty apartments . . ."

She looks at me with those big doe's eyes. Her soul reaches out to me.

"All right," I tell her. "Listen: I'll ask around the apartments, but you two darlings take the park. There's no stairs to climb, but still, don't strain yourself. Make sure Demetrio does all the heavy lifting."

"Thanks," says Demetrio. "You know, Filomena, I've had to call the cops a few times on some of those kids in the park. They won't talk to me."

"So don't talk. Just hang out in the background and listen. *¿Comprendes?*"

"*Sí.*" He nods.

"You see, Filomena?" says Flormaría. "Only you know what to do."

Then why did I just commit myself to this?

Three hours later I've covered two dozen apartments and come away with nothing but buckets of sympathy and a few bad attitudes. Maybe tomorrow.

By 11:00 P.M., I've read to the kid, brushed her teeth and put her to bed, and I'm unwinding my brain with a *Burns and Allen* rerun on Channel 9. Let me tell you, Gracie could teach logic to the bureaucrats who run things in Ecuador. I also like these old shows because I feel I'm not missing the color. During the commercial, I flip to the public network and get a sound bite on "Superdads of Today." And there goes one of them now: A superdad is feeding a kid while the voice-over says, "With the exception of giving birth and breastfeeding, there's nothing a mother can do for a child that you can't."

Well, whadaya know! And with the exception of writing poetry and peeing standing up there's nothing Lord Byron can do that I can't!

I flip back, when the downstairs intercom buzzes. It's Janette Ivins. Doesn't anybody do business during regular hours? Maybe I *should* open an office. I tell her to come on in, the downstairs lock's broken anyway.

After she's sat down and exchanged a few obligatory pleasantries, asking questions about the kid that allow me to discuss my experience with sleep deprivation as a key element of Third World torture, she gets right to it: "What do you know about Santiago Guzmán?"

"I could tell you his life story."

"Stick to the last couple of years."

"He was the first Dominican to break into the bail bond racket. His nephew Humberto would befriend brokedown fools rotting in jail 'cause they couldn't make bail. Such a friendly guy, he would 'refer' them to a good bail bondsman, who they would end up owing for the rest of their lives, which usually wasn't too long after that."

"What else?"

"He prints a newspaper, *El Tiempo*, which editorializes against mob racketeering, championing free enterprise and competition—as long as it's not competition with *him*. If so, threats turn up in the form of dead rabbits in your morning newspaper, you know, Hollywood stuff. They all think they've gotta live the part, like old man Corleone. Not that Guzmán didn't earn it. When he first started cutting out pieces of Mafia territory, four of *Don* Boronali's foot soldiers cornered Guzmán in a phony office and were about to blow him away when he confessed his guilt and, as a matter of honor, stated his last request: to be allowed to take his own life. They actually fell for that 'code of honor' bit and obliged him by handing his gun back. He turned on them, killing one and wounding the other three before kicking his way out a fifth-floor window."

Janette's eyebrows raise. "*That* wasn't in his file."

"I'll bet. Why the questions?"

There's a space in our conversation that gets filled by the intro music to a rerun of *Sergeant Bilko*. Cops never volunteer information. I'm content to watch a few minutes of Phil Silvers trying to smuggle a roulette wheel onto the base in a jeep until Officer Ivins remembers why she came. I point to the TV and tell her this must be one of the first American situation comedies with a regular black cast member who's not a butler or a maid, but a soldier just like the other guys. Leave it to a Jew to give a black his first break on TV, I tell her. Of course, this was back in the fifties. She takes the hint and gets real.

"The Pérez investigation is going nowhere."

Oh.

"Well, that doesn't follow type," I say. "When a couple of street punks blow someone away, half the time they get caught because one of them's so goddamn cocky and stupid he can't help bragging about it. You got your ears open?"

"Wide open."

I nod. "Unless someone's telling them to be quiet."

"Exactly: no street punks mouthing off. So they think maybe it *was* mob-related, but if they press it, the mob will dig in and we'll get nowhere on that angle, too. So publicly we're still looking for two street punks, hoping the mob will keep its guard down."

"And the lieutenant doesn't think Guzmán already has that information from some Departmental informant who's falling behind in his swimming pool payments?"

"I'm the low person in this PR game."

"So where *do* you fit in?"

"They want me to find a runaway."

"A what?"

"You know, a renegade. Some street-level soldier who's pissed off at his bosses for not promoting him fast enough."

"Are we talking about a cop or a mobster?" I say. She

shrugs. She must have heard that one already. "Let me get this: They expect *you* to single-handedly infiltrate the Dominican mob? That's absurd."

"And I'm getting no help from anybody. This is supposed to be my first chance to show what I've got, and the lieutenant's handed me a job the attorney general's office can't even handle." That still doesn't sound right.

"Words cannot describe the lieutenant," I say. Janette nods. "Though 'asshole' comes close."

Janette laughs. That breaks some of the tension.

"Somebody got it in for you?" I ask. "You know, somebody who wants to see you screw up?"

"Maybe."

"One thing I learned working for the lieutenant," I say, "is that whatever line of investigation you're pursuing, no matter how well thought out, if it isn't producing results, it's wrong. Change your approach."

"That's why I came to you. I need your help."

"An unemployed mother living off somebody else's food stamps and you need *my* help?"

"Sergeant Nichols said you'd help me. She said you'd have some ideas."

She came armed with the right artillery, didn't she?

"Besides," she goes on, "it's a class B misdemeanor to refuse to aid a police officer if he or she has been identified as such."

"Section 195.10, Penal Law," I say.

She smiles.

"I'll ask around," I say.

"I really appreciate this, Detective Buscarsela."

"Call me Fil."

"Thanks, Fil. You know, I came to you 'cause I didn't want the Department to see me sweating this out."

"I understand."

I'm showing her out the door when she turns and says in a hushed voice, "So I'd sure appreciate it if you didn't let it get out that you're doing this for me."

"Sure. It'll probably be easier on my own, anyway. Some of it."

I come back in and flop down in front of the tiny TV in time to hear Sergeant Bilko boast, "Somebody's got to take care of the South Pacific: Audie Murphy's in Europe!"

CHAPTER THREE

"Steal wisely."
— Alexander Pope

ALL RIGHT, I'm investigating a possible mob murder, without having examined the body or the scene of the crime, with no leads, no physical evidence, no witnesses. Who in all the wide world should I suspect? Where do I begin? Imagine searching all the libraries in the world for one particular book, without knowing the author, title, subject, or call number— just a vague sense that the cover *might* be dark blue or brown. Cops are trained to size up any sort of behavior deviating from the norm as being suspicious. Someone wearing a long-sleeved shirt on a hot day is supposed to make us think: intra-venous drug user. But I always asked, Who decides what's "suspicious" and what's "normal" behavior? You? Me? The *generalísimo's* Minister of Propaganda? Men with combat boots and guns? At what point does individuality bleed over into abnormality? I know I would have a hell of a time trying to explain some of the things I do when I think nobody's watching.

It's true, a cop has to have an incredible ability to read people, to step onto a subway car at two in the morning and scan the whole scene before deciding it's cool and moving on or spotting the one lunatic with the meat cleaver under his coat. It's just that when you deal with people who lie for a living, you tend to look at everyone as liars and everything as one big lie, or, as my first partner Artie Lieberman once put it, "Like that Roman philosopher said, in the end, everything we believe in is bullshit, or something like that."

I corrected him: "That was Socrates, a Greek, and what he said was, 'The only thing I know is that I know nothing.'"

He'd shake his head and laugh saying, "A cop with a classical education . . . Jee*zus*!"

I spend the morning covering the rest of the apartments above and adjacent to Lázaro and Flormaría's store and come up with the same nothing I got last night. I realize it's time to listen to the advice I gave Janette Ivins: If the line of investigation you're pursuing isn't producing results, try something else.

I decide to start with Ernesto Oliveira. He owns a restaurant called Ollie's. Ernesto was beaten up for declining protection and thrown through his front window onto Dyckman Street under the big smiling face of Oliver Hardy. I don't bother him with stupid questions like, "Why do you think Guzmán would want Pérez dead?" But he knows me well enough, and after about twenty minutes of hushed, sincere coaxing in the back of his storage room while Antonia plays with the empty egg cartons, I get a description of some of the "crew" who sent him through the picture window. I know one of them immediately. He's a scar-faced eighth-grade dropout who thinks that an eight-cylinder engine is a direct extension of his penis. Yeah, there's one in every neighborhood. It's pretty hard to miss a guy who treats Seaman Avenue like a drag strip and thinks of pedestrians and other traffic as obstacles in an exceptionally colorful video game.

Fortunately, my mother taught me never to fight with an ugly person. "They go for your face," she said. Plus I'm with the kid.

So I call the 34th Precinct to leave a message with Officer Ivins describing the vehicle and driver, with instructions to watch him closely for traffic violations (thirty seconds behind the wheel ought to be enough) then take him in and grill the hell out of him. He's tough, but like most of his kind thinks he's a lot tougher than he really is, and will be easily frightened by the thought of spending the rest of his postadolescent sexual peak behind bars. But Ivins is not there, and the cop who answers recognizes my voice and starts playing games: "Could you repeat that, ma'am?" I repeat that I want to leave a message for Police Officer Ivins. "Could you repeat that in Latin, ma'am?" he jokes. I'm torn between shouting at him that I'm trying to help Ivins solve a fucking murder, asshole, or playing to his game, that is, letting chauvinism work for me, a game I grew pretty damn sick of after a while. I hang up to try back later.

I'm taking Antonia to the playground when I remember we need baby wipes. While in the store I'm trying to think of anything else we need, but my mind is preoccupied with getting the old news to Janette Ivins and what my next step should be, and all I can think of is lighter fluid for my Zippo. (My pal Artie used to say that the only reason the Allies won World War II is because of the Zippo lighter. The Germans had the Luger, the Messerschmitt, the Panzer and the V-2 rocket. But we had the Zippo.) I don't buy from this store very often, and here I am buying baby wipes and lighter fluid. The cashier looks at me like I'm a South American terrorist working on a devastating successor to the Molotov cocktail.

Back in our apartment I'm already sweating. I take a two-minute cold shower, because this is the year of the big drought. A wet June and July eventually bail us out, but for four months the most powerful city in the west is at the mercy of nature, just like my "underdeveloped" country of origin. Talk about a blow to the ego. The yups down at the world financial center were positively insulted by this. They're so used to overcontrolled climates that when Hurricane Gloria came crashing through a few years back they didn't even suspend the Staten Island Ferry! Yet they laugh at the English king who thought he could command the tides.

There are a couple of messages from Flormaría on my

machine, so I call her. She wants to know how it's going. I tell her I've got nothing yet, but I'm beginning to feel that something's out there. That's not good enough for her.

"I'm working on it," I say.

"Demetrio's getting nowhere, too."

"He's only been out there one day, give it time."

"Why?"

"Okay, listen: It's pretty likely that those two *malditos* planned the robbery in some way. They probably checked the place out a few times, maybe even while you were there. You want to come down to the precinct with me to look at mugshots?"

"I did that already. I spent two days doing that. It was no good."

"Do me a favor and do it again."

"Only if you go with me."

I had to bring it up.

So we go waste a few more hours looking through eighteen miles of mugshots. Nothing. Then finally she thinks she may recognize a face or two. That doesn't mean it's them. Anybody can stop into a store for a soda. But it gives her something to hold on to. Since Ivins isn't in, I show the photos to the desk sergeant for a check. One of the mugs is busy waiting out a three-year stretch at Ossining for grand larceny (car theft). The other one is out on the streets, but he hasn't gotten into any trouble lately. That worries Flormaría, but I get a copy of the photo and tell her to have Demetrio switch from hanging out in the park to hanging out in some of the many undesirable locations in the neighborhood, cautioning her to tell him *not to flash the picture* in those places if she wants him to come back alive. It's a poor choice of words, but it gets the point across. I figure that project will keep them out of my hair for a while, and maybe even provide a good lead.

I'm wrong.

I started my new job at the EAF this week. So far, it's been pretty slow, but that's to be expected. I mean, I figured that "administrative" meant "secretarial," but the job description didn't say anything about arranging paper clips in size order. Good thing they've got an elementary school grad like me on the job. Not that I haven't sat and stuffed envelopes for hours on end for a worthy cause, but one thing I've learned not just as a cop but from every job is that helping out a cause by doing the grunt work is *still* doing the grunt work, that being a secretary for the EAF is as boring and demeaning as being a secretary for any profit-driven martinet only the pay is sixty-five percent lower, and that *any* subordinate's job most often consists of keeping the boss from showing the world what an incompetent schmuck he is. And my two bosses, Paul Bartlett and Josiah S. Carberry, are both leftover leftists with that misplaced sixties attitude that efficiency is a sign of untrustworthiness, that only capitalists are shrewd businessmen, therefore all good anti-capitalists must be absentminded, computer illiterate spendthrifts. So much for the "homey" quality. Being secretary to these guys is a hell-and-a-half. Even for a cause.

They mean well, I guess, but they're still bosses, and charitable or not, bosses always want a little more work out of employees than they're prepared to pay for.

My other problem is my immediate superior, Dick Zirkelback, an assistant administrator with the personality of a plastic ashtray. Only ten years younger than me, his earliest memory seems to be of the day our current president, George H.W. Bush, took office, and his vision of the world is correspondingly shallow. He's going for a Masters in Circulating Memos, and likes to brag about the books he's reading in class.

"Man, *The Iliad*, it's just like our office!"

I guess he means the disruptive infighting, because I tell him I don't see anyone throwing eighteen-foot bronze-tipped ash spears at each other in this office. I think I've made an enemy. What can he do to me? When they were handing out brains, Zirkelback was standing on the wrong line.

There are six other women who sit near me, chained to the same oars that keep this slave galley moving forward: their word processors. Ten years ago, they would have been called the "typing pool." Sophia's a Greek immigrant working her way through college, Jennifer's a paper-thin Long Island kid straight out of high school, Liz is a vivacious Argentine-American, and Helena is an efficient but reserved visitor from what they now call the Czech Republic. Ellie and Francie are a whole different breed. They're not that much older than me, but they inhabit another world. Their minds were molded in all-white suburbia before the women's movement of the seventies. They *want* to be secretaries.

On our coffee break, I meet some of the fundraising staff, and strike up a conversation with a woman named Lydia. It turns out Lydia is studying to be a commercial graphic designer, and this is just a day-job that pays the rent. She's got a kittenish figure, reddish-brown hair and a husky-sexy Lauren Bacall/Kathleen Turner-type voice that must have the men battering down the door to her apartment.

"Yes, but not the right ones," she says.

We share a brief discussion on the difficulty of locating the three decent men out there before Zirkelback taps his watch to remind everyone that it's time to get back to work.

Besides the six keypunch operators whose backs are towards me most of the time, the only person whose face I can actually see while I'm sitting at the keyboard is a projects coordinator (that means fundraiser) named Jeff Cohen. When I step into his cubicle to introduce myself he's on the phone, waving me stiffly away. "This is a private conversation," he says. I reserve comment about people who expect privacy in open-air office cubicles, since I'm trying to limit myself to making one new enemy per day. The only other nice person I meet my first day is the guy who handles the nonprofit bulk mail, a light-complexioned black man named Kwame. Turns out he's from Eritrea, and I have to verbally dance on eggs to find out if Eritreans consider their homeland a province of Ethiopia or a separate country. He says they *are* a separate country. I placate him with talk about Ecuador's peculiar status, too, on the losing end of a fifty-year-old border dispute with Peru, and right away we're fellow travelers.

We take our awful machine-made coffee back to his work area, which, curiously enough, is in a sort of "third world" area of this fancy office. Way in the back, beyond the carpeted cubicles, we come to a makeshift storage area overflowing with cardboard boxes full of God knows what. Behind that even, down a dark hallway with no ceiling tiles, exposed pipes, next to the toilets, is the bulk mail maintenance room. Oh, he's got a desk, a phone, computerized mailing lists, and some nice maps on the walls showing the extent of worldwide environmental disaster, but a fire could break out down here and it would be days before anyone in the front office took notice. And I smell chemicals.

"It comes through the vents from the garment sweatshop downstairs," he says, sitting at his desk. He's wearing a knitted vest. I guess where he comes from, this is cold weather. But he likes it better than Miami, where he first lived after fleeing ethnic oppression at home, only to be harassed by the Dade County Police:

"One day," he says, "I was walking away from the shops on Eighth Street near Overtown and a cop car pull up, they jump out and *throw* me against the wall! They ask me, What are you doing here? What is your name? They want to see my identification, but they are slapping my legs for concealed weapons. Then they are jabbing their billy clubs into my kidneys! That never happen to me in Ethiopia! And it never happen to me up here."

"That's because you wear a shirt and a tie and you work in midtown."

"No, up here it's better. New Yorkers gave very generously to feed my country."

"But somehow we can't fund housing for thirty thousand homeless people."

"Yes. You have so much wealth to share with my poor country. Why do these problems exist here?"

I'm saved from having to answer that one, but the cure is worse than the disease. Zirkelback leans his face in the door and says, "Mr. Bartlett is looking for you."

Yeah, he probably wants me to straighten out all the bent staples so we can reuse them.

I take Antonia to the park. On the way, one of life's little inconveniences broadcasts his desire to copulate incessantly with me. I decline.

Some of the other mothers and a few fathers are out on the playground, being vigilant of their children while gossiping in the sun. You can see Pérez's store from the playground. It's still closed. I'm there about twenty minutes, pushing Antonia on the swing and spotting her on the slide, catching up on what new mischief the other toddlers have managed to come up with, when I look up and see Janette Ivins watching us from behind the chain-link fence. I don't know how long she's been there, or why she might not want to be seen approaching me, so I lead Antonia by the hand and join Janette for a walk around the park at the speed of Antonia's size-two feet.

Janette says, "I heard you were trying to reach me."

I'm surprised the message got delivered at all. I tell her how and why she should apprehend our hot-rodding young mercenary.

"I can't bring someone down to the station on a traffic violation," she says.

"That's a rookie cop talking," I say. "Where this punk comes from, the police do whatever they want. Sure, he's heard about Constitutional rights, but he'll forget about them quick if you remind him what the boys back home would do to him if they ever saw him again."

Janette is unconvinced. They forgot to teach her that at the Academy. I say, "Just stop him for excessive horn blowing,

35

Section 151 of Traffic Regulations. Once you've got him check out the inside of the car. If there isn't something illegal in plain sight I'll wash your feet next Holy Thursday. Or catch him when he leaves his car idling. More than three minutes and you're authorized to tag the steering wheel, remove the key and deliver it to the station house."

"I'm impressed," says Janette.

"You can play by the rules if you want, but you've got to know how to make the rules work for you."

"I hear you," she says.

We complete a circuit of the soccer field and walk up the hill to the baseball diamonds. Two games are going. On the far field it looks like O'Farrell's Pub is clobbering the boys from Mehan's Garage. On the near field it's Juanita's Supermarket versus the *Al Paraíso* Grocery. I can't tell who's winning. This is about as far as integration gets. Sharing opposite fields, but not really mixing. I guess that's better than some neighborhoods. This whole diamond is Dominican, the sidelines too. Not as large or loud as the turnout for the Irish game, but pretty good.

I'm not a real softball fan. The ball's too damn easy to hit. *Everybody* gets a hit, for Christ's sake. Give me baseball or soccer. Softball is all in the fielding. Middle-aged men with potbellies and two-pack-a-day smoker's hacks are getting hits off this pitcher and running down the fumbling short-stop for singles. The next batter up makes my head jolt back out of reflex.

"What up, girl?" says Janette.

"Check out who's batting for Juanita's Supermarket."

Janette looks over at a tallish man in his late thirties, top-heavy with a combination of muscle and fat, fat cheeks, and a moustache bordering on walrus. I tell her, "That's Alejandro Pliego. One of Guzmán's lieutenants. He might even be friendly about it if you catch him in the right mood."

"So you don't think I should take his car keys down to the station house?"

"Not if you want to keep your job. A guy like Pliego might

see you openly to work out a deal. 'Course, you'd have to have something for him."

"You ain't suggesting I bribe a mob lieutenant to talk?"

"Not a chance. I mean you've got to have something *on* him, something big enough to be a real bother, but you'll forget it if he remembers a couple of names for you."

"Oh, all I gotta do is get something on him, huh? And all you gotta do to bring about world peace is stop everybody from fighting all the time."

"Sounds simple, right? Tell you what, you go after the drag racer, and I'll see if I can help you dig up something to irritate Guzmán's gang into cooperating."

"Easy to say."

"I'm not just yakking, Janette, I *know* what I'm offering. And I don't get overtime, backup or a pension."

"I didn't mean it like that."

"You better not."

"So give me some background on this Pliego dude, maybe I can use it on our friend the drag racer."

"I just said I don't have anything you can use. Not yet." I reconsider. "He's got a pretty conventional criminal background: the son of a Dominican sugar cane worker, emigrated here in sixty-five, which would have made him ten or twelve years old maybe, provided schools with a disciplinary nightmare until he dropped out the week before his sixteenth birthday, arrested eight or nine times by his eighteenth. Graduated to the big league with the help of a violent taxi strike a couple of years back."

"I remember that."

"Yeah. The taxi drivers were easy targets, so some idiot decided to hire some Cuban and Dominican muscle, strictly as temp labor. But they had no loyalty to the strikers, the bosses had the money, so they switched sides and helped the bosses break the strike. There were some deaths. Anyway, once in, they couldn't be gotten out, and the taxi and limo racket was a mighty fine stepping-stone to bigger and better things. The Cubans' corporation made most of its money from drugs, but this gave them a good hold on previously legitimate trades. For Pliego, it must have come as a blessing—which would fit in with his unique interpretation of Christianity."

"Like what?"

"The old Robin Hood act. Two or three times a year he flies down first class to hand out ten-dollar bills in his old *barrio*. The people know it's blood money, but when's the last time the law did anything for them? Hell, Guzmán built a low-income housing development outside of Puerto Plata! Two hundred fifty units. That's more than the government's *ever* done for them."

"So to them he's a hero."

"Sure is." I'm watching Antonia playing around with the ballplayers' children. Another run scores. "I always thought the playground bullies'd be different when I grew up, that they'd learn to stop taking advantage of their size and strength. That's how a kid sees things. Always optimistic, full of possibilities. Well, I've grown up. They haven't."

"The bullies grew up, all right, but they ain't changed none. That's why they're running things."

"Anyway, they've been trying to pin a string of felonies on Pliego for years. He's got a smartass lawyer who manages to delay trial every time the cops get all the witnesses together, and you can imagine how tough it is to get seven people to agree to testify against a mobster, even a mid-level one like Pliego, only to have the whole thing be rescheduled half a dozen times. Then when they finally get to trial, the prosecutor makes deliberate reference to Pliego's refusal to testify, thereby unconstitutionally implying his guilt before the jury, so the judge *has* to call a mistrial."

"Smooth."

"They must have pumped that prosecutor plenty," I say.

"Sounds like he's just making the rules work for him."

"Ah, shaddap."

Our conversation is cut off by the familiar wall-shaking sonic thrust of a particular flashy red sports car.

"That's him!" I tell Janette. "Move it."

She starts to run, turns back and yells, "Let me know what you find—"

"Go go go!" I tell her, trying to keep her from telling the whole neighborhood I'm working with her.

I watch Pliego for a while through the chain link of the backstop. The sides have changed and he's playing third. Two guys in a row are walked, which might be a record in softball. The next batter hits a grounder and runs it out with the help of some especially lousy fielding. So now it's bases loaded. The next man up connects for a soaring line drive over Pliego's head. He's taller than I thought, because he jumps up, makes the catch, lands on the bag doubling out the runner from third, then throws the ball to second where the other runner slides too late and is called out for a triple play. I'll say this for Pliego, he can sure play softball.

I carry Antonia away from the diamond down towards the Harlem River inlet. Joggers sidestep us impatiently. I envy them. No more running—doctor's orders. I give Antonia some bread for the ducks and stand for a while watching the Hudson in full spring flood roll along the Jerseyside Palisades and under the majestic Henry Hudson Bridge. We walk along the marshy edge of the inlet to the woods. Antonia wants to explore. Just like her mom. I follow her down a path, lift her over a drainage ditch and down to the water's edge. She throws some stones in, giggling with each splash, then I convince her to head back with me. Just before the drainage ditch I spot something I hadn't noticed the first time: more Voodoo in the park. Five wax candles burned down to their stubs, arranged in a cross, red, brown, green, blue, yellow in the center, and some brightly colored pieces of cloth tied around a whole chicken carcass.

That reminds me of what old Marco said at the candlelight vigil about Papa Legba. Just for the sheer hell of it I decide to ask him what he knows about Pliego or Guzmán that might help solve Lázaro's murder. Marco is revered in this neighborhood. People swear by his home remedies, for which he refuses payment. He makes what living he does selling ices, and is easy to spot over by the basketball court with his dirty straw hat, scraping away with sunburnt sinewy arms on a forty-pound block of ice with a razor-sharp slicer. We talk in Spanish.

"What flavor for the little girl?" he asks.

"Ooh, lacky," says Antonia.

"He doesn't have chocolate," I say, scanning the array of bottled colors.

"Sure I do," says Marco, reaching inside his wagon and taking out some home-made chocolate syrup.

"All right," I say, reaching for my money.

He stops my hand as he gives Antonia the ice. "No money," he says. "I've been waiting for you to come see me."

"You have?"

"Sure. I know you can't rest until Lázaro's killers are caught."

"Well, that's a bit extreme—"

"And you know I say Papa Legba help you to find them."

"Okay," I say. He nods firmly.

"You good woman. Good soul. Good spirit."

"Knock it off, you're giving me a swelled head."

He smiles a wizened smile, his gold teeth flashing in the setting sun. "*El Don* Guzmán come to me for magic baths," says Marco.

"Magic baths?"

"Oh, is very strong baths. I put jasmine, orgeat, almond, holy water, *trago*—well, most times I use *trago*, he insist on Champagne, pay extra for it—pineapple, mushrooms, some cock's blood—"

I clear my throat. "What is this used for?"

He looks at me as if I've asked what day of the week comes after Saturday. "To protect him from the evil that others wish him! Very strong baths. He pay me well for them." Now he lowers his voice for the real thing. "I make an herb tea that helps him relax. It sometimes loosens the tongue. Some men yes, some men no. Guzmán, yes. I tell him he must unburden his mind in bath. He say, 'Damn *chinos* damage car.' Cost him plenty to replace whole car before Monday."

Chinos. That's a word they use for greenhorn newcomers.

"Thanks, Marco," I say, and we start to go.

"Wait," he says. I turn around and before I can say or do anything, quickly, almost imperceptibly, he rubs a root or maybe it's an herb on the four points of a cross across my chest. "You protected now. Papa Legba protect those who do His work." He means it.

It's a funny feeling. If Marco were in the Church, he'd be a bishop by now. And a blessing is a blessing no matter what side of the street it comes from. I tell him, "Thanks." And I mean it too.

Sunday I skip Mass at the Good Shepherd Church, west of Broadway, to hear the Spanish Mass at St. Jude's, *east* of Broadway, across Tenth Avenue from the 205th Street Gasetería, a red brick windowless church that looks like a factory from the outside, where sunglassed anonymous mobsters get themselves blessed before moving on to the day's more profitable duties.

I pray for the Lord to help me understand better, communicate better, live better, to help me find a path other than violence.

Both Guzmán and Pliego are there. After Mass, when they're all filing out, I notice the dark unfamiliar face of a nervous-looking man of medium build as he squeezes through to get closer to Guzmán, who brushes by without looking at him. The man edges sideways towards Pliego through a pew full of people who haven't finished praying. It looks like there is eye contact between them, and Pliego shakes his head once in what might be a succinct "No." I think I see him indicate his watch. Later? I don't know what the connection could be between this shuffling character and *Don* Guzmán, but I figure my disguise of mother and child to be pretty impenetrable.

The guy heads straight from the church to a sandwich place down on Dyckman Street, which is fine with me because Antonia's getting hungry. After lunch, the guy hangs out with some very dark-skinned Dominicans for nearly forty-five minutes, and I have a hell of a time pretending I'm window shopping up and down the block the whole time. They split a six-pack of beer, watch the women, finally the guy splits off and heads west towards the Hudson. I follow him the length of Dyckman Street to a garage half a block from the abandoned substation under the highway.

The proverbial bell goes off in my brain. Old Marco had said Guzmán's complaint was of inexperienced help damaging a car. At this point my motherly instinct is to leave Antonia with *mamita* Viki and come back later alone, but my detective's instinct keeps me moving towards the garage at an eighteen-month-old's pace, racking my brain for a cover that'll let me look the place over. By the time I get there I've decided to tell them I'm thinking of buying a 1975 Duster for $250, and could I bring it in so they might have a look under the hood? They go for that. I stand around and play the role of the woman who needs help understanding car engines, and they are perfectly content to let me hang around and talk, and—God, I really don't like doing this!—I let Antonia loose so she can run free through the place. That supplies me with sufficient cover to go snooping around pretending to chase after her.

I don't know what I'm looking for, of course, except "suspicious" vehicles of some kind. A clean license on a dirty car, maybe, or a real screamer like a New York inspection sticker and Jersey plates. After a while I figure my luck has already been too good for one day, and the act is beginning to wear a little thin. I lie in wait and ambush Antonia in front of a rancid chartreuse-colored BMW. I can't believe the poor taste of some of the yuppies moving into this neighborhood's newly sprouting co-ops. I've never seen a BMW this color.

A single nerve ending somewhere inside me twitches, and makes me get down on one knee, all the while mouthing a monologue about, Oh, Antonia, how could you let *both* of your shoes get untied? when I'm actually restraining her with one hand and looking at the BMW's grille. The underlip of the hood looks dark, but I can't be sure in this light. I take out my compact mirror and hold it up to the grille, trying to catch a little fluorescent light from above, but it's no good. Then I remember the Zippo. I ignite the flame, align the mirror with it and there it is: a quick job, something the real owner would never stand for, particularly since the original color was a nice royal blue. Stolen? Kind of sloppy for mob work, but I'm in the right place, certainly.

What did I say about those Zippos?

Eight phone calls later I finally reach Janette Ivins. She says, "Filomena, I didn't get nothin'."

I tell her, "I did."

CHAPTER FOUR

> "I believe in getting into hot water.
> I think it keeps you clean."
> — G.K. Chesterton

MONDAY starts a bad week for cops. First, federal officials open an investigation into whether tens of thousands of dollars that were being used by the NYPD to arrange stings, drug buys and the like were milked for private use by some of the arrangers. That's bad for public relations. Then I'm riding the subway to work, and I open the paper to find a twenty-three-year-old *latina*—who frankly looks a lot like me before I started letting my hair grow naturally—a cop's daughter, is accusing two Queens police officers of sexual and verbal abuse. I scan the text for the facts. She was with her black boyfriend; it's unclear how the trouble started, but it ended when the cops beat the guy to the ground, arrested her and dragged their new prisoner into the patrol car where they proceeded to punch, kick, fondle, and prod her with a night stick. The two officers have been put on modified duty, while the vice-president of the Patrolmen's Benevolent Association is considering counter-charges against the woman. "The officers accused will be completely exonerated," he says. "Unfortunately, the officers of the 113th Precinct are now fair game for anyone who feels inclined to make bizarre charges against them."

My blood boils at the thought of a man who thinks that

a woman would "feel inclined" to invent charges that only bring embarrassing exposure and a long and ugly litigation process. Oh yeah, it must be a lot of fun to come forward and say, "They shoved a night stick into my crotch," and have this desk jockey laugh it off with one of those just-between-us-guys bullshits. I'd like to catch this guy *in flagrante delicto* with a non-mammalian life form.

I get out at 34th Street and walk through Penn Station to use the public restrooms, but two of the stalls have been roped off with that yellow plastic CRIME SCENE: DO NOT CROSS tape. Oh, *great*.

There's a foul smell at work that no one else seems to notice. I worry. We once had a case where a gardener beat a woman to death, then claimed the fumes from some ingredient in the insecticide he was using was the cause of his temporary, violent outbreaks. An expert toxicologist upheld his testimony, but the judge overruled it. Still . . . Then I notice how all the visitors to my boss's office keep saying, "Oh, it smells so *new*." I go and see for myself. He's gotten new carpeting, and that smell is the contact cement underneath evaporating. I can't believe this. Here I am supposedly working for an environmental organization, meanwhile I'm breathing in industrial glue and it's making me sick. And I'm nowhere near a window. I complain to Francie, the secretary in charge of supplies, and she fishes around in her desk for a can of "air freshener." I tell her more chemicals is not what I had in mind. Boy, I'm just making one friend after another in this place.

By mid-morning, it's time to begin seriously questioning reality. I'm detecting erratic behavior from some of the professional staff, but I can't tell if it's really them or just my own dizziness. Normally I can make that distinction.

One of the Foundation's programs involves getting tourists to send in their leftover foreign currency so that we can send it back to the country of origin as a mass charitable donation. My bosses are nonplussed that the Peruvians don't *want* to buy back their currency with dollars, even at a greatly reduced exchange rate, because, weak as the dollar is everywhere else in the world, it's the solidest currency in the Americas. I could have told them it was time to begin questioning reality.

Meanwhile I'm trying to type with increasingly unresponsive fingers and eyes that keep unfocusing. The phone rings.

"EAF," I say. A woman laughs.

"That's funny," she says. "I always answer the phone with, 'EPA.'"

Anyone who starts out by sharing a laugh sounds like a human being to me. I ask her, "*The* EPA? The U.S. Environmental Protection Agency?"

"That's us," she says. "You must be the new assistant director."

"Director's assistant. There's a world of difference."

"You don't have to tell me," she says. "They call me a Remedial Project Manager, which sounds like I'm teaching juvenile delinquents how to read."

She can't see my smile, but there's amusement in my voice. "My name's Filomena. What's yours?"

"Gina. Gina Lucchese."

"You work with the Environmental Action Foundation?"

"Only unofficially."

"Jesus, doesn't anybody do anything officially?"

"Only when we don't want to get anything done."

I chuckle. "Mm-hmm. I used to work for the city."

"Doing what?"

"It's a long story."

"I'd like to hear it sometime."

Just then Mr. Bartlett steps out of his office. "Who is that?" he asks me.

I tell him.

"Transfer that into my office," he says, and shuts the door behind him.

"Gotta go," I say, and transfer the call. Damn. The one interesting voice I've heard in this place besides my new Eritrean friend Kwame and a couple of my sister galley slaves and the boss decides she's too important to have her waste time talking to me. It's time for a break anyway. Just as I'm getting up, Mr. Bartlett opens his office door, still on the phone, and says to me, "Filomena, did an envelope arrive from the EPA in this morning's mail?"

"I haven't seen it."

"Well, would you look?"

"Nothing came this morning."

"What about the late morning mail?"

"I'll have to check the mailroom."

"So do it."

Using job skills I mastered sometime around the second grade, I go down to the mailroom and wait for the mid-morning delivery to be sorted. The fast-moving shape glistening with sweat turns out to be a heavy-set, medium-dark black man who hands me the envelope without looking up and gets right back to work, his arms swishing from mail bag to tray, tray to slot so quickly it makes me dizzy, or maybe that's the residual glue vapor.

I open the envelope and take the long way back so I can have a look at what Ms. Lucchese does. Wow! She's a full-fledged Superfund investigator authorized, like the proverbial five-hundred-pound gorilla, to go *anywhere she wants*, at any time, for whatever reason. Her specialty seems to be Superfund Priority Cleanup sites that are owned by the U.S. Government. Her list has such familiar names on it as the Livermore Lab in California, army depots and ammunition plants, a few Air Force bases, contractor-operated rocket missile test sites, and a place called the U.S. Mint. All in all there are thirty-two sites on the list, eight of which are her responsibility. I've got to get to know Ms. Gina Lucchese better.

I get back upstairs, knock on Bartlett's door. He opens it a crack, grabs the envelope and shuts the door in my face. I quiet the inner voice from saying something obscene, take a deep breath and let it out slowly.

I'm getting ready to break for lunch when Janette Ivins

finally calls. I told her to watch the Dyckman Street garage for any unusual activity and especially to keep an eye out for a chartreuse BMW for which I supplied the license plate. She tells me the owner of the vehicle picked up the car at 8:00 A.M. this morning, only it wasn't chartreuse, it was dark blue. She says she traced it, and the man was the legitimate owner of the vehicle.

"What was wrong with it and when did he bring it into the garage?" I ask. Embarrassed silence. "Officer Ivins, the lieutenant would have canned me for not getting the engine serial number, the mileage, date of last oil change and a more exact description of the color than 'dark blue' since repainting jobs are our primary evidence. You better start earning your pay." Suddenly I am aware of a few keypunch operators turning my way. Let them turn.

"Sorry," says Janette Ivins. "I got caught up in following the owner."

"You could have verified ownership simply by asking to see his license and registration. It would have taken about ten seconds. Save your detective work for the tough ones."

More silence. Then I ask her, "How soon can you call me back with that other information?"

"I'll get right on it," she says.

"Okay. I'm going to lunch, but I'll be back. The air in this place is making me sick."

I hang up and ride the hiccupping elevator down eight floors to street level and go munch on my homemade tuna salad in one of those little cubes of green they reclaimed from between the concrete skyscrapers. The air upstairs must be pretty bad if a twenty-five-foot-wide break in midtown Manhattan smells like Appalachian spring to me. I finish my lunch quickly enough, then sit there just trying to breathe in the air and clear my head. Goddamn that chemical smell! It really has fogged my thinking. The murderers are getting away, but my boss has a new carpet! I've got to get back in case Janette calls, but clearing my head is important too, so I stay ten more minutes breathing as deeply as I can. A city like this should have public oxygen bottles on every corner. I walk around the block a couple of times to see if increasing my metabolic rate will work the stuff out of my system quicker. It seems to help a little. I head back inside.

One o'clock passes. Two, three o'clock. Still no call. At three fifteen, when I'm busily typing the millionth set of corrections to the new appeal letter (that's junk mail to you), Zirkelback sticks his narrow head over the top of the partition and says, "Those corrections ready yet?"

"I'll be ready to print out in five minutes."

"No you won't. There's a line for the printer."

"Whatever."

"It's got to get done," he says, as if I've spent the afternoon reading *Playgirl*. He starts to leave. "Oh, by the way, you got a call. Janel—no—Janet?"

"Janette?"

"Right." He snaps his finger at me and disappears.

"Did she leave a number?" I call out. No answer. It takes nearly all the resistance I've got in me not to break the keyboard over Zirkelback's head, but that would only bring down assault and battery charges, plus property damages. Sometimes knowing the law sucks. I dial the 34th Precinct. Ivins is out on patrol I'm told, try back at four o'clock.

A very slow hour passes during which I complete the damn corrections, put the file in electronic line for printout, and call up *mamita* Viki while waiting, to say hello to Antonia. *Mamita* Viki puts her on, and when she says "Mommy!" to me over the phone, emotionally so close but half a city away, so tender in her recognition and me sitting in this drop-ceilinged pneumatic office space, my heart wells up with the urge to smother my baby with big wet kisses, hold her close, and never let her go. I talk some baby talk back to her, giving the heads another reason to turn.

It's a quarter to five before I get Janette on the phone.

"The BMW was brought in Friday for a twenty-thousand-mile tune-up," she says.

"And got two paint jobs?"

"That's how it looks."

"And the owner didn't notice?"

"He says the garage told him they scratched the paint while they were working on it so they repainted it no charge."

Hmmm. I cup my chin with my free hand.

"Filomena? You there?" she asks.

"I'm thinking." I don't really know how much time goes by before I say, "Will the Department stretch to a stakeout?"

"What's the justification?"

I lower my voice further. "Tell them you have probable cause to believe that Guzmán's mob is using the garage as a source for untraceable cars. You have material evidence that non-participatory citizens are having their cars used to pull mob crimes. The customers, who are themselves innocent of any crime, leave the cars off on Friday, the garage paints it another color for a job on Saturday, then paints it back the original color so it's ready to go back to the customer by Monday morning. And that they have even gone to the length of replacing an entire car when one was inadvertently damaged beyond twenty-four-hour repair."

There's a pause during which I can hear Janette Ivins whispering "shit" to herself.

"It's okay to be impressed," I tell her. "My mind's been askewed all day long. Think you can do it?"

"You bet, Fil."

"Oh, and, uh, by the way, Officer Ivins, getting that testimony from the owner about the scratched paint? That was pretty good police work."

"Thanks."

We say goodbye. I think now maybe we're getting somewhere.

Only now do I look up and notice the time: 5:30. From out of nowhere Zirkelback waltzes by, sees me still sitting at my typing table, and says, "Staying late? That's the spirit."

I mumble, "Get a personality!"

I still believe that honesty is the best policy, but when you move in the circles I move in, playing by the rules doesn't always accomplish much. That doesn't mean breaking and entering, which you can only get away with if you're organized like the CIA or Stasi or Ecuador's own *Escuadron Volante*, but it *does* mean lying an awful lot. When dealing with crooks or corporations, extracting the simplest information is impossible without lying. I understand Laurence Olivier once said that acting was a series of lies that added up to the truth. Sounds a lot like police work.

The problem with most law enforcement agencies is they are no good at the little lies. The only way they know how to do it is the patented Phil Spector Wall of Lies—you know, spend three years and $8 million trying to pass off three undercover agents as big-time dope dealers. But in order to pass, the undercovers have to flash so much cash and generally emulate the real drug dealers for so long that by the time they make the bust, the undercovers *are* drug dealers. Not an efficient system. And the Feds spend years trying to infiltrate these tremendous, bureaucratic and stratified mob organizations. When I'm on a job, I can be myself, as long as I conceal some of my intentions behind half-truths.

I decide to call Pliego in person. I'm mildly astonished to find him listed in the phone book, on Nagle Avenue across from Fort Tryon Park. It's the first thing Tuesday morning and I'm taking a break from typing in the corrections to a computerized mailing list of high-dollar contributors who are going to be invited to a $100-a-ticket-minimum gala event. (The good seats are $1,000.) A woman answers. I ask to speak to Mr. Pliego.

She says, "He's on another line right now, can I have him call you back?"

Pretty polite, considering she's working for an indicted felon. Try calling up a government agency sometime.

I can play this politeness game too: "I'd like to make an appointment to see him."

"And you are—?"

"Filomena Buscarsela. I'm with the Neighborhood Watch group that's trying to get local businesses to cooperate in finding Lázaro Pérez's killers. We're taking steps to prevent such crimes in the future." Pretty good for a spontaneous rap, and I haven't even had my coffee yet.

"Is tomorrow good? At four-thirty?"

"How about five-thirty?"

"Certainly. He'll be glad to see you." End of conversation.

Well, *that* was easy. Getting through the rest of the day isn't. It seems that the invitations to this gala event must go out by five o'clock today, and they haven't even been printed yet because my bosses couldn't agree on the wording until three days after the absolute, final deadline. So I have to go to the bank and get a check certified in the amount of the printing bill because the Environmental Action Foundation has such a lousy credit rating with this printer for past foul-ups, hand deliver it to the printer, stand there while they run three thousand of these things through their fold-and-stuff machines, then schlep eight boxes of stuffed invitations back to the office for postage. I opt for a cab, and I don't take cabs very often.

Back in the office, Zirkelback tells me to take the cab receipt over to Petty Cash for reimbursement. I tell him it was my choice to take the cab, that I don't want donors' money paying for my cab rides. He shrugs and says, "Suit yourself," as if I've just won the lottery but refuse to accept the money because I disapprove of gambling.

I handle a lot of the incoming checks. At least half of them come from retired couples who probably braved axe handle-wielding thugs back in 1936, and younger generation activists for whom $10 is three days' food. The higher administrators who spend three-quarters of their time wooing $50,000 donations from the fourth-generation descendants of nineteenth-century robber barons tend to forget that half the money comes in in the form of $5 and $10 checks.

So I thought the envelopes were all stuffed, and all I had to do was drop them off in the mailroom so they could feed the three thousand envelopes through the postage meters in about four minutes. Wrong. These invited guests are so-o-o special, their invitations must be sealed with colorful, commemorative first-class stamps that have to be applied by hand. I've got a B.A. in Spanish Literature from the *Universidad Estatal del Ecuador* in Guayaquil, five years' experience as a beat cop for the NYPD; I've chased gun-crazy rapists down active subway tunnels, rescued victims overcome by toxic fumes, talked a borderline psychotic holding up a pet store into handing me his gun (yes, a pet store—you don't want to know); but all of this was just preparation for the challenge of spending twenty minutes being told by this blond-haired Dan Quayle clone the correct way to put commemorative stamps on 100-percent rag cream-colored envelopes. They can't go just any old way, I learn. They must be right side up, and absolutely parallel with the edges of the envelope. Crooked ones have to be done over. And he actually checks back every ten minutes to look through the finished pile like he's an industrial quality controller.

I almost quit right there, but I'm over a barrel. When I was by myself, I wouldn't think twice about bagging some bogus employment. Notice, hell! When my paycheck *bounces*, I don't give notice. The only reason I'm still sitting here is an eighteen-month-old girl named Antonia. I feel bad enough having to leave her alone ten hours a day, and I owe it to her to take a job that I'm likely to come home from alive. But there's a big part of me that would rather be tending sheep in the Andes.

So halfway through this sticky task, when I'm just falling into that stride where I know exactly how many I can do in a minute and how many more minutes it'll take me to finish this stupid task, Mr. Bartlett comes rushing up to me, looking at the pile of envelopes with a half-crazed look in his eyes as if I've decided to take a perfumed bubble bath in the middle of the office floor and says, "Filomena! You're still here? I told you to pick up Liz Crowell's plane tickets by two-thirty!"

I'm about to say, No you didn't, but what's the point?

Ms. Crowell is one of those next-generation rich kids I was telling you about. This one sits on the board of directors, which means no formal salary, but she gets to jet all over the goddamn world on the excuse that only she floats comfortably in those big-money circles where the bosses are always scheming and dreaming that if only they could get a million from this celebrity, a half million from that oil sheik, *then* we could *really* get the job done! Obviously, Ms. Crowell's plane tickets are more important than three thousand potential donors, so I've got to head back out to run some more errands, and while I'm out there, could I pick up some vitamins for Mr. Bartlett at this one health food store down on 17th and Broadway? Normally I'd leap at the chance to spend the better part of the afternoon outside, strolling down Broadway and taking my own sweet time about getting back, but—call it crazy—I feel an obligation to the prime reason for the Foundation's existence, a commitment to defending the environment. So I spend some more of my money on cabs, and get back to the office in time to finish stamping the damn envelopes while screening calls that range from senators sponsoring pro-environmental legislation to lonely sick people somewhere in the Midwest whose idea of reaching out and touching someone is calling the main switchboard of a "charitable organization" and staying on the line until somebody talks to them. Sheeesh!

The stuff gets mailed on time, Ms. Crowell makes her plane (L.A. this time) and I go home exhausted.

Antonia's in an awful, bratty mood today, and I don't get anything done for myself, just spend the whole evening trying to satisfy her constantly shifting, whining whims. Guilt is its own punishment. I leave today's paper unopened. By the time I get her to bed, there's nothing left I can do but turn on the TV and wait for its tranquilizing effect to sink into my brain. The last twenty minutes of the Colombia-Uruguay *Copa de America* qualifying match does the job with a 1–1 tie.

Wednesday morning I ask my boss if I can take a few hours out of the afternoon to read some of the Foundation's literature, because I feel like I don't even know what the organization really stands for. He says sure, it's great that I want to learn about the subject, but of course it doesn't work out that way. The day careens by in another endless streak of self-made crises that started small as tasks, graduated to problems and today are unleashed as screaming calamities because somebody wasn't doing their job. Zirkelback points fingers in every direction but up his nose, only I know from working a *real* job that the superior officer is held accountable for any screw-up on the part of his or her subordinates, whether s/he knew about it or not.

I'm not complaining about being a harried secretary. It's just that this place is wasting good people's money. When bills aren't paid on time and late fees are incurred, when things that could have been done cheaply three months ago are done at top-dollar last-minute rush prices, hell, if this were a for-profit corporation somebody's head would be rolling across the bloody carpet! It's as if the object is to spend as much as we take in, but on what? On protecting the environment or on paying late fees and buying a new line of color-coordinated swivel chairs?

That afternoon I meet with a *real* businessman. Pliego's office is nicely done, not ostentatious, not too tacky in that way that some of my people go for when they have money. You know, the phony Baroque gold spray-painted cherubs and curlicues and stuff. His legitimate front is an import-export business serving the community, which is actually necessary, because when immigrants send money or sorely needed American products like medicines that are unavailable in their poor home countries, the packages have a way of never reaching their destinations unless sent through a private company that guarantees their arrival.

I told *mamita* Viki I would be a little late today. Antonia's not going to like it, but I promise I'll take her out for the biggest ice cream sundae there is. I don't want to bring the kid in here. I'm at that stage where every night when I put her to bed I pray that she'll still be breathing the next time I see her. They always try to make you think that parenthood is primarily financial responsibility. They never tell you how emotionally helpless you really are sometimes.

A little after 5:30 the middle-aged Dominican couple who were in Pliego's office before me are shown out. They thank him profusely, bless him *(bless* him!) and back out of the office. He turns to me, a big smile on his face, clean-shaven except for the semi-walrus moustache. The air conditioning's up so he can wear a suit and a tie. He extends his hand cordially as I get up and enter his office. We talk the whole time in Spanish.

He sits down behind his desk and says, "Now, *Señorita* Buscarsela, of the—"

"The Neighborhood Watch. We organized the candlelight vigil for Lázaro Pérez."

"*Sí, sí, por supuesto.* Of course. How terrible. You were friends?"

"Yes."

"Close friends?" What's it to him?

"He was a good man."

"I see. So what can I do for you?"

"That was a great catch you made on Sunday," I say.

"Oh, you saw me?" he says, unable to resist preening a bit. Let him preen.

"Great play. If you had chased down that runner from second, you could have retired the side single-handedly."

"Maybe I should have done that." He laughs.

"The neighborhood is increasingly concerned that the Dominican mob killed Pérez in retribution for some undisclosed transgression."

The laugh freezes, cracks, and falls into a brittle heap on the floor. Five years of busting pimps and junkies and you learn these moves. Or else. But his face quickly smooths to show the concern of any legitimate businessman who is reminded of a painful subject. He's a smooth one, all right.

He says, "I think that's unfounded. Why should the mob go after Pérez? He meant nothing to them. Now take *me*, they give me problems all the time—you know, because I handle a lot of cash, and have a lot of packages going back and forth—you understand?"

"The mob gives you a hard time."

"Yes."

"Why don't you go to the police, then?"

"Oh, *señorita*, you do not know how they operate. There is no way around them. They work with the police. Why, without corrupt politicians and police, the mob would be unable to operate."

"The only difference is the politicians have to run for re-election every couple of years."

He smiles at me.

"Well, I'm glad you're telling me this," I say.

"You are?"

I'm beginning to see why he's just a mob lieutenant. At the risk of sounding immodest, he's starting to get too interested in checking me out from top to bottom to notice where the conversation is taking him. The real shrewd ones are too cold. They don't let *anything* make them forget about protecting their interests.

I say, "Yes, because I've been contending all along that poor Lázaro's murderers were a couple of street kids after crack money. It was much too sloppy and stupid to be a mob job."

That pleases him very much. I'm leading away from his trail, so he opens up.

"So what did you want to see me about?"

"Well, even though the mob is clearly not responsible, they have feelers out in every level of criminal activity. I bet they would be able to find Pérez's killers if they were asked to, or forced to."

"How could anyone force the mob to do anything?"

"Say, by threatening to break one of their rackets—like that garage over on West Dyckman that uses innocent people's repainted cars for midnight jobs then gets them back on the street again and into the legitimate owners' hands within twenty-four hours."

The corners of his mouth take a dip, then turn right back up again. "The police have known about that little operation for months."

"They *have?*" I say.

"As God is my witness."

Well, there goes my lead in this race. I go on, "So you don't think threatening to expose that would exert any co-operation from the mob."

"Anyone who threatened to expose that operation would probably have many more problems coming from the Police Department."

"I see. Perhaps if some bigger operation were to be exposed?"

"*Señorita*, we are speaking in parables. None of this will ever happen."

"But with your help—"

"How can I help? These mobsters have no respect for American laws. How can they? The Americans used those laws to overthrow our government."

I see something new in his face. The painful remnants of a very old scar. I ask him about it. He's looking right through me, replaying the scenes in his head.

I change direction: "Is that just for decoration?" I say, pointing to a walnut and glass liquor cart. He gets quickly to his feet and crosses to the moveable bar, gets out the liquor and offers me a drink. I accept a sherry with a lemon peel. He takes whiskey and ice. After a while he tells me.

"When I was ten years old, they came in the middle of the night. They kicked down the door, put a mask over my father's head, and took him up to a ridge overlooking the city and told him to run in any direction. When he refused, they doubled him over with a rifle jab to the belly, stuck the barrel to his head, and told him, 'We don't know what to do with you.' He told them to go ahead and kill him if they wanted, but to take his mask off so he could see them, so they would have to look at his face when they pulled the trigger. The cowardly bastards shot him in the back of the head from point-blank range. Blew the entire front of his face away."

"That's— How terrible."

"When you become a citizen here, they tell you horror stories from the days when King George the Third of England sent his soldiers bursting into homes without warrants to look for illegal property—"

"Yes, I know."

"—but they support it every day in our countries."

"Yes, they do."

"May I ask you something? Are you married?"

"Why, no," I say, a bit taken aback.

"Then perhaps you would accompany me to dinner some night?"

"I've got a baby girl."

"Bring her, too."

The intercom rings. He answers it. The receptionist's voice says, "*Señor* Pliego, the gentlemen from Stencorp are here to see you."

"Just a moment," he says. To me: "Think about it?"

I thank him for the flattering invitation, and walk out of there not knowing what I should be thinking.

I *thought* I got to the bottom of that crooked garage business too easily. I'm going to have to revise my theory about lies leading to the truth. I call up Janette Ivins and give her the bad news. The only thing she's sorry about is that she didn't figure it out first. I take Antonia out for one of the largest ice cream sundaes in the Western hemisphere. It takes another half an hour to clean it off her.

There are four messages on my machine from Flormaría, so I call her up and she tells me that Demetrio is getting nowhere hanging out in those nasty places waiting for a particular face to walk in, and that she's going to start making the rounds herself.

"I don't want you doing that," I say. "Considering who might be involved, it could get dangerous."

"The trail is getting cold, Filomena."

Dammit, she got that phrase from me. I promise her if there's anything out there, I'll find it. She practically asks me to make a vow before God. I tell her that it's a sin to make such a vow and not to fulfill it, and that I have no desire to be smitten by the Almighty for failing to solve a crime with no clear motive, clues or witnesses.

That holds her. For now.

Thursday is another bad day for cops everywhere when the 113th Precinct files counter-charges against the woman they mishandled. I've got an urge to jump in and help her, too, but I'm spreading myself too thin as it is.

I do manage to set aside a chunk of the morning at work for going through the Foundation's backlog of position papers. The stuff is very well written and touches on all the right points. It inspires me to go in and tell Mr. Bartlett I'd like to get involved in bigger stuff, say, like working with that EPA investigator. He tries to be polite about it, but basically he says, Yeah, right, when pigs fly.

"Could you get me a budget projection for next year based on this year's budget?" he says, tossing me a sheaf of spread-sheet-size computer paper as thick as three Manhattan phone books. "I need it for Monday's meeting."

I spend the next five hours accessing the budget data-base, working vertically to separate blanket funding outlays into their itemized programs, and horizontally to tally the quarterly totals. In case you've never done it, let me tell you it's a thrill a minute. A roller coaster ride is nothing compared to an unfamiliar computer program that devours huge chunks of carefully double-checked figures at the slip of a finger. Plus it's hard to project a budget when they have gala events like the "Hawaiian Pineapple Bash" that apparently cost more money than it raised. But then I start seeing millions coming in from a place called Samuelson Graphics, which I happen to know is a division of Morse, Inc., and a queasy feeling engulfs my viscera. All in all, nearly $7 million came in out of a total income of $30 million, which is quite a chunk, with about $500,000 taking the scenic route back to Morse, Inc., in "costs." Like Ms. Crowell's "costs," I suppose.

When I just about can't take it anymore I take a much-needed coffee break (I'm bringing *real* coffee from my *barrio* now) and join my fellow inmates by the coffee machine. Amid complaints from the Americans that my coffee is too strong, I confirm my rising doubts when Jeff Cohen actually listens to what I've got to say, takes me back to his desk, and shows it to me. I've only been here a week and a half, and spent most of that swamped under gathering mounds of data, so I can almost be excused, I guess. It's a complete list of the board of directors of the Environmental Action Foundation, including generous celebrities, a few congressmen, some unfamiliar others, and one name, Samuel Morse. I ask to see his affiliations, and it's the same guy. Someone had a perverse sense of humor when they named him Samuel. What hath God wrought, indeed. I figure anything this guy's connected with has got to be fishy.

I pick up the phone and call Gina Lucchese. Jeff is standing over my shoulder, but I don't care.

"EPA."

"Gina, this is Filomena, from the EAF."

"Oh? Oh, yes, Filomena? What do you want?"

"I think I've got something here. I'd like to check with you on it."

"Sure. On what?"

I talk lower. "You know anything special about Samuel Morse?"

"Other than that he's on your board and he owns Komputer King? No."

"He owns Komputer King?" Jesus.

"You know him?"

"You could say that. He once tried to kill me."

CHAPTER FIVE

"Don't quote me."
— Anonymous

"WELL, twice, actually."

"You're not serious," says Gina.

"Want to see my X-rays? My lungs are still scarred."

"From what?"

"Methyl Isocyanate."

The correct naming of the chemical changes everything.

"How severe was your exposure?"

"It was meant to be lethal. Can you meet me at the office?"

"I can't leave the building. Can you come down here?"

"Only if you tell Mr. Bartlett you must have me."

"Put him on."

Bartlett okays my afternoon at the EPA, but only if I get him the preliminary budget projection first. It's already 2:30 and I haven't had lunch yet. I sift through the significant figures for another half an hour and produce a projection that is good enough for his purposes. He doesn't let me go until I promise to do a more thorough job tomorrow. I tell him that'll be no problem *if* he lets me work on it. He doesn't pick up on what I'm saying. I rush out, hoping to get an hour with Gina and still make it uptown in time for Tonia.

Just downwind of the piss-rancid subway stairs I step

into a suitcase-sized deli for a sandwich. (I woke up this morning, mixed up a bowl of salmon salad, and left it on the kitchen counter.) A man standing in front of me turns. He's wearing one of those fluorescent spandex racing outfits that reveals every goose bump, with an upturned cap over his blond crew cut. He looks me in the eye and says, "Yes?" with a smile. I say, "Hi," and look at the sandwich board.

He says, "Oh, you're here to *buy* something." He gets out of the way. Now what was *he* selling? I don't want to know. I decide to buy food that came here in a package. It costs more, but I've got enough problems without bringing home an incurable disease. Factory-sealed yogurt and shrink-wrapped peanuts, and I'm down the stairs into the clammy pissy subway. This 34th Street station is really the pits.

At Canal Street, a smell-evangelist gets on and announces to me, "I have come for your soul!"

I tell him I don't carry it around with me. Fortunately, I get off at the next stop.

The EPA is hidden in the monolithic labyrinth of 26 Federal Plaza. There's a large, featureless object that some-body apparently thinks is a sculpture blocking half the open space out front. I'm not sure, but I think it's that big slab of concrete The Who were pissing on for the cover of *Who's Next*. I stand in line with the rest of the stooges who actually believe that government is there to serve us, pass through the metal detector and the baggage inspection and I'm in. Elevator up to the seventh floor, signs lead along the corridor to a seemingly endless office space partitioned off into a maze within a maze, a behaviorist's wet dream.

The office is surprisingly like any other office. Tenth-generation Xeroxed cartoons laughingly proclaim, YOU WANT IT WHEN? alongside other familiar icons of secretariana. I have to ask for Gina Lucchese's office. Turns out she doesn't have an office. This government inspector who makes indus-trial violators lose sleep in contemplation of one of her sur-prise visits works out of a partitioned cubicle much like the one I'm assigned to over in *our* rat maze.

Gina Lucchese has something else working against her, considering her opponents. On the force, they all said I was too small to "take" burly males unresponsive to psychological methods, but I'm five inches taller than this bird-boned example of transplanted Mediterranean womanhood. She's a beauty, too, however you define that subjective term. Dark hair, dark eyes, light skin from spending too much time in front of a computer.

"Filomena?" she says, getting up from her screen.

"Gina?" We shake hands. "What do the PR execs from an industrial polluter do when they're expecting The Government to show up with an eighteen-person moon-suit crew and they get you instead?"

"It causes some problems," she says. "They think trying to buy me dinner might save them $3 million in clean-up costs."

"Where are they taking you for dinner? Japan? I can't imagine the restaurants near a toxic waste disposal site are truly first class."

"Try truckstop steak houses."

"So we're talking about a fifteen-dollar dinner of road kill."

"Not that I can accept gratuities in any amount from a PRP, but I get the feeling they'd spend a lot more trying to buy a male inspector."

"Yeah. On another kind of meat. PRP?"

"Sorry. Potentially responsible party."

"Like the suspect."

"Right."

"They really try to buy you?"

"Once the subject turns to economics I usually get them to understand that they would save a lot more money by just complying with the statutes now, rather than face $25,000 a day in fines later."

"Twenty-five thousand a day? I know that sounds like a lot, but it's chickenshit to a corporation."

"I can triple it to seventy-five a day if they make us sue for it."

"So it's *cow* shit."

"Were you born in a barn?"

"There was no room at the inn."

Gina laughs. I ask her, "How extensive is your authority?"

"EPA Region Two covers New York, New Jersey, Puerto Rico, and the Virgin Islands."

"And I thought fifty blocks of Northern Manhattan was a tough beat. Doing the toxic waste detail in New Jersey must be like running the Welcoming Committee in Hell. Puerto Rico?"

"Nice in winter, torture in summer."

"What's going on down there?"

"A lot of companies locate there to avoid taxes."

"I bet the wages are lower, too."

"I'm investigating a pharmaceutical company that's using underground storage tanks that have leaked pure carbon tetrachloride into the groundwater."

"You mean *legal* drugs are poisoning the environment?"

"You could put it that way, I suppose. Or they dump industrial chemicals into evaporation pits. Trouble is, only half the stuff evaporates. The rest sinks into the ground. The bedrock is so porous down there the stuff is leaking right into the ocean."

"Great. What industrial chemicals?"

"Oh, benzene, carbon tet, trichloroethylene, vinyl chloride—"

"I mean what are they used for?"

"Solvents and cleaning fluids, for cutting through metals, shaping, refining. They do in a few hours what used to take days of stamping, filing, and buffing by hand."

"But the only offensive by-product of manual labor washes off in soap and water."

"Pretty much. But today's marketplace expects a certain level of precision, speed, and ease of manufacture for machine parts. This is supposed to preserve our 'edge' over the competition."

"What's the cost to the environment of trying to maintain that edge?"

"You want to see the report?"

"Sure."

Gina saves the computer file she was working on and opens the top drawer of one of her filing cabinets. Half the contents of the drawer are marked, "La Torrecilla."

"That's the name of the site," Gina explains, handing me a thin folder.

I examine the cover document. Titled, "Problem Alert," it comes from a Dr. S. Guncler, Director, OVRO. More alphabits. Basically, it gives an ungrammatical listing of dates, times, locations, and reference numbers, all oddly familiar, like the unnatural language of a police report, before getting down to a complete sentence concluding, "The water system serving the La Torrecilla community was found to be contaminated (carbon tetrachloride 440 µg/1, trichloroethylene 120 µg/1, PCBs 1.3 µg/1 and trace elements of others BDT [see below]). The community has been advised not to drink the water. 601, 503.1, Priority Pollutants . . . "

I ask, "What's four hundred forty ug slash one?"

"Ug? That's not U-G, that's micrograms. Four hundred forty parts per million."

"Oh. *Du-u-h.*"

"Don't feel bad. You should see their faces when we dump a bale of this stuff on some judge's bench."

"What's all this? '601, 503.1 BDT—'"

"Those are tests for specific pollutants. BDT is Below Detection Level."

"Is one point three parts per million a lot?"

"Of PCBs? It's plenty."

"*Shit.* So what do you do with these results?"

"First a public notice," she says, flipping through the pages for me.

"This notice is for New Jersey, not Puerto Rico," I say.

"It's a sample notice."

"Oh? This happens so often you've got a standard form for it?" I guess we're all going to have to get used to it: the standardization of disaster.

"It's a big country. Not big enough to bury all our chemicals, though. About one-quarter of all public water supply wells have detectable levels of at least one of these chemicals."

"What? Why isn't the EAF *screaming* about this?"

"Beats me. I gave them the info. I don't know why they're not pushing this story, here. Excess nitrates in the water can reduce an infant's ability to process oxygen, producing 'blue baby' syndrome. Suffocation. And boiling the water like common sense dictates only makes it worse, by *increasing* the concentration of nitrites."

I have to sit down. "This is getting to be too much like police work. The combined weight of the total problem is too much for one person to bear—if you stop and think about what you're doing."

"Ex-cop, huh?" says Gina.

"Career burnout."

"So now you're typing Cunningham's letters to rock stars?"

"It's a little thing called a kid to support."

"A kid? Got any pictures?"

"Have I got pictures? Is the Pope a Polish peasant?" I pull out a wallet-size of Tonia qualifying for the "under 2" category of the New York Marathon, running through the grass in a toddler tracksuit.

Gina exudes the requisite ooh-how-cutes. I tell her, "You realize she calls the alphabet the 'Ay-bee,' because she knows the first few letters. Well, one night I was up late, couldn't sleep, actually, and it came to me that 'alpha-bet' means 'A-B' in Greek. I mean, the 'Ay-bee' is the literal English translation of the 'alpha-bet'! Isn't that something?" Gina the non-mother listens unthrilled. I guess you have to be a parent. I look down at the collection of documents. "What's 'OVRO'?"

"That's the Organic Volatile Research Organization. A private contractor we use."

"You use private contractors?"

"All the time. This isn't the Department of Justice. We're really very small. Frankly, it softens our credibility—our reliance on paid-for information from private testing labs."

"And if EPA inspectors can't be bought, private testing labs can be."

"Well, I think we'd find out about that—"

"Don't be so sure. The Police Department can't send forensic evidence outside for analysis unless they establish an unbroken chain of police possession of the evidence. They have to stand guard over it every step of the way 'til they get the results. Otherwise, it wouldn't stand up in court."

Gina's phone rings. "Just a minute," she says to me, answering it. She attends to her business, I flip through the documentation. Gina has compiled a report that states, "Polluted water is not new. Throughout history water supplies have been endangered by microbial organisms, but today's contaminants are far worse. The human body has *no* protection from modern chemical contaminants and radionuclides, and the effects of such modern compounds (nervous system breakdown, kidney and liver breakdown, bone cancer) take much longer to reveal themselves than do microbial infections, so isolating the cause becomes extremely difficult." Her conclusion is that whatever you dump into the ocean eventually comes back to be a part of *you*. Didn't I have this nightmare once?

"Why did you want to see me?"

I look up. Gina's off the phone. Where do I begin? I ask, "What do you think of Paul Bartlett and Josiah Carberry?"

She looks at me, not quite sure what to make of this retired police detective sitting in front of her, who's so full of questions. She fiddles aimlessly with some papers.

"Just between us," I say.

"Honestly?"

"*Real* honestly."

Her investigator's instincts seem satisfied.

"Carberry's got a heart of gold but his head up his ass, and Bartlett's the same, only a bit more severe. Sometimes he doesn't know what he wants, but he can get pretty nasty if you don't give it to him."

That's what I wanted to hear. I need to know where her sympathies lie. "And if that Zirkelback were any more anal retentive, objects in space would start disappearing into the black hole of his—gravity curve."

Gina laughs at my scathing capsule description. She continues, "They get paid for generating good will and putting out opinion papers that tell everyone else what they should be doing. I've actually got to confront the dumpers. I could quadruple my salary by just switching sides. The big oil companies get some of their best hydrogeologists from the EPA."

"Just like a crooked cop makes five times what an honest one does—"

"You still haven't told me why you came to me."

"A few years ago I had a run-in with Samuel Morse. Tried to prevent him from illegally shipping toxic waste to Africa and South America. The only reason the charge didn't stick was that I committed criminal trespass to get the evidence."

"That was stupid of you."

"Sure was. I was younger, crazier."

So you're telling me the same Samuel Morse who's on the Environmental Action Foundation's board of directors tried to kill you?"

"Twice. He hired an assassin to shoot me off a subway train, and when that didn't work, they locked me in a room full of concentrated insecticide."

"This is on record?"

"Yeah. Things have changed over the years. I've got more control over my life now—more or less. Except I can't run anymore: it rips my lungs apart. And I can't smoke anything. Even secondhand smoke's a serious pain. I just can't believe Morse has cleaned up his act that much. His name's all over the income half of the budget, and I can't help thinking he's only involved with this environmental organization to polish his image so he can continue to foul the earth in some less visible way."

"So what do you want me to do, investigate all his holdings?" She's kidding.

"No, just the likely ones." I'm serious.

***

It takes time, but Gina agrees to be my partner in an investigation into the possible EPA violations of all likely Morse, Inc., subsidiaries. At least I'm doing it from the right side of the fence this time. Only during the long subway ride home do I consider how I must reexamine that budget the first thing tomorrow morning. And do it right this time.

Last stop, all off but a homeless man trying to sleep lengthwise on three of those new individually contoured seats that seem to have been designed specifically to keep homeless people from stretching out on them. I saw him in this morning's rush hour, slouching at a window seat, jacket pulled up over his face to keep out the light, and he's still here, about to embark on another trip to nowhere.

I trudge up to street level, where a pair of buses idling on the corner of Broadway and 207th Street accurately reproduce the air quality of midtown that I came up here to escape. I duck through the cloud and head towards *mamita* Viki's.

I pick up Tonia and stop off on the way home to get the second-best fried chicken in the universe at a cramped butcher shop that's done more for affirmative action than our last two presidents. Three men sweat year round in front of two enormous revolving barbecue spits and deep fryers. The owner is a white-haired Russian Jew and the two younger men are black and *latino*. And the *latino* guy looks half-Chinese.

Upstairs, I take my eyes off Tonia for a minute to wash the salad vegetables, only to find she's thrown today's paper in the toilet. I've been after the super for six months to put a latch on the bathroom door, but he expects a ten-dollar tip just for coming up and having a look at it. I keep writing on endless lists of things to do to get a latch and put it on myself already, but I just never seem to get around to doing it.

I cut some chicken into kid-sized pieces and we sit down to eat. My paper having been prematurely recycled back into wood pulp, I turn on the TV to watch the Spanish news, only to discover that the A train two trains after mine jumped a switch just north of 59th Street, ripping a car in half and throwing a woman onto the tracks, breaking her ankle. I am about to conclude that perhaps this city is falling apart, but no, the next story is one of development on the Upper West Side. A twenty-story luxury high-rise is to be built north of 91st Street. There follows a description of planning committee acrobatics that are difficult to explain to someone who lives in a sane society.

When Thursday afternoon feels like Monday morning, you know you're getting older. I'm so beat I just lie on the bed for half an hour after eating while Antonia shreds some magazines. I clean up in a semi-stupor, then finally get my third wind of the day around 9:00 P.M. Now I'm really in a bind. It's Tonia's bedtime, yet I feel a pervading impulse to get outside and get some answers. I've been letting Lázaro's killers party on their stolen money long enough, and I feel bad about it. But if I put the kid to bed, I'm trapped inside; if I take her with me, she'll become a dead weight within fifteen minutes and I don't need the extra strain of canvassing the *barrio* with her in my arms. The big, heavy stroller is out of the question. I'm not carrying that Duesenberg up and down five flights of stairs.

I'm about to call up one of the other mothers to see if I can drop Antonia off asleep and pick her up later, but I hang up before I finish dialing. I hit upon a compromise. I've been thinking too much like an American, you see, which after all these years in the country and changing my citizenship is almost forgivable. Back in Solano, a tiny mountain village nine thousand feet up in the Andes whose claims to four streets are considerably exaggerated, they don't have strollers and snugglis and car seats and sassy seats and rock'n'rides and . . . and . . . and. I dig around in the closet for my faded winter shawl, wrap Antonia in it and tie her around my back the way all the Cañari Indian women do it. This method is really for infants, not toddlers, but the night is cooling off, and I think I can hit a few of the late-night convenience stores before I collapse.

I walk an angular figure eight, covering the blocks, taking Broadway across the bridge into Marble Hill, squaring back along the river's edge and returning home via two side streets. I cover fourteen open-'til-midnight convenience stores. Nobody knows anything, nobody's seen anything. Sure they were concerned, but that was ten days ago, and they can't be scared all their lives. They've already put Lázaro behind them. Seems like I'm the only one who can't stop thinking that if I don't get these punks soon, one of them could be next.

My unpracticed shoulder muscles complain as I ease Antonia off my back into her bed. This I do for you, Lázaro.

Friday morning they're still cleaning up the mess on the A train so I have to take the number 1 Broadway local, which stops about every five blocks for an hour-long 175-block ride to midtown. I show up half an hour late to work and lose all the time I was hoping to get on the budget, since the bosses don't usually start distracting me from my more important duties with their assignments until about 9:30. I try anyway.

Something's wrong. The budget access password keeps sending me back an invalid message. I catch Zirkelback on his next strafing mission through subordinate territory and explain the problem.

He says the budget access password has been changed, "But you don't need to know it. Mr. Bartlett realized that working with it was beyond your capacity. Come on over to my office in about ten minutes and I'll give you your instructions for today. I need you to work on gala prep. Monday's the big night, and there's a lot we've got to do before then!"

Now Mr. Bartlett's a decent-enough soul, I guess, but he's the kind of guy so lacking in technical skills that opening a fortune cookie presents him with a challenge. He wouldn't realize *anything* about my working on a computer program. Somebody *put* that idea in his head. Who? Zirkelback? Acting on information from Cohen? I decide to talk to Mr. Cohen.

"You're not expecting overtime this weekend, are you?" I ask Zirkelback. "There's a lot I need to take care of at home."

"There's a lot of work that's got to get done," he replies, implying my job is on the line if I don't come through. "Can't you get a babysitter?"

He doesn't wait around for my answer, which would probably involve orificial obscenities anyway.

I knock on the shellacked wooden edge of Jeff Cohen's cubicle. He hides what he's reading under a pile of papers and says, "Yes, what do you want?"

"Can I talk to you for a second?"

"About what?"

I approach his desk. "I was wondering if it would be all right for me to bring my daughter Monday night. I mean, I don't have to pay a hundred dollars to get her in, do I?"

"That's entirely up to you. Will she keep you from fulfilling your duties?"

"What duties am I going to have besides handing out literature and keeping an eye on the cash box?"

"We need people serving drinks—"

"I'm not bartending for three thousand people."

"In the first place, we'll be lucky if five hundred show up— but all right. You can just take tickets at the door. Must you bring your child?"

"Can I call you Jeff?"

"Sure, I—"

"Look, Jeff. I'm working two jobs. I don't see my kid enough as it is. Besides, she won't be a bother." Not compared to you people, she won't.

"Okay. As long as she doesn't interfere with your job."

I'm working a whim as it is. I decide to push it. "She interferes with *everything*. That's why her father abandoned us. In our *machista* culture, caring about how someone else feels is a sign of feminine weakness. Stay out all night

73

drinking up your paycheck and you're a *man*. Bring that pay-check home to your wife in time for dinner and you're a fag. Among *latinos*, that's the worst insult there is. Call a man a *maricón* and you better be good with a knife."

He's listening. I go on: "It's easy for men like him. All they want is a nice long list of conquests, some hard, some easy, to be savored in memory or swapped like playing cards around the club table. Women like me are stuck with the kids while looking for the romance, the love, the commitment to something besides an opening in my body, to something that consumes all, yet endures, sometimes forever."

It works. Jeff Cohen looks up at me with new eyes. There was something about his manner and the fact that he was the only man in the office who didn't fluoroscope me every time I went by. I figured he was a romantic, of sorts. And I can see that the pamphlet he tried to stuff under some papers is a Gay Men's Health Crisis report on AIDS.

There are still a lot of folks in the closet, even in New York.

I tell him, "AIDS has put sex back into the nineteenth century: You mess around, *you die*."

"And there's no cure," he says. "No cure."

I sit down on the edge of his desk. "It's one thing for cigarettes to cause lung cancer, but when the fountain of life becomes the sower of death . . ." I let that image drift down and settle between us. "Well, it's a cruel twist." An angel passes. "Are you free for lunch? Or even just fifteen minutes? Out of this office."

Somebody close to him must be dying, and I've caught him during one of those rare moments when men actually allow themselves to feel vulnerable, human. I never expected this. He might even be fighting to keep his tear glands from giving him away. He swallows and says, "Sure."

"Whenever you feel hungry," I say, getting up.

As I'm walking out I hear him whisper, "I haven't felt hungry in three months."

Gala preparation means the exceedingly beat business of arranging hotel and plane reservations for celebrities who are flying in to "entertain" the $100-a-ticket-minimum guests. And do I expect a top country singer who does a live Christmas special every year on NBC to take a cab from JFK to midtown? Not on your life! He gets a limo. They *all* get limos. Now, I understand this is the lifestyle they've grown accustomed to, but why doesn't somebody in this office have the guts to confront these stars and say, Look: Donating your talents is not enough. Why can't you donate your travel and accommodations, too? It's all tax-deductible for them, isn't it? And I'm beginning to see how this organization takes in $30 million a year and still manages to dip into the red once a month. They hope to raise between $150,000 and $500,000 Monday night. But with a full-scale sound system (can't the stars tone it down for charity?), lights, union technicians running it all, a full-priced wait staff and first-class treatment for six stars and their complete entourages, this event is already costing over $120,000. And you don't pack a crowd like that into the back room at CBGB's. Hall rental alone clears $10,000, and that's at a break. This gala now *has* to raise a minimum of $240,000 or be in violation of federal laws regarding charitable organizations—namely, that to qualify for tax-exempt status at least fifty cents out of every dollar donated must actually go to the programs. But I expect it's pretty easy to bury these costs inside program expenses. I still don't see where $30 million goes. I've got to get another look at that budget.

At lunchtime, Jeff Cohen waits behind me while I try to save enough money to feed an Ecuadorian family for six months by seeing if two stars arriving at Kennedy Airport at the same time could possibly share a limo. They'd like to, but—sorry—they can't. Their entourages are too big. Jesus.

The rattling elevator, overloaded with the lunchtime crowd, keeps getting stuck with its doors open on each floor, but eventually Jeff and I ride down to the filthy, smelly street and walk two blocks south to a glassed-in, watered-down-Italian place.

I tell him, "I think the *bread* here is out of my budget."

"You're covered," he says, leading me to a table by a window looking out on a brick wall that the restaurant owners have painted white to keep the "view" from being just a little too depressing. He calls the waiter over. We order.

I break the ice the best way I know with a gay New York Jew: "So you don't think the president will be championing gay rights in the next election?" I ask.

"I thought Reagan was bad, but *this* guy's brain is so spooked he has to ask his advisors what his position is on every issue except China, as far as I can tell."

"He says he's an environmentalist," I say.

"Right. And he shows it by planting a tree for some photographers, and saying that if everyone would just plant a tree, there would be no more environmental problems in this country, and that we didn't need any 'fancy studies' to tell us this. Of course, deep down everyone knows if it weren't for 'fancy studies' the polluters would have buried us by now under all their garbage, but it plays in Peoria."

"So tell me why the Foundation is paying the travel expenses for six wealthy celebrities coming to Monday's gala, when five of them openly supported the ex-oil-company-president's election campaign?"

"That's the charity biz for you. They sell tickets," he says.

"I wouldn't pay two cents to see these assholes."

"You, my dear, are a rarity."

"Yeah, I double in value every five years. And I always thought I was just an average—"

He sniffs. "What's that awful smell?"

I look around and see a bag woman has pushed her way through the front door and is busy stuffing toothpicks and breath mints into her pockets. Jeff calls the waiter over, hands him a few dollars and says, "Give her a cup of soup and a sandwich to go and get her out of here."

"Yes, sir."

Jeff is quite a paradox. Caring and nasty, generous but contemptuous, socially conscious but cynical—well, I guess that's *not* a paradox.

Our food arrives. We're halfway through it before I ask, "Who in the office knew I was working on the budget?"

He looks at me as if I've brought up an unpleasant subject that I promised I wouldn't. But I didn't make any promises. He says, "The whole area knew, that's at least ten people."

"Do *you* know the new access code?"

"Why, yes . . ."

"Will you tell it to me?"

I can see I've put him in a tough spot ethically. "That could be a problem," he admits.

"Okay, I understand. What if you access the budget, and just happen to leave it on your screen for half an hour?" We eat on in silence. "Fifteen minutes?"

He's almost finished with his eggplant parmigiana. He carefully trims some wayward stretches of mozzarella with his knife. Then he looks me in the eye and says, "Okay."

"Thanks."

He cleans off his plate before he says, "But you'll never get a chance today. It'll have to be Monday."

"Fine."

He wipes his mouth and says, "Plato was right. Check, please!"

I spend the rest of the afternoon arranging for balloons, booze, plastic cups—"Plastic cups?" I shout. "I thought this was an environmental organization!"

"There's no time to arrange for glasses," explains Zirkelback, "we'll recycle."

Translation: More work for me—and all the other garbage I've got to do to show I'm doing my part. But I'm adamant about going home no later than six o'clock and not coming back until 8:00 A.M. Monday morning.

"Make it seven," says Zirkelback. Dickhead.

Friday night! What that phrase used to mean to me when I was younger! Now it means collapsing in a chair while the kid uses me for a trampoline. The hell with everything else, this is what really matters. Taking care of her, making sure she grows up loved. And it gives me a chance to catch up on my gibberish.

"Who's the iggy-biggy baby? Who's the iggy-biggy baby? The ooky, the tooky, the ooky-tooky-tooky?" It sounds silly now but it means a lot to her.

Three twenty-five A.M. the phone rings. Feeling like someone's cracked my cranium on cement, I get up and answer the phone. It's Janette Ivins. She sounds a bit drunk.

"They took me off the case!" she complains. I hear music behind her. Jukebox?

"Can we talk about this tomorrow?"

"The fuckin' bastards took me off the fuckin' case!"

"Can this wait until tomorrow?"

"What time tomorrow?"

"Whenever you can get here," I say. "Good night."

"Two cops are dead. I'll be right over."

CHAPTER SIX

"Think of the opportunities here in Florida. Three years ago I came to Florida without a nickel in my pocket. Now I've got a nickel in my pocket."
— Groucho Marx, in *The Cocoanuts*

WHEN THEY INVENTED the term "pain in the ass," *this* is what they had in mind. I'm up for the night, now. If I've learned anything from half a decade as a cop and my first two years as a mother, it's how my body's sleep clock works. If I am awakened between 1:00 and 3:00 A.M. I can usually get back to sleep. Three to 3:30 A.M. is a neutral zone that can go either way. Anything later than 3:30 A.M. and it's hopeless. My body decides it's gotten enough sleep and there's nothing left to do but wait for the rest of the world to get around to starting another day.

So I've got plenty of time to lie there in the darkness, waiting to see if Janette Ivins really shows up or not, reflecting on where I stand so far in all this. Police coverage of Lázaro's murder has evaporated to nothing. PR to the contrary, the cops have obviously filed the Pérez case under Unsolved Murder #2018. It's not a cover-up, they just can't get any further and don't particularly give a shit. Why bust your butt for a nobody? It's time to settle the mob angle once and for all. Even if it really was two crackheads, the mob may still be the best way to get at them. But I have to smell out something big enough to make them go along without sticking my nose too deep into their shit. How I'm supposed to do that, I don't know. Not yet, anyway.

The Dominican branch of the organized crime network isn't as codified yet as its older, better-known brother organizations. There are still a few cracks in the surface I might be able to drive a wedge into.

Funny, isn't it? Now I'm beginning to welcome this rude awakening. I have no time to think during the day. Sure, I've been asking around, but without any purpose. Now it's becoming clear: Either way, my trail leads to the local mob. But what can I possibly pin on them that's big enough to bargain for without catching my death of it first? I'd have to have the whole case ready to go out via certified mail to the district attorney's office in order to pitch it to Guzmán and walk out alive. I've got to build a case to that point without anybody catching on to me. And right now I've got nothing, except that previously owned getaway car business, which the mob lawyers would plea bargain down from grand larceny to theft of services anyway. If that. Someone would still have to testify against them. And someones don't testify. No, I'm right back where I started: nowhere.

And sure, I'm also pissed that my job has turned out to be just another shitty job, but it's better than biting the heads off chickens for a living, I guess. But that cancerous excuse for a human, Samuel Morse! All these years and I still gag on my own vomit when I walk into a windowless room that's been sprayed with insecticide. Some of that nausea comes from disgust with myself at my own botched mishandling of that business. I keep torturing myself with a million if onlys, like if only I'd had the patience to do it right, the guy might be in jail on four counts of attempted murder. But I'm still madder at him. I *know* he's on the board of the EAF to help cover up *something*. Maybe I can stick him with it this time. I'd like to stick him with a poisoned sword. Something is rotten in the state, all right.

It's a little before 4:00 A.M. when the intercom buzzes. I leap out of bed to stop it before it wakes Antonia, but Janette leans on the buzzer like a raging drunk who doesn't care that it's 4:00 A.M. and people have lives. She's becoming a cop, all right.

I buzz her in, open the door, step out into the hallway to look down the progressively shrinking flights of stairs to guide her up if necessary. The blue-black fragment of her body completes five circuits before she gets to me, still in uniform, looking like she hasn't had *that* bad of a night, and that some of whatever she was drowning her sorrows in has worn off with the walk over here. Don't get me wrong. She's still bleary-eyed and gin-breathed.

"You got anything to drink?" she asks.

"Nothing for you but water," I say, filling her a big glass from the tap. "Help yourself." She slurps half the contents in one draught. At least she's replenishing her liquids. Less pain tomorrow.

Janette flops down in a chair, and I remind her to be quiet, I've got a kid sleeping. It's a wonder she hasn't woken up crying already. My reminder is useless. Ignoring my requests to lower her voice, Janette tells me what I already know, that she's been removed from the Pérez case. She asks me, "Can't you go talk to the motherfuckin' lieutenant, tell him all that we've been doin' on our own?"

"I have no voice in there, Janette. Never did. Isn't there anybody else? I can't be the only friend you have in this precinct."

Every third word an obscene modifier, she explodes with lamentation over the two NYPD cops who got shot in unrelated incidents just a few hours apart. Officer John Paul Salerno, an undercover with the 34th Precinct, was shot after going into a building down on 161st Street to buy a gram of cocaine. Right now they figure the perps didn't know he was a cop, that it was a standard crooked drug deal turned robbery. The other, Officer Tim Stroczek of the Manhattan North Precinct, was shot in uniform while his partner was trying to make a routine arrest on East 116th Street, one of the worst blocks in the world.

The fact that Janette saw Salerno a few times around the 34th is what's getting her. When a cop dies on duty every one of them feels it, but usually the situation got out of hand on the other side of town somewhere. There's some distance involved. This happened on her beat. The commissioner has ordered all New York City cops to wear bulletproof vests at all times, which is not going to be easy with summer coming, and the politicians have all jumped in calling for a national death penalty for drug dealers who kill cops. It's a nice idea, but since drug dealers risk death every waking minute of their lives from far more efficient and ruthless pursuers than the U.S. government, I don't expect that to be much of a deterrent. Janette launches into an angry, drunken tirade that, minus the modifiers, basically puts forth the idea that the U.S. "war on drugs" translates into a war on blacks and other minorities, the housing projects are raided without proper search warrants, the neighborhoods are subjected to near-martial law, and workers are terrorized into submitting to constitutionally questionable drug tests while their job security and safety erodes with each passing day.

"I've got no faith in the courts, neither," she says. "They're good at puttin' away poor folks, but I sure as hell don't ever see them puttin' away any rich folks."

"And you've only been a cop three months," I say. "It took me half a year to learn that."

"Well, I'm not gonna let them win, Fil. I want to work with you, no badge, no protocol, no nothin'."

"Careful, Janette, I've done that scene. It sounds great in rehearsal but it can bomb on opening night."

"Screw the critics, sugar. I'm talkin' 'bout guerrilla theater."

"Now there's a thought. Undercover police work as a form of theater. It sure takes acting skill. And if you're not convincing, the audience'll kill you. Like, uh, the—*como el teatro invisible*." In my hasty 4:30 A.M. thinking, I can't find the English for what I want to say.

"What are you talkin' about?" says Janette.

"It came about during the worst years of the Brazilian dictatorship. Theaters were closed, even street theater was suppressed. So they came up with the idea of starting an argument or a discussion in a restaurant or a train station that got everybody in the place talking about high food prices or the transit strike and no one ever knew that they were actors pretending to be customers, otherwise they would have gotten arrested."

"Hey: I'm serious. Tomorrow let's you and me knock on some doors—"

"And if we don't get answers we start knocking heads?"

"Now that's the first sense you've made all night, girl," she says.

"Forget it, Janette. Without the city backing you, you can't pull those stunts. I know. You're off duty tomorrow?"

"Yeah?"

"So you've got no authority around here without the uniform. And if it gets back to the lieutenant you're misrepresenting the precinct—"

"Stop talkin' shit, girl! How the hell are these punks gonna know I'm off duty 'less you tell 'em?"

"You think every cop in the Three-four is on your side? I mean, by as much as you're going to need?"

There's a pause now. "I've only been there three months," she admits.

"That's the first sense you've made. Now why don't you sleep for a few hours and I'll wake you up around nine?"

She shrugs. "Where's your bathroom?"

I watch Janette drift off into that open-mouthed snoring sleep of the passed-out drunk. As an ex-abuser, I'm repulsed by Janette's quick caving in (it took me five years), yet jealous of not having that catch-all psychic safety net of the temporarily soul-spilling drunk. I've been through it enough to know it's a lie, that you always feel worse after the painkiller wears off, plus I've got a little someone depending on me now. I mustn't fall in again, yet I still catch myself craving the complete letting go from time to time. Not like I "need" it, but that I "want" it, which is worse in a way, to help release the mounting pressure of a job, motherhood and, yes, detecting, to help me unfocus on the minute details in order to see the missing links in the case as a whole and figure out whodunit. Any good criminologist will tell you that Sherlock Holmes by his own admission sometimes unraveled a case by spending the night "sitting upon five pillows and consuming an ounce of shag."

You're not going to make drugs go away by burning Peru to the ground and building more prisons. Aah, I could go on and on. Meanwhile two murderers still walk free. And cops are dying. And working people are dying. I sit and stroke little Tonia's head. I wouldn't want her to get caught in some stupid drug-related crossfire because the cops are too busy keeping back the crowds at a half-price sale at Bloomingdale's.

The unexamined life may not be worth living, but the examined life can be hell on earth. I think about somebody hurting my kid, the wrenching fear, the supreme innocence of the child, the supreme vulnerability. She has no reason not to trust anyone yet—no street smarts. Isn't that how they should be? What a world! That one must teach a baby how to *distrust*.

I endure the pain of imagining what might happen if *I* should disappear from *her* life now. At her age, Tonia wouldn't even remember me! By the time she grew up she'd probably have no recollection of me at all. She might never search for evidence of me because she wouldn't even know I'd been lost. And I certainly don't want Raúl to get her.

Teenage killers aren't parents. They can't understand how everybody, no matter how bad, started as a baby, that when somebody loves a baby, and has fed it and cared for it for years, they will never recover from having it taken away.

A lot of friends have lost children, mostly in Ecuador. The poor die younger and in greater numbers. Parenthood. If it means anything it means that your kids are supposed to outlive you. I can't think of those little lost lives without some faith going out of me: If you can lose something as innocent as a baby, what *can't* you lose?

I tried explaining all this to my newborn baby girl, still blood-red and smeared with white streaks of slippery, stretchy smegma. But they had already taken her away. I didn't get to hold her for six hours. Now I say a prayer over her.

Saturday morning brings clear skies, a cool breeze skirting off the river, and a child in a good mood—she senses right away by a lack of the usual tension that today is the day she gets to have me all day. I get Janette around some food stamp—bought orange juice. Coffee and eggs get her into the shower. I make her uniform look like it hasn't been slept in by lugging out the iron. Christ! I haven't had time to iron any of *our* clothes in almost a month, and here I am pulling on it to make a hung-over cop look like the real thing.

Janette pulls on her clothes and wants to bug out immediately. I need another half hour. She gets all blustery with me about why the hell I need so much time.

I laugh. "This from a woman who just spent twenty minutes using up the hot water while I was ironing her uniform. Who needs a man in the house when I've got you around?"

Janette sees the joke and laughs. Hardly a trace of hangover. I was never that lucky.

I call Flormaría and talk to her in Spanish, which I've noticed Janette does not understand, but I still talk as fast as possible just to make sure. I tell her to come right over, that I'm with the cop who was working on the case, and explain that Officer Ivins is a bit of a loose cannon who could fuck things up, which is why I need her help. She says she'll be right over.

What takes me half an hour is getting Antonia dressed presentably and packing a bag filled with snacks, bottles, spare diapers, toys, and baby wipes. Janette doesn't know that all of this stuff is required for any excursion lasting more than fifteen minutes. I have to lean against the clothes and other junk clogging the closet so I can get the stroller out.

I buzz Flormaría up and give everyone their orders. I tell Janette, "Since you're in uniform, we'd better work separately."

"Doing what?" she asks.

"Flormaría and I can slink around the 'hood chatting with storekeepers without drawing a crowd. I bet the local mob has their hooks into a lot more places than we like to think."

"And what do I do?"

"You cover the legitimate 'cop' beat and try to coerce it out of them."

"Out of who?"

I tell her, "The Rusty Scupper has two teenagers without work permits washing dishes in the kitchen, the Last Stop Bar and Grill on 207th and Broadway has a burnt-out Exit sign, I'm pretty sure Delgado's fish market doesn't have sanitary conditions in the rear freezer, and if you can't find some violations at the corner *bodegas* then you're not worthy of that badge, Officer Ivins. Tell them you'll overlook it if they give you something we can use."

"And if they don't?"

"So you'll make your quota early."

I tell Flormaría where we've been so far. She likes the fact that I'm trying a new angle. She's confident we'll get results. That makes one of us.

I take Antonia and the diaper bag, Janette carries the Duesenberg down five flights to the street, and we're off. It's only 10:00 A.M. and things are just starting to jump. For the next four hours we cover every principal avenue in the neighborhood, from Dyckman to 218th Street, from Tenth Avenue to Seaman to the park, where Flormaría and I come across more melted wax and chicken feathers, also female underclothes and used condoms strewn around the paths just inside the woods. I can understand dumping the used condoms, but how do you sneak back home without your underwear? Antonia says, "Peebo messy," but doesn't get more specific than that, thank God.

Nearly everyone we talk to has had some contact with the local mob, but their attitudes run the full gamut from (1) pride, as in, One of ours made it. See what nice cars they drive? to (2) approval, sort of a *Pax Dominicana*, as in, They keep the *barrio* from being shot up by small crooks and warring gangs (this in the face of contradictory evidence), to (3) acceptance, by far the most common, as in, What am I supposed to do, defy them? My wife doesn't look good in black, to (4) ignorance, of this and all problems, ending with (5) disgust, as in, "I am proud of my family name," says an unrelated Guzmán, "And this *hijo de perra* ruins it!" There are those who came here just as poor, just as oppressed, who chose the hard way, working every day for a lousy wage. One kid's working his way through college washing dishes in a restaurant. He hopes to graduate to a "decent" job. His ideal? Washing bottles in a medical laboratory.

But through all our sifting we begin to unearth something that runs far deeper than the glossy attitudes whose faces are turned to the outside world, something that undercuts the superficial variations in appearance: fear. Not the obvious fear one sees a thousand times over when dealing with witnesses against the Mafia, that palpitating, back-watching, nerve-racking fear that a cop sees and feels from a block away. This is more subtle. The local mob has rarely crossed the line into physical punishment. We can't get a single person to admit to a threat that would hold up in court, and yet they are truly terrified, though in a way I don't pick up on at first. Talking to Mafia victims is like having a car alarm piercing the air at all times, its high-pitched wail stabbing into your brain like a knitting needle through the eardrum. Talking to the *dominicanos* is like someone's turned the pitch up so it's just out of range, not piercing your ears, not even measurable by any standard acceptable means, no, just getting under your skin until you go mad from irritation without ever knowing what's causing it.

Nobody will say it, but looking back through dozens of conversations I finally begin to notice at least one pattern.

People are afraid to speak out against Guzmán's crew, of course, but nobody has been threatened, either, at least not with direct violence.

We meet on the corner of 207th and Academy, in front of a grocery with stands outside brimming over with such non–A & P fare as *yuca*, plantain, raw sugar cane, okra, and a few things I don't even recognize myself, since the Caribbean is not my home culture.

"I wonder if Guzmán isn't using enforcement of a different kind," I tell Janette.

"You got something on your mind, why don't you just tell it to me?" she says.

"He rarely resorts to muscle. His old muscle has gone soft—too 'respectable' to bother murdering some grocer whose daily profits barely run to three figures. The mercenaries are such undisciplined trigger-happy juveniles they make a mess of everything they touch—definitely not what's needed to keep a whole neighborhood knuckled under."

"Yeah? So talk to me."

"There's an old man in this neighborhood who's a practicing *brujo*."

"A what?"

"A witch doctor," Flormaría translates.

"Uh-huh. My grandmother went for that stuff. Killing a bluebird's bad luck, or if a spider comes down out of her web, don't let it back up or somebody's gonna die. You trying to tell me Guzmán's throwing hexes on these people?"

"He wouldn't have to do it, just threaten to. Threaten in a way we wouldn't understand, and could *never* toss up to a judge."

"So you think this witch doctor might be Guzmán's enforcer?"

"Not Old Marco," says Flormaría.

"No, not Old Marco. But he's not the only one around. I bet Guzmán's got one working for him, and everyone knows it but nobody'll say. The fear in their eyes is real enough."

Flormaría nods in agreement, her features tightening

into the gaunt, angry mask of one who knows that there is a great evil out there that may be too powerful for us to punish. I tell her to take it easy; she is almost eight months pregnant.

"I don't remember seeing 'fear in the eyes' in the chapter on admissible evidence," Janette says.

"Maybe we should rewrite the chapter. If I recall correctly, the key element of extortion involves the *threat* of physical or psychological harm. Voodoo seems like both."

"So what do we do now? Go around trying to sell these folks some black cat oil?"

"No, but there's a small, unassuming bookstore hidden away on a piece of Ninth Avenue in a high-turnover storefront that used to be a pot store, then a thrift shop, and which now sells dream books, candles, and other artifacts that keep turning up alongside the chicken carcasses."

Flormaría knows where it is. I tell her to go check it out, and to give them a story about wanting to protect her unborn child from hexes, or something. "Just let them know you're looking for a powerful *brujo*."

She says, "Leave it to me," and disappears up the block. That leaves us: the law firm of Buscarsela, Buscarsela & Ivins.

Halfway to Sherman Avenue, a record store owner is violating the city's anti-noise laws by blasting red-hot *merengue* outside his store, which is a bullshit ordinance in this neighborhood, but it gives me an idea.

I go into the store first, wheeling Antonia in the stroller. The owner asks if he can help me. I ask if he has any Ecuadorian music, knowing he doesn't, but it gives me an excuse to stay inside and browse through the racks of records featuring extreme close-ups of solo artists on some and repetitive photos of women wearing string bikinis or less in provocative poses on the compilations.

Ten minutes later, Janette comes in and plays her part well. Whipping out her ticket book and talking like a criminal law book in rapid, deliberately impenetrable English, she traps the store owner in a face-reddening emotional discussion of the fact that no one has ever given him a ticket for playing music outside the store. Janette talks a Harlem mile about nobody giving him a ticket before not meaning shit, the law is the law, and the law says he gets a forty-five-dollar fine.

"¡Cuarenta y cinco pesos!" the owner boils over.

My turn to step in. I know, it's an old, old cop routine. What do you expect from an old cop? I play the good guy in this scene, interceding on behalf of the owner, trying to explain to this hot-blooded rookie cop fresh out of the Academy that loud music is part of the Caribbean culture, that people enjoy hearing his music on the street, that he's never had a complaint in five years of doing business, and aren't good community relations better than racking up her monthly ticket quota like this? I tell her she could easily meet her quota in half an hour ticketing the double-parked cars along Seaman Avenue any morning before 7:00 A.M.

Seeing an opening, the owner does his best to cool off and agree with me. Janette wavers, then returns to her original conviction. The ticket gets written. We vacillate back and forth like this for a while before I prevail in convincing Janette that the record store owner is a good citizen and member of the community. Janette says if he's such a good member of the community, how come he didn't cooperate with the police when they were coming through trying to get information about the mob after Pérez's death? The owner contends no police ever came to him about Pérez, that he must have left the store with his brother-in-law that day, that of course he would like to help in any way possible.

Janette says she'll tear up the ticket if he tells her how come everyone's afraid to give statements about the local mob.

"You want me to make a statement?" says the owner, fearfully.

"You can just put your statement right in my ear," she says, leaning in to him. He whispers something. After a while, Janette nods, then tears up the ticket as promised. She leaves. The owner thanks me. I tell him it was nothing, really. Janette and I meet two blocks away on 204th and Vermilyea.

"What did he say?" I ask.

"You were right," says Janette. "People who are even *thinking* about testifying against Guzmán suddenly get sick. This guy says his cousin was in bed for three days coughing up blood until he sent a message to Guzmán saying he would never open his mouth to the cops. He was back on his feet the next morning."

"Naturally."

At least we've got some kind of confirmation of our angle. I tell Janette that we can't be seen together after that show we put on in the music store, that we'll meet at my place later. Then I go to find Flormaría.

"No luck," says Flormaría. "They know who I am. They knew right away why I was there and didn't want to say nothing. Why don't you go?"

I can see she's about to go into her pushy mode, so I tell her, "They saw through you, they'll see through me, too. I'm not going in there 'til I know what I'm looking for. Okay?"

"Well..."

"*Okay.*"

With Antonia asleep, we spend another hour striking up conversations with the folks chilling on the benches outside Dyckman House. A few of the older Dominicans close in around us as I tell them how Old Marco covered me with a protective root. I've seen a lot of second-hand belief in *brujería*, or witchcraft, up in the hills of Ecuador. But these are communities with dirt roads and one hour of water service a day. Utterly incongruous in this pulsating burg, I am taken aback by the fact that *everyone* has a story to tell about his or her encounter with Voodoo magic. A curly-headed man in his fifties tells me in all sincerity how Legba showed him how to swim the moment he fell off a boat in the tidewaters off Samaná. A twenty-two-year-old medical student at Lehman College tells me how her neighbor's wife was jealous of her shapely legs and how she woke up one morning paralyzed from the waist down. Her family went and got a *bruja* who confirmed that her legs had been cursed by a jealous woman. The *bruja* performed some herbal magic that she is unable to describe in any detail, but it worked. As proof she shows me how pretty and supple her legs are.

An old woman says that some of the ornaments needed to be a powerful *brujo* cost so much the truly great *brujos* go broke paying for them. Sometimes they rob to have the money to buy them, and, yes, some of the younger ones who are too impatient to wait until the proper time kill for them.

The banks don't exactly give out small business start-up loans to these guys.

I tell Flormaría she's done enough for one day, that she'd better go home and take it easy. She's not crazy about it, but she goes.

I head back to my place. Janette is rather conspicuously waiting in the lobby, which kind of ticks me off. I tell her the part about the hotheaded young *brujos* who rob and kill seeking a shortcut to Voodoo mastery.

"Now there's a new angle on this murder. What do you think?"

"I think we're lost in this shit, Janette. You had time to make any Dominican friends down at the precinct house?"

"The Three-four is full of Dominican police officers, but—"

"Let's go."

CHAPTER SEVEN

"PHILOMENA (Virgin Saint) Martyr. July 5. Died before
A.D. 500. A saint venerated at San Severino (*Septempeda*)
near Ancona. Nothing is now known of her."
— *The Book of Saints*

THE 34TH PRECINCT house is not one of those rustic old brownstones with the arching windows and doorways with globular gas lamps that they have in some of the nice precincts downtown. It's a modern post-bunker-era cube of industrial brick that was built to withstand a siege. The only swatch of color comes from the purple-and-black funerary bunting flapping mournfully in the hot breeze drifting up Broadway. But for that you could mistake the building for a phone company relay station.

Up the steps inside the building is a five-foot memorial wreath: a floral cross standing atop a tripod of ribbon-wrapped palm leaves, leaning against The Wall. The Wall enshrines the framed photos of seven other officers who gave their lives for this precinct. The first photo dates from the days when Charlie Chaplin was a bigger draw than Eddie Murphy, the next three are old enough for the officers to be wearing those parallel-buttoned dress uniforms they did away with before I learned to speak English. The most recent one is a black police officer I never knew who was killed just three years ago. Immediately to his left is a smiling official portrait of Police Officer Francisco Carrera, whom I *did* know.

He disagreed with the administration's misdirected anti-drug tactics, too, but a police officer does not enact the laws she or he is required to enforce. Carrera responded the way he was ordered to. The dealers just saw the uniform.

The shifts are changing, officers are scuttling in and out, looking through me to the nasty streets outside where four cops have been blown away so far this year in northern Manhattan alone. They've all got black strips across their badges obscuring the upper half of the seal of the City of New York.

I turn the stroller around, stand behind it, and lift the wheels up one step at a time. By the time I get to the landing, Antonia's awake, so I unstrap her and change her diaper right there with uniformed cops running up and down the stairs. I fold up the stroller and Antonia climbs the rest of the way under her own power. I want an officer who's coming off shift, so I stand watching them sign out and approach the likely ones. Five men and two women ignore me, can't stop, or are otherwise uninterested in my dilemma before Officer Eduardo T. Corona stands and listens to me. He's a five-foot ten-inch muscular man who's blacker than Janette but considers himself *latino*. I tell him Janette's waiting down the street. She can't come up because she's in uniform on her day off.

"Why's that?" he asks me.

"Killers don't knock off at four," I say. "It's like bird-watching: You have to be out there when *they're* out there."

"That rookie's working to catch two killers on her own time?"

"Yeah. And we need your help."

He takes the "we" rather literally, looking down at my toddler with raised eyebrows.

"This is Eduardo," I tell Tonia. "Aren't you going to say 'Hi' to Eduardo?"

"Hi, Dardo," she says.

"Hey there," he says, kneeling down.

I tell him three syllables is more than most people get. He agrees to talk to Janette, and goes off to change. In a few minutes he's back, and we start down the stairs. In a squad-room of my former buddies, nobody's even noticed me. On the way down I ask Eduardo, "What's the 'T' for?"

"Tagliaferro," he says. Now there's a name with magic in it.

It's two votes we go to a bar and one against. Antonia, the tying vote, demands the park. Concession to her superior diplomatic skill breaks the tie. She threatens to scream all afternoon unless we head for the park. We take the 190th Street IND elevator up to Fort Tryon Park and discuss the case walking among the freshly planted flowers. Of course Eduardo heard about the Pérez case, but it was pretty much filed away under "Forget" as far as he knew. We enlighten him to the most relevant aspects of our investigation, to the possibility of getting at the local mob. Eduardo has his own special memories of dealings with the mob.

"Alejandro Pliego," he says. "Sure I remember him. We went to the same grammar school. I was helping out in my dad's store for lunch money while he was mugging kids for theirs. I stayed up late studying to graduate with honors so I could get the scholarship that was the only way I was gonna get to college. He drops out in the eighth grade and women throw themselves at him 'cause he drives a Jaguar. What'd straight A's get me?"

"A mandatory bulletproof vest," I say.

"I was still sweating out midterms while he was strut-ting around consolidating command and respect of the whole *barrio*. The respect is what got me. Bum couldn't spell his own name but everybody admires him because 'he made some-thing big of himself.' Somebody important, *que tiene palancas, que vale*. I swore I'd work my way through law school just to ride his ass to prison where he belongs and show the commu-nity what's really making something of yourself and what's not. But Papa keeled over on a huge crate of fruit he was too proud to admit he couldn't lift anymore, and I had to drop the dreams of law school and start bringing in the money fast. You know how it is."

"Sure do," I say.

"Uh-huh," says Janette.

I turn the subject around to his island's culture. "We think Guzmán's got a bad *brujo* under him keeping people scared."

"*La brujería* is a bunch of garbage. It's all in the mind."

"All fear is in the mind," I say. "The law even allows for that. If people *believe* they are threatened, then they *are* threatened."

"I suppose so," he says.

"If I hold an empty gun to your head and tell you to hand over your wallet or I'll blow your brains out, your fear of death is real, *amigo*, it doesn't matter the gun isn't loaded."

"Don't talk about that, please," says Eduardo.

"Sorry."

"But I see your point."

"Then you'll help us?" asks Janette.

"Help you? How?"

"Guzmán believes in *la brujería*," I say. "There's one in my *barrio* who he goes to for magic baths. He obviously believes Old Marco is a good *brujo* with command of positive, restorative powers. He must be using someone else as an enforcer of evil *brujería*, because Marco would never consent to that, no matter how well he was paid."

"How do you know that?" asks Eduardo.

"Okay, so I don't know it. He sells ices to the kids for a living. Why would he do that? An enforcer makes good money, and the hours are pretty good, too."

Eduardo nods, agreeing. "Okay, so you want some help identifying Guzmán's alleged *bruja* enforcer."

"You got it," says Janette.

"This is crazy," says Eduardo.

"Antonia, get out of the flower bed!"

It's almost 6:30 P.M. when we go to the bar all the off-duty cops hang out in, strengthening their reserve against inevitable death with the old barleycorn. Somebody actually gives me a hard time about bringing a kid in there, then his pal recognizes me from the old days and a few of them crowd around to pat Antonia's head and pinch her cheek. I am offered enough drinks to topple a redwood but restrict myself to ginger ale with a splash of Tabasco sauce.

"One alky special," says the bartender. Thanks. It looks like beer and bites like hell, but it keeps the craving beast at bay. Some of the assholes suggest getting Antonia drunk just to get a rise out of me. Genteel readers can skip this line where I tell the assholes to fuck off.

We spend almost an hour there, me listening to the usual cop gripes about chasing suspects through streets jammed with shoppers and shouting for somebody to just stick out a leg to trip the guy so they can catch him and nobody does anything, while Janette and Eduardo wade into the crowd asking questions. A tap on the shoulder and a finger crooked towards the door relieve me. I say my goodbyes and note that it's a quarter to eight as we're back on the street.

"Come on," says Eduardo, leading us north up Broadway. We veer off northeast at Nagle Avenue, proceed five blocks to Dyckman, then two more under the el train, to a social club. Janette's still in uniform, so she stays outside while Eduardo goes in. Five minutes later he comes back out.

"They haven't seen him," he says.

"Seen who?"

"Raymundo Samaniega. I busted him for car-chopping a couple of months back. We all knew he had mob connections 'cause he was too damn dumb to set up a shop that smooth without getting caught sooner—"

"Ain't it always that way?" says Janette.

"—and he threatened me with *brujería* when I took him in."

"Ohh," I say, finally realizing why we're wasting all this time. "You expecting him to come by here?"

"Saturday nights he always hangs out here."

"They expect him?"

"Sometime," says Eduardo.

"Sometime," I say. "Well, I've got to feed Tonia and I'm all out of snacks. If you guys want to sit stakeout that's fine, but I'm taking her home."

"I can't stake this place out in uniform," says Janette. "I shouldn't even be standing here now."

"Well I'm not staying here all alone when it's your damn investigation," complains Eduardo.

"All right, I'll stay," I say, handing Janette the keys to my apartment. "But you've got to take Tonia with you, feed her and bring her back. And while you're there change into some plain clothes."

"You've got nothing in my size," says Janette.

"There's a floral print dress in the closet my aunt gave me. I never wear it. It should fit you."

I give her detailed instructions about Antonia's likes and dislikes, and explain to Antonia in complete adult sentences how Janette is going to take her back and feed her, then take her back here to me right away. Okay? I guess it's okay, she doesn't fuss. Janette leaves Eduardo and me alone. I don't like it, but I don't seem to have much choice. We sit down on a stoop a few doors up from the social club and wait.

"Stakeouts really suck," I tell Eduardo. "I always hated them. You can't read, you can't listen to music. Just sit and watch a doorway for seven hours. The guy's probably on a three-week vacation in the Bahamas, and you're watching his front door."

We talk cop talk for half an hour, still no Janette. I'm starting to get edgy.

"She'll be along soon," he says in that we'll-take-care-of-everything-ma'am cop-to-citizen kind of voice.

A couple of young men try to look cool as they pass by making kissing sounds at me, despite the fact that I'm obviously sitting with a man.

After an hour and fifteen minutes Janette finally returns with Antonia, who's ready to be put to bed. I want to go home, but Janette tells me to unfold the stroller and put Antonia to sleep in it. I tell her it won't work, but she convinces me to try. Antonia is now cranky as hell, is screaming for her own bed and favorite stuffed animal, when Eduardo whisper-shouts, "There he is!" and leaps to his feet. I take Antonia in my arms and rock her, telling her to calm down, I'm going to take her home right away. I walk up and down the sidewalk, rocking Antonia in my arms, passing Eduardo and Raymundo often enough to hear most of it. That clipped Dominican Spanish is full of Caribbean slang and hard to follow in little snippets, but I get the idea. "I got an honest job now," says Raymundo.

"That's good," says Eduardo. "Doing what?"

"Waste management."

"Management? You?"

"It means clean-up, cop."

"Oh? Who for?"

Raymundo digs into his pocket and hands Eduardo a business card. Eduardo looks it over and says, "Congratulations."

"What you want with me, man? I'm clean."

"What was the name of that bad one you promised to put on me for sending you up?"

"I'm not talking about that, man."

"All I want is a name, Ray. There's no harm in that. Or do you want me to take you in and have the lab verify if your piss'll pass your parole requirements?"

"You want to talk to *La Dama de Hierro*," says Raymundo.

"The Iron Lady? Give me her name, Ray."

"You didn't get this from me, okay?"

"Her name, Ray."

"Oh, come on, man, be reasonable—"

"This is me being reasonable, Raymundo, you want to see me when I get mad?"

I finally get Antonia to understand I'm taking her home to bed in just a minute. I'm looking the other way but all my listening is directed backwards so I can hear Raymundo say the name, "Lucille Ferrer."

"Thank you," says Eduardo. "It's been a challenge working with you."

Janette wants me to spend Sunday with her tracking down the Iron Lady. I say no. She has no need of me for a routine name search, and I need to spend the day with my child. Janette pleads with me to assist her, saying that I know this beat better than she does. I tell her then it's time she started learning. Besides, we can cover more ground if we split up. And I've got some people I want to talk to without a cop standing next to me. Once I put it that way, Janette regretfully agrees to pursue Ms. Ferrer as if she really exists. We'll meet back at my apartment at the end of the day.

Once again I cross the neighborhood with Tonia to hear Mass at St. Jude's. The priest there is so long-winded and irrelevant I find myself wondering if "parable" comes from the same root as "parabolic." And I usually pay close attention. Today I find myself staring emptily at the minimal decorations inside this brick box church. The way they have set up the hymn numbers on display boards under the statues of the saints makes them look like the stats on a baseball card: St. Teresa's having a good season, with 128 souls saved and 38 souls batted in, St. Cecilia's in second with 118 saves and 22 souls batted in, 11 while in scoring position.

My new friend Pliego is in the crowd again today. I don't see Guzmán, but then, these hardcore Spanish parishes give five or six masses on Sunday, not like those air-conditioned suburban parishes with one 10:30 A.M. service; show up or else the minister's wife will see to it that you don't get the fruit cup at tea time afterwards. These priests make their living the old-fashioned way: they work for it. I wipe the floor with a rag so Tonia can climb under the pew to play. She's too young to pay attention to the service anyway. I'm not one of these parents who force a two-year-old to sit up straight and cross herself at the right moment. It'll come.

After Mass I scan the faces, and it looks like *everybody's* making eye contact with Pliego. So how did I get that first lead? Divine Providence? I'm no proselyte, but I had it beaten into me that nothing happens unless God wills it—and it happened, so He must have willed it.

I take the slow route back towards the park, passing by all the stores with the latest children's fashions. I stand in front of the windows, picturing Antonia in each one of the outfits I don't reject out of hand because they either look like Day-Glo crinoline versions of seventeenth-century Spanish royal costumes or are imported from one of the many countries that don't require infant clothes to be flame retardant. The rest I reject simply because they're too damn expensive. Of course I'd like to take Tonia to the gala tomorrow and have her look better than the high-dollar donors who are all probably beating their brows at this very moment trying to decide which outfit will beat out the competition tomorrow night. But it'll have to be in something she already has. Naturally I think she's the cutest baby on the East Coast when she's dressed in nothing but a diaper, but then, like I said before, I'm biased. Still, I have some free entertainment walking up the street, stopping every ten feet to picture her in the latest outfits.

I'm looking through one window when a reflection appears behind me. It's Pliego, watching us from a few feet back. I don't turn. Let it be his move. I'm caught up in asking Antonia which dress she likes best, going over our new vocabulary from *Sesame Street* involving relative sizes, and adding my own regarding color. I guess the creators of *Sesame Street* know there are still a lot of kids out there without color TV, because it's the one subject they don't touch that often. Speaking as one of the Neanderthals who still has black-and-white TV, I appreciate their concern.

So I'm showing her all the different colors when Pliego creeps up and says, "Such a beautiful little lady!"

I'm thinking, Great, here comes the threat about if I want my kid to grow up I'd better keep my nose out of his business.

"But then, she has a beautiful mother," he says.

All right, I admit it. Maybe because I hear so many crude remarks, or maybe because I'm reaching the age when the first cracks are threatening to break the previously smooth surface, but I have to admit that polite compliments, even from guys who use hit men instead of fax machines, are hard to ignore.

"Antonia, say *gracias* to the nice man."

"Ga-ca."

"She's still working on that one," I say.

"Buying a new dress for the little lady?" he asks.

"Just looking. Got a big party tomorrow."

"A private affair, or may anyone come?"

"It's part of my job."

"Just what is your job?"

I tell him I work for a nonprofit organization dedicated to informing people about the need to protect the environment, and how tomorrow I have to work a $100-a-ticket gala.

"Then sign me up for five tickets," he says.

"You don't have to do that."

"And you don't have to tell me what I should and should not do with my money. Put Pliego Import-Export down for five tickets."

"I don't have any of the ticketing information with me," I say.

"I can telephone your organization tomorrow and reserve five tickets?"

"Sure you can, but—"

The sneak. He pulls out his appointment book, opens it to Monday and clicks his ballpoint out. I give him the EAF's number.

"It will be an honor to support so worthy a cause," he says. "And I can expect to see you there?"

"I'll probably be taking your ticket."

"But surely they will let you take a moment away from that so that you can dance?"

"I think it's more of a variety show."

"Ah! These Americans don't know how to throw a party. Food and table talk is all they know. What is a party without dancing?"

I have to agree with him.

"So you're looking for a special outfit for this beautiful little lady to wear tomorrow?" he asks.

"Like I said, just looking—"

"*¿Cual quieres?*" he asks Antonia. "*¿El rojo? ¿El azul?*"

Antonia giggles. "Don't get her hopes up," I say. "She hasn't learned a lot about economics yet."

"Which one do you want?"

"None of them. They're all too expensive."

"The pink one?"

"With her skin color? Men! Dark jewel colors: blues, reds, evergreen, sometimes purple. She looks good in purple."

"All right, here's a nice purple one," he says, getting ready to go inside the store.

"Oh no, please, I mean it. Don't offer her things she can't have."

"Who says she can't have it? It's my offer."

I look at the price. Eighty-five dollars. For a size two.

"No, really," I say. "We were just window shopping. She has plenty of clothes at home."

"How do I know that if I've never seen your home?"

This guy is swifter than I've been giving him credit for, in this department anyway. He goes inside the store. I go in after him, trying to explain how there's a great store right near our apartment that sells used children's toys and clothes in good condition for one-quarter the price of this place. I've gotten a lot of Antonia's stuff there, then when she grows out of them I bring them back and get the next largest size, but Pliego's insistence crosses the line from friendly offer into that sort of macho shut-your-mouth-woman-I-know-what-I'm-doing bit, and before I can walk out of there and disappear down the block the purchase is made and this ex-strike-breaker is handing me a newly paid for child's dress that costs more than any dress I'd buy for myself these days.

"Okay," I say, accepting the gift. "Thank you. Say thank you, Antonia."

"There's only one condition," he says. Ah, here it comes. "She must wear it tomorrow night."

"No conditions," I say, walking out of the store.

We walk the steamy length of Broadway, turn left towards the park.

There's a *bodega* on the corner of Cooper Street a block from the park that always has a couple of good-for-nothings strutting around in front of it looking to peck at something. As I'm crossing the street to avoid them, a minor menace to society leaning against a car he wants the girls to think is paid for tells me, "You're my kind of woman."

I try to avoid him. No smart comments. I'm not in the mood. But he keeps getting in front of me, saying, "What's the matter, you're too good for me?" I'm carrying a kid, so it's a real pain in the ass trying to get away from him. He gets in front of me again: "I said you're my kind of woman."

I'm too tired and too preoccupied with solving crimes against humanity to come up with a snappy retort, so I just tell him, "Oh shut up, you worthless prick!" and cross Cooper towards the park. Okay, so maybe I'm not a poet like Gabriela Mistral. No surprise there.

But he storms across the street after me blurting, "What the *fuck* do you *fucking* mean by that? Come back here!" Oh, Jesus.

The light on Seaman Avenue is against me, so he catches me before I can cross into the park. He stands a nose's length from me, screaming in my face with beer-fueled ferocity. I try to alert him to the fact that if he's so macho, why is he picking a fight with a woman and a child, but I might as well be sending semaphore code in a dense fog.

This guy is really overdoing it. I put Antonia down and shove her behind me because this guy is seriously scratching to punch me. Some macho man. I decide to pursue a rare course of action: I keep my mouth shut. His beer breath and foul-spitting tongue wet my face, and I stand there taking it, cringing—oh, *dying*—to send him to the pavement with two quick chops and maybe break a few teeth too for assaulting me in front of my baby child. And I know the law's behind me on this one—Justifiable Violence, they call it—because I have withdrawn from the encounter only to have him continue the incident by the threatened imminent use of unlawful force. But I neither want Antonia to learn the path of violence, nor do I want to tip off the mob informants who just might be watching that I am more than just another pretty single mother. Yes, this primate can thank Pliego's un-asked-for attentions for the fact that he can still use his genitals.

Eventually his esteemed friends manage to sidle up the block and convince him to walk away, that obviously I didn't mean it and certainly won't do it again, and the guy backs away like he's won some tempestuous battle, yelling that I'd *better* not do it again, or I'll *really* learn what it's like to feel the force of a *real* man. This he punctuates with a phallic forearm salute that hits me as hard as a rapist's knife to the throat— and I know what that feels like—and that snaps it. I look around for some kind stranger to hold Antonia for a second so I can make this guy understand that he is never to threaten a woman with rape as long as he breathes, but what can I say? I never fully figured on the immeasurable responsibility of having a little person look to *me* for her clues as to how to live.

So, vowing to firebomb this jerkoff's car some night when Antonia's not around, I take between ten and twenty long, deep breaths and take the kid across the street into the park. That son-of-a-bitch. If it weren't broad daylight I'd have put him in traction. What really gets me is he'll never know how goddamn lucky he was.

Still fuming from enforced impotence, I push Tonia on the swing a bit harder than usual, then let her get her Sunday clothes covered with sand while she plays with the other kids, all of whom have parents too diligent to let their kids play without having taken them home for a change first. But we're here already, so the hell with it. It's only sand.

I talk with some of the mothers and the two fathers who are pulling Sunday child-watch duty. The women admire Antonia's new purple dress, still in the package, but there is some probing in their voices about how I came to acquire it. Not that they disapprove, quite the contrary, in fact. A lot of my working-class friends always seem to have the shiniest cars and the hippest clothes, meanwhile they're living eighteen to a room. It's appearances, and different values. And they know I don't subscribe to those values as much. It's that mountain girl upbringing. So why the change? Is some man providing me with a little extra spending money? I acknowledge that it was a gift, but refuse to divulge any further information. That satisfies their smiling curiosity.

I look up at the sound of tinkling bells. Old Marco is pushing his ice cart up to the playground. He fends off the advances of a dozen or more tiny outstretched hands, supplying them with their demands with surprising agility on that thick block of ice, but much slower than the kids would ever tolerate from a mere Good Humor man selling prepackaged ices. So there is still some respect for manual labor in this nation's youth. I was beginning to lose faith. After the second wave subsides, I take Antonia over for an ice.

Marco scoops it out, waves away the currency, and tells me, "Legba say you looking in wrong place."

"Oh? Did Legba get more specific than that?" I ask.

"Legba answers every question, but we do not always understand the answer."

"Okay." I nod.

He leans closer. "You must let me uncross you."

"What do you mean, 'uncross' me?"

"There are powers. They do not know who you are yet, but they will find out soon. They know somebody is looking for them, uncovering what they desire to keep hidden. They will put many bad curses on your head. That is why you must let me uncross you."

"Sort of like preventative medicine."

"You say it yourself."

"When?"

"Now."

"Now?"

"There is no time to waste. The powers are strong. They will find out who you are. I must protect you first."

"Where?"

"Not here. Let us go deeper into the park."

Marco unlocks the wheels and pushes his cart past the

victory garden, down the hill behind the baseball diamonds and the soccer field and up into the cavernous overgrown darkness of the heart of the park. Hundred-foot tulip trees blanket the sky with a translucent dark green, and the bald face of the Manhattan schist rises abruptly to one of the highest natural spots on the island. They turned this into a park because they couldn't develop this wild, glacier-cut stretch of rock if they tried. Midway up the hill to an over-look of the Cloisters, Marco turns off the broken paving into the woods. I follow him through the branches into a clearing covered over by a thick canopy of foliage. A tree in the center of the clearing stands like a central post holding up the leafy roof of this naturally occurring vaulted chamber.

Marco opens a side hatch on his cart and removes a color photo of the president that he tacks to the central tree trunk.

"What's that for?" I ask.

"He is the chosen representative of God in this country."

I'm suppressing laughter, and I apologize to Marco.

He says, "He owes his position to the divine intervention of the Voodoo gods."

I say, "That explains a lot. I knew there was some trick to how he did it."

Marco says, "It is better to refuse Legba's services than to scorn them."

The seriousness in Marco's tone is surprisingly convinc-ing. Marco lights a candle at the base of the tree and fills a metal bowl with water in front of the candle so the darting flame reflects off the water. He takes a stick and traces some patterns on the dirt in front of the bowl that look like those scanning electron micrographs of atoms smashing apart in cloud chambers. He reaches inside his cart and after some struggling with string and paper, pulls out a live white pigeon.

"Wait a minute," I say. "I was expecting you to give me some of that uncrossing powder or something."

"Erzulie likes perfumes and powders. Legba favors the bones of animals. And you must share in the meat with him if you want the magic to take hold."

I swallow. Raw New York City pigeon? Maybe it's time to stop this charade. I've learned in life to pray to God for the strength to carry on, but not to expect him to balance my checkbook and remove the landlord from my life. (All right, so maybe I did ask for that last one once or twice.) And yet, Marco means well. I may need his strength and skill on my side. I weigh the options. He stands there, cradling the cooing pigeon and waiting for my verdict. Finally:

"I don't want Antonia to watch this."

I'm sitting watching the evening sun go down from my fifth-floor window when Janette buzzes herself in. She says she hasn't identified her yet, but thinks this Iron Lady could be our woman because people are scared shitless of her. She wants to know how my day went. I don't know where to begin. I take a minute.

I begin with two words.

"Bird guts."

CHAPTER EIGHT

"You call this evolution?"
— Charles Darwin

I LIKE THE CITY when it rains. It keeps some of the scum-bags off the street, washes some of the grime away, and notice-ably freshens the air. It also rains the poetry of change. It alters the face of the harshness, polishes the drab until it reflects a hundred different aspects of neon, headlights and work-lights, and transforms the surface of the gritty into something magical and rarefied. For a moment everything is suffused with the soft glow of a natural haze. Then a downpour soaks you to the skin. But for a while there, you were really living.

Either way, nobody gets to enjoy it, we're all too busy dashing for the subway entrance. Monday morning. Enough said.

It's one of those days where the only available seats are free because they've collected a puddle's worth of cold water in their precontoured depressions. Another design flaw some engineer in La-La Land never considered. I stand with my back against the connecting door, which on these new cars never opens, so I don't have to be bothered with the guys who think a subway train is their apartment, and try not to get the paper too wet as I read my way down to midtown.

I see I'm not the only one who had a busy weekend. A

few weeks ago the president got on TV with a bag of crack cocaine and told the world it was "seized a few days ago in a park across the street from the White House . . . it could easily have been heroin or PCP." Well, that started it. The NYPD Tactical Narcotics Team (TNT) swooped down on an entire block of West 160th Street between Amsterdam Avenue and Broadway, sealed it off and frisked everyone in sight. The ones caught with drugs were arrested on the spot. But a woman who lives on the block says, "All of the drug dealers came back the next day. The raid didn't scare them. It scared the people who were minding their own business." More PR trouble for the cops.

And if that isn't enough, Legal Aid lawyers are now saying that the rapid expansion of new drug cases stemming from the Police Department's war on crack means that by this summer there will be no place to prosecute those arrested or incarcerate those found guilty. In other words, drug dealers know that *because* of the "War on Drugs" the likelihood of prosecution and jail time is actually getting weaker and weaker.

Now it turns out that the president's drug prop, in the words of the headline, was NOT ALL IT WAS CRACKED UP TO BE. Ha ha. It seems DEA agents practically had to drag a crack dealer from the other side of town just so they could bust him across the street from the White House so the prez could fit it into his speech. Well, they say history is written by the victors. Another item in the paper details how a broken front door is blamed in a fatal stabbing in the lobby of a high-rent East 78th Street building. The tenants blame the landlord and guess what? He's my landlord, too! The other paper doesn't carry the story. Why? Because my landlord owns it.

I take a break from this wonderful way to start off the day, check out the crowd surging in at 125th Street, just in case that one lone nut with the meat cleaver is working this morning. I don't see him, but two women about my age whom I peg as secretaries from New Jersey (they must have gotten on at 175th Street while I was absorbed in newsprint) are talking about their Saturday night out. One is telling the other in that displaced-Bronx-to-Jersey nasal whine, "After what you did, I'd be ashamed to show my face." It appears that alcohol was involved. I wonder what she did?

Congestion in the express tunnel holds the train in the station long enough for the car to fill up like one of those buses in Nairobi or something. I can't even turn the page in my newspaper, it's that crowded. I'm forced to read page B3 of the *New York Times* that the man next to me is reading, where I learn that a fifteen-year-old boy who turned an aerosol spray can into a blow torch has been indicted as an adult for spraying swastikas and setting fire to a synagogue in Brooklyn in which five Torahs were reduced to ashes. Further down is an analysis of the TNT's new tactic of putting a cop on every blasted corner in the high drug-use zones. I remember when we tried that with Operation Pressure Point, and the neighborhood went cold. We got rid of the drug dealers all right, but we got rid of everything else, too, by turning the streets into a maximum security gulag. No life at all. So what did we do? We did what we were told.

Thanks to the delays I'm late for work, but nobody seems to notice. They're all running around like mad making the last-minute arrangements for tonight's gala. I strip off my dripping wet raincoat and flip through the morning pile of mail. It's the usual mix of bills, bank statements, journals, junk mail, and a curious postcard from an exterminating service whose motto is, "We Kill with Skill." I check the postmark. Brooklyn. Well whadaya know? Back in the 1640s, the Dutch called the place *Breuckelen*. I looked it up once. *Breuk* means "break," so I figure that "Brooklyn" means "broken, crumbling." If there's a lesson there, it's too early in the morning for me to spot it.

Funny. In a way, today is rather enjoyable. After a weekend of playing cop with a baby under one arm, this place is almost a welcome relief, but it helps too that everyone is running around in such a craze that they don't have as much time to bug me with their trivial commands. Or maybe they're just so preoccupied that I can ignore a lot of what they tell me and they won't notice. Call it crazy, it puts me in a good mood. At least an eight o'clock curtain puts a specific deadline on all their nonsense, so they've actually got to *think* for a change about which decisions to make, which tasks are really important and which ones to ignore. They generally have the luxury of indulging every ridiculous whim that drifts up from the sweatshop down below. Literally. I am convinced that there are chemical fumes in the office at all times—only rarely getting so bad that you actually notice them—that are affecting their brains and making my bosses and co-workers act forgetful and scatterbrained (the fumes only give me headaches). That might explain why the bosses give such muddled directions and make the same misstatements four times in a row, and why one time Zirkelback, while taking a stack of copier paper from my lap, brushed his hand against the nerve of my crotch. I attribute that to stupidity, not sexism. I can't imagine that gawky white boy thinking up something like that on purpose. Maybe I'm too forgiving. After all, if assholes could fly, he'd be a jet.

Things are heated up today. Every message is urgent, every package crucial. The fax machine runs out of paper and you'd think the Visigoths were sweeping south across the Canadian border. Grown men with paisley ties clipped to their button-down shirts lie on their backs on the floor trying desperately to unclog an overheated Xerox machine jam. Frantic calls to the copier company bring the response that we are exceeding this model's capacity. When the sales supervisor is loudly informed that this model was bought with the understanding that it would be able to handle just such a work load, the supervisor admits that his sales rep might have "oversold" the model. I guess that's "lied" to you and me.

Faxes are down, phones are busy, important people who we've got to reach are in meetings (imagine that, people in meetings on a Monday morning!) so it's time to call out the messengers, costing this nonprofit organization fifteen dollars to deliver a message that would have cost us a dime if somebody had thought of it a week ago. As Bartlett's "administrative assistant," I get to deal with this mess.

A tall black bike messenger advances through the human and paper whirlwind to my typing desk. Sweat drips from his brow and rain drips from his shiny black helmet and rainsuit. He pulls an envelope from his bag and shoves it at me. This must be the missing Letter of Agreement for the union guitarist who's supposed to play tonight.

I ask the messenger, "Do they give you anything special for showing up to work on a day like today?" I mean like extra pay.

"Yeah. They let you keep your job," he says, leaving, and somewhere a door slams.

My phone rings for the millionth time today. It's Flormaría. I tell her this isn't a good week for me. She doesn't like that. I remind her that I have some good leads and I promise I'll chase them down within the next couple of days and let her know what I find, then I kind of politely tell her never to call me at work again.

At coffee break I actually get a few minutes to chat with my cellmates.

Lydia's wearing a dress that looks like a painting by Jackson Pollock.

"It is," she says. "I got it at the Guggenheim gift shop. I did the alterations myself."

With a chainsaw?

"Nice. It reminds me a little of Wilson McCullough's style."

"Do you *believe* they've got *three* of them here, the lucky bastards? You know what they're worth now?"

Yeah. I do.

"They must be early works," I say. "For one thing, they've got some color in them. His later style was exclusively black."

Lydia looks at me approvingly. I look up at the paintings. The thick strokes of dark, swirling madness are pure McCullough, but each one has some flashy highlights in one bold color: from left to right, the first one has some orange, the next has some yellow, and finally, red.

"They've got them arranged wrong," says Lydia. "It should go: yellow, orange, red. Progressively darker."

I contemplate the paintings some more. "You're right. That would suit Wilson's temperament."

"'Wilson'? Are you friends with 'Bobby' Rauschenberg, too?"

I tell her a bit about my experiences in the world of art before Zirkelback blows in like a storm out of the south and encourages everybody to get the hell back to work before he starts taking names.

Midway through the mayhem, Jeff Cohen brushes past my station and lets me know he's going to lunch now. I ask out loud if he'd like me to program his phone over to mine, or something like that, and he says sure, so I get up and head for his cubicle. I don't know how long I've got, or how I can even justify staying here with all that's going on outside, but here goes.

Jeff has accessed the Foundation's budget and left it on his computer screen just like he said he would. I've learned enough about this program now to manipulate it a bit better than before. I call up a search for every mention of "Morse," but that just gives me what I already know. He's all over the income half, on record for $7 million worth of tax-deductible donations. Only $500,000 is disbursed to him, for a total of $6.5 million donated, which no matter how you slice it is real money. I just can't believe a guy who would kill to protect $54 million in illegal waste disposal income would be the type to donate $6.5 million to the Environmental Action Foundation.

I check the expenditures side. I've seen enough of the way this place works to know that I do not see $30 million being put to use here. Something is missing from the expenditures, but I can't find it. Pressure, tension, and the fact that I don't know what I'm looking for all contribute.

I return to the income side and note down all the major contributors and other sources of income, then I search the expenditures again using the same list. Fifteen minutes later

I think I've found something. Six million dollars was deposited in a rollover account, one of the ways organizations such as this make some risk-free interest income, probably tax-free too. Or tax-limited, anyway. Naturally, this money was never withdrawn and put to use, which is why the six million should be missing from the expenditures side. But it isn't. It seems like all the money was spent, yet no more is said of the account, and I go back and discover that the account seems never to have yielded the Foundation any interest. Ba-da-bing!

The hell with this computer shit. Now I'm hot on the trail, and I know what I'm after for a change. There's a file cabinet with all the bank statements. A steel brace runs up the front of the cabinet, secured by a hardened push-key lock. I could pop it in a second with a heavy screwdriver, but that would be a bit noisy. So I go over to Jeff's desk, fish out some paper clips, and quickly bend and pinch a few into the right shapes. I look around again, then employ some useful job skills that are *not* on my resume.

Nobody bothers me as I pull the folders for the rollover account, spread them out on a table, and start going through the statements. At last accounting, the rollover fund was only $10,000! Looking back through the statements, it's easy to see that over the course of six months, between 1,500 and 2,000 checks were drawn in amounts small enough to pass unnoticed but large enough and frequently enough to deplete a $60 million account. Sixty million dollars! Twice the total budget!

I start going through the expense checks. They're made out to a thousand different payees, many of whom I recognize from the direct costs in the budget. But more than half of them have been endorsed by the same parent company. To my blurring eyes some of the stamps look like they say, "Unemployed." But I find some good ones and what they say is "Unisystems." The income checks tell the same story. I don't have to dig through another nine miles of bank statements or infiltrate another forbidden computer program. I put all the stuff back and go to the reference shelves to pull down a heavy book on corporate responsibility that, among other things, is an excellent tool for finding out who is covering up what by assigning all their problems to a subsidiary. It takes me about twelve seconds to find out that Unisystems is a primary subsidiary of Morse, Inc.

So that's it. Morse visibly donates $7 million to the Environmental Action Foundation and funnels the other $53 million through the sewers or something. Then they give it all back to him, except for about $500,000 that they get to keep for saving him the trouble of having to pay taxes on the $53 million (plus he also gets to deduct his $7 million "donation"). That's a mighty big tax break. It must be worth $15 to $20 million. God knows what other fees he's saving on by having the EAF do his banking for him. And all the EAF gets out of it is $500,000. Morse even gets the interest. Considering the lengths I've seen them go to just to secure such sizeable donations from other unlikely sources, this little scam would appear completely justified to them. It may take some fiddling, but $500,000 is worth a little fiddling. On the other hand, $7 million is almost twenty-five percent of their total operating budget. People do a lot of messy things for that kind of money. The bastards. And Zirkelback wants me to come in on weekends for them. Shit!

I tell Zirkelback I'm going for lunch. He tells me to be back in fifteen minutes, there's no lunch breaks today. I decline to tell him to go take a flying fuck, and I go call Gina from a street-level pay phone. "You get anything on Morse yet?" I ask her.

"I just got in, Filomena," she says. "I've got other cases, you know. You find anything?"

"Some shit you wouldn't believe."

"I'm listening."

"Start looking for everything you can find about a company called Unisystems."

That night I take off work at six and ride the subway north to get Antonia. The train is one of those aging sixties models that pounds like the drive shaft is about to shoot up through the floor. It takes over an hour to get home and I'm already sweating. I'm due back downtown in twenty minutes. I grab the kid, run over to the apartment, take a thirty-second shower, change into a plain black cotton dress that hugs me with a low-cut top and billows out into a dance skirt below. Every woman in the city has one of these, right off the rack. There's nothing else to do but grab Antonia's new purple dress and jump back onto the subway.

We're lucky this time. The train's a new model with air-conditioning, and rush hour is past, so the train makes a smooth voyage to midtown in twenty-two minutes, during which time I feed Tonia some snacks (thank God for *mamita* Viki's three-course lunches) and change her into her hideous purple party dress. It actually looks terrific on her, but I resent that it was paid for by an extortionist. I'm funny that way.

It's already a quarter to showtime when I ride the elevator up to the reception hall, and Zirkelback is stage whispering holy hell because the guests are already arriving. He says something about this is what they have day care for that under different circumstances would have gotten him a bloody lip.

I take my place next to the cashier and the ticket-taker, and let Tonia loose behind the table where she won't get into trouble. My job turns out to be taking the checks from the people who reserved without paying and don't happen to have $500 cash on them. I hope these checks are good. There are some names I recognize, not big names, but those supporting names you sometimes see if you actually sit there and read the credits rolling up the TV screen after the show is over. Assistant producers from New York's television scene, and other media people lucky enough to work for corporations who like to make $100 donations provided we put on a good show and keep refilling the glasses.

A couple of advertising casting directors check Antonia

out and tell me to give their office a call later in the week. Yeah, right. But will your couch fit both of us?

Before long, hundreds of Beautiful People are jamming the narrow corridor leading into the hall, and they're already losing their cool at actually having to wait in line for two minutes. This is probably a first for some of these media execs who get served morning, noon, and night by doormen, limo drivers, caterers, administrative assistants, messengers, and secretaries, just so they can sit in their sky-high offices and reject some struggling writer's story idea because "It's not connected to reality."

There are a few friendly-looking faces who seem to enjoy this "slumming," and more than a few women wearing Imelda Marcos cast-offs and enough jewelry to pay off Ecuador's external debt. One of them nearly takes out my eye as she bends forward ungracefully to fill out a check.

"Made out to whom?"

"The Environmental Action Foundation. Just put EAF," I say, thinking, you want to make a *real* contribution, send your jewelry to Ecuador's Treasury Department.

It only takes a few minutes for the hallway to empty, and the next thing I know the lights have already gone low in the theatre. What? No introductory speech about why we're all here—to save the environment from corporate irresponsibility? It must be part of the show. Zirkelback comes out and tells us it's okay to stand inside to watch the show, but to stay near the door to take care of late-comers. I ask the cashier if she can watch Antonia for a minute while I go to the kitchen to get her some real food for dinner. The cashier looks at me like I'm asking her to watch my pet python for six months 'til I get back from Borneo, so I lift Antonia out of the field of adult legs oriented towards the stage, navigate this slalom myself, and sneak off down the hall to get the kid some deli cuts from the reception plates.

When I get back, the cashier is taking a couple's check. They take their tickets and go inside. "Where were you?" the cashier says to me with an edge that would chop open a can of peas (and *still* slice a tomato). This evening is not starting off well.

We get back inside the darkened theatre, and the second-to-last comedian on earth is on stage:

"I tell ya, times are changing," says the comedian. "My uncle put in fifty years and he was replaced by a machine. All right, so that machine was a staplegun." The audience of office execs laughs politely as the comedian describes how his uncle used to do the work of *two* stapleguns when he was really going strong.

He continues: "I tell ya times are changing. Have you heard about the new Jewish motorcycle gang? —Hell's Boychicks. They wear leather *yarmulkes* with metal studs."

Some laughter as he mimes his words. "You ever wonder if Hitler really got out of Germany alive? Some say he went to Bolivia. I am *convinced* that Hitler was a janitor at my elementary school."

A chuckle escapes from my throat. Okay, so the guy's *almost* funny. Antonia's more interested in the balloons decorating the stage than the famous-for-being-famous personalities they bring out to sing a few forgettable numbers with the backup band and dancers who I happen to know cost this environmental organization nearly $30,000 to transport, feed, and house for this twenty-minute set. Still no speech about the environment.

That act finishes to thunderous applause. What can I say? It's a star whose career has been in troubled waters for four or five years already, playing a "charity" gala to a roomful of media producers and execs. Sounds like her motives are none too altruistic here.

The emcee announces that this next act is for anyone out there who doesn't realize just how sexy clear-cutting and strip-mining can be. The lights change impressively to a cool blue moonlight and a hot spotlight hits the undulating figure of a woman whose costume reveals so much flesh the blinding glare could start a brush fire in the frozen tundra, cause cracks to form in the reinforced concrete foundation of a high-rise office tower, and unleash pandemonium at a conference of Dominican monks. More parody? No! This is the real thing! A stripper! A goddamn stripper! And the band is playing an anaesthetized version of "Night Train," and the stripper is working the balloons, and the men in the audience are getting rowdy, and I'm embarrassed for civilization. Five billion years of evolution. For this.

I leave the theatre as I hear one exec tell his neighbor, "I wouldn't mind trapping *that* endangered creature." Guffaw.

I take Antonia over the power cables, behind the sound board, and flash my ID to get backstage. A guy who turns out to be the stripper's boyfriend sits quietly reading Flaubert in a straight-backed wooden chair. Flaubert!

I watch about a minute of the show from the wings before a union stagehand getting eighteen times what I'm getting for being here tells me to get the fuck out of his way. Guess he didn't see my ID.

I go back out front and sit through the rest of the glitzy-but-boring show, waiting for that break that never comes when somebody is supposed to stop the show, turn on the lights, and talk to this roomful of well-connected media people about the dangers threatening our earth. It never happens. The show's over, the applause triumphant, and the lights come up in time for everyone to raid the reception tables, which have perfectly ordinary deli fare. From the way they attack it, you'd think they were starving in the wilderness and the cold cuts were manna from heaven.

I watch in increasing confusion as non-recyclable Styrofoam plates are loaded up with grain-wasting steroid-injected meats and non-recyclable plastic cups are filled with multi-colored sugar water and blended alcohols. Now the film is wiped away and the conversation reveals the donors' true characters. Wing-tipped execs whose company expense accounts paid for their tickets are standing around cradling misting cocktail cups, nostalgically lamenting the bygone days of Reagan when everything was booming. Now it's all bust, they say. But they fail to see what went wrong. "I should have grabbed *more* while I had the chance" is the gist of their lament.

I circulate, nod my head at the co-workers I see awash in a sea of corporate faces trying to milk them for a few more bucks. No, not enough drinks in them yet. Give them another hour.

About eighty percent of the conversations have to do with television, but not the business of television that you would expect from this crowd. Huddles of thirty-something yuppies dressed to the nines are standing around sharing memories of specific episodes of the *Brady Bunch*, and testing each other on who can remember both versions of the theme to *Gilligan's Island*. (They changed "and the rest" to "the Professor and Mary Anne" in the second season, I discover.)

And in the midst of this swirling sound and fury twenty-five stories over New York, I am overcome by a feeling of emptiness. We live in such a rootless society that the only thing we've got in common is an episode of *Charlie's Angels* that we all saw fifteen years ago.

Edith Wharton warned of the brain-sapping dangers of radio. What kind of perception of the world is my child developing, with eighty-seven-channel color TVs, satellite dishes, programmable VCRs? Well, I guess I survived the advent of radio, huh?

I spot my new friend Lydia through the bobbing faces. She's really dressed up, looks gorgeous, and is surrounded by five execs who are trying not to be too obvious about the fact that they are staring down the front of her dress. I close in, lifting Antonia into my arms to keep the men at bay, in time to hear one of them tell Lydia, "Now y'all got to admit George Wallace was a *great* American!"

Lydia turns to him, all smiles, and says, "There is no doubt that Governor Wallace was a—*significant* American. Ah, Filomena!"

She seizes my arm and the opportunity to walk me away from the group, leaning close and confiding, "Let's get out of here before I puke."

We try to blend into the wallpaper behind one of the speakers pounding out gutted disco versions of safe old Motown hits so this crowd can get down about as much as anyone can in full formal wear. Give me a genuine Bacchanalia any day.

"Who picked this band?" asks Lydia.

"Please, I know how much we're paying for them," I say.

"How much?"

"I don't even want to think about it. Let's just say if this thing goes past midnight they're getting double overtime."

"Good deal. I should have brought my art school mates up here to take over the stage. They'd blow the wigs off these coneheads."

"You could just pull the plug on the sound board."

"Jesus, the Rice University marching band rocks harder than these phonies."

"You went to Rice?"

"Well, I spent a *lot* of nights there," says Lydia, winking at me.

"Uh-oh."

"What?"

I've been spotted. Alejandro Pliego actually came! Two hours late, of course, Latin time. He's gesturing like a deep-sea fisherman pulling on a five-hundred-pound tuna for me to join him on the dance floor. I shake my head no, indicating the kid. Don't ask me how, but Zirkelback appears between us, gesturing for me to come over to him. What is it now? I go over to him and he tells me in clear-cut terms that if a man pays $500 to get in here and he wants to dance with one of the staff, then one of the staff better dance with him.

"You're staff, you dance with him," I say.

Nothing doing. This is too much of a scene for me to make my own scene. Zirkelback wins. Lydia gets Antonia. Pliego gets me. I'm trying to find the throbbing bass line that's supposed to be in this funky song's original version, but it's just not there. I move around, but there's nothing there to move to. Wouldn't you know it, the band doesn't stop, but segues right into a slow number about a woman who wants a man, and Pliego puts his softball player's arms around me and gains total control over my body for the next seven grueling minutes. I do the best I can, putting my right hand in his and getting my left arm folded up between us halfway to his shoulder so there's *some* distance between our bodies, praise God. But that still leaves him with one hand free to do some exploring.

I guess I could call myself lucky that he doesn't take excessive advantage of this situation, and I manage to pull him off of me every time he circles near a potentially erogenous zone. It's an accident of design that I have these spots that can become involuntarily stimulated in virtually the same degree by someone I actually love and care for as by some sleaze who used to bust the heads of my brothers-and-sisters-in-solidarity. Of course emotional entanglement heightens the sensations when all goes right, but the primary signal is the same. I sure wish God would consider a design change on that one.

So I survive the dance, and beg off another with the excuse of having to go use the women's room to change my child's diapers, which is probably true anyway. I retrieve Tonia from Lydia's watch, and head out of the noise and smoke to the brightly lit hallway that leads to the restrooms. I push open the door and look at my face in the mirror over the sink. I still look pretty. Somewhere a picture of me just aged five years.

Antonia wants to pee. I'm still trying to toilet train her, but I never have the time, so I figure why not now? I open a stall and nearly break my neck on the ceramic tile floor, slipping on empty crack vials. A shudder of pain shoots up my spine and I look up and see two men who paid $100 to get in sitting on the tank in what is supposed to be the women's bathroom. The glass pipe is blackened and smoking. Their eyes are fluid and opaque.

"Want some?" says one, holding the pipe out to me.

I lean forward trying to get to my feet.

"Hey!" says the other. "I'd like to dive into those tits and not come up for air for a week."

They both laugh those puffball-inflated laughs of the freebase rushing around their brains looking for some electrons to adhere to.

I swat the pipe out of my face. I think I hear the tinkle of breaking glass as I exit the bathroom. The gala is breaking up, and not one word has been said about the environment.

After midnight, the subway train turns into a pumpkin and Antonia turns into a sandbag. They're doing track work, the train goes local and the ride home takes nearly two hours. I have to get up in five hours.

And somebody's in trouble.

CHAPTER NINE

"I am not a slut, though I thank the gods I am foul."
— Audrey in *As You Like It* (III, iii, 38–39)

I DON'T SLEEP WELL, I don't eat well, I don't ride the subway well. All the time I'm steeling myself for what I've got to say to my bosses. Bartlett keeps me away from his office as long as he can before I walk right in and tell him I want a word with him.

"Sure," he says, heading out the door. "You want some coffee?"

No, I *don't* want some coffee, but he's already gone. He knows I'm ready to explode, so I wish he'd just sit down and have me let it out rather than making with the false politeness. Bartlett gives me a few more minutes to seethe before he comes back, and he's got Zirkelback with him. Good. Let him hear this, too. The only one who's missing is Carberry, who never seems to be around when people are looking for him.

I start off looking straight at Zirkelback: "First of all, I don't appreciate having my immediate superior pimping for me."

Zirkelback is first out of the gate with, "It's not my fault."

"Nothing is ever your fault," I say. "You should have someone permanently on staff whose job it is just to get fired every day so he can take the blame for your screw-ups."

"Now, wait a minute, what's going on here?" says Bartlett. Hey, he noticed something is actually going on around him.

I tell him, "What's going on here is that I choose my own dance partners."

"The guy paid $500 to get in—" begins Zirkelback.

"So that makes it all right? I don't care if he paid $5,000 to get in. *You* don't make that kind of decision for me."

"Mr. Zirkelback is authorized to direct the staff as he sees fit at these events, Miss Buscarsela," says Bartlett.

Oh, so that's how it is. Okay. Drop the infantry back, bring out the cavalry.

"You blew the prime directive," I say.

"What do you mean?" says Bartlett. He knows what I mean.

"The literature that you had lying out on all the tables last night that nobody bothered to read states that the primary purpose of this organization is"—and I pick up a brochure and read right from it—"'to inform the public about the need to protect our environment from the dangers that threaten it.' I didn't hear one word about the environment last night."

"We don't control these events—" says Bartlett.

"Then I want nothing to do with them."

"—the stars do," says Bartlett.

"Well, *we* should," I say.

"You must understand," says Zirkelback, "that we raised nearly $300,000 last night that will go to funding the other work we do."

"What other work? As for as I can tell, you only publish position papers. Where are you on the drinking water issue that the EPA has been loading this office with data on? I mean, Greenpeace is out there hanging off bridges and chaining themselves to submarines! I kept waiting for the lights to come up and for somebody to get on stage, talk about the issue, and pass the hat a little more. You could have brought in another twenty to thirty thousand."

"Uh, true—" begins Bartlett.

"I would have even gotten on stage to talk. People were

putting *drinks* down on your position papers! I busted my butt—not for the environment, but so some media execs could party."

"This isn't the crowd for it," says Bartlett. "These are TV people, they have a thirty-second attention span."

"All the more reason we should have talked to them—at least for thirty seconds, anyway."

"Well, we're all very tired from the late night," says Zirkelback. Pitiful.

"If there's one more event where nobody talks about the issue, I quit."

"I think your reaction is way out of proportion to the cause," says Zirkelback.

I say, "You may not know it, but your staff agonizes over wasting so much as a rubber band because we've got to be environmentally conscientious, and you had a roomful of five hundred rich, highly placed, environmentally ignorant media people, and you blew it—you didn't talk to them about the environment!"

"Well, it's got to be on their level," says Zirkelback. "If you're suggesting we squander our resources on creating slick media displays—"

"Slick? Who cares? One guy was even nasty to me."

"Well, I wouldn't condemn the event on account of one guy getting fresh," says Zirkelback.

How does he know the guy was fresh? No time to think about that one now, I'm losing the big one.

"We'll have to talk about this later," says Bartlett. "We've all got a lot to do."

"Not later," I say. "Now."

"No, later," says Bartlett picking up the phone like he's got some unbelievably urgent business going on that I'm just too small-minded to grasp.

"Hey," says Zirkelback. "It was even worse last year."

"I don't give a damn." That's me talking.

"Later?" says Bartlett, beginning to dial.

Okay. Cavalry retreat. Artillery time.

"Why are you letting Samuel Morse launder $60 million through the EAF's bank accounts?" Ah, *that* gets their attention. First there's the usual I-don't-know-what-you're-talking-abouts bouncing around like rubber balls in this tiny, glue-smelling office, but I go calmly forward into the hailstorm of words, for I have the Lord with me, and "a fool's voice is known by a multitude of words." That's Ecclesiastes. Bosses should learn that they can't intimidate someone who was raised on angry prophets. I cut through this clumsily thrown up verbal smog by explaining that I have had dealings before with Mr. Samuel Morse and I know what kind of a businessman he is, and that I have already photocopied both sides of all the checks drawn on the rollover account, so I know where the money's gone. Okay, so I'm lying about the photocopies. I've got to throw everything at them.

It works. They finally admit that this is happening, that they are in fact allowing Morse to "avoid some taxes" by depositing some of his money through the EAF, but it's only fifty million dollars, not sixty million, like that's supposed to make a freaking difference.

"It's probably worth seventy-five million to him," I say.

"And it's worth one million to us!" Bartlett spits the words at me. "Thanks to the new tax laws reducing the deductibility of charitable donations, more and more charities are hustling for the same dollars."

"Or fewer dollars," adds Zirkelback.

"So that makes it all right?" I say.

"This organization would be unable to function without the money Morse donates," says Bartlett, expanding the term "donates" rather beyond its dictionary definition.

"He gave us thirty computers *at cost,*" says Zirkelback.

"Oh, *that's* worth thirty mil," I say. "I never knew the commandment read, 'Thou shalt not lie—without a *very* good reason.'" I love the Bible. It gets them every time.

Bartlett chops at the air in front of him with the edge of his hand. "You're very new here, and very idealistic, young lady. We know what Mr. Morse is doing, we accept what

Mr. Morse is doing. You may not realize it, but he gives us almost one quarter of our working capital. Most of the funds we get are pre-allocated. The funds we receive from Morse Incorporated are soft money—non-allocated—we can do anything we want with it."

"Like give most of it back."

"When we're strapped we pay our bills with that."

I'm about to say then they should do some preventative planning and not get strapped so often, but Bartlett goes on, "Including your salary."

I think my face cringes like I've just eaten some titanium.

"Ah, you see? Sobering thought," says Bartlett. "But then, that's business. And if you blow the whistle on us, you'll get yourself and this organization in big trouble. That is our organization's position."

"Yes, but what's the truth?" I ask. No answer. "All right. I'll keep quiet. But let me tell you something I've learned about the truth: My dad was born in 1890 in the Ecuadorian Andes. Yes, he had me when he was nearly seventy. And in case you don't know what those two facts add up to, they add up to me getting my ass whipped bloody for breaking a commandment. As a kid, the worst trouble I ever got in was for telling a lie. As an adult, it seems like the worst trouble I ever get in is for telling the truth."

I get up to leave, stop at the door and face them. "And about that $6,000 we spent bringing Liz Crowell back from L.A. in time for last night's show: You could build a *school* in Ecuador for $6,000."

I turn to go, but one of the gossipy fashion-conscious secretaries blocks me on her way in with some coffee. Nerves stripped raw and I've lost my insulation. So it must be me who tells her, gratingly, "Get out of my way!" and heads for the phone without my usual Catholic schoolgirl poise. With one officer newly dead, maybe the 34th Precinct has an opening.

"I've got to see you, Janette. Now."

"Can't do that, Fil. There's some racial shit goin' down, lieutenant's got us all pulling overtime."

"Racial shit?"

"Six dudes jumped three Jewish guys from Yeshiva University. They think it's retaliation for that kid who got sent up for torching that synagogue."

"Jumped?"

"Beat them unconscious and continued to stomp on them after they fell to the ground."

"Sheesh."

"The neighborhood's gonna fly apart unless we get out there and ease tension."

"Ease tension? You're outgunned and outnumbered by the perps, untrusted by the public, and handcuffed to outdated crowd-control techniques by a bunch of fat-assed bureaucrats who think innovation is a *threat,* and you're just supposed to go out there and 'ease tension'?"

"I really gotta go, Fil."

"Come by when you get off shift."

"Only if you put some beer in that refrigerator."

"I could go for a couple of kegs myself."

"See ya."

I hang up and redial the EPA, reconsidering about going back to being a cop. The tension is tremendous. The city is getting ready to explode with racial violence, so what does the brass do? Send in the cops to block off streets the angry folk consider to be theirs with wooden police line barricades from the sixties, nightsticks drawn and some mounted police added for extra intimidation, like the *picadores* who jab the bull to remind him he's supposed to fight if he looks like he's getting a bit lethargic.

I hear wailing laughter coming from Bartlett's office.

"EPA."

"This is Filomena. You find anything yet?"

"I've got nine full-time cases. Who's paying me to work overtime? You?"

"Gina, I've got proof that Morse is using the EAF to launder money from questionable sources. You've *got* to investigate his Unisystems holdings."

"Look, I'm trying to build some cases that'll actually *stick* to some of the biggest offenders in the country. We're talking about Superfund violations, the National Priorities List. I just don't have the time to open a new investigation."

"You don't have time for a new investigation or you don't have time for something that's not a sure thing?"

"Okay, okay. So I'm a little quota conscious. You happy? I've got to bring two of these cases to prosecution by September or they're going to start wondering why they keep me on staff."

"How much evidence would you need to justify a full-scale investigation?"

"What are you driving at?"

"You say you don't have the time to check into it yourself. Okay, what if I come down there and you just open your files and give me a shove in the right direction?"

"You want to come down here? Now?"

"Hey, it's all public information anyway. I can always get it through the Freedom of Information Act, couldn't I? Now what's it going to be?"

"Man, who lit the fire under you?"

"Murderous scumbags who know how to use a lumbering, cooperative bureaucracy to bury their crimes"

"Okay. When are you coming?"

"As soon as I can get the hell out of here."

I knock on my boss's door to go right in.

"I feel sick. I'm going home," I say.

He says, "Yes, take the rest of the day off, Filomena. I'm sure you'll feel better tomorrow."

I wish I could be so sure.

People in the movement used to say, "If you're not part of the solution, you're part of the problem." The Environmental

Action Foundation is neither. Sometimes, when I'm feeling charitable, I wonder if maybe inaction *is* better than being a total swine, but—I don't know. What would Jesus the rule-breaker have said? I know what my old revolutionary comrades-in-arms would have said: they would have purged me the old-fashioned way just for questioning them.

I'm waiting for the subway to take me down to the EPA building, thinking about that turd Zirkelback and what I'd like to do to *him*. Actually, I wish no worse on him than what he did to me, which in my case is quite a curse: for him to be pimped off and humiliated by his immediate superior someday while he's making a salary he can barely live on and the rest of his life is in total turmoil.

I curse him for his "by the book" attitude, which is really a cover for what a *putz* he is. I once asked him if it would be possible for me to take a box full of programs home and transfer them to a cheap computer so I could work at home once in a while and be with my kid. His answer? "If you did, you'd be liable for prosecution and could spend ten years in jail for software copyright violation." Yes, the word is *putz*.

He's lived too short and privileged a life to understand that The Rule Book doesn't cover it all. The Rule Book doesn't cover what to do when you take a one-week temp job after being promised $250, and Friday afternoon the manager vanishes, leaving three guys with baseball bats telling you to get out of there. The Rule Book doesn't cover working for a cocaine addict who keeps endangering your life by cutting corners and who takes in $20,000 a week but passes out rubber paychecks.

The train pulls in and I get on, thinking about all the lies they fed me about the social mobility this society offers, about how anyone can make it if you work hard and study, if you try. In reality, the system fears innovation and only rewards those who play along by whitewashing their alternative cultural values. And what if your "alternative" values include teaching peasants how to read a utility bill and figure out if the merchants are cheating them? Unprofitable. Pastoral work in the rice paddies? A living wage for all? Feeding the hungry? Meaningless. Smile and pretend you *love* doing everything the boss tells you. *Lie* at the interview. It works.

Chambers Street already? I get out and head for the back exit.

I think Gina did it on purpose. In the hour since I spoke to her, she has called up about a thousand miles' worth of computer printout from the records library and requisitioned eight bank boxes full of files for me to look through.

"This is everything we know about Morse, Inc., and its subsidiary Unisystems," says Gina.

"So the government *can* get moving when it has to. Where do I start?"

"By opening a box," she says, turning away and heading for her cubicle.

I know this move. Please, ma'am, it's just a purse snatching, you sure you wanna press charges? It means three hours' extra paperwork for me. Okay, ma'am, but you gotta look through these mug shots first to see if you can identify him. *Slam!* Eighty-five pounds of paper is dropped in front of the plaintiff. But once in a while she actually sifts through all eighty-five pounds of it and comes up with a positive ID.

I sift. I sift through old deeds to land Morse's present factories are built upon; local investigations showing that some of the killer compounds leaking from his sites are attributable to the previous owners; even the visa applications for a couple of German rocket scientists (dated 1946), if you can get to that. All the small-scale stuff handed up from the State EPA; floorplans; blueprints; what look like chemical abstracts; and acres and acres of legalese, the general gist of which I manage to picture in my mind, even though I don't fully understand a single sentence. Morse has broken his empire up into a thousand fragments loosely connected by the incomprehensible fine print of legal-size documents.

I sift 'til five and call out for Chinese. Gina's staying late putting together her case against some Long Island tungsten manufacturer. It's a tough case because tungsten is an essential metal for the defense industry, which means it's the Environmental Protection Agency versus the Department of Defense, and one underfunded, politically unpopular branch of the government doesn't particularly want to take on a massively overfunded, politically untouchable branch of the government because it's liable to get as messy as a Manson family reunion. I call up *mamita* Viki and tell her I'll be a couple of hours late. I don't like doing it, but I'm driven, frenzied even. And none of these documents can leave the building.

It takes me seven hours. Towards the end, my sifting becomes more like shoveling. I cover all eight boxes and about half of the computer printout A little after 8:00 P.M., I walk into Gina's cubicle with a handful of photocopies. I stand there and lay them on her desk in front of her one by one as I make my case.

"Box Five, Folder C: In 1985, Tronix Corp., a subsidiary of Unisystems, in turn a subsidiary of Morse, Inc., bought half of the Pythias Township test site. Box Two, Folder F and page one twenty-eight of the Internal Records Documentation: This site was previously owned by the federal government and sub-contracted out to defense industries for the testing of rocket engines. Page two-oh-four: The site was sold to the State of New York, which in turn—Box Three, Folder M—sold half of it to Tronix. Box Six, Folder D-Two: In 1988, workers at the site brought a complaint to the county water authority about a funny taste in the water at the site's drinking fountains. Now, I figured the results of that should really be somewhere in the files, but I'll be damned if I can find them. However, I did find a reference to it on page three sixty-seven of the Records: The county responded to the complaint, and called in the State EPA, who drilled a few holes and took samples straight from the water fountains, as far as I can tell from this technical jargon. The Records *did* refer me to Box Eight, Folder C-two, and if my reading of this chemical analysis chart with all its peaks and troughs is in any way correct—I was absent the day they taught Magnetic Resonance Imaging at the police academy—the water seems to have tested positive for excessive quantities of half a dozen can-cer-causing chemicals. It was right there in your files. Kind of spread around, though."

She looks at me. "So we missed it."

"Don't take it too hard. Son of Sam was on file for months before a beat cop gave him a ticket for double parking."

The A train has a seizure, gasps and dies just before the 145th Street station. It takes twenty minutes to bring the power back so we can lurch into motion and disgorge into the station to wait for a second train. The next A train has to be switched to the local track, so this takes another twenty minutes before we're in motion again, and it's a quarter to ten by the time I pick up Antonia, who has already been asleep for two hours. Earlier, when this day was going so badly, I just wanted to head home and spend the rest of the afternoon with her. Now I feel like she's playing the part of an extra in the drama of these past few weeks, when in fact she is, has been and will always be the major character in my life for as long as it lasts.

I wonder if I really should become a cop again. It wouldn't take long to get reinstated as a detective. Then I could chase crooks on the city's time, instead of wandering around in strange people's offices, up to my waist in barrels of docu-ments whose primary purpose is to circumvent comprehen-sion. To say nothing of all the other unpaid investigating I'm doing to help someone who is, after all, dead.

The first six months with Antonia were a wonderful pain, a sweet hell of stumbling around at 2:00 A.M., changing her diapers every forty-five minutes, and having her drain the life out of me into herself so fast I could swear I actually saw her growing before my eyes while she sucked at my breast, the way Popeye's muscles used to balloon out right after he sucked down that can of spinach.

Oh, there was a man around, but he wasn't much good even then. Sure, he'd hold her for a minute now and then when something was boiling over on the stove, but usually he was too busy buying and selling stereo equipment and VCRs of questionable pedigree. I said nothing because when you're lying in a sleep-deprived semi-psychotic state with a twelve-pound human breast pump at your tit there's not much else your running-on-empty brain can handle besides staring into the phosphorescent glow of the latest video trash.

Then she finally started sleeping through the night and I felt like a werewolf the day *after* a full moon. No more fangs, no claws, no furry coat, no bloody footprints, I was human again. And she became fun. She learned to make her wishes known in her bilingual baby talk, and I read to her constantly in both languages. Maybe she'll get a job at the U.N. one day if her mother doesn't drop one of the grenades she's juggling.

Antonia wakes up just long enough to recognize that I'm putting her in our bed, then turns over and goes back to sleep. I take her shoes off, take off her day clothes, kiss her my blessing.

I'm getting ready for bed when there's a knock at the door. I go to the hallway, stand an arm's length beside the eyepiece and flip it open with my finger. When nobody shoots my finger off, I move over and look out. It's one of the tenants from the other half of the building: a third-generation Irish kid who decided to stay. I open the door for him. He's got a petition of complaint against the slumlord's tactics and a statement of support for the forming of a Tenants' Association. I sign both. He tells me there's a meeting tomorrow in the lobby to discuss the fact that the front door locks still haven't been repaired, how the boiler can't even get hot water up to the sixth floor, and all the rest of it. I tell him I'll be there if I can make it.

"Think the place'll really go co-op?" I ask.

"We're fighting it. Got one-fifth of the tenants' signatures."

That's not enough. I want to ask, "Who would buy into this dump?" but that's not the right thing to say to someone whose grandfather still lives here.

Back to the bathroom to brush the teeth, wash the face and take a rather cool shower of piss-soft pressure. He was right about that boiler. I expect this in Guayaquil, not New York. I'm still under the water when I hear the door again. Normally I wouldn't hear it, if the water pressure were up. I wrap a towel around my hair and throw on an old terrycloth bathrobe that's still stained from baby vomit. I've washed it a hundred times, but the semi-digested beets just never seem to come out.

I'm a little more cautious this time. I take the broom and lift the eyepiece cover from a safer distance. More knocks and Janette's voice, shouting, "Come on, Fil, open up!" Just what I need.

I peek anyway before letting her in.

"Make it quick, will you, it's been a long day," I say.

"Hey, you were the one who told me to come by after shift, remember?"

"You're right. Sorry."

"And I bet you don't have any beer, either."

"Just one. It's yours."

"Hot damn," she says, opening the fridge. "Don't you be telling me about no long days."

She settles into a chair. "I pulled a double shift today on account of three Jewboys getting beat up."

Jewboys? I decide to let it go. "Bad day, huh?"

"The worst."

"If you can sit here and say it was the worst then it *wasn't* the worst." I copped that line from Willie the S.

"My worst so far. Holding a line all day with brothers and sisters all glaring at me like I was some kind of Uncle Tom traitor—"

"I got the same thing from the *latino* junkies I used to pull in. You get used to it."

"What are they staring at, anyway? I could be making better money doing a whole lot of worse stuff."

"So could we all be."

"Like that *broo-hah* stuff you were talking about. You were saying that this old man Marco doesn't charge for his services."

"He says God works free of charge."

"But this Iron Lady, she charges, right?"

"Probably, yeah."

"So there's got to be some kind of record of the transaction."

"I wouldn't know."

"Well, you see I got this tip from Eduardo. He says anyone cutting the volume of business like this Iron Lady's supposed to be doing's gotta be taking in stuff she can use, you hear me?"

"Keep talking."

"I mean, like live animals. Chickens, goats, he said maybe even big stuff like a bull or two. Well, she's gotta keep all those animals somewhere, doesn't she?"

"You're telling me that Lucy Ferrer has got a barn full of livestock somewhere in the Inwood-Heights area?"

"Why not? You've heard of stranger things, right?"

"Okay . . ."

"Well that gives us something to look for!"

"Or smell out."

"I've been smelling already." She finishes the beer and goes for another, doesn't find one. "Damn! So anyway, I hear there's this storefront down on Academy, see? Always locked up with a big iron gate, two big padlocks. Folks say they never see anybody go in or out, but they do hear animal noises coming from inside."

"What kind of animal noises?"

"I don't know! Isn't that enough?"

"Enough for what? A legal warrant? You're out of your mind."

"Enough for a little late-night visit of our own . . ."

"Not a chance."

"But Fil—"

"Can't you get somebody else?"

"You're the only one I trust."

I sit there staring at the empty beer bottle Janette left on the table long enough for it to grow some mold.

"How about early, early morning?" I ask.

"Can't. I got shift. Tomorrow night?"

"I guess so. I'll have to see."

"Good enough. So what was it you had to see me about?"

My mind is a clogged vacuum cleaner bag that needs emptying. "I don't even remember."

CHAPTER TEN

"What force or guile could not subdue,
    Through many warlike ages,
Is wrought now by a coward few,
    For hireling traitor wages.
The English steel we could disdain,
    Secure in valour's station;
But English gold has been our bane—
    Such a parcel of rogues in a nation!"
— Robert Burns

"FILOMENA, take this down to the mailroom," Mr. Bartlett commands.

I take a large Jiffy envelope of God-knows-what and gladly abandon my workstation for the comparative diversion of a trip downstairs. Wednesday morning and it's business as usual. Not one word has been said about yesterday's outburst. The guy down in the mailroom is a little less hurried today. He has time to grab the package and joke with me: "All right, what you got for me this time?"

"Search me. Probably a contract on my life."

"Bartlett getting to you?"

"All bosses get to you once in a while. That's normal. It's that weasel Zirkelback I can't stand."

"Stiff, huh?"

"Stiff? Let me put it this way: He's so tight-assed if there were a pin stuck in his butt it would take a derrick to get it out."

He likes that one. Stands up straight to laugh, and the light catches his face. I never really saw his face before now, he was always just a dark blur behind the mesh cage. He's big and muscular in that way that catches a woman's eye if you're only looking for the physical end of it and I see now that he's good-natured in a way that makes him seem even cuter.

"Look at all this junk," he says. "We got eighteen thousand pieces going out first class at twenty-five cents apiece, when they could just as easily have gotten their act together three weeks ago and sent it all out bulk rate at eight and a quarter cents apiece. I mean, what do they think the non-profit rate was invented for? That's three thousand bucks spent on nothing right there."

"Please, I'm sick with this stuff already. I'd like to break into accounting and just start cutting checks and sending them to a priest in one of the poorest parishes in Ecuador—*he'd* know what to do with all this money." Or at least pull the McCullough paintings off the wall and donate them to a public library.

"Y'all don't even have to look as for as Ecuador. Just send the stuff uptown, honey. That's a Third World country right there. Send it to the schools so they can replace those crappy textbooks from the fifties with no covers with some *real* books. Send it to the women's health clinic. Send it to Death Row so some brothers can hire themselves a lawyer who sees in color, not just black and white."

"You mean like green?"

"Maybe I mean blood red. 'Cause if you born black and male in America today, you already got two strikes on you and you're swinging, you hear what I'm saying?"

"What's your name, anyway?" I ask.

"Azani," he says. "Azani Shakur. You?"

"Filomena Buscarsela."

"Ain't we a mouthful of syllables."

"Somehow I didn't figure you for an Azani."

"That's 'cause I used to be a Leroi."

"Oh."

"It's a black thing, you wouldn't understand."

"Maybe I would," I say, waiting. "People said I wouldn't understand English when I first got here, either, but I did all right. You're welcome to try."

He looks at me like, Hmm? Sudden romantic interest?

I speak: "I see we have removed the question of different race and replaced it with the question of different sex."

"We?"

"Why don't we just start slow with lunch sometime."

"You're on."

"Unless you can lift my spirits by figuring out some way to boil Zirkelback in oil and make it look like an accident."

"That slice of white bread? Just send him down here to me. The heavy-duty metal clasp on a bulk rate mail sack will take someone's ear off at four feet, if you know how to use it," he says, and he starts twirling the dangling metal from the end of two feet of frayed rope.

"Too physical. The punishment must fit the crime."

"You wanna fuck with his head?"

"You could put it that way."

He smiles. "I got just the thing. Come on in here."

He opens the mail cage and walks me through the obstacle course of slots, trays, dirty gray third class mail sacks and desks piled high with first class envelopes. Back behind some dripping water pipes is a utility closet. Azani pulls open the door and turns on the light. Next to a battery of fuse boxes is a ganglion of telephone lines.

"What's his extension?"

"6598."

"6598? 6598 . . . Here we go." Azani gives a sharp yank and pulls the wire out. "Mr. Zirkelback just picked up some phone trouble."

"But they'll come right down here and fix it."

"No, they won't. They'll call Bill and Senjai in maintenance, who'll rip apart his office looking for the problem. And you never know, while they're doing that they just might disconnect his fax or his PC."

"I'm beginning to like this," I say.

"But does it earn me lunch tomorrow?"

"I'll let you know in ten minutes."

"Fair enough."

I go back upstairs to find my fondest wish realized. Zirkelback is stomping from office to office, checking everyone's phones and demanding, flush-faced, that somebody call a repairman. He sees me and tells me to do it. I say gladly, call up the boys in building maintenance, and give them the wrong information.

Right around lunchtime Bartlett comes out of his office and says, "Gina Lucchese needs you to go down to the EPA."

Needless to say, I'm doubly glad that Gina is working with me now and that she's giving me a viable reason for splitting this excuse for a nonprofit organization for the rest of the day.

"The case is big, Filomena," says Gina. "Let's go after him."

That's what I like to hear. "What have you got?"

"Enough to say this is a classic case of federal irresponsibility and definitely a Superfund candidate."

"Yeah? So tell me more."

"Morse's subsidiaries aren't responsible for everything, but if we can isolate his footsteps through this mess, I think it'll cost him plenty."

"Go on."

"The U.S. Government established the Pythias Test Station in 1945. They developed the Hermes missile project there, and throughout the fifties conducted rocket and ramjet testing, and R and D related to nuclear propulsion systems. It was the height of the Cold War, and they were pretty much told it was perfectly okay to dump all their corrosive rocket fuels, oxidizers, and monopropellants into the ground. But under the new Superfund law, new owners are partially liable for the mess left over by their predecessors."

"So we can make Morse pay for waste dumped back in the fifties?"

"Well, it's more complicated than that. In 1964, New York State bought the test station through NYSASDA—The New York State Atomic and Space Development Authority. They built what's referred to on this aerial photo as the GE/Exxon-Nuclear Building—"

"Now there's a name that just fills me with confidence."

"—and established a one-mile safety easement around the building for lease to the Iso-Nuclear Corporation. Now have a look at this: This is a blueprint of the site prepared for GE. Notice that all of the structures are within this one-mile radius," she says, fingering the dotted circle around the site. "What's wrong with this picture?"

I examine the blueprint through the eyes of a detective. It looks like a prop from those *Dirty Dozen*–style commando movies. Thin blue-lined roads define the boundaries and connect the thicker blue-lined structures affixed with such labels as "Fuel Magazine," "Bottle Storage," "Control Station," "Power House," "Gas Plant," "Chemical Storage," "Pneumatic Lab," and even "Guard House." Gina has written all over it leaving cryptic markings in red pencil.

"This looks like a job for the Green Berets," I say.

Gina throws the aerial photo down next to the blueprint. "You can see in the photo that although all of the structures lie within the one-mile radius, several unlabeled structures in the photo that are missing from the blueprint lie at the very edge of this circle, *less than one thousand feet from a housing development and a public school.*"

"Is that bad?"

"There was an accidental release of uranium hexafluoride in 1979 that couldn't have done them any good. Finally, in 1985 Morse bought the property. They were clearing away debris for construction of a new shipping and receiving facility when one of his bulldozers punctured a buried container of triethyl aluminum and it exploded."

"What is Morse using the site for?"

"Defense technology. He's only—"

"'Defense technology'? That's pretty broad."

Gina sighs. "Hinge oil. Satisfied?"

"Hinge oil? They can't go down to the hardware store and pick up some 3-in-1 like the rest of us?"

"High-tech hinge oil for very small moving parts in Air Force and Navy jets. The stuff needs to maintain its viscosity under tremendous pressure and temperatures ranging from rocket blasts to stratospheric sub-zeros."

"Right. And I say they just ordered some 3-in-1 in bulk quantities and slapped some new labels on it."

"Anyway, Morse is only using half of the site, the other half still belongs to New York State."

"Does that create a problem?"

"The previous owner can be held liable if contamination took place during their ownership, but if one of the PRPs is the federal government, the EPA—part of the federal government—ends up investigating itself, so we have to go through the DOJ."

"Gina, I'm a civilian, remember?"

"The Department of Justice. It's a lot easier for us to prosecute a private company. Unfortunately, a lot of priority sites are federally owned."

"I noticed."

"If the USAF is a PRP, the DOE will take care of it."

"Gina!"

"I mean, we usually don't have to get involved if a branch of the armed forces, such as the Air Force, is a Potentially Responsible Party. The Department of Energy handles it for us."

"Thank you."

"But then you get into a mess like this"—she says, flipping through the acres of chopped-trees-turned-into-documents—"they had an emergency leak that was so bad we had to send out the OSCs—On Scene Coordinators, all right? The real environmental cowboys, who think of RPMs like me as a bunch of office-bound clock-watchers while they're out there up to their knees in stuff that'll make their urine glow in the dark if they're not careful with it. But I don't want you to think that only the military sites are disasters, the federal government makes a mess of everything else, too."

"Like what?"

"I've got a case pending involving the U.S. Mint. We're redesigning the water treatment ducts because the waste stream from the mint is clogging the system, it's so thick with heavy inks and solvents. We're trying to fit new filters to handle their stream. We've got carbon tetrachloride, trichloroethylene, 1,1,2-trichloroethane, 1,1-dichloroethane, boron, PCBs—I shudder to think of the unskilled labor that subcontractor hires handling PCBs—chloroform, trans-1,2-dichloroethylene, 1,2-dichloroethane, bromomethane, toluene—"

"Do I have to know this for the midterm?"

"And those idiot PR people from Pythias, Stencorp, and Kim Tungsten all act like, 'Hey! What's a little carbon tet? Our men can handle it.' As if environmental safety were some kind of guy thing, and manliness alone a defense against airborne biohazard evaporants. Sometimes I feel like telling them right back: 'Hey! It ain't axle grease, ya know?'" She slips into a flawless imitation of the heavy Brooklyn-Italian accent.

"So what about Morse? Are we going after him?"

"Are we going after him? I'm authorizing a full-scale investigation," Gina says, pinning the Pythias Test Site blueprint to her map-filled bulletin board. "I'm proposing water-level observation wells here, here, here, and here," she says, slapping color-coded stick-ons all over the red markings on the chart. "Shallow monitoring wells here, here, here, here, here, here, here, a-a-a-nd here," stick-ons of another color, "and deep monitoring wells here, here, here, here, here, here—"

She covers the blueprint with so many stick-ons you can hardly read it anymore.

I'm riding a euphoric wave of anticipated vengeance on both houses that weigh on me as I leave Federal Plaza and head for the subway. But at 14th Street the A train's lights go out and we sit there for about half an hour before the garbled announcement comes through that the power has been cut because of a building collapse at 31st Street. Angry and bewildered riders are told to collect transfers from the token booths and walk over to Seventh Avenue for the Broadway line. That's bad advice. The western wall of a six-story building collapsed and knocked out all of the West Side subways, the Long Island Railroad, PATH, NJ Transit, and Amtrak. We have to walk north to 42nd Street if we want to get home. Traffic is jammed from 59th Street to Herald Square waiting for a crane to be brought in from Queens to clear away the rubble. I'm glad I'm not a cop *this* afternoon.

But it sure gives me plenty of time to think: this town is crumbling. Everything for the public—elevators, subways, lavatories—crumbling. Limos are doing rather well, though. The old-school politicians at least kept the machine running while they siphoned off their share. This administration is chopping it up and selling it for scrap!

Tonight is going better. I actually get to spend an hour making a real meal for my daughter and reading complex sentences to her. It's amazing how much she's beginning to understand, even though she doesn't speak that much. They say that's how bilingual kids are. Then Janette shows up. In uniform. She doesn't even say hi to Tonia.

"You ready?" she asks. "Let's go."

At least I was prepared for this and made arrangements with one of the nicer neighbors upstairs—a young Dominican woman with two kids who's married to a New York City cop, by the way—to take Antonia for a couple of hours. This way she'll have kids to play with, not some babysitter doing the crossword puzzle while she's in the bedroom throwing a knotted sheet out the window to escape.

It only takes a few minutes to walk down Academy Street to the bad stretch of abandoned storefronts. The one we want is padlocked shut with two locks, a grimy old combination lock a kid could pick, and a thick, shiny lock of hardened steel that looks like trouble.

"So now what?" asks Janette, like I'm the one who's experienced at illegal break-ins here.

I rattle the gate and say, "Oh, killers, may we come in?"

"What you doin', girl?"

"It's as good a method as any." She looks at me. Darkness has only just begun to veil our activities. "Give me your nightstick."

I take a look at the flimsy combination lock, suppress a giggle and *bash* the lock off with one downward stroke of the stick.

"That was easy," says Janette.

"You do the next one," I say.

Janette tries the same method several times with no visible effect. Next she tries to use the nightstick as a crowbar, inserting it between the lock and an iron crossbar and pulling down with all her weight. You can hear her groans of exertion two streets over. A dark-skinned passerby says, "Yeah, those are tough suckers to pop!" and keeps walking along like this is a perfectly normal activity here. I said it was a bad block. Janette gives up on her stick and reaches for her gun. I stop her.

"Overkill," I tell her. "This lock is stronger than the gate it's attached to."

She gets the idea, and jams the stick into the gate right where one of its rusty hinges is sunk into the cracked concrete. She pulls on it, hard. I join her and we both pull with all our might. With a *crack!* that they probably hear in Rockland County, the hinge flies loose from the wall and we're in.

I ask Janette, "Was it good for you, too?"

She laughs. We push aside the gate and step in. It's as musty as a mausoleum in here. The bales and boxes turn out to be filthy-sheeted cots sprinkled with empty crack vials and trunkloads full of pornographic material.

"Well, here's your Voodoo lodge: a crack shack," I say.

"It sure smells like farm animals have been kept here, though," says Janette. She's right.

Suddenly a shadow blocks the door. A metal blade glistens.

"Excuse me," I say, "is that switchblade sterilized?"

Janette spins around.

"That's right, show him your badge," I say.

The shape tries to make a run for it, but Janette makes a flying tackle and pins whoever it is to the brick wall. The knife starts to come up but Janette lands a well-placed whack of wood on bone and the knife goes flying. By the time I get there, she's got her gun drawn and well-positioned. I'll say this for Janette, she knows how to fight.

"You got a lot of porno here," Janette tells the shape.

"It's all fuckin' legal, you cunt," says the shape.

"What do you know, it talks!" says Janette, being bad. "If you can call it that. We also got a lot of drugs here."

"You didn't see nothing," says the shape.

"You call this nothing?" says Janette, coming up with his knife. "Now this is the way it's gonna be: I make a nice solid crack bust and you spend some time behind bars, or—"

"Or?" asks the shape.

"Tell me where I can find Lucille Ferrer."

The shape shudders. "*¡La Dama de Hierro! ¡Eso no!*"

"Congratulations on your drug bust, Officer Ivins," I put in.

"You sure you don't want to reconsider?" says Janette. "They're not as lenient as they used to be down at the station. These days, pulling a knife on a cop during a drug bust could land you in some serious mess."

Now comes that familiar pause that you know means there's no way this punk is going to do time if there's a way out of it, but the price seems kind of high to him all of a sudden, and he wants to bargain it down some more.

"That *is* the bargain," says Janette, with an air of finality.

"If I were you, I'd take it," I say.

But no. The Iron Lady must be some lady.

The shape sighs and says, "Then I go to jail."

❧

"I had an erotic dream about you. Correction: A *damn* erotic dream about you," says Azani.

"Just keep working," I say.

"All right. Today, we start messing with Zirkelback's fax modem."

"Can't we do something more serious, like trash his hard drive?"

"What you want me to do? Call you up on the phone while you watch and wait for him to perform a system operation so I can cut his power at that exact moment?"

"Say, I like the sound of that."

"Don't you think that might be too obvious?"

"Okay, okay."

It's Thursday already, and we're down in the mailroom plotting how to shred what's left of Zirkelback's placidity.

"Just tell me when he's transmitting or receiving, and I'll yank his modem," says Azani.

"I love it."

Within an hour, Zirkelback puts his modem on line for a transmission. We launch Plan Nine from Outer Space, and Zirkelback's agonizing screams are music to my sadistic ears. Azani and I congratulate ourselves for surviving the elevator ride one more time, but I tell him we can't beat the odds, that each successful trip brings us one trip closer to disaster. He laughs and steers me south on the avenue to a block full of Chinese restaurants.

Azani goes up to a group of Chinese teenagers taking a cigarette break and asks, "Where's a good restaurant?"

One of the kids says Hong Fat's is good.

Then Azani deliberately insults the kid by saying, "Your father work there?"

The unstartled kid answers, "*Your* father."

As we head towards Hong Fat's I ask, "What the hell did you say that for?" He shrugs it off. "That's not very good for a first impression."

"That's 'cause you don't know enough about me yet."

We get to the restaurant and I stand at the counter flipping through the papers while Azani goes upstairs to the men's room. I find today's *Daily News* under two different Chinese newspapers. They've caught Police Officer Salerno's killers. Sorry to say it's two black guys. Why are the cop killers they catch always black? I know at least *some* of the cop killers in this place are white. This is not going to help things this boiling summer. The Feds are seeking a deal. They believe the murder was a hit ordered by a low-level drug boss from his jail cell, and they want the two guys to tell it that way in front of a judge. Facing the maximum sentence of twenty-five years to life, the two guys look like they're considering it.

"Don't you read enough when you're getting paid for it?" says Azani, slipping up behind me.

"Yeah, but it's always fiction—like why we need more donations, or requisitions for reimbursements from Liz Crowell's assistant. Look at this: They're making a TV movie out of that Preppie Murder. That poor girl. They'll never make one about Lázaro Pérez's murder."

"Who?" he says as we sit down.

"That's exactly what I mean. Nobody's ever heard of him, nobody will ever hear of him again. Just a nice guy on a bad block."

"He wasn't your boyfriend, was he?"

"He had a wife and kid back home in the Dominican Republic," I explain.

"So?" Like that's nothing.

"I've had my fill of bums, Azani. At my age I expect a bit more from a man."

"Maybe you expect too much."

"Just an even trade. I give a lot, I need to get a lot back."

"Well, baby, you have come to the right place, because I have a *lot* to give."

"I think I'm talking about more than just that. I meant in general, you know?"

"I give all my women *everything* they need."

Why don't I like the sound of that?

"By the way, those two guys over by the potted palm? Screaming," he adds.

I look over. Nobody's screaming. "What did you say?"

"You know," he flips his hand down at the wrist.

"You're telling me they're gay?"

"Pretty in pink, baby."

"So?" What is that? Suddenly I'm finding myself awfully disappointed with Mr. Azani Shakur, but I can already smell the food coming out of the kitchen and I'm hungry.

Gina, bless her, asks for me to be sent down to the EPA for the rest of the afternoon, but not before I get to see Zirkelback's newly reattached phone die on him in the middle of a crucial conversation.

"The gas chromatograph shows forty peaks that aren't on the list the search was conducted for," says Gina.

"Meaning?"

"Meaning that the Pythias site is going to cost Morse, Inc., maybe $30 or $40 million to clean up. Three times that if they make us sue for it."

"This is getting good."

"Well, if it's a Superfund candidate but not on the National Priorities List, that weakens our case a bit. And it always takes time to figure out how to pierce the corporate veil."

"Hmm?"

"The old bureaucracy game. I request documents and it takes them fifteen months to search their files for it, or they say, 'Our secretary shredded it.'"

"Or 'Our computers went down.' Yeah, I've heard all those high-tech versions of 'My dog ate it.' But getting the bureau-cratic rigmarole shouldn't faze you, you're the government, the biggest bureaucracy there is."

"Yes, but *we're* accountable. I called up Morse, Inc., to ask about Unisystems's holdings and they told me, 'That's our subsidiary.' So I called up Unisystems to ask them directly, and they said—"

"'You want our parent company.'"

"You're clairvoyant."

"It's a gift from my mother. Street punks feed us the same garbage, only they don't blame it on their secretaries."

"Yeah, well, it makes it easy for them when only *we* have to play by the rules. By the time we process a report authorizing a preliminary investigation, they've managed to relocate to Sweden, and no one will tell us where or how they got rid of the eleven million gallons of volatile organics. Too bad you can't go into court and call the earth as a witness."

"Oh, but you can!" I say. "I was on a shit detail once—a *real* shit detail. A group of suspected drug dealers were disrupting the local economy, but every time we busted down the door, they'd flush all the stuff down the toilet. When by the longest shot we found out they had one of the only houses in the precinct that didn't flush into the sewers we leapt on it. It took us a few weeks, but we got us a warrant to pump out their septic tank. We leased a pump truck and dressed up as septic system cleaners, and before the suspects even knew what we were doing we came up with a plastic bag containing $2,000 in twenties and one hundred sixty vials of crack—but *sheeeeeesh!* You don't want to *know* the other stuff we came up with! So the earth *was* our witness, but her testimony stank up my clothes for a week."

Gina likes my story. "Lucky for you New York is geologically stable. You might not have been able to pull that one off back in Ecuador with all the subduction down there."

"What's subduction?"

"The process of one slice of a continental plate pushing under the edge of another. That's what pushed up the Andes, created the Amazon River, and causes all those earthquakes that level whole cities."

"Say, you *are* a geologist, aren't you? But what about squeezing Morse?"

"Stick with me, babe. We always get our man. It's just hard when you're constantly dealing with assistants of representatives of subsidiaries who can all claim they're out of the loop. You have to get ahold of who's in charge, and it's everybody's job to insulate him."

"I'll tell you who's in charge: Morse."

"He won't talk to me."

"He'll talk to *me.*"

Janette comes over, and this time I've got a full six-pack of beer waiting.

"How're they taking it at the precinct?" I ask.

"Not too good. The killers aren't going to make that deal. They know they're dead meat if they go to prison after popping."

"So the judge'll just have to give them the maximum."

"Maybe yes, maybe no."

"My job's going in circles, too. They're wasting millions of dollars that should be going to help clean up the earth."

"I thought that organization was reviewed as one of the most cost-efficient."

"Reviews can be bought. Especially with soft money."

"With what?"

"Forget it." Then, "Contributions not subject to regulation. Seven-figure checks not disclosed publicly. Exempt from the fifty-cents-out-of-every-dollar federal guidelines."

"So they can do anything they want with it."

"Yeah, and I don't like what they're doing."

"You know what our problem is, Fil? Maybe we're just too honest."

"After our little exercise last night—a throwback to the good old days when a vice cop's primary tools were a pickaxe and a sledgehammer?"

Janette gets a laugh out of that. Then she asks me, real serious all of a sudden, "What do you do when somebody hands you a fifty to look the other way?"

"Tell them it's not enough."

"No, really."

"You facing that?" I ask. She nods. "Already? One: Just let the bill fall to the ground, sister. Don't even touch it. Two: Arresting a briber is a good way to get a commendation.

Three: *Now* you can pick up the bill, 'cause at this point it's evidence."

She nods again, slowly this time.

I have one beer, she has the other five and wants to go to sleep in my bed. I apologize but push her out. I need to spend some time with Tonia. I've got a shelf full of unread books that have been waiting all year for me to get to them. Tonight I've got no energy to do anything other than watch an old *Honeymooners* rerun, but I do it holding my daughter close to me and it feels great.

Friday morning I promise Antonia she's going to have me all weekend. She still doesn't grasp time units beyond the next ten minutes, never mind tomorrow. But it makes me feel better anyway.

On the subway, I read that the two cop killers are definitely not going to deal, so they're going to start jury selection. The block they were pulled from hasn't changed any. When a dealer disappears, five take his place. The TNT pulled another block-long bust last night, this time on 145th Street and Broadway. The grainy newsprint photo looks like a shot from the London Blitzkrieg: bright streetlamps and arcade lights bleed out in overexposed white flashpoints while patrol cops stand over dozens of prostrate bodies hugging the filthy sidewalk. Buried at the end of the story's continuation on page 47 is a black civil rights advocate bringing charges of racism against a police officer who pushed him through a plate glass window during the sweep. He says he was just walking along that block when they started the sweep. Police say if he was on the block he was a suspect. The guy says the cops used violence first, without justification, and used racist language. Maybe I should just take Antonia and flee from the city before it explodes in a hail of fire and brimstone.

In the middle of the day I get a call at my workstation. It's Janette, though I don't recognize her at first, her voice is so thin.

"I got a call," she says.

"Janette?"

"It was from her. It was a dude saying he had a message from the Iron Lady: if I didn't stop trying to carve out a piece of her turf, she'd carve out a piece of me."

"Then that means we're on the right track if they're running scared."

"This wasn't just fronting, Fil. This dude was *for real*. I heard death in his voice. Maybe we should lay off this."

"Let's talk later, okay?"

"Just have a six-pack ready."

"No—" I begin, but she's already hung up.

Hmm. As usual, the good news comes hot on the heels of the bad. (My man Willie the S again.) It's a good omen that we're stirring up enough trouble to merit threats. But nobody likes getting threats. And a woman with a child doesn't ever feel totally free.

I call Flormaría to tell her the news that we're definitely onto something with this Lucille Ferrer business, but I warn her that the measure of our success is how much trouble we could be getting into. She likes what she hears, but as usual, expects me to bring it all together no later than three o'clock this afternoon. I tell her to cool it. And she tells me that every moment I delay is another day that her brother's soul has to suffer the torments of Purgatory. Just what I need to hear.

I decide to call Gina. For the first time, I get an administrative runaround, getting a receptionist when I always got her direct before.

When I finally get ahold of her and ask her what's the big idea, she says, "It's over, Filomena."

"What do you mean, it's over?"

"Everything being done at Pythias is classified. The Department of Defense came down on us—hard. And the district supervisor came down on me even *harder*. He even used the 'F' word."

She means *fired*.

"They can't fire you for building a case, goddammit, if you do it right, if you go through the proper channels."

"It'll take years to cut through the paperwork needed to build a case that will only take years of expensive litigation to resolve. I can't take it on right now, and nobody else wants to take it either, with our feeble budget constantly under attack. It's over."

"It is *not* over. Call Morse."

"He's out of town."

"Where?"

"They won't say."

"Make them say."

"I can't."

"Yeah, but they don't know that."

"I can't do that, Filomena."

"Then I'll do it. Wait for me, I'm coming down there."

"Filomena—"

"Just wait there."

"Can I borrow your ID?"

"What?" says Gina, her eyes widening. "This is not trying to fake your way into a bar with your older sister's ID, Filomena."

"And you're not my older sister. Come on."

"I could get in big trouble for this."

"Tell them your purse got snatched."

"If they ask me, I'll have to tell them you took it."

"Fine. I also pulled the Brink's job. And I'll deny everything in court. Now give."

"Okay. What's got into you?"

"The earth is my mother, too."

"So?"

"Well, I don't like it when someone dumps shit on my mother."

I go to a copy shop, borrow one of their X-acto knives,

and slice open Gina's ID. Then I insert a cheap machine-made photo of me over her and have them re-laminate it. There's no time to change the text. I become Gina Lucchese for the next few hours.

I take Gina's License to Kill uptown to that familiar old steel-and-glass erection that's home to the parent company of Morse, Inc. Everybody's too busy trying to make their boss more money to notice that I'm well over five-foot three-inches and I don't weigh 110 pounds like it says on the card, but it's a bad picture of a Mediterranean-looking woman and nobody's looking closely at the photo anyway. They're looking at the U.S. Government's authorization for me to go anywhere I want, spirited along by a few well-aimed lies. I have no problem whatsoever about lying to these people to get what I want. I even tell them to call my supervisor for verification (Gina's working in her office, near the phone). They say that isn't necessary, they recognize my name, they remember dealing with me, I just sound different in person. I guess I'm not quite what they pictured, either. After fifteen minutes the secretary returns with the information. Mr. Morse is spending the weekend out on Long Island, at his favorite country club. She gives me the address and says she'll have to let him know I'm coming to talk with him. I tell her that's the way it's supposed to be done.

I get home a full hour early and take Antonia for a long-awaited walk through the park. It doesn't take long for Old Marco to find me out.

"Legba says you ask too much."

"It's just my way of working, I guess."

"He says you make wrong move."

"I do that sometimes."

"I don't say that you need it, but here's a little something, to protect you against—Death."

He takes out a greasy felt pouch on a length of string and lowers it over my head and around my neck. "Don't take it off until this is over. And it isn't over yet."

"You sure said it." I make the mistake of smelling it. Reflex, I guess.

"Do not open it," he says.

"No. No, I won't. *Gracias,* Marco."

I take Antonia back up to the apartment for a real meal together. There's a message on my answering machine. It's from *her*.

"Te voy a dar un consejo," says the icy cool voice. Dominican accent. "Let me give you some advice. You'd better close your ears to my business. Iron can be very cold and hard." Click. Beep.

Wonderful. At least we're getting out of here tomorrow. Of course, Morse knows I'm coming, but he'll be expecting Ms. Gina Lucchese, RPM of the EPA, not a ghost from his past protected by a genuine Voodoo talisman.

CHAPTER ELEVEN

"Point that thing somewhere else."
—Grace Slick

WE HAVE a saying in Ecuador, *De todo puede burlarse el hombre, menos de la muerte.* Man can laugh at anything except death. And what of death? I'll tell you: Death laughs at us. Oh yes, death is quite a prankster. A friendly guide who leads you through the forking branches of life, out to the very tips, where buds drop the seeds for another tree of life. An unforgiving loan shark who does not collect until we have spent it all. Death diverts us all, existing always and everywhere, nowhere and never, the omnicidal maniac, the original terminator, the surprise guest at every appearance, this cutup will cut you up, split your sides, pull your leg, leave you in stitches, death will crack you up.

Yes, death is a funny thing. We deal with other fears every day, keeping the big one at bay, but when death comes, it wipes away all fears, as it wipes away everything. It's the impassable wall at the end of every alley of life, the nasty finish that awaits every human joyride.

Nasty thoughts indeed as Antonia and I board the Long Island Rail Road for a trip out to Sandy Pointe Village. Don't ask me whose idea it was to put the extra "e" at the end of "Pointe." Probably some real estate speculator trying to chicify the place by making it sound French. The only thing French on Long Island gets deep fried in animal fat and served up alongside the greaseburgers at the drive-thrus.

Oh God, death, death, death. How much of our dread and awe of you is the result of the human mind's inability to comprehend the nature of its own non-existence, and how much is plain instinctive animal fear? Do animals fear death? My first partner, Artie, always used to say, "If the assholes don't get you then the idiots will," meaning it's bad enough that there are creeps out there who are *trying* to kill you, but there are also all those nincompoops who accidentally cut off each other's arms with chainsaws while trying to trim their hedges or who think it's *fun* to scare cyclists by forcing them off the road or to throw beer bottles at pedestrians from speeding cars.

I mean, you can watch your back for killers every day of your life only to have some dork on Quaaludes try to clean your rug with kerosene instead of rug shampoo, or you run across some snot-faced kid with a week-old driver's license who thinks his reflexes are perfect 'cause he saw all those Tom Cruise movies and those bad things could never happen to him, or some drunk who finishes six martinis and still thinks he can drive. I think about it all the time lately, how nowhere is safe. I've had a lot of close calls, and while there's always a part of you denying its omnipresence, somewhere inside of everyone is a little voice saying, "If the assholes don't get you, then the idiots will."

Plus I'm not as streetwise as I used to be. Too much time away from the street, too many other concerns, too often I never notice the corner 'til I've painted myself into it, and one of these days my number's going to hit. What is it about men, never being able to admit they're wrong or don't know something? Nobody knows everything. I didn't know until I overheard two truckers talking about it that the metal brace that's supposed to keep cars from going under the rear of the rig is called a "Jayne Mansfield." There I go thinking about *death* again!

I try to divert myself by looking out the window as we pass the Elmhurst Tanks, those trafficopter landmarks. Who would want to live this close to these enormous gas tanks? What if they—never mind.

Nobody knows everything, all right, and what I don't know right now is filling up a book. Somebody out there knows more than they're telling me. I can't nail it down, but if I know anything, it's that one of the people who I think I'm working with is leading me on. Why else would I be on this train? I'm supposed to be tracking down Lázaro's killers. He'll never know I'm doing this for him, and wherever he is now, he's probably forgiven them anyway. And here I am: dressed in nothing but a T-shirt and shorts because it's so hot today, I don't cut such a terrifying image.

We're starting to get out into the real suburbs. Girls sporting that Long Island Hair—you know, the kind that looks like they emptied a year's supply of hair gel into it and then stood in front of an exhaust fan for an hour until it dried—crowd the platform heading into the city for a fun-filled Saturday waiting in line to get into clubs that must have signs insisting, "Your hair must be at least three feet high to enter."

The suburbs. Some of the sickos you meet out here are worse than anything you'd ever meet in New York. In the city, you've got a fighting chance. There are places to hide, stores open all night to duck into, and when the average slob totes a weapon it has usually been, until the unfortunate advent of crack, a cheap Saturday Night Special that doesn't have the range or the accuracy to be a threat as long as you can run a serpentine seventy-five-yard dash in under 9.3 seconds. The loonies with the forty-eight-piece arsenals of legally purchased assault weaponry tend to come from the suburbs. We pass swiftly over rooftops and highway overpasses, and I hope some disgruntled outcast out there isn't aiming a high-powered rifle at my face.

I feel the talisman I'm wearing. What is this thing? I'm not supposed to look inside the pouch. It's alternately hard and soft. The hard things feel like thin tubes maybe an inch long that seem to widen at the ends, the soft things too shape-less to define, like hair, or feathers or even tufts of aspirin-bottle cotton for all I know. I'm about to yank it from my neck—and then stop myself. This whole business is crazy. But then, if this is the kind of weapon they are using against me, I suppose I have to fight with the same weaponry. Suddenly I feel like the thing *is* protecting me, but from what? Not against a train wreck, or a sociopathic multimillionaire who has used murder before to protect his investments. So from what, then?

Just as the fractured gray industrial plants start to give way to tailored green industrial parks, I watch a few miles of budding green woods go by, and our stop is called. Why am I bringing Antonia? I'm only figuring on ten minutes with Morse, and then maybe I can take her to a beach, or a park, or anywhere that has air you can breathe without special filters. In reality, I don't know what I'm figuring on.

Sandy Pointe Village has a compellingly dreary train station like something out of an existentialist novel, all blind-ingly bleached concrete and scrub-filled sand. The topsoil was stripped away and sold at a profit somewhere else, and all I can say is: you'd have to *sentence* me to live in Sandy Pointe Village.

There's no public transportation, of course, so we have to take a cab to the country club. The guy looks at me like I'm one of those illegal Central Americans who stand around downtown Hempstead waiting for day work (just like in the market square back home), whom the rich like to use because they work for less and don't complain because they can't com-plain. But he takes me there.

The Sandy Pointe Country Club looks like the exterior location for one of those old horror movies set in a dilapidated mansion in the Louisiana bayou, with tall white pillars and hanging vines clinging to them. Now the *truly* classy places treat you like royalty no matter who you are or what you look like. By this definition, there are almost no truly classy places in the United States. The staff here look me up and down like they can't imagine where I got the money to pay for a taxi, and what am I doing using the front door instead of the kitchen entrance?

I tell them Mr. Samuel Morse is expecting me, and fork over one of Gina's business cards. The guy makes quite a show out of checking the reception desk appointment book. I think he's one of those retired Berlin Wall guards who's trying to adjust to a new line of work.

"You'll find Mr. Morse in the gaming room."

"Great. Where's that?"

A withered finger showing intense disgust points me in the right direction. How can a finger show disgust, you ask? Beats me, but this guy managed it.

The carpet in the gaming room is thick enough to stalk rhinos in, or at least swallow up quarters forever should you drop one. The games consist mostly of card tables. There's a chess set that hasn't been used since the advent of gunpowder and the pool table is covered with a thick leather protector. Morse is sitting at the table by the window playing something involving dice with a cigar-puffing club member. I close in and see that it's backgammon.

"I figured you more for a crap shooter," I say.

Morse looks up. Sees me. Almost goes back to his game like he can't understand why one of the maids isn't in uniform before I see it change his eyes. Yeah, those eyes. Tanned body and parti-colored leisure clothes say the good life, but the eyes are those of a cold fish.

"Officer Buscarsela! I thought you were dead."

"What? And leave you my stamp collection?"

Morse laughs so his companion will laugh, but he leans close to whisper in that sick treacly voice, "Gaining access to restricted property using false identification is a crime, isn't it, Officer Buscarsela?"

"It's called Criminal Impersonation, and if you want to get nasty, I could file counter charges against you for calling yourself the Komputer King."

"Under what statute?"

"It's a little-known statute in the U.S. Constitution:

Article One, Section Nine, 'No title of nobility shall be granted by the United States.' But don't feel bad: It's how we got Elvis. And we'll get those burger people, too."

There's a moment's lapse, then Morse laughs again. His companion says, "I can see you two have a lot to talk about," and he gets up from the game in spite of Morse's insistence that they keep playing.

"All right," Morse says, abandoning the game. "Let's go to the bar, then, shall we? What was yours again? Whiskey, I believe. Lots and lots of whiskey. I'm not sure we carry your brand. Charles stocks only the finest."

"Nothing for me, thanks."

"Oh, reformed have we? Or just not while you're on duty?"

"I'm not on duty."

"Not on duty? Oh no, not more of your reckless vigilant-ism I hope. Charles!" Morse signals for the bartender to bring him his usual, which turns out to be an Absolut martini, very dry. Charles asks what the lady will have. At least there's one gentleman here.

"Just some ice water," I say.

Now this Charles has class. He serves me a highball glass full of ice water as if he were pouring White Star for the Princess of Wales.

"And who is this little lady?" asks Morse. "Not some prop from the undercover department?"

I'm already regretting that I brought Antonia with me, but at least the rug is clean enough to let her play on it.

"I told you I'm not on duty. She's my daughter."

"Oh, doing some extracurricular activity, are we, Officer Buscarsela?"

"Look, you might as well shut up with this Officer Buscarsela stuff. You know I haven't been a cop for a couple of years. And my correct title would be Detective."

"Why should I know anything about you? Then what are you bothering me here for?"

"Oh, am I bothering you? Terribly sorry."

"Get with it, miss. What's the story?"

Ah, now the real Morse is beginning to emerge.

"If you think me showing up at your club is a bother, then you'd better get ready for some serious pain."

"Why's that?"

"Because your messy methods are about to be found out by the U.S. EPA. Could end up costing you fifty to a hundred million dollars." All right, so I exaggerate.

"What messy methods?"

"The crimes against nature you've attempted to mask by delegating them to your subsidiary Unisystems."

"That nonsense? Not a chance. My lawyers'll tie up that EPA investigation for *years*. It's so easy to screw up those public bureaucracies. They're there to serve *us*. All we've got to do is send in a hundred broad requests for information under FOIA. The bums won't have time to investigate because they'll be chasing down memos that were issued twelve years ago 'cause the law requires them to do it."

"You forget they have me helping them out."

"Unofficially."

"I can still testify to your pattern of willful neglect and deliberate misconduct."

"Ooh, you shouldn't use that word 'testify' around here, Officer—Miss Buscarsela. I happen to know that if a witness were to become unavailable because of, say, death, even *after* testifying in court, his—or in some cases, her—testimony would not be admitted in evidence if the defense did not have the opportunity to cross-examine."

"Too bad I'm not wired. You just committed a felony."

He laughs. "Your word against mine . . ."

"Well, since you're going to quote law at me I might as well quote you the second paragraph of the same law: 'If a witness dies, his—or in some cases, her—testimony at a *prior* trial may be read into evidence if the defense at *that* trial had the opportunity to cross-examine the witness.' You should always read the second paragraph, too, Sammy."

He knows what I'm talking about. His brow wrinkles a bit.

"The problem with fu—with tree-huggers like you is you try to impose your narrow, politically correct views on everyone else, like somehow only *you* know what questionable procedures should be made illegal."

He's trying to get a rise out of me by using this presidential debate tactic of turning my belief system on its head.

"If by 'questionable procedures' you mean extortion, bribery, physical abuse, and murder—yes, I think those particular business practices should be made illegal."

"I got the law on my side, Buscarsela. The Department of Defense says everything connected with Pythias is classified."

How did he know I was talking about the Pythias site? I haven't mentioned a word about it. Now I *know* someone's working both sides of the field. Morse eyes me like he's reading my very thoughts. He chuckles and takes a big gulp of his martini.

"Well, the law should be changed," I say. "I've got a lot of problems with a law that says a gun store owner who sells a gun to a man who *he knows* intends to kill his wife with it is *not* guilty of Criminal Facilitation because he did not *intend* the crime to be committed. If you ask me the gun store owner should get ten years."

"You planning to take on the Department of Defense? No one's that crazy, not even you, Buscarsela."

Well, there's always Plan Nine from Outer Space. "Well, it's a crazy country. It's kind of a weird system: A crook makes sixty million illegally. They can't get him for that But, he should have paid *tax* on the sixty million. *That* they can get him on."

"What are you saying here?"

"I know all about your using the EAF to launder your mucky money. I don't care about that, but you shouldn't have defrauded the IRS like that, Sammy. The IRS is *very* particular about that sort of thing. And they never forget a face. It's the only thing they ever pinned on Al Capone. Spiro Agnew, too."

Morse hesitates, takes a sip from his martini that lasts about a minute.

"You seem to be ignorant on one crucial fact here," says Morse.

"Oh? What's that?"

"That I already know that you have no intention of exposing the EAF's improper use of funds."

"What?" It just comes right out of me.

"Therefore you cannot expose my dealings to the IRS."

He's done it. I've survived twenty-one passes before he's skewered me. I'm caught without words to say it. He smiles now, long and leisurely. "All the phones at the EAF are monitored. Board members have access to all the data."

"Sacred shit!" I don't usually speak my thoughts when I'm losing, but it happens.

"Mommy?" says Antonia, looking up at me concerned.

I pat her head, saying, "Yes, honey, Mommy's all right." At least I know where my leak is.

"Don't feel bad, Buscarsela. You did good, considering you were playing against the house. But it's time to cash in and go home. I'm one hundred percent covered."

It's beginning to look like he is, too. How can this be? How did this happen? There's a whole lotta complicity going on, more than I can see from where I'm sitting. I can't just let him get off *again*.

"Not quite one hundred percent Sammy. Ninety-eight maybe, but not a hundred."

"Why? You still got more? Okay, let's hear it."

"The government may be slow, but they've got nothing else to do but investigate guys like you. So it'll take them years, they'll still get you, and when they do, it'll cost you even more for making them take so long, because when they win—and they will win, there's no statute on this sort of thing—you'll have to pay all the fines *plus* all the legal costs that your investigation-slowing tactics piled up."

It's a pinprick, but it's the only thing that penetrates the bodyguard of laws that surrounds him. He orders another martini, drinks half of it, contemplates the nature of the olive, drinks the rest. Then: "I'll make you a wager, Buscarsela. If you win, let's say I make that $3.5 million donation to the EAF. A real donation, no strings attached. And you leave me the hell alone."

"And if you win?"

"Then you just leave me the hell alone."

"What are we playing?"

"Come here, I'll show you."

He climbs off his bar stool, signs the tab and walks me out the back door, across a level flagstone walk through a manicured lawn towards a long, low building set back into the woods where it sounds like people are hammering boxes together with mallets.

"What's that?" I ask.

"Target range."

"Oh, no. I'm not taking Antonia in there."

"Relax. We got day care here." He signals to one of the waiters covering the grounds with a tray of drinks to take Antonia to the playcare room, but I insist on going there myself before leaving my child in the hands of strangers.

The playcare room seems legitimate enough. Several trained staff members are entertaining, feeding and generally watching over the toddlers and infants of parents who presumably don't want their poolside sunbathing to be interrupted by such inconveniences as keeping their children from drowning.

"Okay," I say, after making sure it's okay with Antonia to leave her for a while.

"So it's a go?" asks Morse.

"Let's see what you've got first."

"Now that's exactly what I was going to say to you."

We go out to the target range.

"Handguns or rifles?" asks the attendant, ever so delicately.

"I'm not too quick with these things," I say, picking up a .22-caliber single-shot rifle.

"Handguns," says Morse. "The .38-caliber police special, Officer Buscarsela?"

"That's fine with me." *Detective,* you asshole.

We get ourselves fitted with earplugs and goggles and enter the firing range. Would-be marksmen line the lanes taking shots at movable paper targets. Morse picks out a lane and loads his revolver. With real bullets.

"Any setting you prefer?" he asks me.

"It's your call."

He calls for two standard targets to be set at the maximum distance. Then he takes careful, measured aim, and unhurriedly squeezes off all six shots. They all hit the target. Three are in the white border, which doesn't count; two are in the outermost black ring, one point each; and one is in the second ring from the center, a mortal wound. But his grouping is terrible. Unsteady hand.

I don't bother with this deliberate shit. You never get thirty seconds to get into stance, take aim and shoot on the street. I load my revolver, spin the chamber and look Morse in the eye before facing the target, dropping into position, both arms extended in front of me and firing all six shots in under three seconds. The first five all pierce the black rings from mild to mortal, closely grouped, the last one lands just inside the first circle for a bull's eye. Not bad.

Morse takes stock of the situation and quips, "James Bond would have gotten it on the first try."

"Yeah, and Leatherstocking could have done it at a hundred yards, if you can believe Fenimore Cooper."

Morse now explains his proposition to me. This country club has swimming, golf, tennis, and all the rest, but it also has twenty-three and a half acres of wooded wilderness behind the target range, where stressed-out executives on holiday come to relieve their daily anxieties by facing the ultimate anxiety of having a killer stalk them with a loaded gun. But the gun is only a plastic plaything that uses compressed air to shoot soft globules of nontoxic washable paint. I still don't like the idea.

"Whatever happened to water pistols?" I ask.

"Those are for kids," he says. "Unless you prefer to—"

"Die in a flood? No, that happened to me in a previous life. So what are the rules?"

"To waste your opponent," he says, cracking a smile.

"Oh, a realistic game, eh?"

And he takes me over to a large colorful map showing the twenty-three and a half acres of woods and how they're laid out, with paths, ponds and a few structures.

"What are those?" I ask.

"Huts and shacks. Built just for this game. We've tried to make it as realistic as possible."

"Uh-huh." I'm beginning not to like this in a big way.

"Two attendants lead us separately into the woods, then we radio each other that we're ready to go."

"Oh, we carry radios?"

"You know, walkie-talkies. Then it's just us two out there in the forest, and whoever splatters the other one wins. So it's a wager?"

I have serious doubts about the impartiality of the attendants, but since Morse is unassailable every other way, and is offering me a chance to at least show him who stands to win if it ever comes to a real showdown and maybe even give some of his funny money back, I agree to this grim charade. His face lights up with glee in anticipation of "wasting" me, at least symbolically.

Ten minutes later I'm in the middle of what passes for wilderness an hour from New York City, and the attendant leaves me to my fate. The radio crackles with Morse's confident hunter's voice: "You ready, Buscarsela?"

I bring it to my mouth and push the TALK button. "Yeah. Go ahead."

"Let the games begin!" he bellows.

I look around at the trees and discover as if for the first time that I'm alone in the woods, half a mile from anyone within listening range, with a guy who's tried to kill me twice. If that's not proof I should have myself committed right away, I don't know what is. What am I doing here? This guy uses gunmen to get what he wants, and here I am playing "shoot me" with him. And since he was brought into these woods separately, for all I know he could have his armed hitmen with him, and all I've got is a stupid fucking plastic pop gun. How did I get myself into this? Maybe there's some drug in this damn pouch that I've absorbed through my skin that's caused me to lose touch with reality, bringing my kid to a place like this. At least she's not here to see me panic like that night I spent stalking a felon through the Reptiles and Amphibians House, never knowing where I was going to put my foot down (it's what you don't see that scares you). Even all the pressure from the week isn't enough to explain this goof-up. I've been trusting everyone since the beginning, now I find out that they're all a bunch of liars who are only in it for themselves, using me as some kind of gofer, and *still* I keep trusting them!

"Here I come, Buscarsela, I'm coming to get you!" he taunts me from the radio. His egomania is his undoing. During the next several minutes he continues to taunt me. But the radio is cheap and the signal weakens appreciably when I turn away from the source, allowing me to get his general position. We spend about twenty minutes playing this silly game, him taunting me with adolescent gleefulness, me continually moving perpendicular to the direction of his radio signal until I can get a bead on his strategy. Maybe I can get back to the clubhouse and get the hell out of here—but now he's between me and the house.

I come to a dirt path that allows me to move towards him without giving away my position by stepping on twigs or something. I move as close as I dare, and stay there.

"I'm closing in on you, Buscarsela, you better get moving!" says the radio.

How does he know I'm not moving? Shit! This "radio" is sending out a signal telling him where I am! Don't ask me what high-tech weaponry he has at his fingertips, but his bold overeagerness has given it away. And given me my out.

Within a minute or so from his last transmission, Morse tramples through the vines. It sounds like he's alone. At least he's playing that part fair. The pounding gets louder, he's running now like he's real sure of where to find me, then he steps onto the dirt path and waits. He listens, then checks this wallet-sized folding case that looks like a hand-held computer game. I thought as much. Morse slowly stalks me along the path, staying near to the cover of the thick tree trunks, then finally jumps through the bushes into a small clearing and fires his pellet pistol.

A bright orange paintball bursts across the face of the radio I have hung from a low-hanging branch. He turns around just in time to get a dark blue burst from my pellet gun right where his heart would be, if he had one. He looks down at the spreading stain, then over at me. I step out from behind the bushes, feeling like a jerk with this plastic plaything between my fingers.

"You got me," Morse says. Then: "My turn." And he levels his pellet gun at me. I know it's just an air gun, I've just seen him fire a harmless paintball with it. But it still gives me a creepy feeling to have this leech point that thing at my face. He holds that position for the longest time, drinking in the pleasure from my discomfort. He squeezes. A bright orange smear hits me right across the goggles. Would have been right through my forehead. I wipe off the paint just in time to see him reach into his belt and pull out the real thing: the .38 service revolver he was using back at the target range. I can see the resistance his arm needs to lift this one instead of that stupid plastic thing. Boy, is he enjoying this.

"Come on, Morse, you'd never get away with it. You know that. We'll just call it a draw, all right?"

"You're scared, aren't you?"

"Of you? Morse, I'd almost give my life to land you with a murder charge. But I've got a kid now. Things are different."

He keeps the gun aimed at me. We're close enough for him to take my head apart with one shot. It's not a pretty thought.

"Okay," he says, lowering the gun. "It's a draw, Buscarsela. Again. But you keep your butt out of my business!"

I start to turn. I catch a chuckle with a flicker of movement

—I dive and shoulder-roll into the bushes in time to hear a distinctive *click*. I look up from a carpet of what I hope isn't poison oak or something to see Mr. Morse clicking the empty revolver five more times at my head. He laughs.

Oh, how he laughs.

Still hyperventilating from fear-fed anger, I enter the club-house from the back lawn and have to pass through the bar. It must be the air conditioning. A shiver shakes my spine and I keep my eyes straight ahead of me while passing the sound of clinking glasses. I never want to turn into one of those poor fools who shows up drunk to the rehab classes. I ask the front desk to send for a cab. Then I go upstairs to find Antonia playing happily with two other kids. I let her play for a while, then I need to sit down. She sees me and drops everything.

"Mommy here," she says, running over to me. I hug her with my cold, quivering arms. "Mommy?" she asks.

"Yes, *mi hija,* we're going."

"Bye-bye," she says in that sweetest voice of hers to all the other children and staff.

We're waiting for a cab out front when one of the main-tenance boys drives up in one of those humongous off-road trucks with the fourteen-foot-high cab. He offers me a ride to wherever I'm going.

"Are there a lot of mountain roads on Long Island?" I ask.

I don't think he understands my humor. I get in anyway. When we're out of sight of the club he offers me some pot. What can I say? I want it. But the kid. My damaged lungs. I can't. I tell him no, and realize I'm shaking again, which thank God is camouflaged by the jolting ride.

"Where to?" he asks.

"I hear Spain is nice this time of year."

All right, so it isn't Spain, it's a rocky North Shore beach near enough to the city to have a few plastic bags and other objects floating in with the seaweed, but it's a change. A few wet and wild hours later and we're back on the train heading into the city with me wondering what hole in fate got me through this day alive. Maybe Morse didn't believe I would be stupid enough to be acting entirely on my own again. What does that say about me? Maybe it's better this way. He knows I won the bet, that he'd lose again if it ever got real, that he cheated me. Yeah, it's better this way, with him knowing that I'm still one up on him, that *someday* he's going to get it There's an Ecuadorian proverb, *Mala yerba nunca muere.* Evil weeds never die. And the richer you are, the more fertilizer you can buy.

The bad guys always go for their guns first in the movies so the heroes can blow them away with a clear conscience. They never mention that the handful of cops who actually do kill somebody in the line of duty usually need a couple of years of therapy before they can keep a meal down or have sex or any kind of steady relationship ever again. That might be the only thing keeping me from killing Morse. So far.

I watch the commuters smoking on the platform, like there isn't enough carbon monoxide in New York City, they have to toke up here first; or maybe they're just chain smoking to prepare themselves for the shock of the "air" in NYC, the way a diver slowly works her way back up to the surface so as not to get the bends.

We get back to our apartment and get a call from Flormaría. I tell her I've had a rough day and I don't feel like talking about it. But she always wants to know every detail, so I end up telling her—although she interrupts constantly to question me and to tell me that she is not impressed. Why did I spend the day on Long Island? I try to explain to her that sometimes I need to use an indirect approach. And she starts in again on how none of this is bringing comfort to her brother's tormented soul. She is really starting to get on my nerves with that stuff. I mean, I'm doing the best I can without the luxury of a salary, a health plan and official backup (how can I bill a dead man?). I let her go on for a while, then I tell her I'll talk to her later and I hang up.

I've almost gotten over my rage and frustration when the phone rings again. I don't feel like answering it.

Oh, what the hell. It's Janette.

"What's new?" she asks.

"Well, the sex was good but the room was expensive."

"What?"

"Just kidding."

"How'd it go?"

"The bastard got off clean. Again."

"That sucks."

"Yup."

"Can we talk?"

"How about tomorrow? After Mass?"

"When the heck is that?"

"Eleven-thirty. And leave the uniform at home, okay?"

"I'll be waiting at the front door."

"You can come inside."

"No, that's okay."

I go to sleep loving Antonia to death in my arms.

I skip the Mass at St. Jude's—there are some faces I don't feel like seeing today—and return to my usual church, the Good Shepherd. The young Dominican priest is speaking today, not the old Irishman.

He reads from the Book of Ezekiel, one of the heavier prophets. God is hammering away at His Israeli children for their infidelity to him, calling them harlots, and promising the longest list of sufferings for their abominable and lascivious transgressions. First come the endless and unspeakable punishments for His chosen people, the Jews: Then come the punishments for the people He *doesn't* like! Just in case there was any doubt. For in the end, God is merciful on His people, and ultimately forgives them for their forgetfulness, their fleshly failings, and gives them His word that there shall come a time when His wrath shall be appeased, when all their suffering shall end and they shall enter into His eternal grace and know once more the bliss that they strayed from, distracted like little children by the evil and costly trappings of the material world.

You can't buy *this* guy off with soft money.

I walk down the aisle with Antonia to take Communion. As I bend over, Old Marco's pouch swings down between the wafer in the priest's hand and my open, receiving mouth. I press the pouch to my chest and swallow the wafer.

Janette's waiting for me at the front door.

"You're in big trouble," she says.

CHAPTER TWELVE

**"Wherever you find injustice, the proper
form of politeness is attack."**
—T-Bone Slim

"WITH YOU or with God?" I ask.

"With Lucille Ferrer," says Janette.

"Fuck her. I'm not buying this Voodoo jazz. Either she's threatening us or she's not. If she is, I say we hit her and hit her hard. Teach her to fuck with us." I realize that I've let my tongue waggle into cop-talk right here on the church steps and in front of my kid, too.

"Fukwithus," Antonia says, imitating me.

"Oh, great."

"Another *bodega* was hit last night," says Janette.

"How bad?"

"Four people shot and their throats slit."

"Throats slit?"

"Think it's related?"

"Who were the victims?"

"All people who worked at the store."

"Shit. Let's go have a look."

"Now?"

"After I take Tonia to the babysitter."

Antonia starts to cry when *mamita* Viki opens the door. She knows this is supposed to be our day together. I try

178

explaining to her that Mommy has to do this and the place I'm going is not for kids, but she's starting to throw a tantrum already. *Mamita* Viki says to go, that Antonia will be fine in a few minutes. Feeling like the worst mother on earth and not a much better detective, I take Janette down to the street and catch a gypsy cab to Gun Hill Road in the Bronx.

The *bodega* is like many others, bedecked with triangular plastic bunting and bright signs with red-and-yellow lettering advertising such ethnic specials as FRESH GOAT MEAT and JAMAICAN PATTIES.

The cops have roped off the sidewalk out front with yellow crime scene tape and are going over the interior with methodical precision. Janette identifies herself as an off-duty cop and gets to stand and listen while they question neighbors. The general idea is that the place was a drug store. I look at the pretty young face of one of the victims smiling up at me from today's paper and I find that hard to believe. Anyone who's a college freshman working in a store like this and hoping to go to medical school someday sounds too smart to screw with that stuff, but what do I know? I'm the forgiving type. How many "One more chances" did I give Raúl? A hundred? Two hundred?

Some of the detectives seem to agree. The store was stocked with fresh goods, including the hard-to-find ethnic items—an expensive proposition atypical of your basic aspiring drug store, which is usually content to leave the same four cans of peas and tomato paste in the window until the sun fades the labels blank.

So it could have been a holdup gone bad, then made deliberately violent to appear like a drug-related killing. Under the hot June sun, I shiver.

At the moment the scene is such a focal point of activity that neighbors are pressing in at the edges volunteering to talk to police, who have to tell them to wait, there's so many of them. But all their testimony covers the same generalities about the store owners, and nobody actually saw or heard anything last night. I decide to reverse my thinking, a tactic that frequently paid off in the old days, and I start scanning the perimeter of the crowd to see who's *not* volunteering to talk. Most of the folk are simple passersby who naturally stop to gawk and crane their necks for a look inside where there's absolutely nothing to see, and then move on.

I scan one spot three times before I notice a man so shabby and dusty he just about blends in with the battered, worn-out stoop he's resting on just a few doors down. Except for the white beard stubble, this grizzled old man is the same color as the brown stones. Closer in, I see why: dark glasses, white cane, pint bottle in a brown paper bag, shoes so old they look like he should have replaced them sometime around 1968.

"They already aksed me, but I tole them I ain't seen nothin'," he says. "Not a damn thing."

"How's your hearing?" I ask, pulling out a crinkly $10 bill and smoothing it out on my knee.

"Hmm, I do perceive the currency of the land bein' unfu'led."

"What denomination?"

"What denomination? Dat's when they's a-swearin' in the president—Heh heh heh!"

I press the bill into his hand. He runs his fingers over it.

"Hmm, I do perceive an o-fficial portrait of Andrew Hamilton."

"Pretty sensitive fingers."

"Try me sometime, honeychile."

"Okay, so you didn't see anything. Tell me what you heard."

"I ain't heard nothin' but some shots and a car drive away, that's the God's honest truth."

"How many shots?"

"Might have been five or six. I covered my ears, you know. Dem shots hurt my ears."

"Yeah, yeah. Here's something you might be able to tell me—did all the shots sound the same? Like they were all fired from the same gun?"

"I 'spose they might have been the same. They was real rapid."

"Like nobody else had time to pull a gun and shoot back?" I ask.

"Like I say, dat's all I heard."

I take a deep breath of sooty Bronx air and let it out. I start to turn away when his raspy voice calls me back.

"Y'all done aksed me what I saw, and y'all done aksed me what I heard, but ain't nobody aksed me what I *smelled*."

I come back to him. "What did you smell?"

He holds his hand out, twitching his fingers together for more money. I explain to him that I'm not working for the Police Department, I'm a poor mother trying to solve a similar murder in my neighborhood, and as proof I let him feel one of my ill-gotten food stamps.

"Okay," he says. "It was a Cadillac car. A old model, late seventies. Seventy-eight maybe."

"And how do you know that?"

"Honeychile, I know dem cars by the way dey smell."

"Great."

"Don't believe me, do you?"

"Yeah, I might be having a tough time of it now that you mention it."

"Come here," he says, getting to his feet with the help of my arm and the cane. He leaves his bottle behind on the stairs, which at least indicates that he is the fixture on that stoop I thought he was. That bodes well, I suppose. He walks me across the sidewalk to the curb, sits himself down on a parked car. Traffic is moderate, and moving. Vrroom!

"That was a Cutlass Ciera," he says. It was. "Eighty-four." I can't tell that.

Vrroom! "That was one o' them Japanese American things, what's the name of it? Not a Pinto—A Colt! Dodge Colt. Them things make enough stink like four cars put together. 'Specially the mid-eighties models." It was a Colt.

Vrroom! No hesitation this time: "Mercedes D-class Diesel. They's no mistaking them." Right again.

Vrroom! "Checker cab! Didn't think they was hardly none o' them left on the road."

"A man who can identify cars by their exhaust smell," I say, incredulous. He laughs. I can see his teeth are none too good. "'Course I don't figure it would stand up in court . . . So you're telling me you heard five or six shots, and two men drove off in a seventy-eight Cadillac?" He didn't say anything about two men, of course, I just throw that in to see.

"A *white* Cadillac."

"Oh, now wait a minute—!"

"Those two dudes, they was in some real hurry. Scraped that Cadillac right up against this here car tryin' to pull away. Owner was cussin' his ol' head off 'bout the dent and the paint scrapes."

He's pointing to the street side of the bright red car he's sitting on. I walk around and discover a busted taillight and dented fender, ringed around the edges with traces of—white paint.

"I'll be damned," I whisper.

"Heh heh heh."

I hand the old man the rest of the food stamps.

I tell Janette to tell the police to start asking the neighbors if anyone saw a white Cadillac, then we walk past the Veterans Memorial Hospital and down the hill together to the University Heights Bridge into Manhattan, talking the whole way about our only clue.

"Never mind how I got it," I say, "it tells us a lot. No big mobster or dealer would bother with an aging battleship like a twelve-year-old Cadillac. Too damn bulky to be maneuverable on these narrow streets. They all drive BMWs and shit."

"So they borrowed it from one of those garages."

"It wouldn't hurt to watch the garages again, but the same logic applies. If you're going to borrow a car, grab a fuel-injected compact, not a white warhorse visible from a mile away. There's only one crowd that goes in heavy for big, *big* American cars around here."

"And who's that?"

"The car services."

"You're saying we're looking for a gypsy cab driver?"

I take a moment to enjoy the panorama of the Inwood-Heights Precinct in full spring bloom as we come down Fordham Road. Then I tell Janette, "The local mob has a pretty tight grip on the car services."

"So you're saying maybe it is the mob?"

"It's beginning to look like a good bet."

"You know how many car services cover the Bronx? Dozens!"

"Yeah, but only three are based in Inwood."

"That helps. Which one do we start with?"

"Whichever one you want. I'm not pursuing that end. That's what we have cops for."

"No, wait, Fil, you're not gonna bag on me, are you?"

"I've got to get home to my kid, Janette. Call up Sergeant Betty if you don't know how—"

"No. I mean, she's got enough problems down in her precinct. You hear about it? I guess not: A Vietnamese guy was attacked by a crowd of ten or twelve bloods who mistook him for a Korean whose store they're boycotting."

"How do they know that?"

"The crowd was chanting, 'Go home you fucking Korean!'"

"Oh."

"They hit him with a claw hammer."

"Shit."

We get to a corner where I'm going one way and Janette's going another.

"Well, I guess I'll start checking the dispatchers."

"Look for a white Cadillac with a dent in the right side."

"How'd you cop that clue, girl? Voodoo?"

"Just about."

I pick up Antonia and sit talking to *mamita* Viki for a while. She tells me I need a man in my life.

"Thanks," I say.

"You had one, but he was a lazy. He didn't get on his balls."

"That's 'on the ball,' *Mamita*."

"Whatever."

I have to laugh. Actually Raúl got on his balls *too much*. He never understood that having an affair is not lying to one person, it's lying to three: Me, the other woman, *and* himself. Above all, himself. Sure, I thought about other men when I was with him. I don't know why God made us this way, all I know is an affair is doomed to failure because when it's not true love, you can't give a hundred percent, and in love even ninety-nine percent seems fake—to me, anyway. Never did to him. I guess that's one of the differences.

Raúl never noticed how energetic our lovemaking was after we had spent the evening with a circle of friends that included someone more desirable than he. I should have known something was wrong the time I confessed to him how when he was away I was out with this guy almost all night, and ended up on his floor massaging his bare back, but I didn't sleep with him. I went home. And Raúl says, "Why didn't you, you fool?" And I said, "What?" because I had this crazy idea about being faithful. And he says, "I would have," meaning if the roles had been reversed.

Maybe it was sleep deprivation. But I only had that excuse for six months. The first time I had to work late, I was worried about leaving him in charge of the kid. I asked him, "What if three friends come over to play poker and you forget about the baby?" And he said, "We won't forget about the baby, we'll deal the baby in!" I have to admit I laughed. He wasn't *such* a bad guy before he joined the Reptile-of-the-Month Club.

Maybe we should drop in on him. It's Sunday afternoon. Maybe it won't be so bad now that some time has passed.

Two blocks from home a group of men liming their *cerveza Presidente* and slapping the ivories whistle their approval. One of them ventures to politely verbalize his desire to sample my fruits.

"You couldn't handle it," I tell him. That livens things up a bit.

Back in our apartment I'm packing a snack for Antonia so we can go out. I'm about to toast some slices of whole wheat when I notice that the toaster is missing. I look around and find that my tape player is missing too. I take a careful look around and can't seem to find anything else missing. My jewelry, such as it is, is safe in its appropriately small hiding place, and no thief would bother to walk off with that worthless TV, but someone has definitely been in here, and the door was locked. The fire escape window is still securely locked. I check the other window, which has to be kept open in this weather. Someone would have to be pretty determined to jump six feet from the fire escape into this window in broad daylight. For a lousy toaster and a boom box? Well, that'll translate into ten or twenty bucks, which to these goddamn crackheads is an afternoon's high.

First I call the police. I tell them I used to work at the precinct, but they still want me to come down and report the theft in person. I tell them I'll do it tomorrow. "Knock yourself out," the guy says.

I shut and lock the window and take Antonia outside. She gets in her time on the swings, and the requisite ice cream cone. I don't see Marco around today.

Then we head over to Raúl's building, just for the heck of it. His downstairs door's broken too, so I just walk right up to his apartment and ring the bell. This week's hot young babe opens the door and lets me in after giving me a stare as blank as the face on one of those inflatable dolls.

Maybe Raúl hasn't changed that much. He's in the other room lying on the couch, can of beer resting on his belly, copying some porno video with his two-VCR-rigged system. When he sees me he jumps up so fast he nearly sends his beer can out the window.

"Filomena!" he says, rushing to greet me in the doorway of his entertainment center, leading me back into the kitchen. "You must be hot, get her a beer, Conchita!"

"Just some juice, if you have any."

Conchita slams a beer down on the counter in front of me.

"Thanks," I say, resolving not to have more than a third of it.

"Hey, you brought my little girl to see me, eh?" he says, picking up Antonia and showing her off to Conchita because it takes a *man* to make a baby, and this proves he's a *man*. Right. Any idiot can *make* a baby. You can prove you're a man by sticking around to help raise one.

"She's not Filomena's Revenge anymore, is she?" he says to me. Then he turns to his girlfriend. "That's the way you women get back at us—by having babies who puke and shit all over us!" He laughs.

"Isn't that my toaster?" I say. I don't think about it. It's a reflex. Sitting right there on the windowsill is my toaster. Raúl falls silent. "That's my fucking toaster, isn't it?" I say.

"Now take it easy, Filomena—"

"What are you stealing from me now? You don't have enough with your big-screen TV and your Car That Goes Boom—"

"It wasn't me."

"Oh? Then who was it?"

"Enrique and Jorge. They must have taken my copy of your keys."

"You mean you *gave* it to them. Didn't you? So they could steal stuff to sell. I don't see my box around, how much did they get for it? What are you doing?"

"Hey, *Twilight Zone* goes on come hell or high water."

"At a time like this you're going to watch TV?"

"Not TV—*The Twilight Zone*. TZ is not TV."

He's running to change the channel. I rush to confront him and look at the screen. He actually yells "No!" and tries to stop me but it's too late. I've seen it. It's *me*. Or rather, it's us. Last year. The son of a bitch is copying some hidden camera video he made of us having sex, and suddenly it gets awfully quiet in here, except for me on the tape.

"So that's why you kept the camcorder in the closet," I say.

"Filomena, listen—"

"How many of these have you made? Who are they for?

Your friends? Your motherfucking friends who break into my apartment to steal what little I've got left?" I punch the STOP button then hit EJECT, break the thin, protective tape cover in half and rip twenty or thirty feet of the tape to shreds. Then I do the same to the master.

He tries to stop me, and Antonia comes up and yells "No!" at him and hits him on the leg. He raises his hand to strike her and I knock him away from her.

"Don't you *dare* touch her!" I say. He comes at me and I throw the broken cassette at him as hard as I can, which is pretty damn hard. Antonia's crying. I pick her up and tell her, "Don't hit your father. You should respect him. Even if he's wrong, you should respect him. Even if he acts like a jerk, you should respect him. Even though he's a worthless, lazy, good-for-nothing, womanizing *asshole*—you should respect him. Now say bye-bye."

"Bye-bye." She waves.

We leave without further incident. I go right out and buy two fresh locks, a brace and a plate, plus that damn latch for the bathroom door, all of which sets me back $125. Just when I'm looking forward to a little relief, we get back to our apartment and there's a little matchstick figure pinned to our door with a note taped to it.

It reads: WE WARNED YOU.

There's a piece of fabric tied around the figure's throat. I recognize the pattern. It's—oh, God—cut from one of Antonia's dresses.

I turn the keys and push the door open. Sunlight fills the hall and everything seems normal. There aren't that many places to hide in my two small rooms.

There's a message on my answering machine from Pliego. "I missed you in church today."

I wish they had left me my music and stolen this machine instead.

Now I have to spend hours that I do not have turning the place upside down while Antonia naps, to make sure that there are no more "surprises" here. At least she feels safe. Two rooms suddenly seem awfully big when your level of detail has shifted to trying to find out if someone has left a few tiny specks of mercury in your milk.

Much later I determine that, aside from the ruined dress, which they left hanging halfway out of her drawer, everything's where it should be. They just wanted me to know that they were here.

How nice.

I spend the rest of Sunday evening fitting the shiny new armaments into my door and, yes, I even get hyped up enough to put that latch on the bathroom door and drive a few screws into both window frames so they can only be opened about six inches.

Monday morning I have to hang up the phone to stop Antonia from dialing Morocco, then carry my daughter down the stairs and walk her over to *mamita* Viki's. An elderly man is standing in a fourth-floor window overlooking Seaman Avenue taking his first morning air. The way he's inflating his chest and stretching his arms makes me think of Mussolini on his balcony overlooking the *piazza*. Now *there's* a cultural stereotype with more lives than a sackful of cats. The Italians gave the world its share of poets, philosophers, and artists for the ages, and all they're known for in Hollywood is being the best-organized criminals. I kind of respect those murderers, in a way. Remember a few years back when they whacked "Big Paul" Castellano in the middle of 46th Street near Third Avenue at 5:30 in the afternoon? I'm not saying that isn't among the most reprehensible of acts—succession by assassination—but in this age of escalating random terrorism that sneers "There are no innocents" after a ten-week-old baby gets sucked out of a hole blown in the side of a passenger jet, I must admit I have a certain deranged respect for hit men who can walk down one of the most crowded blocks in the world at that time of day, pick off the one guy they're there to get, and vanish back into the crowd without anyone else even getting a hair blown out of place. Today's terrorists would have taken out the whole block. So you see, it's all relative. And it reminds me I've got a few things to say to Gina Lucchese.

Down in the subway I learn the unpleasant news that a federal appeals court has overturned the convictions of the two baby food company executives who distributed that phony apple juice. That blows. So the guys walk and the company pays the $2 million fine for them. And we end up paying more for baby food. There oughta be a law. Ooops! My mistake: There *is* one! It just doesn't apply to everyone. Comedians are joking that the two guys should be rewarded because by replacing the apples that should have been in the juice with sugar water they ended up protecting kids from the insecticide, alar, wax, and preservatives they put in *real* apples! Funny, huh?

From page six, I learn that a global bank linked with prominent Iran-contra figures was indicted for laundering $32 million in drug profits for Colombia's Medellín cocaine cartel. The bank is pleading that they were "Wholly unaware of any violations of law that allegedly have been committed." This is a highbrow version of "You ain't got nothin' on me, man, I didn't do nothin'!" This, after we caught the guy trying to knife some senior citizen for his Social Security money. Just deny it all, the lawyers'll work out a deal later. It'll take *years* to get a conviction.

I take the Kamikaze pilot's flight trainer they call an elevator up to the EAF, along with three Salvadoran women four feet high with moon-shaped faces and straight black Indian hair going to the illegal garment shop on the floor below us. Then I type some shit for three hours, then Zirkelback comes up behind my left shoulder and says, "Can I see you in my office?"

I follow him in wondering, What now, no more rides for me on Air Force One?

"I know what's been going on here," he says.

I just look at him. Never confess anything until you know what you're being accused of.

"So you think I'm anal retentive?" he says.

Is that all? "Gina told you I said that?"

"It doesn't matter who—"

"Because this organization's business priorities offend me, not personal stuff—"

"It doesn't matter! What matters is that you have been abusing this organization's trust to ignore your *very important* duties to go down there to that EPA, just because some mistakes were made—that is, because you *think* some mistakes were made, you go starting up some ridiculous investigation into the private business dealings of one of our executive board members."

Christ, he even talks like the president.

"I was doing it for a sick friend," I say.

"I work for my bosses, Miss Buscarsela. And my bosses include Mr. Samuel Morse, who doesn't like the way you've been working for us, so I might as well be totally honest with you and tell you that we're going to be keeping a *very* close watch on you, miss, and you may just want to leave voluntarily before it gets worse."

This guy is a scream. Like the "voluntary" confessions I've seen them squeeze out of hardcore dirtbags.

"I'm not quitting. I've got a child to support."

"Well, maybe you should have thought about that before you got pregnant."

Hey, this is getting personal. Maybe I was so convinced he was a boob I was blind to his racism, but now I see it written all over his face. Chalk up another loss to thinking the best of people. I lean closer to him. "Are you saying there's too many of us in the world already, Mr. Zirkelback?"

He's not sure what to say to that. In letting his emotion gain control of his mouth, he has imprudently revealed his true nastiness. I continue: "Maybe we should all learn English? Why don't you just say it, Mr. I-work-for-my-bosses? Go ahead. Call me a spic to my face. It's what you're thinking, isn't it? Yeah. But you couldn't do that—no, that wouldn't be prudent, and the bosses wouldn't like that. So you just do it in subtle little ways like dishing me out like a whore. I don't know what part of the country you come from, pal, but this is New York, and one day we will rule here. So give me your damn letters to type. But stay out of my life!"

"I think we've said all there is to say."

Great. Now I've got someone else to curse out. But she beats me to it. I pick up my phone and it's Gina. No hellos, no how are yous, just, "What did you do? Morse burned his files, cleared his dump, and the Navy is stonewalling me about any involvement with Pythias!"

"Yeah, well *you* seem to have covered your ass pretty well, too, Gina. Zirkelback pushed you for details of our conversations so you told him personal shit that doesn't even matter? He fed Morse information that almost cost me my life, dammit!"

"It was public information."

"But he got it in less than twenty-four hours. On a Friday! That's pretty good service coming from the federal government. So you told Zirkelback everything and he's such a good little boy he told his boss Mr. Morse because he'll do anything to please his boss Mr. Morse, and I walked into a fucking rat trap."

I'm not even sure at what point she hangs up.

I go downstairs to see Azani.

"Zirkelback giving you problems again?" he says. "I don't know how he manages. That boy wouldn't know how to find his own ass without a set of calipers and some surveying equipment."

I'm so edgy I welcome the relief of a laugh.

"I'm surprised you let a guy like that get to you. He ain't much thicker than a sheet of tissue paper, and his skin's about the same color. My old boss used to follow me into the men's room."

"Doesn't sound so bad to me."

He gets that look in his eye again. Then: "It wasn't nothing like that. He'd be talkin' to me like, 'I want you to help move up production, get that production movin',' and I'd be, 'Yes sir, yes sir,' and go into the bathroom, and this clown would follow me in and stand there talkin' to me while I'm takin' a piss."

"So why didn't you just turn around to answer him and piss all over him?"

Azani bursts out laughing. "I shoulda done that. Woulda whupped him good! Ha ha ha ha!"

"'Whupped him,' huh?"

"It's a handful." We share a short moment of angst-relieving laughter, then he says, "You free for dinner?"

"You like Spanish food?"

We take the subway up to my neighborhood. I manage to shop for food, pick up Antonia, take everyone up to my place and fry up a simple dinner of *carne asada*, rice and beans with *patacones*—smashed green plantains—or *tostones*, as the Dominicans call them. By some miracle there's even beer in the house. After I put Antonia to bed, we talk.

"I'm glad we don't live two hundred years ago," I say, "when masters could make the servants do *anything*."

"Yeah, but anyone who was rich two hundred years ago, their kids are still rich today. Nothing's changed. If your ancestors were servants, most likely you're still a servant today."

"Not the same way. They're still our bosses, but only for eight hours a day."

"That's where you wrong, girl!"

"They don't have the right to screw the servant women first on their wedding nights anymore—"

"They still own everything! Look at the fuckin' Jews, man, they fuckin' *run* Wall Street!"

"Azani, we have to talk . . ."

I send Azani home before 9:00 P.M. because I do not want Tonia waking up in the morning and finding *him* in our bed.

There's the usual half dozen messages from Flormaría on my machine, so I call her up and she asks me point blank what I'm doing to ease her poor brother's tormented soul, and I guess I just lose it.

"Will you shut the hell up with that? I'm working on it, goddammit!"

But she gets me right back: "And if Lázaro hadn't stayed open late for people like you, he'd still be alive, *carajo*!" Slam.

Sheesh.

CHAPTER THIRTEEN

**"I wish the rent
Was heaven sent."**
— Langston Hughes

TODAY a man with a system of wires concealed under his shirt running to makeshift detonators in his pockets stepped onto the IRT subway platform at 125th Street and Lexington Avenue and blew himself up. Nobody knows where he was headed. Two transit cops standing less than twelve feet away said they "didn't notice him until he exploded." I guess that makes a certain amount of sense.

Morning at work passes in a stony silence. I've become an unperson, just like when a cop's being deloused by Internal Affairs—the rest of the squad keeps their distance. Innocent until proven guilty, my ass. My friend Jeff restricts his inter-action to a short hello on his way into his cubicle. The secre-taries gather at coffee break in their little huddle-ettes, only this time they're gossiping about me. Lydia hasn't come in today, the one person I feel like talking to.

It occurs to me that I haven't spoken to Kwame in a while, and it feels wrong. Pursuing these cases has so consumed my psyche that I've ignored anybody who can't help me further my case, including my own child, and that makes me feel bad. I certainly don't like it when people treat me real nice until they find out I'm not important.

Kwame's in his Third World office, still wearing a knitted sweater vest. Doesn't he know it's summertime in New York?

"He-e-e-y, Filomena! What a miracle, you coming to visit me. It's been so long."

"What a miracle: you're the only person who's speaking to me."

"Oh, that, eh? Let me tell you something you may not know: You're the third secretary to Messers Zirkelback and Bartlett since January. Nobody can stand the way those two do business, playing politics while the ecosystem goes up in flames."

"Yeah, it's pretty frustrating. The money this place wastes on messenger services could subsidize a hospital in Ecuador."

"I don't particularly care for Mr. Zirkelback's methods, either. Fortunately, our paths rarely cross in this office. I just do my job, and try to do it right And you know, you're right. The spectre of my home country keeps me dedicated to working here, not because I like to see my name in print next to some vaguely environmentally conscious country singer."

"There's just so many dedicated people here, putting in so much time, and for what? So Zirkelback can kiss some millionaire's ass? He's more of an enemy to the people working for him down in the mailroom than he is to the ruthless industrialists who are raping the rainforests."

"True. You mention the mailroom. There is something there that is not always polite to bring up."

"Go ahead."

"Forgive me, but—you are seeing Mr. Shakur outside of work?"

"Well, it hasn't really—uh—you know . . ."

"It is not really my place to get involved—"

"It's okay. What have you got to say?"

"It is not my business, but I thought perhaps you were unaware that Mr. Shakur lives with a woman who is the mother of their four children."

"Oh." That's all that was missing.

"Forgive me."

"No, I thank you."

"I was only concerned about you."

"Thanks. He's not getting what he's after anyway. There's no room for racists in my bed."

"I should not even have mentioned it."

"You're doing me a favor, Kwame. I'm too forgiving. No telling what might have happened."

I return to my workstation. Forget Azani. I don't have the stomach for another confrontation this morning.

Lydia comes to work late with a bruise under her left eye. Gossip circulates. Nobody gets a word out of her until an impromptu coffee break around 3:15. She tells me her boyfriend hit her.

"I didn't know you had a boyfriend," I say.

"I thought you knew. I don't tell people." There's logic for you.

"I can see why. You're not going back to him."

"Well, we live together."

"Oh." Didn't tell me that, either. "Then you're coming home with me." We elbow our way onto the subway and ride home together. She shows me a picture of her boyfriend, who I find out has money and education, which just shows you that girlfriend abuse knows no class boundaries. I convince her to stay the night by explaining to her that love is sometimes like a *pointilliste* painting: you can sometimes see what's going on better farther away from it than close up. She says maybe she should put him out of her mind and invites me to go dredging for guys in clubs dressed in our lowest-cut outfits.

I tell her, "You only catch *fish* with hooks, honey."

Back in my apartment I feed her some warmed-over rice and beans, and she opens up to me about her art studies.

"I was born at the wrong time," she complains. "Twenty years earlier and I'd have been a pop-expressionist painter, a feminist collagist, a destructivist. Twenty years later and I'd be writing the first software to successfully transfer any image the brain conjures up—dreams, nightmares, psych-edelic hallucinations—to digitized, reproducible form. But no, I had to be born now, and get trapped between the paint-brush and the microchip. One of them obsolete, the next one still in diapers."

"Yeah, well sometimes I feel like I was born at the wrong time, in the wrong place, to the wrong parents. We didn't have diapers, just rags, and we never heard of any of those artistic movements," I tell her as I'm gathering up the dishes. "Every generation is transitional. Antonia's going to have opportunities that I never had. Sure I wish I had some of today's things when I was a kid, but Einstein's theories are still holding up and all *my* attempts at time travel have failed miserably up to now. That's just the way it is."

"But that's exactly what I mean," she says. "You must have had some incredible experiences growing up in a com-pletely different society." Oh yeah. "And the only way you can share them with your daughter is by telling her about them, maybe showing her the old family album."

"I don't have much to show her," I say, stacking the dishes in the sink. "And she's not old enough to understand what I've been through. Some day I'll get up the money and take her to Ecuador. Until then, I'm teaching her Spanish, feeding her *arroz con menestra* with fried *yuca* and *patacones*, taking her to church, and telling her *never* to take up with an abusive lover."

"You're telling her that? Really?"

"I figure it's never too early. Kind of like subliminal adver-tising, I guess."

I look at her while I'm running the water, waiting for it to warm up.

"So you try to evoke feeling. But the great dilemma of every artist," she explains, "is, how do you *record* feeling? You can record impressions of feelings, or images of people undergoing feelings, but you can't record the actual feelings themselves."

"Yeah, well maybe someday neurologists will be able to do that too," I say.

"I just resent it because the first guy who's going to get to do it—to realize my lifelong fantasy of being able to transfer brain-made images directly onto a computer screen—is going to be some techno-nerd, not an artist like me," she says. Then she starts going on about cybernetics and the body and some other postmodernist shit that I just tune right out while I'm washing the dishes until the phone interrupts me. It's Janette.

"Can you come out and play?" she asks.

"Let me check."

I ask Lydia if she wouldn't mind watching Antonia for a while so I can go help out a friend.

"Sure," says Lydia.

"Where are you?" I ask Janette.

"How soon can you meet me at the Dyckman Car Service dispatchery on the corner of Payson?"

"Give me ten minutes."

I give Lydia the usual speech about helping herself to anything, which is not much of an offer, really, and that Antonia should make no trouble about going to bed in half an hour so she won't have to baby-sit that much. And the TV works best if you stick the antenna out the window.

"No problem," says Lydia.

But it's a problem for Antonia. She doesn't know why I keep going out nights. I try to explain once again how Mommy needs to do this, but these are abstract concepts that don't enter a child's brain until they're four or five years old (if ever).

So I hit the streets again. I find Janette sitting on a park bench across the street from the dispatchery.

"Found our white Cadillac with the dented right side," she says.

"Fast work, Officer Ivins," I say, sitting down next to her. "Now what?"

"Well, I was waiting for you to get here so we could talk to the dispatcher. You're from the *barrio* and you're a little bit better at this sort of shit anyhow."

"I'm glad somebody notices," I say, and we cross the street into the dispatchery.

The dispatcher's cage is lit up by two of those colorless

fluorescent tubes that make everything beneath it look flat and bloodless. A wiry guy with a white T-shirt flashes back and forth under those lights. We go up to the cage and wait.

"With you in a minute," says the dispatcher, emptying and filing 11 × 14 manila envelopes. When he finally turns to us I see a familiar though oddly robust-looking face.

"Juan Aguila!" I say.

He looks at me. "Filomena?"

"You guys know each other?" asks Janette.

"What are you doing here?" I ask.

"Making an honest living."

"I see that. You made it back."

"Yeah."

"Congratulations."

"Thanks. What can I do for you?"

"Who took out the white Cadillac on Saturday?"

He slows it down: "What is this?"

I introduce Officer Janette Ivins of the 34th Precinct.

"We believe that car was used to commit a crime last Saturday night," says Janette.

"Wish I could help you," he says. "But I wasn't on duty, and the sheet says it was released to a collective."

"A collective?"

"Sure. We got lots of them. Immigrants fresh off the boat. They don't have the money to make the fees themselves, so four or five of them pool their money and split the fares."

"So you got five guys who could have been the driver?" I ask.

"Yeah."

"Can I see their names?"

"Yeah, yeah, okay. It'll take me a few minutes." Something in his voice says he wouldn't be doing this for just anybody, but he still remembers back when I gave him a chance, when nobody else would. And the favor has collected interest since then.

Janette whispers to me, "I don't trust this turkey. I say we hit him."

"No, he's on the level."

"You know what your problem is? You got too much faith in people. Why should this guy be helping us?"

"Because he's got his life back together."

"What? Just because he isn't hooked on anything anymore? That don't mean shit. Maybe it just doesn't show."

"No, I can tell. You should have seen him years ago: a skeleton. He wouldn't be in this cage if he was still into that shit. Sure they don't all clean up. He has. I can just feel it."

"If you say so, but if you don't mind, I'll just keep watching our backs."

It takes Juan nearly fifteen minutes, but he comes back with the list. Janette and I both pore over it.

"There," I say. "The third name." Raymundo Samaniega. "You got his address?"

"I'm not supposed to give that out," says Juan.

"And you're not supposed to play the numbers, either," I say, pointing to the receipt sticking out of his pocket. "Do it and we're even." I don't particularly enjoy reminding him that way, but that's life on an investigation. Squeeze what you can out of them and move on to the next person. I promise myself to make it up to him sometime later.

Raymundo's not home yet, so we hang out across the street. And wait. One of the old women who I sometimes help with her groceries comes out of the building and strikes up a conversation with us. She asks where Antonia is. I tell her with a babysitter. Nice of her to draw attention to how guilty I should be feeling.

"So what do you hear from Ecuador?" I ask.

"It's bad," she says. "Prices are up, crime is up. *Hay muchos asaltos*. All those *ladrones colombianos y peruanos* are sneaking into our *lindo* Ecuador. There's nothing worse than a violent foreign criminal, they have a hatred for their victims that our own humble pickpockets don't have."

Now there's a curious thought. Not curious enough to keep my mind occupied during the three and a half hours it takes for Raymundo to come home.

"*Aquí está*," I say, forgetting in my absorption that English is supposed to be the native language here.

Raymundo's just getting his keys into the lock.

"Getting home awfully late, aren't you, Raymundo?" asks Janette.

"I work late. Who the hell are you?"

"That's no way to talk to a police officer," I tell him.

"Where were you Saturday night between 9:00 and 9:30 P.M.?" asks Janette, sounding like she means business.

"Which one of you was driving the white Cadillac?" I say. "Was it you or one of these other guys?"

I hold a handwritten copy of the list in front of him.

"Hey, what is this?" he asks.

"Say, he's finally decided this is something," I say.

"Just answer my question, man. Either you were driving the car or you weren't. Now which is it?"

"I wasn't driving, I was at work."

"You work very unusual hours," I say.

"Doing what?" asks Janette.

"Like I told you before. Waste management. We gotta be ready to go out twenty-four hours a day in case there's an emergency spill."

"*Phew!* Smells like you just came from one."

"You do that *and* drive a car?" I ask.

"So I work two jobs. What are *you* doing?"

"So if you weren't driving, who was?" asks Janette.

"How should I know?" says Raymundo.

"Take him in," I say.

Janette falters. "If he was at work—and we'll be checking on that, Raymundo—then why should he know who was driving?"

"Take him in for questioning. He's a perfectly legitimate suspect."

"Let's check these other guys first," she says. "All right, Raymundo. But if your alibi falls through, we'll be back."

And she lets him go. After we put half a block behind us I say, "What the hell did you do that for? You've let him know we're on to him and you've given him plenty of time to warn all his friends to make up stories to hide their own tracks, too."

"That's the trouble with freelance police work, Fil, I've got no authority to take him in."

"Sure you do!"

"Let's just do this part my way, okay?"

Maybe I have been pulling rank on her. "It's your shot," I tell her.

But I'm right. By the time we get ahold of the other four guys—and they're easy enough to find now that our angle is shot—they've all got alibis.

"Great," I say. "Nobody was driving the car. That's just great."

"That's the way it goes," says Janette.

Yeah, when you screw up. It's almost midnight. "I'm going home."

We promise to pick up where we left off tomorrow, and I go home, climb five flights of familiar stairs and open the door.

At first I think I've got the wrong apartment and I nearly excuse myself and step back out, but that's ridiculous. Of course it's my apartment. I just put on these new locks. Music is blaring, Antonia's running around, still not in bed, because Lydia's using the bed to fuck her boyfriend. He's the one in the picture—remember?—the one who blackened her eye. I step in, slam the door shut.

"What the hell is going on here?" I ask, shutting off the music. The bed stops jittering.

Lydia hastily pulls the sheet up to cover their asses.

"Oh, it's okay for Antonia to see that but not me?" I demand to know.

"We made up," says Lydia.

"Get out of here," I say. The next few moments pass like a blur. I don't really know how I do it but somehow I pull the two of them out of bed still wrapped in the cover sheet and push them both out into the hallway, throwing their boom box and clothes and things after them. Slam.

Antonia thinks it's nothing but a party, which I accept as

better than her being traumatized for life or something like that. I rip the offending sheet off the bed, only to remember that I haven't had time for such banalities of daily life as laundry, so I have to pull a set of "relatively" clean sheets from the dirty laundry bag and put them back on the bed, thinking about all the times I promised some battered woman or rape victim, "Don't worry, we'll get him in court" and have her trust me, only to have the stupid judge dismiss the freaking case on some shit-kicking technicality. It's the ones you tried so hard to help but couldn't that always get you. Still do.

Jesus, the place stinks, too! Maybe it's the bitter bile in my throat, but I never knew someone else's sex could smell as rancid as the open-air meat market in downtown Machala.

It's only after I put Tonia to bed for the night that I open the door to the other room to go open a window. The place smells like a—

I step on something warm and wet.

I step back.

I smell blood.

My hand finds the light switch.

It looks like they've ransacked the place and killed the superintendent. My posters are torn and bloody. The bookshelf and plants have been knocked over and the ashtray broken. There's blood and chicken feathers three feet up the wall and all over the rug. So much for the rug. The headless chicken that I stepped on is lying in a pool of its own blood, staining the hell out of my floor with a sticky mess that is going to take me a *long* time to clean up.

My heart nearly stopped when I first smelled the blood.

It looks like there's been a fight to the death here. But within a few minutes I've reconstructed it all and realize that someone's taken a live chicken, cut off its head right on the windowsill and tossed the body inside, where it clearly ran around for a while knocking things over, shedding feathers everywhere and spattering my walls and books with its blood. It looks far worse than it really is, and, headless, the chicken wouldn't have made that much noise, which is probably why my fucking friends didn't notice it.

On the window by the fire escape, using bright red lipstick or greasepaint, that same someone has scrawled: FLY OR DIE.

I'm not even sure what that means.

I suppose I needed a new rug anyway, but rolling it up reveals years of dirt that I would have preferred not to have to confront right now. I set everything back up, brush off the chicken feathers and sweep them up with the dirt. Then I have to fill a plastic pail with hot water six times during the course of the night, getting down on my knees with a stiff brush to scrub the drying blood out of all the little corners and cracks—and believe me, there are a lot of them in these old floorboards—or else the place will truly smell like Hell's meat market by tomorrow. I'll still probably have to burn incense in here all summer long 'til the smell goes away.

This shit is really starting to piss me off.

How can I fight them with First World justice? Maybe it's getting late and I'm going just a little bit crazy, maybe it's getting up-close and personal with the sacrificial blood on my hands, maybe it's the smell that brings it all back; maybe it's the sheer, primal rage at being pushed around like this and knowing that I can't fight them alone: I feel a voice from decades ago calling inside me. And I actually think of sending for them. But no, it's not really practical. The inter-Amazonian communications network is not good from this distance, and there's the harsh reality of visas and plane fares. Yeah, right: "I'd like visas for three deadly Shuar assassins who tend to favor the use of spears and blowguns, please." Besides, I don't think they'd adjust. Far from their sources, their magic wouldn't work quickly enough here. And I doubt I could lure Samuel Morse or this Iron Lady down to the Amazon jungle.

I wash up.

But before going to sleep, I sharpen the big kitchen knife and leave it by the bed.

In my dreams a hook-nosed, white-haired hag threatens me, her mouth gaping open to swallow me while her booming voice echoes across the topless Andean peaks. She curses me in fluent Quichua, which I hardly even understand anymore. And then I do understand it. In the language of thunder, she declares that I have innocent blood on my hands. I look down and my hands betray me, red and glistening. The icy mountain wind blows through me, leaving one last kernel of warmth where my heart should be, fading, fading . . . I look to my friends for help. They are there, more than a dozen of the old gang, forming a ring around these events, their faces elongated in a way that I know, in the logic of my dream, means that they are observers only, that they will not help me. I call to them not to let me die like this, pinned down to a slaughter stone, to remember all those times we rode together into the subterranean depths of the human thirst for blood, at least to let me die on my feet with a long blade in my hands, but they are too far away from all that now. I am on my own. The hag is about to sacrifice me to the sun god with a twelve-inch kitchen knife when I spring awake.

Antonia's lying next to me, moaning and drenching the sheets with her sweat. I put my lips to her forehead. She's burning up. I give her some baby aspirin and apply cold compresses, and after about forty-five minutes her temperature goes down a few degrees. I let myself fall back asleep only to be awakened minutes later by her hysterical crying. She's boiling.

I call the Dyckman Car Service. The dispatcher refuses to send a car out at this hour until I use Juan's name. He says to be ready in five minutes. Only now do I see that it's 3:27 A.M. I've had maybe an hour's sleep. I throw on some clothes, wrap Tonia up, and lock the door behind me as I run down to the street.

"Columbia Presbyterian, please—fast!"

The guy floors it. At this hour of the night it should take about seven minutes. But the lights screw us up and it takes more like twelve. I pay the driver some money and run into the Emergency Room, clutching my child to me.

It's many harrowing minutes before Antonia gets examined, and the doctor determines she has food poisoning. They immerse her in cold water to bring her fever down and hook her up to an intravenous unit. It takes them several tries to get the needle into one of her tiny veins.

About a quarter to five in the morning they make me put on hospital "scrubs" so I can accompany Antonia up to a recovery room.

They transfer her to a child's bed and tell me I can stay with her for as long as I want, but they can't set up a bed for me to sleep next to her.

The sky is still dark when I sit down to watch my sleeping child breathe peacefully. Kids. You've got to watch them every second. I don't even watch myself that much. Now that the panic is past I get to deal with the guilt of bringing on her condition. Food poisoning? I don't care how much of a modern woman you think you are, when your kid has to go to the hospital because you've been too busy running around playing Joan of Arc to make her a decent meal you feel shitty about it. Was it the leftover beans? What should I have done? Why am I giving myself this wrenching mother's guilt? It could have been Lydia and her boyfriend fed her something. Could it be Lucy Ferrer? Naah, that's my tired mind.

I look at my little girl here, so small in size, yet so large she fills up my life. The more I think about it—and I've got *plenty* of time to think about it—I still find it hard to believe that she was once a tiny sac of cells clinging to the wall of my uterus. I watched for what instincts she might show first, which turned out to be eating and shitting. The first crucial thing a baby actually learns is the difference between "day" and "night," just as the first decision God makes in the Bible after the creation of light is the separation of light from dark. I wonder at the parallel. We are all God's children.

I figure in all the hospital costs and calculate that, at birth, she cost over $1,000 a pound. And I drench myself in the cruel joy of contemplating her empty clothes while she's asleep. Such innocence. Such fragility. Such life. Such fragile life.

Who am I kidding? I'm just as fragile, in my way. Do I really want her to grow up to be like me? To go through all the crap I've gone through? And she will, unless we do some serious improving on this place. I was taught that we were put here to give back more than we were given, that if life means anything it means leaving this place better than we found it.

Or to die trying.

Cutting into reality hurts. Place your soft skin too close to the sharp pyramid of reality's edge and it will gash you open. Reach out with the soft pyramid of your feeling and the hard, scalding surface of reality will grind you flat.

These are the thoughts that crowd my brain and only begin to scatter as the daylight scatters the darkness from the sky. I'm so sorry for what has happened. In Spanish it's "*Lo siento.*" I feel it. I feel this, all right. *Nothing* would have any meaning anymore if anything were to happen to her. I'd find no pleasure in anything. There'd be nothing left of me but total pain of the soul. And I realize this doesn't even come close to what Flormaría must be feeling. I shouldn't have snapped at her like that.

Antonia's a long way from such thoughts herself, sleeping like a little angel. She's going to get more love than I had. My father? My father was a piece of the nineteenth century. He believed that children were basically animals and that if you didn't keep them down with an iron fist they'd grow up to be beasts and whores. Work was the only thing for them. Work in the fields all day, table scraps for lunch, a beating for dinner if you protested. Never loved me. Son-of-a-bitch didn't know how to love. Well, maybe he felt it for my brother but he never felt it for me. My mother? He treated her like the baby-producing cow all women were to him. Threatened to have me whipped in the central square if I persisted in defying him with my absurd desire of wanting to go to high school. Fortunately the high school was ten miles away down a dangerous mountain road in the city of Cuenca. So I ran away. Some cousins took me in and it would have caused too much trouble to come after me. But eventually he did come, with murder in his eyes, so I ran away again and spent some time with a pretty reckless crowd. I learned a lot. Then came college. And college was hundreds of miles away on the coast in the city of Guayaquil. And now I'm here. Glad I'm not an insecure fourteen-year-old anymore. Not that I'm secure now, I've just learned to deal with insecurity as part of my life.

My poor mother died so young. God forgive me, but why couldn't *he* have died at thirty-five and *she* have lived beyond eighty? I still remember some of the lullabies she used to sing me. I sing one to my child:

> *Duermase mi vida, duermase mi amor,*
> *¿Que tengo que hacer? Lavar tus pañales*
> *Duermase mi vida, duermase mi amor*
> *Porque dormidita se aparece un sol . . .*

Why are all lullabies so sad? Because our mothers sang them to us in a childhood long since gone. Boyfriends come and go, but a mother's love is forever.

And when I start to cry, my whole body shakes, every cell in me gives up a shudder and retches a tear that travels to my eyes. A deep soul-shaking cry that is a physically exhausting experience.

I overhear a nurse in the hall ask, "Is it a terminal illness?" I think, Yes, it is. I have this disease called "Life." It's one hundred percent fatal. Music, books, food, art, sex, drinks—all pleasure—it's all just to distract us from the fact that we're miserable. That life is a pointless trek from here to there with no meaning at all whatsoever.

It's funny how a real cry purges you like a thousand hot lancets.

Brightening light is flowing into the room, and I get to my feet, wiping my eyes and blowing my nose. The nurses tell me to go home and get some rest, that I can probably come back and get Antonia later today, around 4:00 P.M.

Brushing some of the cobwebs from my brain, I rub my bleary eyes and wander around till I find somebody who knows how to give accurate directions to the elevator. While I'm waiting for the elevator down, one on its way up stops and a family gets out. Seeing me in the scrub suit, the guy thinks I work here or something and he asks me, "Which way to Neonatal?"

It takes me many seconds to tell him I'm not sure.

He says, "Take another valium," and they walk away from me laughing.

It's not until I'm in the elevator lurching downwards that I shake my addled head and think, Why are people such assholes? I rushed to the Emergency Room at 3:35 A.M., haven't slept since, and since I'm wearing scrubs this idiot thinks I'm a doc and when I'm too slow answering him he insults me. What the *fuck* does *he* know about what I've been through? You see, I try to assume people are good. They have to go out of their way to prove they're assholes to me. Most jerks assume you're a jerk too, and you have to *prove* you're cool to them. Fuck that.

I get off on the wrong floor and decide I need some coffee or I'll never make it home alive. I ask an orderly where the nearest caffeine is, and he takes me to a closet crammed from floor to ceiling with bottles labeled with every color and polysyllabic name there is.

"Go ahead," he says. "Take what you want."

I figure right now would be a good time to black out rather than confront my weakness, but I don't get that easy way out. I have to turn my back and walk the hardest walk I know down the corridor and away from that closet. And nobody's there to give me that pat on the back that I need so much.

CHAPTER FOURTEEN

"El diablo no sabe por diablo, sino por viejo."
(The devil isn't clever because he's the
devil, but because he's old.)
— Ecuadorian proverb

I AM AWAKENED at about 9:00 A.M. by the sound of the phone ringing. I don't normally spring out of bed to answer it, but I do now. It's Janette.

"Bad news, Fil. Two cops killed a dude while his family watched. I got riot duty today."

"Why are you calling me with this?"

"The dude was black, Fil. He didn't get his hands up fast enough so they fired nine bullets into him. One cop was firing from point-blank range. The dude was hit and fell down on one knee, but the cop kept shooting."

"His family told it that way?"

"Yeah."

"Shit. That's fourteen people killed by city cops this year."

"Half of them black."

And the rest *latino*, I'm thinking.

She doesn't say it, but it's in her voice: She wants advice. I warn her, "Just remember that the courts have recently held that the terms 'jackass' and 'go fuck yourself' do *not* constitute harassment of a police officer."

She laughs. The best medicine. "Now take it easy," I tell her.

"Thanks, Fil."

Still, I worry. A black policing blacks is going to involve emotional complications beyond my feeble comprehension. I stifle the urge to call the lieutenant and call up Sergeant Betty instead. She's on desk duty, so I get her right away. We talk for a minute about whether the city is going to go up in flames today or not, then I get around to the point:

"Can you pull some strings at the Three-four and get Janette Ivins taken off crowd control duty today?"

"I doubt it. Not today. What for?"

"'Cause she's still green, and I'm not sure she'll be able to handle it."

"Then she'd better learn fast."

"It's not just that. We're making progress in our unofficial pursuit. If she could cover her regular beat or even work a desk, she'd take us a step closer to catching some killers."

"I don't think so, Fil. They're calling cops in off double shifts."

"Damn! Why'd they ever take Janette off the case?"

"What case?"

"The Pérez murder."

"The Pérez murder? She was never on that case."

"You mean they took her off it."

"She was off it when you met her, Fil."

"Sure, I remember that. Then she told me she was put back on it."

"I don't know what she told you, Fil. But she was never put back on that case."

"Oh. Thanks."

"Sorry I can't help. Not today."

"Forget about it." I call up the 34th and ask for Officer Ivins. The cop handling the phones gives me a seriously hard time about it, but I eventually get her.

"Filomena?" There's haste in her voice.

"Damn it, you lied to me."

"I didn't lie to you—"

"All right, you just 'oversold' yourself, okay? But the new translation says, 'Thou shalt not oversell yourself.'"

"What are you talking about?"

"I'm talking about you getting me to track down two killers so you could get all the credit. No wonder you didn't bring in Raymundo. It would have blown your cover. Well congratulations, you may have just blown the whole case."

"Now, Fil—"

"I *told* you that hotdogging stuff doesn't work—hell, it nearly got me killed! And what do you do? You go and try to pull it on me!"

"Maybe I—uh—"

"Goodbye, Janette. And good luck." I hang up on somebody for a change. And unplug the phone.

Now I'm worried. What about Eduardo? He works in the same damn squadroom. He must have known Janette wasn't on the case, which means either he was willing to help her pull off this scheme or maybe—just maybe—*he's* the one who's been feeding half our leads to the enemy camp. Great. Just great.

I've got nothing better to do than go back to the hospital. But first, a shower to make me human again. Then I heat up yesterday's coffee and sit down to reflect. I don't think there's anyone in this whole dizzy business who hasn't betrayed me in some way. I'm running through the list: Raúl—check; Gina, Azani, Lydia—check; Janette—check; even Flormaría and I had a falling out because I haven't worked a miracle yet and brought in her brother's killers; (Eduardo?)—check; Zirkelback and the whole of the Environmental Action Foundation—check; and me, that's right, my own blind trust has led me to betray myself—when I hear a sound behind me. I'm not usually supposed to be in at this hour. Somebody knows my habits pretty well.

I put the coffee cup down, sink to the floor and peep around the corner. The shades are still drawn, but the windows are open six inches. Somebody is on the fire escape. Sounds like they're scrawling another message on my window. I pick up the kitchen knife and I creep into the bathroom to get my secret weapon and a towel to wrap around my fist.

I expect the infiltrator is quite surprised when my towel-wrapped fist drives a baseball bat through the window and leaves his unfinished message indecipherably shattered across dozens of triangular fragments. I've never seen the guy before. It's not one of Raúl's rowdies. He tries to run but I manage to club him in the shins, bringing him down, and brush him back with a few swipes at his head while telling him to fuck off. "Lucy send you?" I demand. He doesn't answer. He can't attack me because of the triangular shards of glass sticking up between us. I start breaking them off with the bat so I can get at him.

He recoils as I aim several blows at his kneecaps while yelling, "I—said—FUCK—OFF!" Then he tries to make a break for it. Luckily, I've got him off balance, while I'm solidly anchored on both feet. I push the bat between his legs and trip him. He lands face first on the rusty iron steps with a *clang!* Ouch. But he's momentarily stunned. I jump through the window, get the bat under his throat in a very illegal stranglehold, dig my knees into his kidneys, and manage to put the knife right in front of his eyes with a nearly free hand. I don't know where I found the strength to do that. I feel like I'm seventeen again, riding with the wild crowd, sweeping down from the mountains on a moonlit night, fearless. *Fearless.*

Sleep deprivation will do funny things to you. Then there's the primal biological response: I've heard of momma birds attacking poisonous snakes to protect their young. But I'm without my child now, and I'm irrational, not thinking of the future, for once, and they're bringing out a part of me I haven't seen in years, and they clearly didn't count on me going *this* crazy.

I spit into his ear: "Take me to her!"

He manages to laugh. Blood comes out of his mouth.

"Take me to her or I'll cut your fucking throat and throw you off the fire escape."

It's a five-story drop. That would get just about anybody's attention. I position the knife for a deadly thrust.

And then I realize: why the hell am I bargaining with *this* peon? I haul him up by his neck and convince him to take the easy way down. Alive.

I'm able to leave the bat at home, and we make a rather strange sight walking out the front door of my building, like two mating mantises, a couple so in love that I won't unwrap my arms from around him, even though it makes it a little hard to walk. I've got one arm around him, holding both of his hands with my right hand, and keeping the kitchen knife under his jacket, pinned between his second and third ribs, with my left.

"*¡Lo vas a pagar caro!*" he curses me. "You'll pay for this!"

"Just take me to her."

They want me to lose the knife.

"No."

"Then you must be blindfolded," says the gatekeeper.

"Fine."

And now I suppose we make an even stranger sight, two lovers, one blindfolded, being led across the street in broad daylight by a grocery-store owner. The *barrio*'s grapevine is going to dispatch this one to all points pretty quickly. Well, maybe it's time to bring things to a head.

I am led through a maze of exceedingly strange sensations. They know I'm trying to keep track of where we're going, building a mental map and storing it for the future, so naturally they do their best to make that map fall apart. It's very hard—all the sounds seem weirdly amplified, the smells full of meaning, but confounded by unexpected interference. I know we're passing the pizza place, but the curb seems awfully big and unfamiliar to me now. They take me through front doors and back doors, up and down flights of stairs, through dank, chilly basements and over sweltering rooftops and down again, spinning me around, until I tell them, "Okay, enough, I've lost the trail. Believe me. Now just take me there."

They do.

Somebody tells me I can take off the blindfold now.

I can't do it without letting him go.

I let him go and I take off the blindfold. I'm still holding the knife, standing alone in the center of a room. The room is dark, smoky and red. I'm not sure where the light is coming from. Faces surround me. Unfriendly faces. I scan them, looking for the face I just brought in here, looking for Eduardo's face. I don't see them. I see the faces of people I've seen a thousand times in this neighborhood, seeing them for the first time, hauntingly new and unfamiliar. I know them. I even know some of their names, but I can't remember a single one right now. My mind is empty except for two things: blood and survival.

A man's voice rises behind me, above me, near, far: "It's time for a test."

Dark figures set out a cage full of pigeons: nine gray, one white.

"We are going to release them. You are to kill the white one with one stroke. If you can do that, she will talk to you. Agreed?"

"Agreed." I used to hunt for my own food in the Andes. I think I can handle this.

I take a wider stance, knees bent, not locked. I steel myself. They let them go. I leap, ready to skewer the white one with a single thrust, but it flies right in front of the watchers' faces and I halt right there, letting it fly away.

I think a sound reaches me from the planet earth, somewhere above, below, like a diesel truck's distant Klaxon, somewhere out there. Then it's gone.

"That was the moment, my child," says the voice.

"I know."

"Why did you not throw?"

"I would have hit someone."

"They know that," says the voice.

Do they really expect me to kill someone?

I defy them: "I can meet your challenge."

I see a faint flutter at the edge of my vision. I turn, ready to throw. Someone is holding the white pigeon above his head, its wings spread between his fingertips. He lets it go. I take aim, draw a bead, but it would mean letting the knife out of my hands. I don't move.

No one moves.

The pigeon circles, flutters, considers perching on a rafter but thinks better of it, zig-zags back and forth above their heads, then flies to the far corner and circles back, coming in right above me. I launch the knife straight up. It pierces the bird's chest and this horrible carnal union drops like a dead weight into my hand. I've got the knife back, the dead white bird impaled upon it, oozing warm blood onto my fingers.

And in the silence, I swear I feel someone smiling at me. I turn. It's her. She's deep in the smoky red shadows. She's in her twenties, thirties, forties, fifties, sixties, seventies. She's pale and dark, fleshy and bony, her skin is rough, smooth, sinewy. I get rid of the bird.

All of our speech is in very formal Spanish:

"Yes . . . yes . . . my child . . . I see that you have finally come."

I cross my arms, keeping the knife pointed away from her. It's almost a bow.

"I am not here to threaten your power," I say.

"Yet you are powerful. You have seen many throats cut."

"I do not seek to undermine you."

"That is wise."

"I seek the ones who are guilty of the unfeeling murder of a good man, a good brother, a good husband, a good father."

"Lázaro Pérez."

"May his soul rest in peace," I say reflexively, deferentially. My mind is empty.

"You have been asking many questions."

"I do not wish to confront you, only to sweep up the poor remains of this one, small corner of the great, wide world, this one terrible thing that has been done, this terrible, stupid thing that did not need to be done."

"But you seek my children's names."

"You know that I do."

"Yes. They are part of my terrain."

"You know who they are?"

"Yes."

"Then you are my enemy if you do not tell me their names."

"And you know that I cannot."

"Yes. I know."

Pause.

"Perhaps you would like something to drink?"

"I'm trying to cut down."

"Yes. You are, aren't you? Yes. You have strength, young one."

Christ, I'm almost starting to respect her.

"Hear what I say," she decrees.

"Yes."

"If you are able to discover their names in the next three days, they are yours. If you cannot, that part of this world is closed to you, forever."

"You mean the idea of catching them?"

"Yes."

Pause.

"Meanwhile the threats stop?"

"Yes."

A longer pause. Then:

"Give me 'til Monday."

She thinks. She strokes her chin.

She nods.

I take the leftover nails from my last hardware purchase and the huge piece of plywood I keep under the mattress to stiffen it and nail it over the broken window. It's a half-assed job, but I'm kind of pressed right now. And I'll have to replace those shades.

I get on the subway for the hospital. No emergency this time, thank God. I pick up a paper that's been left on the seat from the morning rush hour and look it over. There's a photo of the dead man's wife being supported in her grief by two friends as she leaves a storefront Church of God on 155th Street. Jesse Jackson was there. There's a drop quote from him in the middle of the page in large, eighteen-point italic white letters in a black box: "Be angry, but don't commit suicide. Be angry but do not attack anybody else. An eye for an eye and a tooth for a tooth will leave you blind and disfigured."

But nobody's listening. The train stops at 175th Street and refuses to go any farther. After a series of back-and-forth calls between the motorman and the conductor trying to find out the source of the trouble, I get out to walk the seven remaining blocks to the hospital. A transit cop stationed at the turnstiles to deter fare-beaters advises me, "Don't go out there."

What choice do I have? I've got to see my kid. She has to see me. I ascend to street level, and I can forget about a leisurely walk down Broadway to 168th. Every side street in every direction is closed off by blue Police Line sawhorses. It takes me nearly fifteen minutes to squeeze through the crowds pressed against the walls, then walk several blocks out of my way down Audubon Avenue to get there.

The main entrance to the hospital is right on 168th, which, slightly farther east, is one of the worst streets in the precinct. And I'd say there's well over three thousand angry demonstrators crowded into Mitchell Square. Every cop in the precinct has been called out or risks facing charges. In Ecuador it's the opposite. Student attendance at the protests was mandatory, which always amazed me, since it sort of defies the idea of protest.

The crowd continues to press against the police line. Why are they gathered here anyway? I ask around and discover one of the cops involved in the shooting was taken here because in all the confusion his partner shot him in the hand. Some of the chants are pretty ugly. And all those rookie cops don't know what to do. They're losing control of the situation. The crowd knows this and increases their vitriolic taunting.

Someone yells, "Why don't you go arrest some *white* people!" And many nearby voices agree with a united burst of cheers and applause.

There's a lot of pushing and shoving, then the police decide on a show of strength and start marching new units in. While I'm watching that, a thrown rock or something clips one of the young white cops, because he spins around and cracks somebody. That breaks it. The crowd surges forward and overruns the floodgates, spilling out into the street, trampling the police barriers and running after a few cops. There's the sound of something shattering and cops pour into the square from every conceivable accessway, closing in on the crowd from all sides. Most of the people try to break through and scatter down the street. There's a pileup at the subway entrance. Those who can't get out of the way are beaten to the ground.

Police try to move their vans into position but people are crawling along the street right in front of their wheels trying to dodge the nightsticks, trying to protect their heads with their hands. The people who have nowhere else to go attack the van. Even as cops close in, ruthlessly beating away at the outer ring of protesters, they manage to smash every window in the van, turn it over and set it on fire. A team of 34th Precinct cops whom I know to be Vietnam veterans, equipped not with nightsticks but with assault rifles and bulletproof clothing, plunge their phalanx into this crowd to pull the two cops from the van before it explodes.

I see a black girl—she can't be more than seventeen—putting her whole body behind hurling half a brick at the cops with more hatred than she could *ever* show for any imagined enemies like the Russians, the Libyans, or whoever this week's enemies are supposed to be.

People are trying to make a break for it through the barricades I'm caught behind. I get pressed half to death in the crush. Then there's a kind of a *pop!* and three dozen heavily protected riot police charge *me*. Everyone tries to run. I try to press myself flat against a wall.

Ever notice how a blow always hurts more when you don't see it coming? You can't prepare yourself, anticipate, compensate. Out of nowhere, a hard slam to the head knocks me to the sidewalk. I look up and see a cop towering over me ready to bring a yard-long nightstick down on my skull. I'm about to yell "I'm a cop!" but like in a bad dream I can't get the words out of my mouth. Only a split-second recognition saves me: It's one of the cops from the 34th! Cursing the hell out of me, he lifts me up and pushes me against a doorway. Then a protester grabs him from behind and three cops rush to his aid, beating the guy into a bloody fetus position.

Head wounds bleed like hell. Warm blood is gushing from a cut over my eye. I came to get my kid out of the hospital and now I need one.

A cop on horseback galloping at full speed takes a swipe at me as I duck under the awning of a *bodega* and dive behind the oranges. I catch my breath for a second, then plunge unseeingly back into the churning stream and run the mad, chaotic gauntlet that leads to the Emergency Room, which is packed with hurting people. The poor triage nurse is about to have a coronary. I think it's her first day. I figure my wound is superficial, this isn't the place for me. I slip through to the main hallway, duck into a bathroom to wash some of the blood off and put a bunch of paper towels over the wound, which I hold in place as I head to the desk and tell the receptionist I'm here to visit Antonia Buscarsela in room 712. I have to show some ID to prove I'm her mother.

Some kind of fight-or-flight reflex has gotten me through the last few minutes, because once I'm in the elevator the pain hammers me like a six-inch spike being driven into my brain and I nearly fall to the floor.

The nurse's station up in Pediatrics sees me and insists on cleaning and bandaging the wound before I go in to see Antonia. They ask me what happened, and I guess I'm in mild shock because instead of explaining that I was just trying to get in to see my kid and I got caught in the riot, I find myself demanding something for the extreme pain. They think I need to see a doctor, but there's a lightning bolt jammed through the thinking part of my brain, my hands grab on to one of them and my voice screams something like, "*Please* give me some painkillers *now*, damn it!" Blinding pain, then some hands push me back into the chair and my head is covered and my arm is pinched and then—everything's all right. A bricklayer slaps some mortar on my head with a trowel and then pats it down till the cement dries, and the next thing I know I'm asking the nurses, "Which weighs more, a pound of feathers or a pound of nails?"

They're about to answer when I answer that one myself: "You bet your *ass* a pound of nails weighs more—you ever been hit with one?"

"No, I haven't," says the nurse. "Let me take you to your daughter's room."

"I doneed any help," I say, trying to get up. "Whooops!"

I guess I do need help. Maybe it's that winning combination of too little sleep, no breakfast, and getting hit in the head. Plus that nice dose of whatever they gave me that's making me feel awfully warm and flushed all over, and— *fuzzy*. I find it all rather funny.

Antonia's sitting up in bed and she doubles in brightness when she sees me. I get the best hug in the world, and Antonia has a ball because Mommy is rolling around on the bed with her acting like a two-year-old. I speak baby talk, toss her around and generally act in a manner that would definitely get me arrested under other circumstances, but somehow this sort of behavior is justifiable when done in conjunction with a toddler. Wheeeee! I am having fun! Antonia understands every word of my baby talk. I look into her eyes: yup, she understands, all right.

"Okaayy, let's go," I say.

"Ma'am, the doctor said you need to lie down for a while," says the nurse.

"Noooo problem," I assure her. Silly woman. What could possibly happen to us? Look, someone's even taken the trouble to install rubber walls just to keep me from hurting myself.

KENNETH WISHNIA

"Good," she says. "I'll go get a gurney to take you down to outpatient recovery."

Gurney? Oh, no. No gurneys for me. As soon as she's gone I take Antonia and sneak out. The elevator's more like a roller coaster, but it gets us to the bottom. I find the minutiae of filling out Antonia's discharge papers hilarious. The cashier wants to call a cab but I insist on the subway. She has an orderly escort us to the subway entrance. I give the orderly a big juicy kiss of thanks on his surprised lips and Antonia gets me down the stairs all right and onto the platform. We sing a song together while waiting for a train. She carries it better than I do.

The train comes. I never noticed how soft and comfortable these subway seats are! Mmmmm, nice. A heavy-set young black man is involved in an argument with a scrawny pale white guy.

"Yeah, well what the fuck does *that* shit mean, man?!" says the black guy, pinching the Nazi swastika sewn onto the other guy's jacket. Ooh, that brings me back for a moment. I love my child and I hug her to me.

"It's not what you think, man," says the white guy. "It means, like, 'fuck authority.'"

"Aww, you just be burnin' my flag, man. You shittin' me, man!"

"Listen, man, you can't fuel a movement on anger alone."

"I give less than a fuck, man! Y'hear me? I give less than a fuck!" My roving eye lands on the considerable bulge in the black dude's pants, and dwells on it. He gives less than a fuck. I stop my mouth from saying something out loud I would definitely regret. Guess I'm still a bit light-headed. A bit? We get to 207th Street and Antonia practically has to get me up the stairs to street level herself. I do have the presence of mind to make sure we're always walking on the sidewalk against oncoming traffic, which should give us a few feet or seconds more if anyone happens to be driving around with a loaded shotgun.

I'm starting to get dizzy, which is not a good thing in

the middle of the street. I'm lucid enough to pull the lack of food from the sea of possibilities as the likely culprit, and we stop into the nearest restaurant, a homey place serving Caribbean delights. I order a *batido de fruta* (fruit shake) called a *"morir soñando"* ("to die dreaming") and let Antonia decide for herself what she wants. But when it comes the sight of it sickens me, even though I know it's delicious. I let Antonia have as much of it as she wants, and we put the rest in a bag to take home.

My system attacks what little nutrition it can squeeze out of a fruit shake, half the remaining blood draining from my head and traveling down to my stomach to start absorbing it. This does not help me think any clearer.

I take Antonia to the park to let her play and to get some fresh air. I lie back on a park bench staring at the pink tufts dry-brushing texture into the silvery clouds. I don't know how long I watch the hypnotic patterns drift across the sky, until I finally start to come down a bit, or at least am able to handle what is happening to me, which is no fun because I realize I can't turn to anyone right now. That is, until I hear the familiar jangling of the heavy copper cowbells.

I insist on paying Marco for the ice, then I tell him:

"I'm ready. I want the full treatment."

He smiles his golden-toothed smile and nods his agreement. "It is about time," he says. "Meet me back here in one hour."

CHAPTER FIFTEEN

"A job is fine, but it interferes with your time."
— Yiddish proverb

WHAT THE HELL. In Ecuador we eat twelve grapes on New Year's for good luck. That's about the same level of trust in the paranormal as what I'm about to go through. It would be hypocritical of me to perform one and ridicule the other, since one quasi-miraculous phenomenon is every bit as likely as another.

I get *mamita* Viki to take Antonia for a couple of hours and I return to the park, no longer floating on air, but still a bit shot through with giggle juice. Maybe that explains some of my what-the-hell attitude. Maybe it doesn't. I don't know.

Marco takes me to an apartment house I've never been to overlooking the green basin of the Columbia University football stadium and the murky waters of the Harlem River. Beyond that loom the immense blocks of Bronx housing projects.

Flormaría comes in from the kitchen. We look at each other. We breathe in and out a couple of times, then we both start talking at nearly the same time, me apologizing for losing my temper with her, she telling me, "After I hung up I sat there and talked with Demetrio and thought about all you've done for me and I realized how wrong I was to say those things to you."

"Never mind about all that now," I say. "Peace."

"Peace." We hug, her huge belly cradled between us.

Marco has engaged the aid of three helpers: a middle-aged, boxshaped woman whose apartment this is, and two younger men, both very dark-skinned Dominicans. Apparently Marco and Flormaría have already told them about me, because they greet me with all the reverence due someone taking on the dreaded Iron Lucy.

My problem, then, has already been diagnosed. The woman begins laying out playing cards to determine the treatment.

"Three spirits have been sent against you," the woman professes. And she's right. More playing cards reveal other detailed information that they do not share with me. They merely nod in agreement, like doctors conferring over the lab results outside a patient's room.

The two young men supply the rhythm for the ceremony. At the woman's signal, one of them starts beating a drum while the other shakes a gourd filled with hollow beads or something. She takes a sack of corn flour, and Flormaría helps spread it out all over the wooden floor. Then she traces the shape of a coffin in it with her finger and she and Marco lay two straw mats over it. She asks me to lie down over the spot where she has traced the coffin. Marco takes my hand and leads me to the correct spot.

The rhythmic accompaniment strengthens. I'm resonating with extra vibrations from the floor now that reverberate through my body. Marco takes out a box of .32-caliber bullets and starts screwing the tops off of them with his teeth, making a little pile that he mixes into a glass of *trago*. He offers it to me and commands me to drink all of it. It's an eight-ounce glass of denatured firewater mixed with gunpowder. This is the equivalent of maybe four or five shots of whiskey plus God knows what else. I take a sip and grimace. I tell Marco I don't want the rest. He tells me it is the blood of Papa Legba. It will make me strong, not weak. And to have it all.

I tell him No, I don't want any alcohol. He stresses that

it is *not* alcohol, that the moment it touches my lips it transforms into the blood of Papa Legba. He knows my fears and he reassures me repeatedly until I give in.

The drumming and rattling become part of my body. I don't know how long it takes me to finish the glass. Maybe ten or fifteen minutes, maybe less, maybe more. The little pile of gunpowder grows into a big pile before my glazing eyes. It splits into two shifting piles, and the room starts spinning. Oh, shit! I suddenly tighten up, realizing that somehow I have completely forgotten about the shot of painkiller. And mixing alcohol and drugs is the sort of thing people die from. I'm trying to think, How long ago did I get that shot? I think I see by the window that it's gotten dark outside, so that would put it at nearly seven hours, right? That should be okay, right? Right? O-oh, y-yes-s-s, so-o-o right. Oh, I'm starting to feel very right right now. Very very very right. My mouth parts open so the dentist can take my teeth out. It only takes a few seconds and I hardly feel a thing.

I try to move my arms so I can beat along in rhythm with the drums; they sag like rubber and fall to the floor. Suddenly I feel wet. With sweat? Piss? No, the woman is raining down whole kernels of corn on me. I try to catch some in my mouth but I can only stretch my lips about four feet. Somewhere my head falls back on the mats like I've just fallen off an eighteen-foot ladder. Next I see chickens floating in the air above me and I figure, uh-oh, it's time to go, but all the chickens do is peck at the corns covering my body in perfect rhythm with the drumming. No, that can't be. Not perfect. I try to catch them off beat, but I'm too drunk, the silly chickens! Or too something, too—*whatever* I am. I can't distinguish the beats anymore. They arrive before they hit me and stay with me after they've gone and I'm not ready for them.

The sound of . . . the drumming . . . sounds like Africa . . . Caribbean . . . makes me think of the Esmeraldeñan coast of Ecuador. It's the beat of ten million hearts. Twenty million. One hundred million. Five hundred million. Oohhhh!

All I feel is a warm wave of pulsation washing over me,

lapping at my sides, my breasts, then covering me completely. Somehow in my dissipated body my mentality forms with diamond clarity and sharpness, breaking up and refracting images from today. I see facets of bodies running, blood on the blacktop, blood on the two yellow lines down the middle of the street, the white hospital walls. What makes us split our thoughts so violently? Convinced of something we should be questioning? There's a lot of bumpy road stretching away from me in all directions. Anyone can shoot you. Ignorance. Hatred. Tearing apart our minds, and greed and disregard for our mother the earth, that's why the Bible commands us to honor our parents: the way you treat them colors how you treat everyone and everything else. And I'd swear I see Marco uprooting a tree and burying a live chicken under it.

It's more of a 4-D scrapbook of my mind, moving and changing, recognizing the pieces, trying to flip back. And in that refracting pattern I begin to see tiny mirrors floating in the darkness. They tumble and fall towards me. My face slides in and out of the darkness, riding the rotating mirrors of the deep. I see my face doubled and doubled again. No—it's not my face doubled. It's my face and—a shape. It's *like* a face. On a long, white body that's embracing me from behind. I turn, but there is nothing there but a cold whirlwind, empty mirrors receding into its blackness. I turn back. A mirror with my face smacks into me and I pass through it into a cold, dead place. A vague, shadowy form, white, skeletal, approaches, becoming cloaked with the pale dead skin of Lázaro Pérez. He drifts towards me, then hovers. That's as close as he will come, it seems. I sense that he is trying to say something. Trying to thank me, I feel, I hope, I desire. I call his name. He casts his dead eyes down sadly and raises one arm slightly out to the side. Pointing down. I look. There is nothing there. Then I see it. His hand has begun to drip. Blackish, inky muck. His whole body transforms into drips falling from his hand. He leaves without saying goodbye. But the drips are there. I follow the mucky drips through the darkness, back to the scrapbook of my mind. The drips form a stream of muck flowing from image to image. I recognize them all. These are all images that I have seen before—in dreams, in life, from yesterday, from my deepest unconscious, from years ago, from now, dislodged by these events. Maybe I've been aware of it as they've come along, but I've never quite put them this way, side by side, up and down: plastic grocery bags, drought in the city, Ethiopia, dumping in the ocean, shooting up heroin, all connected by a stream of slurpy green-gray muck, paint fumes, carpet glue, garment factory smells, Raymundo smells, something is rotten smells, thick slurpy muck, alar on apples, babies on nipples, slurp, slurp, the earth as a witness, pump the septic tank, slurp! alar on the apples, thick black muck, fumes in the office, sludge in the groundwater, slurp! spray paint in the garage, tailpipe odor of car, muck that fills the mind, slurp! muck not being cleaned up, mucky money that needs to be laundered, you fool, muck of race, muck of bad sex, slurp! m-muck, muck who make us doormats to wipe the muck from their feet, who make us toilet paper to wipe the muck from their assholes, mmmuck, muck dumped into our brains, mmmuck, muck drips into newsprinting ink, slurp! the m-muck of cruelty, and just me and Gina cleaning up the muck, and the muck flows to Janette, knee-deep in muck, and it flows to the priests who are waist-deep cleaning up the muck, and and and and it flows and it flows and it flows to to *Raymundo* who is neck-deep in muck. The muck. *Raymundo who works for the mob*. The Mint. The muck. *The muck from the Mint. The mob. The Mint. The muck.* What was the name of that contractor? I scan the many-sided images spread out before me. I never took written notes, but I have *these*. What I'd never have remembered, surely have had to check up about, lies before my eyes seeing through clear water: Stencorp. The official EPA contractor for cleaning up the muck from the Mint. But the name Stencorp is written somewhere else in my sparkling pantheon of flying data particles. I search among them, sifting for what some higher removed being, able to flip back and forth through the flight through time that is my life, would have found already.

But eventually I find it: "*Señor Pliego*, the gentlemen from Stencorp are here to see you." A voice from the intercom as I was leaving Pliego's office. And the two gentlemen out there who did not look to be gentlemen. Did one of them have the features I now know to be Raymundo's? I check my file photos, but the image is much too fleeting and the shot is blurry. Mucky. No positive ID. Because of the muck. But I have the mob and Raymundo and the muck, Raymundo and Stencorp and the muck. All I need is the third leg between Stencorp and the mob and the muck. And the muck.

The muck.

The muck.

The muck . . .

Someone is slapping my face repeatedly with watery hands. A large fighting cock is eating cornbread off my bare torso. Marco pours *trago* into his cupped hands, sets it on fire and rubs it rapidly up and down the full length of my body. He takes a bottle of pale reddish water, fills his mouth with it and spits it through his teeth onto my body. Euh! I quiver. The faces around me rejoice. They are saying it is the first sign of conscious activity I have shown in quite some time. Marco takes a red-hot poker out of a candle flame and plunges it into three piles of gunpowder, igniting them. He passes a stone that the woman has soaked in *trago* over the ensuing flames and rubs the flaming stone over my body.

He cups his hands violently around the stone and smothers the fire and the drumming stops with a *bam!*

A dirty window shatters before my eyes. I raise myself up on my elbows, brush the cornbread crumbs away.

"What time is it?" I ask.

"There are no clocks in here," says the woman.

One of the young men looks out the window at the starry sky. "Four in the morning," he says.

"Boy, I really feel like I've been through fire and water," I say. And I don't even feel hung-over.

Marco laughs a wide-mouthed, gold-toothed, deep-throated laugh and slaps me on the thigh, hard. It stings. It feels terrific. I look over by the window and notice the snake. In a cage.

"You didn't use *that* on me, did you?" I ask.

"Did you find what you were after?" he asks.

"I believe I did. You know what else I just realized?"

"What?"

"That I never called my office yesterday to tell them I wasn't coming in."

And the whole room explodes with laughter.

I flop down onto my bed when the phone rings. It's Janette. She's had a few, trying to anaesthetize herself from the pain of being commanded to attack her own people. And she's full of tears over misleading me. I tell her it's all right, but she insists on making it up to me. I tell her she can make it up to me by telling me where that damned business card is that Raymundo gave Eduardo.

"I'll just go ask Eduar—" she begins.

"*No!* Don't tell him anything! You get me?"

"Okay, Fil," she says, perplexed. We say goodbye and hang up.

It's 7:00 A.M. when that familiar heavy-handed steady buzzing at the intercom wakes me from a deep and heavy sleep. When you're as worn-out as I am, two hours' sleep can do the work of six. Which isn't much, but it'll get me through the day. That's all I'm going to need.

I let Janette in.

"Raymundo works for Stencorp," she says. She's still a bit buzzed, and she plops down heavily on the couch and demands a beer.

You'll forgive the cliché, but: bingo. But I don't know where she got it from. I'll have to act fast.

"Come on, Fil, let's get drunk together."

"We've both already done that tonight. There's no need to seal our renewed friendship with some heartfelt ritual bonding."

"I just can't believe what's happening out there," she says, getting up and getting herself a beer. "Shit's comin' at us every which way, and everyone's so afraid of being labeled soft on crime all they can think of doing is sending us into the middle of it to bust heads! High noon on 168th Street. Like a western, Fil. Like a goddamn western!" She breaks down and starts to cry on my shoulder. "I'm tryin' so hard, honey, I'm tryin' *so hard!*"

"I know you are," I say, taking the beer out of her hand and putting it where she can't reach it. "Aren't you the one who said my problem was that I have too much faith in people?" She laughs and sobs at the same time. I take her back to the couch. "But now it's time for you to get your fucking act together."

"What's that you say?"

"You heard me."

"Oh. Yeah."

"Hm-mmm."

"You got a radio?"

"Sorry. It was stolen."

"Huh? No shit. Well, I'll just hum us a tune written about three thousand years ago along the River Niger."

Janette starts to sing me an old-time Mississippi Delta blues song. I didn't know she went for that. After a while she sings herself off to sleep. I slip my arm away and let her fall back onto the headrest. The next ring at the buzzer doesn't even make her twitch.

It's *mamita* Viki bringing Antonia home. I thank her, and ask her if it's okay for Antonia to spend one more day and possibly one more night with her. It's no problem for her, but I kneel down to explain it to Antonia:

"Honey, I need to do this. Help find those bad men. Please understand. Just one more day. After tomorrow, you'll have me every day. After tomorrow."

I think she really does understand me this time, because she kisses me and says, "Bye-bye Mommy," and walks back out the door with *mamita* Viki. I wipe away the tear before it gets a chance to form.

Then it's into the shower to wake up for a busy day. I look at my face in the mirror. The scar over my temple is healing well, but the bruise is big and ugly, and I look like the loser in a head-butting contest. Hmm . . . maybe I can make this look work for me. I call in to work and leave the message that I'll be at the EPA all day, then I call the EPA to leave a message for Gina that if she's not there to meet with me at 10:00 A.M., she might as well pack her bags and move back to Sicily.

I head to the subway and go down into the damp mildewy clamor of a June rush hour. There's a Police Department public relations person's nightmare on the front page. Even though the photo caption tries to soften the blow with the expert surgical use of "unbiased" media language, "Police Subduing a Protestor," it's pretty clear that what it should say is, "Riot Cop Beating Somebody Senseless." It's a *bad* shot.

I feel my own scar. Now that I'm awake I realize how it's still quite sore and sensitive. I should have put some fresh bandages on it. After the train whooshes from 125th to 59th Street in a whirlwind of minutes, I have a sobering experience, the precise opposite of my impromptu meeting with Juan, the recovered junkie: a woman steps on the train. I haven't seen her in four to five years, since she was a young starlet getting her first big break—a small "bit" part on Broadway. Then she did a short-lived cheapie late-night TV comedy that was absolutely dreadful, but there she was on TV and there I was sitting alone in the shadows on the floor of my old apartment with nothing else to do at that hour of the lonely night but watch her.

Now look at her. She looks terrible. She looks fifteen years older, not five. Sadder, saggier and twenty to thirty pounds heavier. What happened? I decide *not* to say hello and remind her I knew her when she was young and pretty, unknown but full of hope. You don't end up looking that bad in four years without some serious substance abuse. I know. I busy myself with my paper. I've got enough to do today.

The first thing I do is stop into a pharmacy and cover my head wound with fresh gauze and Band-Aids.

Gina's still mad at me, more so for having left a perfunctory message.

"I couldn't take the risk of your ignoring me, Gina. There's no time to waste."

"No more taking the law into your hands, Filomena."

"Tell me something. You once told me the waste stream from the Mint is so bad it's got an isolated system that you contracted an outfit called Stencorp to clean up, right?"

"Yeah? So?"

"So why is the stream so bad?"

"Because it's heavy inks and solvents."

"And how much would you need to analyze the contents of that waste stream?"

"A liter is enough."

"And private firms analyze samples no matter who submits them?"

"Yeah."

"Anybody?"

"*Yes*. Filomena, would you get to the point?"

"So theoretically, isn't it possible for a mob employee working for Stencorp to siphon off a sample in his thermos or something for his bosses to analyze for the exact chemicals making up the Mint's printing ink?"

Gina finally sees what I'm driving at. Her face turns serious and she ponders this for a while. Then: "The key ingredients in the inks would *not* be listed in standard analytical charts. They're a guarded secret."

"So you find a crooked chemist. God knows there's plenty of college professors out there cooking up PCP after hours to put their kids through college."

"No, it still seems unlikely. There'd be no way to order all the chemicals, it would bring the inspectors right over. The order wouldn't even get processed."

"Hmm. This is an unforeseen snag."

"There's no other kind, Filomena."

I smile. "Friends?"

"Okay. Friends." We shake on it. Then we think. We go

for coffee, chat about the weather, the progress at the other sites. She says something about "these blacks" rioting and I say, "No, Gina," and I peel back the gauze and show her my scar. Then I sit down and stare at a blank wall for a gap of eighteen minutes. Call it a flashback from last night, but I can't get a scene from the old *Honeymooners* out of my mind. "Norton. *Norton*." Of course: the muck.

"How soon can you get your hands on some moon suits?"

"We've got some Tyvex suits in the building, but I'd have to fill out a requisition—"

"Fuck that. Sorry. If they're doing what I think they're doing, we've got to catch them at it tonight."

"Doing what?"

"You said there's no point stealing a sample for analysis, right?"

"Right."

"So what if they're diverting the whole stream to some other location? Couldn't they extract the chemicals?"

"They could! And that would explain Stencorp's exemplary cleanup record!"

"So go pull the suits—"

"No, Filomena. It's got to be by the book."

"No! If you warn them we're coming, they'll dismantle it, won't they? Won't they?"

"Yeah, yeah."

"So it's got to be tonight. Please . . ."

"Who are we going to get on such short notice?"

"Get one of those cowboys you were telling me about. You must know some of them."

A trace of red floods her face. I didn't mean it *that* way.

"What if he won't come?"

"Then he's not the right guy. And we'll need a city sewer worker," I add.

"We can get the blueprints—"

"Right. We've got no time, they're on to us, and you want to take the time to study blueprints. Just get someone who knows the sewers by the Mint."

"And what do we do?"

"Follow it to wherever it leads."

"Then what?"

"We summon help."

"Let's see, one sewer worker, one OSC, you. I can get four suits. You need anyone else?"

"Yeah, someone who knows the toxic waste business."

"Oh, no. What about your friend Barbie D in Chicago?"

"She's in Chicago. Gina, it's got to be you."

Pause.

"I don't want to preach religion to you, Gina, that's not my style, but Jesus made a point of saying it's okay to break the rules if you're doing the right thing."

She acts like she's thinking about it, but I can tell she's already hooked. She's an investigator. It's in the blood.

She says, "Meet me back here at five-thirty."

I could kiss her.

CHAPTER SIXTEEN

"Up ain't up, down ain't down
Shit don't stink and round ain't round."
— George H. Bass (1938-1990),
IN MEMORIAM

I HEAD STRAIGHT for a three-and-a-half-hour nap in a Chinese porno movie. I can't tell you what I dream. It's one of those sleeps where I wake up more tired than when I went to sleep.

I fortify myself with my first substantial meal in two days at a cheap-but-fiery Hunan restaurant and lots of strong Spanish coffee afterwards at this dirty little place that looks like a laundromat. When the city's racial mix *works*, it's incredible.

At 5:30 Gina meets me at the rear entrance to Federal Plaza, and by 5:45 we're climbing into an official government vehicle.

"Isn't this car a bit too conspicuous?" I ask.

"Official cars drive up to the processing plant all the time. Relax, it's got all the comforts of home."

I look around skeptically at the un-vacuumed interior. "Home must be a blast."

"Home doesn't have a portable water purification kit, mobile phone, and support for four protective suits."

"Does home have three jumbo bags of corn chips, too?" I ask, discovering this evidence on the floor of the back seat.

"You caught me. Yes, it's my shame. I spend all day chasing down chemical violators but when it's time for a brew I just can't wait for that first jolt of polysorbate-60 to kick in."

"Aha, so the truth can finally be told, ya junk food addict."

"Yes, but my boyfriend knows about it and he's very supportive."

"But you gotta ask yourself: is junk food alone enough to build a relationship on?"

Gina laughs.

"Oh yeah, I've heard about sex and chemical additives: they say you haven't done it 'til you've done it on Orange Dye Number Three."

Gina agrees. "You want to drive?"

"I don't have my driver's license with me."

"That's okay, the car's not registered anyway."

"What?"

"Just kidding. Slide over. With my ID, you'd have to run somebody down to get pulled over."

I like the way this woman is starting to think. She hands me the registration. Just for the heck of it, I actually look at the thing. It's the right one.

"Oh, the tyranny of the seventeen-digit vehicle ID code," I lament. "That's enough numbers to cover everyone on earth owning two million cars each."

"That's the government for you."

"Where to first?"

"To pick up our two manly men."

Gina directs me across the Brooklyn Bridge and onto some streets I don't think even the mayor knows about. My old cabbie instincts are resurfacing under pressure, and I run through a recently turned red light.

"It wasn't *very* red," Gina assures me.

"I think I'm having a corrupting influence on you."

We pick up our two passengers. The on-scene coordinator (the "cowboy") is a rusty-haired white guy named Eddie with a thick red moustache and the body build of a fireman. Our liaison with the New York City sewer system is named

Elvin, of medium height and build, kind of lanky even. Sort of a black Ed Norton. We exchange hellos.

"Gina's ruined my Thursday nights before," says Eddie, "but she never told me the reason for tonight's trouble had such pretty dark eyes."

"Down, boy," says Gina.

"Don't stifle his perkiness," I say. "It may save our lives."

"Yeah," Eddie agrees.

"Good. You can take over the driving," I say.

Gina directs Eddie onto the Brooklyn-Queens Expressway.

"We should have taken the Williamsburg Bridge," says the cabbie in me. Soon we're passing over the heavy industry along Newtown and Maspeth Creek on the Kosciuszko Bridge. The road is as pockmarked with potholes as any treacherous mountain road in Ecuador and the car visibly slows as it hits the thick yellow air of Queens County.

"Ah yes, sulphur dioxide," says Gina. "One of the top ten all-time air pollutants. Hard to believe this was once farmland."

Elvin says, "Honey, this was once *wilderness*!"

Forty minutes later I say, "We're halfway to Bayside. Where the heck is this place?"

"Halfway to Bayside," says Eddie.

"Uh-oh, I know I'm in trouble now. Trapped in a carful of jokers."

"What we have here is clearly a cooloquium," says Elvin. "That's a gathering of cool dudes to discuss a subject. Any subject."

Half an hour later we're piling out of the car in front of one of the plants where the U.S. Mint manufactures its inks. Smoke belches into the atmosphere from three towering identical smokestacks. Gina and Eddie's credentials get us in, and we suit up in a coat room.

"Mine doesn't fit me too well," I say. It's built for a six-foot football player.

"So take it back to K-Mart and exchange it," says Eddie.

Gina's suit fits even worse. Somebody hasn't figured out that women wear these things, too. I'm paranoid as hell that news of four loonies wearing protective suits is going to travel to the other side ahead of us and defeat our purpose, but Gina assures me that this sort of sight is routine around here. And she's right. None of the workers really give us a second glance as she leads us down a spindly metal staircase to the sub-basement, where all the wastes gather to fester in a temporary storage tank before being filtered down a grating into the sewer. She reaches a gloved arm into the tank and lifts it up. Golfball-sized globs of dark-greenish ink residue ooze through her fingers.

"There's your soft money for you," she says. "This wretched refuse really fouls the nest."

"Money is poisoning the environment," I say. Literally.

"Yes."

Mind-boggling. Gina leads us down what in less enlightened times they used to call a "manhole" but now call a "maintenance accessway" or something on a grungy straight up-and-down metal ladder.

"Hold tight," she says. "This gook is slippery."

She's right. My fists close around the bars, but even through the gloves I can feel how they don't really get a grip, and my feet slip and slide precariously. We descend into a musty chamber choked with foul smells and two-foot-wide sewer pipes.

"Didn't bring the masks, huh?" says Eddie.

"You want 'em? They're back in the car. We can't talk with them on," Gina explains.

"We can't talk if I'm puking, either," I say. Eddie agrees.

"Can it, you two," says Gina. "None of this is toxic." Eddie straightens up like his masculinity has been questioned, which I suppose it has.

We edge along between the one- and two-inch pipes running flat against the wall and the big one- and two-footers running down the middle of the tunnel.

"Here's the GELT," says Elvin.

"Gelt?" I ask. That's what my first partner always called money.

"Gas, Electric, and Telephone Lines," he says, pointing to the thin rubbery pipes running close to the ceiling.

"Everybody's a comedian," I say.

"That's what they're called," Elvin insists.

"Okay, okay. How much farther?"

"That's what we're here to find out," says Gina. "The branch splits off in another couple of hundred feet."

We shuttle along sideways like sand crabs.

"Know any good ghost stories?" asks Eddie.

"Filomena was a cop for five years, she must have a few good ones," says Gina.

"No kidding? A cop?"

"It's nothing," I say.

"Sure it is. I've always wanted to date a cop."

"Good for you. But it's nothing anymore. So I was a cop five years. Yesterday a guy who's been one fourteen years gave me this to remember him by," I say, showing my bandages.

They ask for details, and I give them. That shuts everyone up for a while. We get to a branching in the tunnel. Gina points to a six-inch pipe made of bright, shiny metal.

"That's the ink waste. They have to use stainless steel because some of the solvents will eventually eat through the regular pipes."

"And this stuff goes out into the bay? Terrific."

"So what do we do?" asks Elvin.

"We follow it," says Gina.

About fifty yards down the pipe Gina stops short and says, "Hold it." She kneels down close to the pipe. "God damn."

"What? What?" we all say, crowding around.

"They've cut through the metal and run a lousy PVC pipe down into the sewer. It's already dissolving."

I lean in close to see what Gina's pointing at. A flimsy tube of white plastic juts out from a poorly sealed hole in the bottom of the drainage pipe.

"I thought we were *in* the sewer," I say.

"No," say Gina and Elvin together. Elvin continues: "This tunnel was cut for the Mint. The real sewer runs under this."

"Under this? You mean it gets worse?"

"I'm afraid so," says Elvin.

"How do we get there to follow this pipe?"

"There should be a connecting shaft along here somewhere."

"Great."

Maybe two hundred yards farther along we come to a spot where thin metal slats stand up to form a cylindrical projection to prevent people from falling through the hole. And down the stepladder we go.

"Oh God! It smells like ten thousand farts down here!" says Eddie.

"More like a million," says Elvin.

"There's no sign of the pipe," says Gina.

"Then it must have gone the other way," says Elvin.

So now we have to retrace the last two hundred yards, knee-deep in Brooklyn's sewer water.

"Shoulda brought a boat," says Eddie.

"There it is, I've picked it up again," says Gina.

"Well maybe you should get a shot of penicillin for it," says Eddie.

"I mean the pipe," says Gina needlessly.

We start following this hitherto undiscovered pipe through the, the—well, when they came up with the term "bowels of the earth," this is what they had in mind. "Large intestine" would be more like it. PYEEWW!!

"So come on, Miss Filomena, entertain us with one of your cop stories," says Eddie.

"Okay, okay," I say, still not quite used to sloughing through thigh-deep waste. "It's rising."

"It sure is," laughs Eddie.

"Just try to keep it bottled up," cautions Gina.

I think. "This was back when cops only spent fifty percent of radio patrol time responding to 911 calls. Now it's ninety-five percent. Anyway, it's a little-known fact that most of our imported pineapples and pineapple juice come from Thailand, even though it's marketed here under a prestigious logo that would rather have you not know their sweet-tasting products come from a country where the per capita income averages around sixty-five dollars a year."

"What's this got to do with anything?" says Eddie.

"Well, back in the days before every logo had a lawyer, there was this grocery store owner, sort of an idiot savant. Well, more idiot than savant. He gets it into his head that these Thai pineapples are some super-special exotic fruit. So he prices them to match, starting at ten dollars each."

"Ten dollars?" says Elvin.

"For the small ones," I say. "Twelve to fifteen dollars for the big ones. Okay, so me and my partner—my *real* partner— are driving along in the patrol car when we get this radio call, Felony in Progress. 'Sacred shit!' he says, and we flip on the sirens."

"I can see he taught you a lot about descriptive linguistics," says Gina.

"What was his name?" asks Eddie.

"Artie Liebermann." Good old Artie. And here I am looking at Elvin and thinking about Ed Norton again. "So we get to the store, and the owner is screaming, 'He stole a pineapple!' So much for our quick response, but technically it's a felony—to him it's a capital offense. 'Could you describe him?' 'No.' 'Then how will we recognize him?' I ask. 'Easy,' says my partner. 'He'll be the one with the pineapple.' So this idiot climbs into the car with us like we've got nothing better to do but drive around the streets scouting for a guy who stole a lousy pineapple when really we should be busting the store owner for price gouging. But like I said, the guy has a screw loose in a big way. Finally we spot the perp; he's a six-foot-two-inch black man with a close-cropped Afro—tinted red— and we've got to jump out of the car and arrest him. We've got no choice. The store owner wants the guy publicly executed. So we take them both over to the station and arrange for a line-up. 'Line-up?' says the store owner. 'But I just identified him.' He figures how many six-foot-two-inch black guys can there be with reddish hair? But he's starting to get on our nerves, and he doesn't know how the two cops on whose nerves he's getting can screw with his head."

"'On whose nerves he's getting'?" says Eddie. "Who'd you learn English from?"

"New Yorkers."

"Figures."

"So we get six of the shortest and whitest white guys we can find and put them in the line-up with the six-foot-two-inch black guy, who's rolling his eyes like, 'Oh, Jesus.'"

My audience is getting pretty amused.

"So the store owner points to the suspect and says 'Him.' And we go 'Who?' and he goes '*Him*' and we go 'Are you sure? Take your time,' and he goes 'He's the only black guy up there!' and right away Officer Newton, who's this six-foot-two-inch black man whose hair we've sprayed with theatrical glitter left over from a Halloween party so it looks red, leans in and says to the guy, 'You ain't picking him out just 'cause he's a six-foot-two-inch black dude with red hair, now, are you?' You should have seen this guy's face: turned beet red *and* went pale at the same time."

My companions all laugh heartily.

"Unfortunately, cops fix line-ups for real all the time," I say.

"That's true," says Elvin.

"You hear that?" I say. "Nowadays the truth is so rare, when people hear it they have to say, 'That's true.'"

"*That's true*," the two guys say in unison. And everybody laughs some more. Maybe it's the fumes. We've been following the pipe for what I calculate to be a half a mile, with no end in sight. And I've got to pee. Must be all that coffee I had before. Oh, no. How much longer? I hold it in for another three-tenths of a mile 'til I can't stand it anymore.

I ask Gina, "How do you pee in these suits?"

"With considerable difficulty," she says. "You've got to pull the whole thing down."

"Yeah, baby," says Eddie. "That's the *last* place you want there to be any openings!"

"The question is not how, but where?"

"We're in the sewer, baby," Elvin reminds me. Like anyone's going to notice.

I hadn't considered this. However, I'm going to need some help. When I absolutely convince them all that I'm going to succumb to an unpleasant accident if I don't relieve myself immediately, the two men consent to keep their backs turned, and Gina agrees to support me by linking her arms together under mine and across my chest so I can lower my protective clothing and squat as close as I dare to the swirling ordure. The procedure is carried out with as much care as two astronauts executing repairs on the outer hull of their spaceship.

"You notice how men are always waitin' for women to go to the bathroom?" says Elvin.

"Yeah, right?" Eddie agrees.

"It's like the first thing they do at a wedding is make the man wait for the woman for about twenty minutes. Like, That's right, you better get used to it now, sucker! You goin' to be doing a lot of waitin' for her!" They both chuckle.

"Man, it's easy for you *guys* to pee," I complain.

"That's right," says Eddie. And they high five each other! I don't believe I'm doing this.

After a few tension-filled moments, I am very much relieved.

"Boy, this is a first," says Eddie.

"For me too," I put in.

Another half mile of wading through this river of shit and our journey nears its end. The pipe disappears up through a hole in the roof of the tunnel.

"Looks like this is it," says Gina. She lowers her flashlight and reads the address of the spot we're standing under off her map. "Start looking for a shaftway."

"Can't we go up to the street already?" I ask.

"No. We've got to establish an unbroken chain of proof."

"Sounds familiar." Too damn familiar.

Ten more minutes of breathing this mustard gas and Elvin locates the shaftway. We climb up one flight and come to a locked door. But the locks date from Prohibition and don't present too much trouble. How many thieves do they expect to come up through here? A well-placed crowbar and we're in the sub-basement of *El Tiempo*, Guzmán's newspaper. The hammering of printing presses shakes the ceiling. Even the floor is vibrating. Nobody's around.

"Printing presses. So that's how they disguised it," I say.

But Gina is following the trail of the pipeline to its final destination: A permanent holding tank. This is no accident.

"So the bastards are counterfeiting," says Gina.

"Counterfeiting," I say. "That's some *real* soft money."

Gina takes out a liter-sized sample container and dips it into the tank. Suddenly we are surrounded by the echoes of loud whistles, and two security guards with their guns drawn start running at us—guns?—shouting things like "*¡No se muevan!*" and "*¿Qué estan haciendo aquí?*" One of them runs right at me. Elvin gets his suddenly big body in front of me and blocks the guy's weapon.

"Get *back*, Jackson," Elvin warns. My feminist friends may argue, but right now I'm not complaining.

Gina and Eddie flash their credentials, and Gina finishes taking the sample.

"*¿Si pueden hacer eso?*" asks one guard.

"What's he saying?" asks Gina.

"He wants to know if we can do this."

"Hey, we're the government," replies Gina. "We can do anything."

I find out the two guards are undocumented immigrants who aren't supposed to be working here, much less carrying guns, so we get them to promise their silence in exchange for ours. Gina says she can get me the results in a few days.

"There are many wonders in this city," she says, as we slip out of our muck-drenched moon suits and call for a car to take us back to the Mint.

Eddie says, "Yeah, the first wonder I check out is going to have a license to sell beer on tap."

CHAPTER SEVENTEEN

"You'll never get the big shots."
— Thomas E. Dewey to racketbusting judge Homer Ferguson

HOLLYWOOD likes to depict top gangsters as suave, calculating, likeable, brutal, reckless, cowardly, dangerous—*extremely* dangerous—but almost always very smart. They aren't so smart. They get what they want with muscle and machinery, not brains. How smart do you have to be when you're holding a submachine gun? But like a lot of businessmen, cool-headedness and obedience is usually the name of their game, with the same self-preservationist concern for making sure that nobody's rocking the boat.

I quit the EAF so I can look for some *other* bullshit job, and spend a few days getting to know my daughter again. At least that operation is a success. While I'm waiting out the weekend, the police drop the charges against my twin sister in Queens, arrest the officer in the shooting death that began the riot, and the two dirtbags who killed Officer Salerno get twenty-five years to life. Janette "celebrates" the sentencing with a bathtubful of gin. I ask her very tactfully if she has ever considered seeing somebody about whether or not she may be the type that has a tendency to develop a drinking problem. She tells me she's got it under control. I wish I were that sure.

Trouble breaks out between the entrenched Chinese

gangs and a newcomer Vietnamese gang hacking out a piece of territory in Chinatown. Jesus. Oh, and the State Attorney General's office and the Better Business Bureau open an investigation into a certain environmental organization that apparently produced a glitzy charity fundraiser from which only nine percent of the proceeds actually went to their programs, in violation of the law. (Wonder how they got *that* info.)

Monday morning I get the call I've been waiting for. Gina's got a package for me. I drop Antonia one last time with *mamita* Viki and head downtown. By 1:30 P.M. I'm staging an unrehearsed meeting with Alejandro Pliego that goes nowhere. The guy is not bright enough to grasp what I'm saying.

"Forget it," I say. "Let me talk to your boss."

"What do you mean, my boss?"

"I mean Guzmán."

"Señor Guzmán is not my boss."

"Sure he is. I've got something big for him."

"How big?"

"Is counterfeiting big enough?"

Half an hour later I'm being ushered into Guzmán's inner office, which I have promised not to describe.

Guzmán doesn't mess around, gets right to the matter at issue. All of this is in Spanish.

"Why are you here?" he asks, glaring at Pliego for having brought me in.

I do my Gina Lucchese imitation, which of course they don't appreciate, opening the contents of her U.S. Government-issue briefcase and placing the documents one by one neatly alongside each other facing Guzmán so he can read them as I speak.

"The original copies of each of these documents with cover letters describing our conclusions are in ten post-dated registered letters. If something happens to me and we don't agree to a deal, starting tomorrow A.M., one letter per day goes to the assistant district attorney."

This is no bluff. It's all there. Inks, printing presses, the works. A very serious crime linked directly to one of Guzmán's major holdings. His best front, too.

"It'll never get to trial," he says.

"Trials are like street theater—no one ever sticks to the script. No, I like this way better."

"And just what are the terms of this deal?"

"You guys know who shot Lázaro Pérez. I want them."

"We have nothing to do with street punks like that."

"Yeah, I bet. But you know who they are. If anyone can find them, you can."

"I see. Are there any other terms to this deal?"

"Yeah: Get that witch Lucy Ferrer off my back, and keep her zombies south of 204th Street."

"And all you want in return for your, uh, cooperation on this little matter of the printing ink is the names of the two drifters who shot Pérez?"

"Not their names, Guzmán. I want *them*."

"How soon?"

"What time's the first mail tomorrow?"

"No double crosses afterwards? I understand there are original copies—"

"That would be very unhealthy for me, wouldn't it, Señor Guzmán? No, I'm looking forward to a longer life than that."

Guzmán nods. "A wise choice. All right. You've got your deal." We shake on it. What, no cigar? "You understand I'm just a simple businessman, trying to provide for my kids so they won't have to struggle the way I did."

"Yeah. And Meyer Lansky sent his kid to West Point. Good day, gentlemen. Nice doing business with you."

On my way out, Pliego stops me and says, "Now that this is all over, maybe you have time now to go out to dinner with me."

I tell him, "I don't date strikebreakers."

"Huh?"

"Two years ago I was a cabbie . . ."

It still doesn't quite sink in. So Guzmán takes a shot at

it. "I think what the lady is trying to say is that in spite of our reconciliation on these minor business matters, she's still an 'us,' and we're still a 'them.'"

Well put for a mobster. Now I have to donate that awful purple dress to charity.

It only takes them three hours.

The shifts are just changing when I march two hunched-over, weasel-eyed crackheads, broken in spirit and gaunt-lipped, who know they won't be seeing daylight for a long, long time, past my open-mouthed former co-workers of the 34th Precinct house and deliver my friend's killers to Police Officer Janette Ivins for booking. Statements, confessions, all go on Janette's record. I don't care for it. As long as the boys in the squadroom know who came through for them.

When it's all over, Janette offers, "Buy you a drink?"

"Sure, but I pick: I know a place that makes a great *batido de fruta.*"

I give Marco back his talisman, with my thanks and his blessing. He tells me Lázaro's soul is now at peace.

Antonia loves having me around. She's getting spoiled from it already.

Flormaría has her baby. A wonderful, healthy, happy seven-pound girl. They name her Lazarina Filomena Ortega Pérez. Shucks.

And Gina's still going after Morse, even if it takes twenty years. The government will still be here.

I think.

"Under the Big Black Sun" first appeared in *And the Dying Is Easy*, edited by Joe Pittman & Annette Riffle (Signet, 2001). It's the story of what should have happened following the toxic leak Union Carbide unleashed in 1984 on Bhopal, India, killing more than two thousand people immediately (with estimates as high as eight thousand within one week of the leak), because at the time I wrote the story, not one high level official at the company had been brought to justice for cutting corners on safety, a major factor in causing the disaster. The title comes from an album by X, one of my favorite punk bands of the era.

UNDER THE BIG BLACK SUN

THE FIRST few days out of detox are always the roughest. But if you can get through them, you're on your way to being all right, and creeping along the well-traveled road from ruin to recovery. At least that's what I told the guy who wandered up from the shoreline and began what seemed like a nice enough conversation, until he found out we were from New York.

"New Yorkers are very intelligent," he says, scratching at the sandy stubble around his chin.

"Well, they have to be—" I begin, trying to be polite.

"Even the way they drink water out of the bottle," he says, pointing at the row tourists posing on the hotel deck fifty yards down the beach from us. "It's a certain angle. Not a wasted movement."

Oh. Why don't the Miami Beach police just issue every visitor a deranged-psycho-is-talking-to-me locator you can activate every time this happens? Then you can sit there smiling and nodding your head, secure in the knowledge that men with tasers and butterfly nets will be turning up in less than three minutes.

He says his name is Trane, and I give him a couple

of quarters so he can "call his doctor," then Antonia and I shake the sand out of our threadbare beach blanket and start walking up the sandy slope towards Ocean Drive.

What is it about South Florida? This place is like the filter in the bottom of a drain, collecting all the gunk that comes sluicing down the coast, having run out of other places to befoul.

There's a dip in the dunes, and my daughter is the first one over the top and down into the trough, where a little boy is happily digging with a green plastic shovel. He's all alone. Antonia plants her knees in the sand in front of him to say hi, and the boy looks up. He's got dark brown skin and wild, wavy hair, big rolling eyes, a runny nose, and the bulbous forehead characteristic of some kind of birth defect. Then he waves hello. The arm not holding the shovel is stunted, three fingers where the elbow should be. Something tells me he's not supposed to be out here alone.

I ask him his mother's name, and get a bunch of meaning-less syllables: "Cooo-cooo-cooo, giggleegeee, giggleegeeee."

Antonia's very mature for a pre-teen. She doesn't recoil, or make a face. She starts helping him dig, while I climb up the rim of the sand pit, shielding my eyes from the sun and start searching the horizon for a missing parent.

I must have left my scanners on the default setting of "female," because I pass by a male figure three times before realizing that he's probably the one. Tall and elegant, he is walking away from the hotel deck turning his sharpened gaze to the east and west, an agile urgency conveyed by his avian movements. You don't need a Ph.D. in body language to know that the man is frantically looking for someone, and he has the same deep-brown skin color and dark wavy hair as the boy. Antonia's watching the kid, so I pad along the dunes towards Mr. Missing, who looks quite cool in a pair of loose white shorts and a light blue polo shirt without a stain on them. I'd be sweating through burlap if I lost sight of Antonia.

"Are you looking for a little boy?" I ask, beads of moisture forming on my upper lip.

"Yes! You have seen him?"

"He's right over there—"

"Thank God," he says, setting off in the direction of my outstretched arm. I try to keep up with him, but in flip-flops on hot sand, I might as well be wading through Jell-O.

"How'd you lose sight of him?" I'm talking to his back.

"Pande! Pande!" His shadow skims over the crest of the sand pit and drops off my radar screen and out of sight.

I come upon the man resting on his heels in the sand with one arm around his son, speaking in a language whose words I do not know but whose pitches are unmistakable as the soothing, universal tones of parental nurturing, interspersed with the sharp, strict tones of a thousand years of parental warning, while Antonia looks on, invisible from four feet away.

"Is that where you're staying?" I ask, pointing at the huge glass slab of the Redmont, the luxury hotel from which he appears to have emerged.

"No." I'm clearly an intrusion in his life, but after staring at me he adds a phrase out of courtesy. "We are in a cheaper place."

"Us, too. We get a week in a prefab on Fifth Street—with cement stairs that somebody painted green—for the price of a bed and room service for one night in that place. But hey, you don't come to Miami Beach to stay in your room, right?"

"No, you don't," he agrees.

"Look at them," I say, watching the wealthy sun-worshippers starting to clear a trail into the cocktail hour with ice tongs and mosquito torches. Some of them are excavating with the precision of paleontologists, others are bushwhacking with the bravado of drunken Ostrogoths. One guy seems bent on clear-cutting his way through with a bulldozer and a log chain. He's a fifty-five-year-old frat boy, well tanned, chest hairs going gray, upper body muscular but sagging, and he's pinching plenty of bikini bottoms and snapping towels at the Speedo-rumps that go with them if they happen to raise a fuss.

Pande grabs my attention by repeatedly smacking his shovel against the sand as if he were swatting at a sudden plague of flies, and loudly trilling with his tongue.

I'm not going to ask: What does he have? So I ask, "So where are you staying?"

"We are just around the corner."

You're more than around the corner if you're in a cheap place, buddy, I think to myself. Antonia and I have a five-block walk to our plebian accommodations.

"Are you from India?" Antonia blurts out.

"Yes."

"Where in India?"

"You wouldn't know it."

"Where?" she insists.

"So many questions from a little girl," he says, but I guess he feels that he owes us an answer. "We are from Vidisha."

"Where's that?"

"It is near the Betwa River," he replies, an answer that would normally prompt a deluge of follow-up questions, but this time it strangely satisfies Antonia's inquisitiveness.

Not mine, however.

"Where's his mother?" I ask politely, glancing around as if I expect to be introduced to her.

He's too educated and polite to tell me to do him a favor and drop dead, but I can see a quiet, smoldering pain darkening his features.

"My Unnati died of complications three months after giving birth to Pande."

"Oh. I'm so sorry." The Third World syndrome. "I didn't mean to pry—"

"Of course you did." It's just a flat statement. No anger. "But I also chose to answer you. I thank you for watching over my Pande, but now I think it's time to head back to our rooms."

He straightens up, and I have to tilt my head up to meet his gaze and study his angular Aryan features. He could pass for Robert Redford dipped in cocoa.

Now there's a thought.

And he's another single parent . . .

We're headed in the same direction, skirting the sandy walkway between the palm trees and the benches filled with the last of the left-wing Jewish workers who fought for the unionization of the garment industry sixty years ago so they could retire here and complain about the weather in Yiddish.

"*Ot geyt an andere kubanitse,*" says one of them, as I walk past.

I want to turn to him and say I'm not Cuban, I'm an Ecuadorian-American living New York City, where I also happened to pick up a little of the *mameloshn*, but I don't want to spend time chatting up a former Stalinist hardliner—as inviting as that is—and lose sight of my new friend, Mr.—

"Hey, I don't even know your name," I say, skipping to catch up with him.

He doesn't break his stride, or even slow down, but keeps going as if trying to shake off a clinging odor in the air. I pull up even with him and introduce myself.

"I'm Filomena. This is my daughter, Antonia. I already met your son, Pande."

He's too well bred to ignore this.

"My name is Vishal. Now please let me take him home."

"All right, but our children were playing very nicely together."

He stops.

"I'm sorry," he says. "I am being rude after you were kind enough to help me. I'm just upset about Pande wandering off and—well—"

"And making you look like a bad parent." I finish his sentence for him.

"Well, yes," he admits.

"That's nothing," Antonia starts to say, but I stop her before she can tell him about the time she watched me burn a hit man's face with a red-hot piece of iron or the time I nearly knifed a government thug who was chasing us through a tropical swamp, or any of the other inappropriate things she has witnessed as part of my demented life as a crime fighter.

I noticed that the Redmont Hotel has a public bar over-looking the water.

Zero hour.

"Would you like to have a drink with us?" I ask.

He follows my gaze towards the hotel, his lips tighten-ing nervously as if he were weighing his chances of being thrown out of the place for having the wrong pedigree. We don't have a caste system here, exactly, but we still have our lords and serfs.

And I still don't know which one is the dessert spoon.

"How about a plain tonic water?" he asks.

"That's fine with me."

They stick us near the maintenance shed, but the ocean view is broad and inviting. Pande behaves very well, sitting quietly the whole time, gently rocking his head back and forth and sucking on the last of his soda with a straw. I wish I could say the same for the Class of '65 Spring Breaker, who's graduated to slapping babes full-handed on the butt, a move I haven't seen a guy get away with in twenty years—but then, I've been dutifully yoked to parenthood for a dozen years myself.

The junior execs seem to sense this alien presence, this motherly office, and throw themselves in deeper, partying while they still can before one of the party girls snags them and they end up chained to a weekly paycheck and a thirty-year mortgage.

I'm just beginning to get lulled by the sound of the waves concussing against the wooden pylons beneath the deck, when the big man crosses over the line and ends up in a T-shirt grabbing scuffle with one of the junior silverbacks. I start to rise out of my seat but Vishal puts his hand across my forearms and cautions me against getting involved.

"You better watch who you mess with!" threatens the young male animal.

"I don't see your name on her," says the dominant male.

Nobody's asking *her* opinion.

The bartender and the pool man dash in and pull the

two men apart, the hotel steward appears, pleading, "Mr. Johnson, Mr. Clancy, please, don't let this get out of hand, this is a friendly place, there are children present."

Mr. Johnson looks up and apparently registers us for the first time, smiles and says, "Sure thing, José. I wasn't going to start anything. It's the kid's problem, anyway, trying to keep his girl."

Mr. Clancy—"the kid"—performs the ritual of struggling to break free so he can slug Mr. Johnson squarely on the jaw, but with two burly men holding him back, he soon has the excuse of cooling off and smoothing out the bunched-up marks made by several fists on his Ralph Lauren shirt.

Mr. Johnson directs the bartender to serve him: "Get me a whiskey sour, Charlo—with plenty of ice this time." And he comes right over and sits down with us as if he were part of the family.

"How you folks doing today?"

"Why, you planning on reading us the specials?" I ask.

"Huh?" he snorts.

"What's your name, anyway?"

"Johnson."

"I heard the Johnson part."

He smiles. "Wally. Wally Johnson." The letters W and J are sewn together on his shirt and shorts. He holds out a big, meaty hand for me to shake, gets a few of my fingers and crushes them, as if that's supposed to impress me.

I tell him my name, then he pulls the same act on Vishal, who meets the man's cast iron grip with surprising stoicism, and says, stiffly, "Vishal. Vishal Chanderdatt," enunciating each syllable clearly as if he expects to have to repeat it several times.

But the guy just turns to me and says, "What are you drinking there?"

"Just club soda with a twist," I explain.

The waiter puts Johnson's drink on the table in front of him and starts to leave. Johnson grabs the waiter's arm and says, "And a Coke chaser—in the bottle."

"Yes, sir."

"So what do you do when you're not fondling women's asses?" I ask.

Johnson laughs as he takes a big gulp from his drink and answers so quickly a fine spray of whiskey sour spatters my shoulder. "I'm a beach bum," he says. "My company went belly-up and I jumped aboard a dot.com—but they're getting ready to toss all the dead fish like me overboard any day now, so I figure I'd better get in shape for my retirement, huh?" and his jaw cracks open in a wide-mouthed lion-hunter's laugh.

"So what do you do?" he asks.

Vishal answers that he is a technician for a local television station. The waiter serves Johnson his bottle of Coke, and I'm thinking, "beach bum" my ass. This is a guy who's used to ordering people around. He's probably just down here getting away from his wife and spoiled-rotten teenage children. I bet he told them he's on a business trip. Probably took off his wedding ring, too. I check for a light band of skin on the fourth finger of his left hand and—yes, indeed—there it is.

He's leaning a little closer to me, his leg hairs are tickling me like a swarm of fever-bearing mosquitoes, and he's suggesting that some kind of get-together should occur later on when the moon is out and the kids are in bed, when Trane, the beggar who bugged me on the beach earlier, looms over us, having miraculously evaded the hotel staff, and asks for a dollar.

"You want something?" says Johnson. "I got something for you."

Trane thrusts out his hand because the security staff have spotted him and he's only got about three seconds left to clinch the deal, but before I know it Johnson is giving the Coke bottle a vigorous shake and popping his thumb off the top as if we're in a junior high school cafeteria and spraying Trane with dark bubbly sheets of sticky brown liquid.

"Har-har," bellows Johnson, while Vishal cringes with embarrassment.

I tell Johnson that I'll probably be seeing him later, and

the two of us get to our feet while the security staff close around Trane and hustle him out of there like a dope dealer at a Catholic school pep rally.

•

A few hours later, the kid's in bed, and I close the flimsy self-locking door on our sparsely furnished by-the-week vacation apartment, relishing a moment of solitude and what passes for freedom these days—a quiet walk under the stars with the damp, gritty sand crunching between my toes and grating pleasantly against the soles of my feet, which have been thickened from pounding the hard pavement of city streets for far too long.

I walk north along the shore until the tension and anxieties start to ease, until my mind stops contracting around all those what-I-should-have-told-this-or-that-client scenarios I thought I left behind and opens up to the vastness of the warm breeze coming across the water. I guess you can carbon-date me by the fact that I still remember the latter-day *Jackie Gleason Show*, which always began with an aerial shot of this beach, and ended with the burlesque house-trained comic's bellow, "The Miami Beach audience is the greatest audience in the world!"

Somewhere between sea and sky I turn about and head back, steering towards my little spot of four-walled solidity and the ever-fixed star of parenthood and all its attendant responsibilities.

But I linger for a moment, anchoring myself at the water's edge and marveling at the wide and unknowable expanse of ocean, its vast blackness seeming all the blacker in contrast to the pinpoints of white light reflected upon its dappled surface, clusters of twinkling white globules suddenly tinged with red and orange and red.

I turn and see an EMS crew scrambling over the deck chairs at the Redmont Hotel, their chaos muffled at this distance by the forceful wind spiriting over the face of the deep.

I'm on my feet, the brightly tinted scene floating closer

to me over the dark and featureless void of sand. And into the melee:

"—no response!"

"—dilation?"

"—no pulse at all—"

"Ma'am, could you stand back, please?"

"Everybody off the deck!"

"Ma'am, could you keep back?"

"Everybody off the deck! Now!"

A hard fist closes around my arm as the Miami Beach police remind me that no matter what my other creditable accomplishments may be, I'm still just a greasy *latina* standing in the way of some big white men. I pick up some splinters as I'm dragged against the dried wooden railing.

"Come on, move it!"

"Everybody inside!"

"—move it, move it, move it!"

"—freakin' ghouls."

The bunch of us are shoved inside the main tavern and the glass doors are slid shut, leaving us to gawk like fish in a tank at the ghastly underwater ballet unrolling before our bulging eyes. A crew of four EMS workers come gurgling out of the maintenance shed, angling a stretcher between them that harbors a semi-human object swathed in plastic wrap and tubes. Tight hands press down a light-green oxygen mask over most of the face, but the hair and coloring look like my old schoolmate, Mr. Wally Johnson.

"What happened?"

"I don't know."

"The guy who cleans the pool found him."

"In the shed?"

"He hit his head or something?"

"I don't know."

"Must've passed out—"

"—had three or four martinis—"

"—more like five or six—"

The flurry of excitement and speculation goes on for a

few minutes, until the sightseers get bored with watching a few yellow ribbons of accident scene tape fluttering around the empty deck and begin to cluster around the bar on the opposite side of the room. I notice the junior exec from this afternoon stretching his elbows out like he's ready to call it a night. He's heading for the door when an unfriendly-looking cop comes in and announces that the victim, who has been identified as Mr. Wally Johnson, has been pronounced dead, and that henceforth, "nobody goes in or out until we talk to them."

Oh, God. This'll take about five hours, with this crowd.

"Oh, that's terrible—"

"Poor *Señor* Johnson—"

"Was it an accident?" asks a concerned middle manager.

"How did it happen?" asks another.

"Did I ask you to say anything?" answers the cop, leaving out the epithet that would normally follow as surely as spring follows winter. I guess he's got to keep it in check when he's dealing with the tourist trade, because he manages to be both rude and crude while keeping the actual obscenities to a minimum, a finesse some New York cops could take a lesson from.

The cop snags the junior exec, since he was the one trying to leave just as they came in. The guy squirms a bit in his chair when it comes out that he was involved in an altercation with the deceased earlier in the day, but it only takes about ten minutes to clear him after nearly twenty witnesses place him in the bar from 7:00 P.M. on.

"Don't go anywhere," they instruct him.

I'm still picking splinters out of my elbow when they call my name.

"Are you just trying to find accident witnesses, or you treating this as a suspicious death?" I ask.

The guy looks at me like he's going to toss me into the hold of the next banana boat back to South America for that one, but he manages to say, "Damn right we are."

"Then why the hell is a precinct cop conducting a murder

investigation?" I say, drawing attention to the insignias on his shirt.

"Buh, this is just a preliminary," he blusters, and is saved from further exposure by the timely arrival of two *real* detectives, who tramp in like their heavy footfalls are the only things keeping the building from floating away. They dispatch a forensics team to the pool shed with cameras, tape measures, air quality monitors, evidence bags, you name it.

Suddenly I think about my kid. I've been here so long, I hope she doesn't wake up and panic when she sees I'm not there. On the other hand, she's used to my disruptive schedule. Just a little while longer.

Naturally the detectives try to keep it from us, but from what I can make out of their movements around the shed and the partial phrases that drift over to me, I can piece together that Johnson's blood-alcohol level was high enough to cause him to pass out—although why he should choose to do it in the pool shed is a bit of a mystery—and that someone disconnected the pool's heating vent, which caused the shed to fill up with lethal amounts of carbon monoxide gas in about three minutes, which is what actually killed him.

They find all kinds of stuff in the shed indicating that someone was living in there, and shortly thereafter they discover Trane cowering under the boardwalk and arrest him on suspicion of murder.

"I was only stayin' there a couple days, man," Trane protests.

"That's the least of your freaking problems, dirt bag. Let's go," one of the cops says.

The detectives come back inside and tell us we're free to go, so naturally I go right up to them and say, "The suspect was living in the maintenance shed?"

"Yes, ma'am," says Detective Thomas, whose name I have picked up through my hypersensitive eavesdropping skills.

"Why kill a man and leave him in your crib?" I ask.

"He's not rational," explains Detective Clarke, as if that covers everything.

Thomas's turn: "Plus we have witnesses who say that earlier today the deceased sprayed him with soda in an attempt to humiliate and degrade him," he says, already translating it into police report language.

"I think he's been treated worse than that over the years," I suggest.

"Yeah," says Clarke, "that's why he'll get five years checking out the nurses' asses in some treatment center instead of fifteen getting reamed in Starke. It'll be good for him."

"Maybe the best thing that ever happened to him," says Thomas, and they both get a good laugh out of that.

So that's it, huh? They've got a body they can shove in front of a judge, and their work is done? Even if it doesn't make too much sense?

I corner the junior exec, who's ordering a drink out of relief.

"Boy, they sure had me sweating, and I don't even have so much as a speeding ticket hanging over me," I say jovially, sighing as if a hugely stressful moment has finally come to an end.

"That's how they work it," he says, matter-of-factly.

"Yeah, I saw them putting the screws to you."

His smile curls up and dries like a time-lapse photo of a withering flower.

"I guess it was on account of what happened between you and Johnson this afternoon over what's-her-name—"

"Tricia can take care of herself," he says, sharply. "She could've broken the guy's arm if she wanted to. She was just being *polite*." He makes the word sound like a crippling Kung Fu move.

"The name's Filomena," I say.

"Chris," he says, not divulging more than he has to. Then, in a shift, he adds his last name as if it were a gentlemanly duty akin to laying his velvet cloak over a mud puddle for me, "Chris Clancy."

That old Southern charm.

We chat for a while, biding my time until he gets

moderately greased, then I let it slip what a dirty old pig Johnson was, and Clancy lets the whole world know that, sure, Johnson was a pig, "But I wouldn't-a gassed him, I'd-a strangled him."

He only met Johnson two days ago, and he already wants him dead. Hmmm.

That gets my wheels turning. The method was gas. The opportunity was that Johnson was a boorish lout and falling-down drunk. What's left? Motive. I think I'll try to find out a bit more about Mr. Wally Johnson, businessman, who was spending a little time down in Florida trying to get away from—what?

I excuse myself from the gaiety of the tavern and head for the comparatively grim and chilly reception desk, where a lonely male in his twenties is watching the minutes tick away, slogging his way through another endless graveyard shift.

"Excuse me," I ask, cocking my head to read his ID tag, which says his name is Roy. "Do you have an Internet terminal I can use?"

Roy says, "Are you a guest at this hotel?"

"Of course I am."

"Room number?"

"Oh, I don't know which number, Chrissy has the key." I get just the blank stare I wanted. "Mr. Chris Clancy?"

Roy punches up Clancy's name on the screen. "Ms. Tricia Lynn?"

"That's me!"

Ask a stupid question…

"There's a computer with Internet access in the conference room, but you need the password to log on."

"So give me the password."

"I can't. It's against our policy."

Then why'd you make me go through the process of identifying myself, you jerk?

I mean: "Then why don't you log on for me? I promise I won't peek at your precious little password."

"I can't leave the front desk unattended."

"Why not? I can watch the desk for two minutes. Nothing's going to happen, I'll be fine."

"I'm sorry, I can't allow that."

"Listen, Roy, you want a wrongful arrest to be blamed on one hotel clerk's irresponsibility? You want the real murderer to get away? How would Mr. Redmont feel about that?"

"Gosh, I—I thought—"

"You thought I just wanted to do some after-midnight shopping for lingerie on the Internet. Now go hook me up."

"Yes, ma'am."

Gee, maybe I should've started out that way.

I finally sit down in front of the terminal and send Roy on his way with a scooting motion of my hand, itching to type in my subject's statistics. First I enter the hotel registry and call up Wally Johnson, Room 1165, and see that he paid with cash, not credit card, and gave his home address as 146 Evergreen Terrace, Springfield, MA., and I'm not laying any money on finding a W. Johnson listed there, folks.

I close the registry and enter a standard ID search and—surprise, surprise—can't get a match for that name and address. I try Wally Johnson, all states, date-of-birth "before 1950," and get several hundred possibilities. Nuts. I've got to narrow the search fields, but to what? What else do I know about him? I exit the standard search and link to a high-security private investigator's site that charges by the minute (maybe I can find a way to bill this to *somebody*), type in the passwords and my account number and call for a search of Wally Johnson, same as above, business executive, married, height and weight estimates, eye color, and other descriptors, and then request the option for field matches for a history of alcohol usage and possible disorderly conduct. Unfortunately there are no subject headings for a chauvinist pig with colonialist tendencies (since he seemed to have no trouble remembering the first names of all the hotel staff).

You know how many business executives named Johnson there are, in their fifties, with drinking problems?

But no match for Wally. I try Walter and Wallace, getting

a couple of hundred matches, but only a few dozen who recently retired or were downsized, and most of them are too old to be my guy. There are a few possibles that I print out and set aside, but there always seems to be something that eliminates each potential subject from my list of possibles. You know: Walter Johnson, 56, of Columbia, MO, recently retired as VP of Marketing at Cyclodyne Corp., so he could spend more time with his grandchildren and work in the nearby soup kitchen at St. Phillip's Episcopal Church every Sunday. Doesn't sound like my guy, right?

Still nothing, and the meter's clicking away.

I've got no reason to believe that Johnson is his real name, either. He gave a fake address, and paid in cash, so what's to keep him from giving a fake name, too? But he didn't seem like the kind of guy who'd put a lot of thought into some diabolical, double-edged pseudonym. He'd probably just turn his name around so he could keep using all those monogrammed shirts.

I try "John Walters" and get more of the same useless garbage. Then I punch in "John Wallace." Score.

There are enough sources on him for me to get off the expensive pay-per-view site and link to a standard who's who.

John Wallace, former Chairman of Amalgamated Compounds, which recently changed its name to AmalCom to erase the association with the old name (so I guess he was only half-lying when he said he worked for a dot.com), has been the subject of a police search for several months now, ever since the legal authorities repeatedly failed to locate him at his last known address in Delaware. After all, you can't serve a summons to an empty house.

AmalCom claims to know nothing of his whereabouts, and furthermore dismisses the summons as warrantless, since "all claims were settled" in the case of—CONTINUED ON NEXT PAGE.

Click.

UNABLE TO DISPLAY PAGE. *Arrgh*!

Okay, it's a big enough story. I ought to be able to find it elsewhere. No, not on the AmalCom site. Maybe from the

Wilmington *News Journal*. Or the RainBeau Network. Hmmm. What's www.India.vs.AmalCom.org?

A field of digital gray-and-white squares gradually resolves into thickly billowing somber clouds as the graphics load first—which is certainly unusual—then the words and the rest of the site build over that.

Of course.

How could I forget?

Fifteen years ago, in one of the world's worst industrial accidents, an explosion at the Amalgamated Compounds pesticide plant in Sehore, India released forty tons of hydrogen cyanide, monomethyl amine and *carbon monoxide gas* into the atmosphere, killing nearly three thousand people within minutes and causing permanent, crippling injury to more than two hundred thousand others. Although Amalgamated Compounds settled for $470 million, which comes to only $600 for each of the injured survivors, the Indian government issued an arrest warrant for Mr. Wallace, charging him with "culpable homicide," after a memo was found in the smoldering ruins of the Sehore plant in which Mr. Wallace instructed the senior staff, who were all Americans, to cut corners at the highly profitable facility by letting the safety systems fall into disrepair, or even, in some cases, to shut them off completely. In response to the charge that he had "demonstrated a depraved indifference to human life in his delegation of operational and maintenance procedures at the Amalgamated Compounds of India location," Wallace blamed the disaster on sabotage committed by a "disgruntled employee," and refused to provide crucial scientific data, claiming that the exact chemical composition of the leaked gasses was a "trade secret."

It also notes that, after all these years, about a dozen victims of the disaster are still dying every month.

I call up a map of north central India. Sehore is about forty miles from Vidisha, where Mr. Chanderdatt told me he comes from. But I bet that's not the whole story. I click and return a few times.

Well.

He comes from a place that woke up one hot, heartless morning to find that the very air had turned against them, a place where there was no refuge under the big black sun, which was blotted out by the thick stinging clouds of night and fog courtesy of Death, Incorporated.

I've been on the machine for far too long and my eyes are getting bleary. I log off and wander bandy-legged out the door, down the hall, and back to the tavern to stare out the sliding glass doors at the naked deck, roped off and guarded until daybreak brings a relief crew to sift the scene for further evidence linking Trane to Johnson's death.

Finding the side exit, I grasp the handrail extra tightly and clomp down the wooden stairs to the beach, the wind blowing my mussy, late-night computer-search hair into my face. I head for home, stumbling with occasional blindness on the uneven sands, until I catch the glow of two bright eyes lurking like a tiger's in the shadow of a low-lying palm tree. I look again and they're gone. But a sudden break in the cloud cover lets a few radiant droplets of moonlight fall earthward, silvering the dark outline of the mysterious stranger's foot-prints retreating up the beach.

I run after him, pushing the fear of smacking face-first into a palm tree trunk to the back of my mind, feet digging into to the cool sand, legs silently pumping and closing the distance between us. In a moment I'm there, at the corner of Fourth Street, but he's gone. Flying on instinct alone, I race five blocks west to a row of cheaper places with neon signs blazing the word "rooms" into the night. There are dozens of cheap rooms on the block, but twenty minutes later I've learned that only two have current registrants with poly-syllabic Indian names. The first one is an extended family of itinerant pilgrims—three aunts, two uncles, six little kids and the hundred-year-old grandfather—all staying together in one room, much to the irritation of the manager.

The second one has a single room rented to "Chirakall V. Shiva and son."

Hmmm.

I find him sitting by the window, staring out at the now-starry, now-cloudy sky.

I wait.

"Now what?" I say.

"Now it's finally over," he answers.

"It's not over. You have to help Trane."

"Who?"

"Trane. The guy Johnson sprayed with soda. He's going down for this murder if you don't—"

"Don't what? Give myself up? Who will take care of my son? You? Take a look at my son!"

And I do look at him, sleeping the deep sleep of the innocent, his huge head crowded between two carefully arranged pillows.

"The people's justice has been served," Vishal insists.

"Not completely. An innocent man is going to be charged with this crime."

"What crime? Johnson didn't even feel any pain," he says, disgustedly. But soon, deep breaths dispel some of his anger. "What do you want me to do about it?"

There's no easy answer.

"You'll find a way. You've obviously been wrestling with plenty of demons," I say, walking out. "I'm sure you can subdue one more."

And I go back to my own child, my own innocent child, and cradle her until the glorious rosy dawn comes up and banishes all my fears of sudden, fleet-footed airborne death to that murky place where the shadows retreat to when the bright bands of daylight erase their presence, where they lie in wait for yet another opportunity to pierce my mortal shell with their poisonous spines of doubt and paranoia.

Happy holidays.

Wish you were here.

ABOUT THE AUTHORS

Kenneth Wishnia was born in Hanover, NH, to a roving band of traveling academics. He earned a B.A. from Brown University (1982) and a Ph.D. in comparative literature from SUNY Stony Brook (1996). He teaches writing, literature, and other deviant forms of thought at Suffolk Community College in Brentwood, Long Island, where he is a professor of English.

Ken's novels have been nominated for the Edgar, Anthony, and Macavity Awards, and have made Best Mystery of the Year lists at *Booklist*, *Library Journal*, and the *Washington Post*. His short stories have appeared in *Ellery Queen's Mystery Magazine*, *Alfred Hitchcock's Mystery Magazine*, *Murder in Vegas*, *Long Island Noir*, *Queens Noir*, *Politics Noir*, *Send My Love and a Molotov Cocktail*, and elsewhere.

His most recent novel, *The Fifth Servant*, was an Indie Notable selection, one of the "Best Jewish Books of 2010" according to the Association of Jewish Libraries, a finalist for the Sue Feder Memorial Historical Mystery Award, and winner of a Premio Letterario ADEI-WIZO, a literary prize awarded by the Associazione Donne Ebree d'Italia, the Italian branch of the Women's International Zionist Organization.

He is married to a wonderful Catholic woman from Ecuador, and they have two children who are completely insane. For more information, go to www.kennethwishnia.com.

Gary Phillips, the son of a mechanic and a librarian, draws on his experiences ranging from labor organizing to delivering dog cages in writing his tales of chicanery and malfeasance. He has been nominated for a Shamus and has won a Chester Himes and a Brody for his writing. His books include *The Jook* and *The Underbelly*. Visit his website at http://gdphillips.com.

ABOUT PM PRESS

PM Press was founded at the end of 2007 by a small collection of folks with decades of publishing, media, and organizing experience. PM Press co-conspirators have published and distributed hundreds of books, pamphlets, CDs, and DVDs. Members of PM have founded enduring book fairs, spearheaded victorious tenant organizing campaigns, and worked closely with bookstores, academic conferences, and even rock bands to deliver political and challenging ideas to all walks of life. We're old enough to know what we're doing and young enough to know what's at stake.

We seek to create radical and stimulating fiction and non-fiction books, pamphlets, T-shirts, visual and audio materials to entertain, educate and inspire you. We aim to distribute these through every available channel with every available technology — whether that means you are seeing anarchist classics at our bookfair stalls; reading our latest vegan cookbook at the café; downloading geeky fiction e-books; or digging new music and timely videos from our website.

PM Press is always on the lookout for talented and skilled volunteers, artists, activists and writers to work with. If you have a great idea for a project or can contribute in some way, please get in touch.

PM Press
PO Box 23912
Oakland, CA 94623
www.pmpress.org

FRIENDS OF PM PRESS

These are indisputably momentous times—the financial system is melting down globally and the Empire is stumbling. Now more than ever there is a vital need for radical ideas.

In the six years since its founding—and on a mere shoestring—PM Press has risen to the formidable challenge of publishing and distributing knowledge and entertainment for the struggles ahead. With over 250 releases to date, we have published an impressive and stimulating array of literature, art, music, politics, and culture. Using every available medium, we've succeeded in connecting those hungry for ideas and information to those putting them into practice.

Friends of PM allows you to directly help impact, amplify, and revitalize the discourse and actions of radical writers, filmmakers, and artists. It provides us with a stable foundation from which we can build upon our early successes and provides a much-needed subsidy for the materials that can't necessarily pay their own way. You can help make that happen—and receive every new title automatically delivered to your door once a month—by joining as a Friend of PM Press. And, we'll throw in a free T-shirt when you sign up.

Here are your options:

- **$25 a month** Get all books and pamphlets plus 50% discount on all webstore purchases

- **$40 a month** Get all PM Press releases (including CDs and DVDs) plus 50% discount on all webstore purchases

- **$100 a month** Superstar—Everything plus PM merchandise, free downloads, and 50% discount on all webstore purchases

For those who can't afford $25 or more a month, we're introducing **Sustainer Rates** at $15, $10 and $5. Sustainers get a free PM Press T-shirt and a 50% discount on all purchases from our website.

Your Visa or Mastercard will be billed once a month, until you tell us to stop. Or until our efforts succeed in bringing the revolution around. Or the financial meltdown of Capital makes plastic redundant. Whichever comes first.

23 Shades of Black

Kenneth Wishnia
with an introduction by
Barbara D'Amato

ISBN: 978-1-60486-587-5
$17.95   300 pages

23 Shades of Black is socially conscious crime
fiction. It takes place in New York City in the
early 1980s, i.e., the Reagan years, and was
written partly in response to the reactionary discourse of the time,
when the current thirty-year assault on the rights of working people
began in earnest, and the divide between rich and poor deepened with
the blessing of the political and corporate elites. But it is not a political
tract, it's a kick-ass novel that was nominated for the Edgar and the
Anthony Awards, and made *Booklist*'s Best First Mysteries of the Year.

The heroine, Filomena Buscarsela, is an immigrant who experienced
tremendous poverty and injustice in her native Ecuador, and who grew
up determined to devote her life to helping others. She tells us that she
really should have been a priest, but since that avenue was closed to
her, she chose to become a cop instead. The problem is that as one
of the first *latinas* on the NYPD, she is not just a woman in a man's
world, she is a woman of color in a white man's world. And it's hell.
Filomena is mistreated and betrayed by her fellow officers, which leads
her to pursue a case independently in the hopes of being promoted to
detective for the Rape Crisis Unit.

Along the way, she is required to enforce unjust drug laws that she
disagrees with, and to betray her own community (which ostracizes her
as a result) in an undercover operation to round up illegal immigrants.
Several scenes are set in the East Village art and punk rock scene of
the time, and the murder case eventually turns into an investigation of
corporate environmental crime from a working class perspective that is
all-too-rare in the genre.

And yet this thing is damn funny, too.

"Packed with enough mayhem and atmosphere for two novels."
— *Booklist*

"From page-turning thriller to mystery story to social investigation, 23
Shades of Black *works on all levels. It's clear from the start that Wishnia is
charting a unique path in crime fiction. Sign me up for the full ride!"*
— Michael Connelly, author of *Lost Light*

The Glass Factory

Kenneth Wishnia
with an introduction by
Reed Farrel Coleman

ISBN: 978-1-60486-762-6
$15.95   256 pages

Ex-NYPD cop Filomena Buscarsela—the
irrepressible urban crime fighter of *23 Shades
of Black* and *Soft Money*—is back. This time, the
tough-talking, street-smart Latina heroine sets her sights on seemingly
idyllic suburbia, where an endless sea of green lawns hides a toxic trail
of money . . . and murder.

But something is rotten on Long Island. When Filomena discovers that a
high-tech Long Island factory is spewing poisons into the water supply,
she's sure that the contaminator is none other than her nemesis, a
cutthroat industrial polluter with an airtight financial empire. Armed
only with an ax to grind, the gutsy Filomena knows she'll have to play
dirty to clean up the neighborhood.

Her search for justice introduces her to the unfamiliar scent of
privilege—from the state-of-the-art chemistry lab of a local university
to the crumbling ruins of a beachfront estate, from a glittering high-
society party to an intimidating high-security chemical plant—and
immerses her in the all-too-familiar stench of political corruption and
personal greed. Once again, Filomena's nose for trouble has drawn
her into a case that's more than a little hazardous to her health. As the
action heats up, she must juggle the dangers of the investigation with
the demands of her adorable three-year-old daughter and the delights
of a surprising new romance.

*"Wishnia writes with brio, energy, rage, passion, and humor. Brash, sassy,
smart, and indomitable, Filomena is purely a force of nature, and* The
Glass Factory *is another winner."*
— *Booklist*

*"Riveting circumstances, a strongly focused plot, and ably described settings
make this essential reading."*
— *Library Journal*

*"Mother and daughter are so appealing, and the case against an
unscrupulous businessman is put together so compellingly, the tale keeps
one reading to its bittersweet end."*
— *Boston Globe*

Send My Love and a Molotov Cocktail: Stories of Crime, Love and Rebellion

Edited by Gary Phillips
and Andrea Gibbons

ISBN: 978-1-60486-096-2
$19.95   368 pages

An incendiary mixture of genres and voices, this collection of short stories compiles a unique set of work that revolves around riots, revolts, and revolution. From the turbulent days of unionism in the streets of New York City during the Great Depression to a group of old women who meet at their local café to plan a radical act that will change the world forever, these original and once out-of-print stories capture the various ways people rise up to challenge the status quo and change up the relationships of power. Ideal for any fan of noir, science fiction, and revolution and mayhem, this collection includes works from Kenneth Wishnia, Paco Ignacio Taibo II, Cory Doctorow, Kim Stanley Robinson, and Summer Brenner.

Full list of contributors:

Summer Brenner
Rick Dakan
Barry Graham
Penny Mickelbury
Gary Phillips
Luis Rodriguez
Benjamin Whitmer
Michael Moorcock
Larry Fondation

Cory Doctorow
Andrea Gibbons
John A Imani
Sarah Paretsky
Kim Stanley Robinson
Paco Ignacio Taibo II
Kenneth Wishnia
Michael Skeet
Tim Wohlforth

"The 18 mostly original stories in this thought-provoking crime anthology offer gritty testament to the violence, cunning, and resilience of people pushed to the brink. Phillips and Gibbons showcase some major talent, notably Sara Paretsky ('Poster Child'), but less well-known authors also make solid contributions. In John A Imani's moving 'Nickels and Dimes,' a black observer of a confrontation between police and protestors in 1972 Los Angeles becomes a reluctant participant and de facto leader. Gibbons's 'The El Rey Bar' brilliantly conveys the chaos, the hopelessness, and the despair engendered during an L.A. riot. SF ace Kim Stanley Robinson's exotic 'The Lunatics' explores the issue of forced labor amid an attempted slave revolt on the moon."
— Publishers Weekly

The Jook

Gary Phillips

ISBN: 978-1-60486-040-5
$15.95   256 pages

Zelmont Raines has slid a long way since his ability to jook, to outmaneuver his opponents on the field, made him a Super Bowl winning wide receiver, earning him lucrative endorsement deals and more than his share of female attention. But Zee hasn't always been good at saying no, so a series of missteps involving drugs, a paternity suit or two, legal entanglements, shaky investments and recurring injuries have virtually sidelined his career.

That is until Los Angeles gets a new pro franchise, the Barons, and Zelmont has one last chance at the big time he dearly misses. Just as it seems he might be getting back in the flow, he's enraptured by Wilma Wells, the leggy and brainy lawyer for the team—who has a ruthless game plan all her own. And it's Zelmont who might get jooked.

"Phillips, author of the acclaimed Ivan Monk series, takes elements of Jim Thompson (the ending), black-exploitation flicks (the profanity-fueled dialogue), and Penthouse *magazine (the sex is anatomically correct) to create an over-the-top violent caper in which there is no honor, no respect, no love, and plenty of money. Anyone who liked George Pelecanos' King Suckerman is going to love this even-grittier take on many of the same themes."*
— Wes Lukowsky, *Booklist*

"Enough gritty gossip, blistering action and trash talk to make real life L.A. seem comparatively wholesome."
— Kirkus Reviews

"Gary Phillips writes tough and gritty parables about life and death on the mean streets—a place where sometimes just surviving is a noble enough cause. His is a voice that should be heard and celebrated. It rings true once again in The Jook, *a story where all of Phillips' talents are on display."*
— Michael Connelly, author of the Harry Bosch books

The Underbelly

Gary Phillips

ISBN: 978-1-60486-206-5
$14.00   160 pages

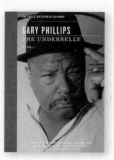

The explosion of wealth and development in downtown L.A. is a thing of wonder. But regardless of how big and shiny our buildings get, we should not forget the ones this wealth and development has overlooked and pushed out. This is the context for Phillips' novella *The Underbelly*, as a semi-homeless Vietnam vet named Magrady searches for a wheelchair-bound friend gone missing from Skid Row—a friend who might be working a dangerous scheme against major players. Magrady's journey is a solo sortie where the flashback-prone protagonist must deal with the impact of gentrification; take-no-prisoners community organizers; an unflinching cop from his past in Vietnam; an elderly sexpot out for his bones; a lusted-after magical skull; chronic-lovin' knuckleheads; and the perils of chili cheese fries at midnight. Combining action, humor and a street level gritty POV, *The Underbelly* is illustrated with photos and drawings.

Plus: a rollicking interview wherein Phillips riffs on Ghetto Lit, politics, noir and the proletariat, the good negroes and bad knee-grows of pop culture, Redd Foxx and Lord Buckley, and wrestles with the future of books in the age of want.

"…honesty, distinctive characters, absurdity and good writing—are here in Phillips's work."
— *The Washington Post*

"Magrady's adventures, with a distinctive noir feeling and appreciation for comic books, started as an online, serialized mystery. Drawings and an interview with Phillips enhance the package, offering a compelling perspective on race and class issues in South Central L.A."
— *Booklist*

"Phillips writes some of the most earnest and engaging crime noir currently being written."
— *Spinetingler*

Nearly Nowhere

Summer Brenner

ISBN: 978-1-60486-306-2
$15.95   192 pages

Fifteen years ago, Kate Ryan and her daughter
Ruby moved to the secluded village of Zamora
in northern New Mexico to find a quiet life
off the grid. But when Kate invites the wrong
drifter home for the night, the delicate peace of
their domain is shattered.

Troy Mason manages to hang onto Kate for a few weeks, though his
charm increasingly fails to offset his lies and delusions of grandeur. It
is only a matter of time before the lies turn abusive, igniting a chain
reaction of violence and murder. Not even a bullet in the leg will keep
Troy from seeking revenge as he chases the missing Ruby over back
roads through the Sangre de Cristo Mountains, down the River of
No Return, and to a white supremacy enclave in Idaho's Bitterroot
Wilderness. *Nearly Nowhere* explores the darkest places of the
American West, emerging with only a fragile hope of redemption in the
maternal ties that bind.

*"With her beautifully wrought sentences and dialogue that bring characters
alive, Summer Brenner weaves a gripping and dark tale of mysterious crime
based in spiritually and naturally rich northern New Mexico and beyond."*
— Roxanne Dunbar-Ortiz, historian and writer, author of *Roots of
Resistance: A History of Land Tenure in New Mexico*

"Summer Brenner's Nearly Nowhere *has the breathless momentum
of the white-water river her characters must navigate en route from a
isolated village in New Mexico to a neo-Nazi camp in Idaho. A flawed but
loving single mother, a troubled teen girl, a good doctor with a secret, a
murderous sociopath—this short novel packs enough into its pages to fight
well above its weight class."*
—Michael Harris, author of *The Chieu Hoi Saloon*

*"To the party, Summer Brenner brings a poet's ear, a woman's awareness,
and a soulful intent, and her attention has enriched every manner of literary
endeavor graced by it."*
—Jim Nisbet, author of *A Moment of Doubt*